CASE FILE
COMPENDIUM
Bing An Ben

3

WRITTEN BY
ROU BAO BU CHI ROU

COVER ILLUSTRATION BY
BOKI, YUBUXIU

INTERIOR ILLUSTRATIONS BY
DanKe

TRANSLATED BY
BEN BINGHAM

Seven Seas

Seven Seas Entertainment

CASE FILE COMPENDIUM: BING AN BEN VOL. 3

Published originally under the title of 《病案本》 (Bing An Ben)
Author © 肉包不吃肉 (Rou Bao Bu Chi Rou)
US English edition rights under license granted by 北京晋江原创网络科技有限公司
(Beijing Jinjiang Original Network Technology Co., Ltd.)
US English edition copyright © 2024 Seven Seas Entertainment, LLC.
Arranged through JS Agency Co., Ltd
All rights reserved

Cover Illustration: Boki, yubuxiu
Interior Illustrations: DanKe

Seven Seas press and purchase enquiries can be sent
to Marketing Manager Lauren Hill at press@gomanga.com.
Information regarding the distribution and purchase of digital editions is available
from Digital Manager CK Russell at digital@gomanga.com.

Seven Seas and the Seven Seas logo are trademarks of
Seven Seas Entertainment. All rights reserved.

Follow Seven Seas Entertainment online at
sevenseasentertainment.com.

TRANSLATION: Ben Bingham
ADAPTATION: Kayce Teo
COVER DESIGN: M. A. Lewife
INTERIOR DESIGN: Clay Gardner
INTERIOR LAYOUT: Karis Page
COPY EDITOR: Rebecca Scoble
PROOFREADER: Kate Kishi, Hnä
EDITOR: Harry Catlin
PREPRESS TECHNICIAN: Melanie Ujimori, Jules Valera
MANAGING EDITOR: Alyssa Scavetta
EDITOR-IN-CHIEF: Julie Davis
PUBLISHER: Lianne Sentar
VICE PRESIDENT: Adam Arnold
PRESIDENT: Jason DeAngelis

ISBN: 978-1-68579-774-4
Printed in Canada
First Printing: October 2024
10 9 8 7 6 5 4 3 2 1

— CASE FILE —

COMPENDIUM

Bing An Ben

3

T A B L E   O F
CONTENTS

60

FEELING HORNY

XIE QINGCHENG LEFT the hospital and returned to his dormitory the next day. He was accompanied by Chen Man, who was rather quiet and seemed somewhat off-kilter.

As they parted ways on the first floor of Xie Qingcheng's dormitory, Chen Man hesitantly called out, "Xie-ge..." But when he was met with Xie Qingcheng's sharp gaze, he just ended up mumbling, "You...you should get some rest. If anything comes up, you can come to me anytime."

Xie Qingcheng found Chen Man's behavior extremely peculiar, but he didn't consider the horrifying prospect that Chen Man might have a secret crush on him. Instead, he assumed Chen Man simply couldn't accept the idea that Xie Qingcheng had had a one-night stand. It was indeed a terrible excuse, but Xie Qingcheng really couldn't think of a more reasonable explanation to mollify his younger friend.

Xie Qingcheng was a grown man; there was no way he could admit that he had been fucked by a boy thirteen years his junior. He felt like a mute person eating bitter melon, forced to suffer in silence.

After a brief pause, Xie Qingcheng said, "You should go. Thank you." He turned to head upstairs.

Standing dazedly in the rain beneath his umbrella, Chen Man called out again. "Xie-ge..."

Xie Qingcheng looked back.

"N-never mind. Take care."

"...What exactly do you want to say?"

Biting his lip, Chen Man did his best to resist the urge to ask, but in the end, he still blurted out, "Are you still in touch with that girl?"

Xie Qingcheng paused. "Would *you* stay in contact with a one-night stand?"

"I...I don't do things like that..." said Chen Man. As soon as the words left his mouth, he realized it sounded like he was criticizing Xie Qingcheng for failing to uphold masculine virtues, so he hastily waved his hands. "Sorry, that's not what I meant."

"You're right. You shouldn't do things like that," Xie Qingcheng said tonelessly. "Right now, I'm also regretting that momentary impulse."

Chen Man stared at him.

"It won't happen again. I find it disgusting." With that, Xie Qingcheng turned to head upstairs.

Only then did Chen Man's lingering pallor regain a hint of color.

It took a whole week for Xie Qingcheng to completely recover from his malaise, and even after so long, the evidence left on his body had still not fully faded. When he was giving lectures or writing on the blackboard at the university, he had to be extra careful that his sleeves were properly fastened because his wrists were still covered in faint rope marks. These marks bore witness to the fact that his hands had been bound when he was wantonly defiled.

Xie Qingcheng didn't contact He Yu again. He Yu had blocked him, while he had straight up deleted He Yu from his contacts. The medical school and Huzhou University were both centuries-old institutions with sprawling campuses that took a long time to circle even by car; avoiding someone was a simple matter, if Xie Qingcheng truly wished it.

Just think of it as a nightmare, he thought, *and don't look back.*

In life, there were many hateful things beyond one's control that would never be dealt with in a satisfactory manner. Sometimes, just escaping in one piece was the best possible result.

Xie Qingcheng had been through a lot in his time, so it wasn't that he didn't understand this principle, no matter how disgusted he felt by what had happened. But he still often startled awake in the dead of night. His illness had receded, his fever was gone, and even his nether regions had slowly begun to heal. But deep down, Xie Qingcheng—who had always been resistant to love and desire—had grown even more frigid than before.

He kept dreaming of He Yu's hateful, lust-filled face and of the things they'd done. Then, he'd suddenly sit bolt upright in his bed. Away from prying eyes, Xie Qingcheng would finally show his panic and weakness, gasping open-mouthed as he buried his face in his hands, sweat soaking through his clothes.

He smoked cigarette after cigarette, and even took sleeping pills.

One day in the shower, he noticed that the hickeys He Yu had given him had finally disappeared completely. But he still couldn't relax. He knew he'd been branded to the bone, and his fear and disgust toward sex grew even more intense. His memories pricked at him constantly, reminding him how he had lost control under He Yu, how he'd vented the desire he always suppressed—a desire that he'd almost managed to quash completely—in a way that he abhorred.

He had screamed, shaken, and lost himself. These memories were like welts left by a whip, stinging him, humiliating him, tormenting him without end.

He had no choice but to turn on his computer, click open his jellyfish videos, and try to divert his attention by watching those ancient, serene life forms float through the water.

He couldn't keep sinking like this.

A few days later, He Yu returned to the He family residence to the rare sight of all the lights switched on. The moment he walked into the entranceway, he furrowed his brows against the warm glow; it was as though he were a vampire who had grown accustomed to desolation, whose most familiar environment was the silence and darkness of an ancient castle.

"You're back," came a familiar voice.

"...Mm."

He Yu was surprised to find both Lü Zhishu and He Jiwei present.

After he'd slept with Xie Qingcheng, He Yu had returned to the villa just once—on the day he tailed Xie Qingcheng to the hospital only to find that there was nothing he could do.

That day, his heart had felt uneasy and especially empty. After all that stimulation, he couldn't help but feel a bit hollow inside when he suddenly found himself all alone. His emotions a mess, he had returned to the main residence, where he could at least find company in the housekeeper and servants.

He knew his parents had recently made a trip back to Huzhou, but agitated as he was, he didn't want to see them, so he had left the residence the next day to stay out of their way. He hadn't returned since. Not until today.

He'd assumed that Lü Zhishu and He Jiwei wouldn't stay for very long, and he hadn't expected they'd still be here when he came back. He wasn't accustomed to receiving this sort of welcome. *Perhaps this is fake, too,* he thought. *Another hallucination.*

But then he realized that he had never once dreamed about his parents coming home to eat dinner with him. They had never appeared in any of his fantasies.

"Is it cold out?" Lü Zhishu asked him. "I've made you some nourishing four-herbs soup with morels and abalone..."

"Mom." He Yu fell briefly quiet. This word, one of the first learned by all humans, was a bit clumsy on his tongue. "I'm allergic to that kind of seafood."

Silence immediately descended upon the hall.

Lü Zhishu felt a bit awkward and shot He Jiwei a glance.

He Jiwei coughed. "It's all right, you can eat something else. I had them make you steamed napa cabbage in supreme soup. The stock's been simmering for hours. It used to be your favorite." He Jiwei wasn't very close to He Yu either, but he was somewhat more reliable than Lü Zhishu. He knew what his son liked.

He Yu didn't have any reason to refuse, so the three of them sat down together at the dining table.

The atmosphere grew even stiffer.

He Yu couldn't remember the last time their family of three had sat down together like this. It had been too long. Looking at He Jiwei and Lü Zhishu's faces, he found them a bit unfamiliar. To him, his parents were more like the two profile pictures in his WeChat contacts, with those slightly flattened voices.

"When do you plan to return to Yanzhou?" He Yu asked.

"There's no rush," Lü Zhishu immediately responded, a sickly-sweet smile plastered onto her corpulent face; it had been stuck on there rather too forcefully and looked like it might fall off at any moment. "Your brother's living on campus now, so we don't need to keep an eye on him all the time. And besides, He Yu, you nearly scared me to death. You mustn't do such dangerous things. What if something happened to you? We'd—" A sob seemed to catch in her throat.

He Yu looked on dispassionately. After the broadcasting tower incident, his heart had become cold and hard. But he didn't feel like wasting words on these two, so he smiled softly and said, "It's all right. I'm doing very well."

Conversation continued idly over dinner. The scene seemed warm and inviting, but chilly undercurrents roiled beneath the surface.

"I'm done. May I go upstairs?" He Yu asked at last.

Although He Yu was making Lü Zhishu a little uncomfortable, she was a businesswoman through and through; she could keep her thoughts tightly hidden, even when it came to her own son. "Ah, okay. Go on, go on. Get some rest. I'll make you chicken soup tomorrow, okay?"

"...Whatever you want," He Yu said indifferently, then got up from the table and went upstairs.

Lü Zhishu watched him disappear into the upstairs corridor with a complicated expression.

He Jiwei asked, "Why are you suddenly being so good to him? Never mind how he's feeling—I can't get used to it either."

"What's wrong with me being good to my son? Isn't that the most natural thing in the world? I'm his mother, after all..."

He Jiwei started to speak, then seemed to think better of it and closed his mouth. He finally got up. "I have some company matters to take care of, so I need to make a trip to Qingdao tomorrow."

"When will you be back?" she asked. "I'm telling you, I thought about it and realized that I really have let him down too often. I ought to make it up to him properly now. You too—don't stay away for too long. Our children are much more important than work..."

He Jiwei sighed. "These words you're saying sure make me nostalgic." Silence fell for a beat before he continued, "You used to say that sort of thing all the time when you first got pregnant with him." He Jiwei smiled, his eyes fathomless yet unexpectedly pained. "It's been a long time since I've heard you say anything like that."

"Lao-He..."

But He Jiwei had already turned and left.

He Yu lay on the bed in his room. Now that he no longer needed to feign courtesy in front of Lü Zhishu and He Jiwei, the look in his eyes had become rather stormy. He gazed up at the ceiling and, just as he had done this past week when he was alone and lost in his thoughts, mulled over things from the past.

A bell tolled.

To He Yu's surprise, the grandfather clock in the old house was sounding again.

Each dull, deeply resounding peal knocked against his heart, just like it had every night that he'd spent all alone, just like when he stood there for so long on his thirteenth birthday, waiting for the companionship of even a single person, only for it to never arrive.

When he remembered the evening of that birthday, he couldn't help but think of Xie Xue again. Not only had his parents never shown much concern for him, but even Xie Xue was nothing more than a partial figment of his imagination, dreamed up by a boy drowning in the depths of loneliness and extreme sickness. She was a real person, but she also wasn't entirely real. Ever since he'd learned the truth, He Yu's feelings toward Xie Xue had become extremely complicated.

Hadn't he always anticipated all this?

He had always felt that Xie Xue's memory was poor. There were certain things that he could remember with perfect clarity, yet she would say that she didn't have any recollection of them. Back then, he had even said to her, *I don't know how you managed to get into university and become a teacher with that memory of yours.*

He'd never suspected that those events he remembered so clearly might have been nothing more than blossoms in a mirror, or the moon on the water—beautiful delusions of his own mind.

That version of her didn't exist at all—she wasn't completely real.

He had known all along that these were acts of self-preservation and self-deception, if only subconsciously. He had once written a story for his screenwriting and directing class about a boy whose spirit returned to the land of the living on the seventh day after his death. The dead boy's soul knocked on his teacher's door and sat down with her to eat some snacks and drink some ginger tea... Yet after the teacher woke up the next morning, not a single cookie on the table was missing, and the warming ginger tea had frozen into ice.

The boy hadn't come at all. He had been imaginary, a ghost without a corporeal form.

The fact that this story had come to his mind so easily... Wasn't it just a projection of the way he had imagined Xie Xue?

In the story, the cookies had never been touched; in reality, the birthday cake had never existed. In the story, the ginger tea had frozen into ice; in reality, his heart was so cold it could hardly beat anymore.

It wasn't that he hadn't known the truth on some level. Now, as he carefully examined his memories with the hindsight of someone who had just woken up, he could distinguish dreams from reality.

In dreams, it was impossible for him to tell if he was dreaming or awake. But once he opened his eyes, he could understand what was real and what was fake.

Just like Xie Qingcheng had said, Xie Xue had indeed been very kind to him, but that kindness was neither exceptional nor unconditional. She treated him like a close friend, but she had plenty of friends—He Yu was merely one among many.

He had never been special.

This truth upset him much more than the realization that Xie Xue liked someone else—his pillar of emotional support had been nothing more than an illusion. For him, even just liking someone, the most normal feeling an ordinary person could experience, was too much to ask for.

With his thoughts running wild, He Yu hadn't had a good night's sleep in a long time. He hadn't been faring much better than Xie Qingcheng that week. The human body wasn't meant to withstand such intense and unrelenting stimulation, so even though He Yu's mind was a mess, he still took a few pills and slowly closed his eyes, falling into his first deep sleep since that night at the club.

He Yu had a dream.

He dreamed of a pair of dangerously bewitching peach-blossom eyes. The Peach Blossom Spring[1] within those eyes had enticed him countless times before, so at first he thought he was dreaming of Xie Xue—that he was in another fantasy, that the pathetic hope in his heart had once again taken on her appearance to comfort him.

But as the dream grew clearer, He Yu saw that those eyes weren't lovely and smiling at all. They were ice-cold, sharp, hostile, and resolute...and also distraught and helpless. He suddenly realized that those were Xie Qingcheng's eyes, the way they looked after he had been drugged with Plum Fragrance 59 in that private room.

---

1   The subject of a fifth century fable by Tao Yuanming, the Peach Blossom Spring is a utopia where people live unaware of the outside world. The phrase can be used to describe an idealized, peaceful location.

The dream was a product of his own subconscious mind, so as soon as he realized whose eyes those were, the full scene began to materialize.

Once again, He Yu saw Xie Qingcheng's body sprawled out on that buttery, black leather sofa. Xie Qingcheng's skin was strikingly pale, like a precious gemstone ensconced in a case lined with black velvet, so fair it seemed almost transparent. What had once been a clean white shirt was now soaked through with red wine. The fabric was plastered to his skin, revealing the lines of his firmly muscled chest as it rose and fell.

He Yu had tormented Xie Qingcheng into a miserable state—he was so drenched in sweat that he looked like he had been fished out of the sea. His body was fully tensed, purely masculine, and ferociously powerful—like a flame struggling as it was doused with water.

The drug coursed relentlessly through Xie Qingcheng until he couldn't take it anymore. He arched his neck helplessly as he clawed at the sofa, staring upward as if he were trying to grab onto something, exposing his wrists and the delicate script on his left wrist that read, *Here lies one whose name was writ in water.*

He Yu stared at that line of text until the clearly distinct words blurred, and finally he couldn't make them out at all anymore. The words were like some kind of demonic curse that was sucking his soul from his body, and he stepped forward like a man possessed... only for Xie Qingcheng to grab his hand with a slap.

Those peach-blossom eyes seemed suffused with a peach blossom miasma.[2]

Once again, that hoarse, impassioned cry, the likes of which He Yu had never heard before, echoed through his dream.

---

2   *Peach blossom miasma is a fictional poison that often appears in wuxia fiction: usually deadly, but with an alluring vapor.*

Xie Qingcheng panted, his lips parted, his eyes misted over, and the veins in his neck shivered hypnotically—like a snake demon that had cast off its molted skin to reveal the vulgar desire beneath, enticing a man to bite and tear into it ruthlessly, to swallow it until that desire melted into his bones. Drawing him into a nightmare that didn't even spare his flesh and blood...

When He Yu woke up, he was still panting for breath.

The watch on his wrist was coldly dormant, a calming weight on his sweat-soaked arm. He lay on the large walnut bed in the villa, the vegetal sweetness of his bamboo sleeping mat flooding his nose with each inhale.

Beyond the window, an edge of grayish blue the color of a crab's shell had begun to peek out from below the horizon. It couldn't even be considered the first rays of dawn—at around four in the morning, it was still too early, and all the servants in the villa were asleep in their respective rooms. He Yu was the only one awake, just surfaced from a dream drenched in cold sweat and shivering from the chill.

A light autumn quilt was draped over his waist. As he stared up at the ceiling, the brass inlay tiles seemed like an array of mirrors; lying on the bed, he could see himself reflected on their surface.

He Yu blinked, his throat bobbing. He was like the empty shell of a body that had just been spat out of a nightmare. But an empty shell would not be affected by the stirrings of desire, and he knew that the thin blanket was concealing the searing evidence of his own debt of sin, yet unrelieved. It had followed him here into the real world, belatedly crossed over from that fantastically vivid dreamscape to desperately seek comfort in something soft, wet, and warm.

He Yu's fingertips twitched, and he was certain that he had truly gone insane. How did he end up dreaming about that night he'd spent with Xie Qingcheng?

When he fucked Xie Qingcheng, he'd believed he wasn't doing it out of any sense of desire. He had lost his mind at the time, and all he knew was that this was the best way to humiliate Xie Qingcheng; completely irrationally, he would follow Xie Qingcheng into the mire if it meant that he could cover him in mud and see that wretched look on his face.

He Ye had originally planned to use the retaliatory madness born of the wine to bring their relationship to an end. After that night of sex, he'd even blocked Xie Qingcheng on WeChat like some booty-calling fuckboy, with no plans of contacting him ever again.

So why would he dream of Xie Qingcheng again, of that hoarse cry that made even the dimples on his back prickle with pleasure? It wasn't like he was gay—how could he get caught up like this?

He Yu closed his eyes and lifted a hand to his temple. The more he tried to evade those memories, the more insistently they rose to the surface, stimulating the desire hidden beneath that thin blanket and teaching him the meaning of primal instinct.

He endured it. But his sweat kept beading, and his breathing grew rough. This masculine instinct disgusted him, and he strove to evade it, but still, it pounced upon him.

He Yu was bloodthirsty, but that night, he'd quenched his thirst with another man. Before then, he had never kissed anyone, much less held someone or sank into the depths of pleasure with them while savoring the taste of passion.

Male virgins around twenty years old who'd just had their first taste of sex were the absolute worst. At that age, they weren't just in their peak condition physically, they were also curious and in possession of a great deal of free time. Every hotel near a university could attest to that fact. He Yu was unique in many aspects, but he was capable of saying such things—much less that his interactions with her brother could be so uncouth.

She was already heartbroken over Xie Qingcheng's recent suffering, so her gege-apologist instincts were on high alert. Seeing that even He Yu had changed his attitude toward Xie Qingcheng, going so far as to figuratively kick him when he was down, she couldn't hold back anymore. She yanked He Yu aside and stood in front of Xie Qingcheng with her arms outstretched, sparks practically flying from her eyes. "Don't you dare insult my brother like that!"

The sight of her all-consuming fury rendered He Yu momentarily speechless. Just who exactly did she think she was? Was it because he'd always yielded to her, protected her, and never failed to help her even if he bullied her in secret? Was that why she felt comfortable throwing her weight around with him, blissfully ignorant of the consequences?

But what if he stopped caring about her? Dealing with her would be no harder than crushing an ant. How dare she stand in front of him, hit him with things, and argue with him? It was seriously a little ridiculous, He Yu thought.

But Xie Xue was still Xie Xue. Even if many of their interactions had been nothing more than his own self-comforting delusions, she was still the person who treated him best out of all his peers. The terrible pain in his heart had faded into numbness. But even if he no longer expected anything from her, he would never actually raise a hand against her.

He looked at her with an air of near indifference, the corners of his mouth twitching slightly, his derision wrapped in apathy. "Can't you recognize someone's good intentions? I'm trying to help him."

"Helping him, my ass! You're just mocking and ridiculing him! I heard everything!" Xie Xue was like a lioness with her hackles raised.

Xie Xue wanted to lower her window and rail at He Yu again, but Xie Qingcheng stopped her. "Don't bother." His eyes were terrifyingly cold. He looked away from He Yu. "Let's go home."

62

IT FEELS GREAT

H E YU WATCHED AS the siblings—this pair of orphans who only had each other—left. Not only had he had a huge falling out with the brother, but he ended up on bad terms with the sister too.

He Yu felt dejected for a long while. He didn't want to admit it, but he had never really been close with other people. Even his relationships with his parents and his little brother were as thin as water. Xie Xue and Xie Qingcheng were the only ones who shared any kind of deeper connection with him.

He'd never felt so disoriented before, not even when he was alone in Europe.

Back then, whenever Xie Xue was upset with Xie Qingcheng, she would call He Yu and complain a little bit about Xie Qingcheng's totalitarianism. The two of them would joke around and talk for a while, and a certain lump in He Yu's heart would slowly melt away.

When he was bored out of his mind, he would post a WeChat moment that only the Xie siblings could see and pretend that he had a headache and slight fever. He knew that any time he posted something along those lines, Xie Qingcheng, out of a sense of professionalism, would doubtless respond with: *Take your medicine.*

Then, He Yu could reply judiciously and with unmatched haughtiness, *I'm fine.* And he would feel delight rise in his heart, as if his mental illness had been suddenly cured without any treatment.

But now none of that would work anymore.

In his loneliness, He Yu got into the habit of searching for and reading all sorts of news about Xie Qingcheng, regardless of whether it was truth or fiction.

He found that even though he was a hacker, he wasn't nearly as deranged as netizens when it came to digging up personal information. He actually ended up learning a lot of new information from these people.

For example, when Xie Qingcheng was in middle school, he was often involved in gang fights.

For example, after Xie Qingcheng's parents passed away, he took a leave of absence from school. Instead of going home and taking care of his sister, he went to Yanzhou all by himself. One of his classmates even heard that while he was there, he hung around at a nightclub. But something must have happened around then, because there was no news of him for more than half a year.

Of course, he could tell that some of these posts were fake at a glance—ones that claimed that Xie Qingcheng's parents were dirty cops and that Xie Qingcheng was actually a criminal mastermind.

Meanwhile, the situation grew increasingly outrageous as more and more of the Xie siblings' personal information was leaked. The number of photos of Xie Qingcheng steadily increased as well. Photos of him at Moyu Alley the other day, photos of him walking on the street, photos of him and Xie Xue eating at a streetside food stall... There was even a school photo obtained from one of his classmates.

There was a brief pause, then He Yu continued in a voice so gentle that it was almost frightening, "Then, have you ever heard of a totally straight man dreaming of having sex with another man?"

Once again, the other boy stared at him blankly. Then, under He Yu's friendly gaze, he resolutely said, "No, never. Who is it? That's hilarious, he's definitely gay. He Yu, I'm telling you, if a straight man tells you that he dreams of men, you gotta remember to steer clear of him. There are way too many dumbasses deep in the closet these days... Hey, what's up with you? What's with that expression?"

He Yu smiled lightly and lowered his eyes so that no one could see the look in them, which was as grim as the underworld. "...I'm fine. It's nothing."

This guy's words can't be trusted either, he thought. *Everyone is different. Besides, he didn't lose his virginity with a man, so of course he wouldn't understand.*

But what made He Yu even moodier was that in recent days, the desire to experience that crazed pleasure again had grown stronger and stronger. He had begun to dream of that night more and more often. Every time he awoke, he saw the evidence of his extreme excitement. He was beginning to think that he really had gone mad.

When a young person, hot-blooded and headstrong, tasted the forbidden fruit for the first time, it was easy for them to become addicted, to sink too deep and find it impossible to stop.

Xie Qingcheng was the first person He Yu had ever slept with, so it was just instinct for him to imprint on Xie Qingcheng's body and regularly reminisce about the events of that night... This was the excuse He Yu used to convince himself every time he woke in the hot, humid morning, lying on his school-standard bedding with his blackout curtains drawn. He would bite his lip and think of Xie Qingcheng's firm, slender body, of his dazed expression on that dark and chaotic night. He would remember how they'd been like two animals in heat as they lost themselves in their messy, sweat-slick coupling. Amidst his roommate's snores, he'd recall the sensations he'd felt and, with sweat dripping down his body, he would silently and violently bring himself to release while looking at those photographs of Xie Qingcheng.

Then, in post-nut clarity, he'd regret it hard and even feel disgusted by himself. There was no way he hadn't gone mad.

The young man wallowed in his depravity until, one day, he felt that it wasn't enough to just look at photos of Xie Qingcheng anymore. After all, he'd only snapped a single photo of the upper half of Xie Qingcheng's body and a few close-ups of his face. The marks he'd left were vivid, but everything else was left to his memory and imagination—it really wasn't enough to satisfy him in the long run.

So he picked up his phone, opened his block list, and, after a brief moment of hesitation, tapped on Xie Qingcheng's profile picture. He wanted to see if Xie Qingcheng had posted any recent updates, and if there were any novelties to be gleaned.

In the end, though, all he discovered was that Xie Qingcheng had locked him out of his WeChat Moments. All that remained on the screen was a pale blue line, just like the thin line of Xie Qingcheng's pursed lips whenever he was displeased or suppressing his desire.

He Yu reached out and stroked his finger over that line with a dangerous look in his eyes. There was no social media platform on Earth that he couldn't break into if he put his mind to it. No status updates were safe from his prying eyes.

This "little hubby," as the netizens called him, may have protected the sanctity of Xie Qingcheng's privacy, but at the end of the day, gods may do what cattle may not. Less than half a minute later, He Yu had shamelessly broken through Xie Qingcheng's WeChat block.

But having put his hacking skills to work and stumbled into Xie Qingcheng's Moments, "little hubby" didn't find anything worth seeing. Xie Qingcheng hadn't posted in ages, and his last update had been a repost of some school business.

Indeed, there were no status updates on Earth that were safe from his prying eyes—unless the target in question hadn't made any such updates in the first place.

In the end, He Yu angrily turned off his phone and spent an extended period stuck in this muddled state, like a drug addict trying to kick the habit. But just like an addict who kept telling himself that he mustn't continue on like this, his body couldn't resist the temptation. He had experienced ecstasy, and it was all too easy to relapse.

In an attempt to go back to some of the standards he set for himself as a straight man, He Yu even visited Pornhub and browsed through some videos of girls. But it turned out to be completely ineffective.

Objectively speaking, the most popular actresses on Pornhub were excellent—they had beautiful faces and lovely figures, and their voices were very pleasing to the ear. But unfortunately, even after browsing through all the top-rated videos, He Yu still felt completely indifferent. He drank an entire cup of coffee with an air of leisure while he watched their performances like some heartless film critic.

What he saw onscreen was nothing like what he'd actually experienced.

His memories from that night could be summed up in four words: hot, wet, crazy, and pleasurable.

He Yu could never have guessed that someone as tall and formidable as Xie Qingcheng could have such a slender waist. Gripping that waist with his hands had kindled a sense of excitement in He Yu; he felt like he could easily crush Xie Qingcheng to pieces.

Xie Qingcheng's skin was prone to bruising too, and the marks on his wrists had lingered long after the ropes were untied. His voice was like spring water in a gully; despite being so light, it could wear through stone. As hard as He Yu's heart was, that low, hoarse male voice had nevertheless chiseled a hole in it, causing heat to stream out in waves.

He Yu never would have imagined that Xie Qingcheng could look so wanton—that this cold, sharp, fiercely unreasonable man, this man's man who always smelled so strongly of tobacco, would lose his mind, that his eyes would grow dazed as he madly tumbled down the abyss of desire into the morass alongside He Yu.

It had been way too hot...which was why He Yu's every attempt to quit this drug ended in dismal failure.

There were several times when He Yu got so upset and angry with himself that he would delete the photos of Xie Qingcheng upon recovering his moral sensibilities in the afterglow of his release. But whenever he got horny again, he couldn't help it—he'd just use his hacking skills to recover them...

Afterward, he just felt pathetic. The pictures featured little more than Xie Qingcheng's face and half of his body; they didn't even capture his waist. Sure, they were pretty to look at, but were they really that arousing? Despite how he'd felt at the time, all "wham-bam-thank-you-ma'am," in retrospect his actions seemed atrociously sentimental, like he'd taken these photos to soothe his desire and feed his yearning for the sleeping visage of his lover the morning after a night of lingering passion. It only made him even more frustrated.

It just so happened that He Yu was addicted to this frustration—so much so that it even stung his haughty self-esteem.

But there was nothing he could do. In the face of that baffling desire, he couldn't bear the temptation of his memories. He wanted to bring his chapped lips to the opium that would eat away at his bones and cloud his mind and suck it down fiercely. With a single breath, the sights and sounds from that night materialized as endless tendrils of dark smoke, wrapping seamlessly around his body into an inescapable cocoon.

He Yu was sure he had fallen far too ill. He was feverishly poisoned and hopelessly addicted.

Who could cure him?

In his heart, he knew the answer.

But there were no signs of life from that person. He Yu only had the handful of photos he'd taken in the darkness and the shattered remains of that night's splendor and desire. That, and the pile of outdated pictures he had looted from random netizens while simultaneously purging them from every corner of the internet.

Unfortunately, those photos weren't very good. They really didn't do a good-looking man like Xie Qingcheng justice. Just how had the netizens managed to take such useless photos? Good-for-nothings.

The "little hubby" was deeply disappointed in them, and truly extremely annoyed. And because increased stimulation only served to push a person's threshold for satisfaction even higher, He Yu could no longer be satisfied by this online Xie Qingcheng, who he could neither see nor touch.

Lying on his dorm room bed, this schoolboy began to experience regret. The thought struck him that, prior to Xie Qingcheng's suspension, it used to take him less than ten minutes to drive from Huzhou University to Huzhou Medical School's offices or classrooms to see that man every day.

This realization left He Yu feeling inexplicably dejected.

Why had he been so unwilling to go before? It wasn't as though just looking at the man would turn him into a homosexual. Why hadn't he allowed himself to take a sip and quench his thirst, if it could have made him feel better?

If only he had gone before, he would have been able to see the man who went mad with him in the darkness, impeccably dressed as he stood at the lectern with not a single hair out of place. He could have heard the mouth that had once panted out those low, shattered gasps right into his own ear calmly delivering a lecture on serious intellectual topics.

He Yu couldn't fall asleep.

Finally, after yet another night of relieving his stress by thinking about Xie Qingcheng, this stupidly addicted young man, who had only just lost his virginity, suddenly got up and locked himself in the shower for a very long time. When he turned off the dorm's cheap showerhead and slowly lifted his head, the look in his eyes was very turbulent.

I can't go on like this, he thought.

He who tied the bell around the tiger's neck should be the one to take it off. If He Yu could take just a few more glances at Xie Qingcheng now, argue with him a bit more, and ideally be duped by the man again, he would definitely revert to feeling the way he did when they'd first met; he would clash with Xie Qingcheng and resent him, find the scent of disinfectant on his body repulsive, and try to stay as far away from him as possible.

Yes, surely that was how it would go.

It was the only solution. He needed to go see Xie Qingcheng again.

An opportunity soon arose.

After multiple rounds of edits and a laborious post-production, the campus film series *The Many Faces of Malady* was scheduled to play at the school theater next Friday. For the occasion, the theater had arranged a joint screening for Huzhou University and Huzhou Medical School students, along with an awards ceremony. Xie Xue was one of the people in charge of this project—her attendance was all but guaranteed.

After making some inquiries, He Yu learned that Xie Qingcheng would also be coming. He even managed to learn his exact seat.

Xie Qingcheng could attend such a bustling event because some news had been released recently about hot-button social issues. Fewer people were following the broadcasting tower affair so closely now that there was fresh meat to swarm over, so it had begun to recede from the center of attention. In any case, Huzhou University's theater was extremely spacious—it was three stories tall and could accommodate several thousand people—and it was unlikely that anyone would notice him in the darkness of the screening.

"Do you need to reserve a seat?" asked the xuejie who'd helped He Yu look into all this. "You're part of the cast, so you should have a VIP seat in the front row, right?"

"My friend is coming," He Yu lied.

"Oh…"

"Could I trouble you to book seat B2230 for me?"

Naturally, the xuejie was very willing to help this handsome youngster out. Using the university's internal ticketing system, she quickly printed out a ticket to the premiere of *The Many Faces of Malady* for He Yu.

B2230 was the seat behind Xie Qingcheng.

He Yu took the ticket and peered at the date that the crappy printer had pecked out, anticipation rising silently in his heart.

On the day of the premiere, he arrived extra early at Huzhou University's theater and sat down in his seat. But he waited for a long time, and the two seats in front of him remained empty.

The movie was about to begin. The lights dimmed all at once, leaving only the scattered gleam of audience members' phones here and there in the theater. A moment later, the huge screen flickered to life and began airing the previews, diffusing vivid light throughout the pitch-dark hall.

It was then that someone arrived at the theater. He Yu couldn't see Xie Qingcheng's face in the darkness, only the indistinct silhouette of his profile, but that alone was enough to recognize him.

What He Yu had failed to anticipate, however, was that Xie Qingcheng hadn't come alone.

The little police officer who was always following him had tagged along.

63

NO, HE'S NOT GREAT

THE CAMPUS PREMIERE of *The Many Faces of Malady* was scheduled on a Friday. The police officer must have deliberately asked for a day off to accompany Xie Qingcheng.

In the dimly lit theater, He Yu stared at the two people in front of him with a blank expression. He was wearing a baseball cap and a black face mask—a combination that wasn't all that unusual at Huzhou University. In fact, it was a standard get-up for the many celebrities who'd debuted as child stars at this fine arts school, and for handsome guys who disliked showing their faces.

Because of this, Xie Qingcheng didn't notice the boy behind him as he moved to his seat.

"Chen Man, your popcorn."

"Thank you."

He Yu crossed his arms, leaned back against his cushioned seat, and raised an eyebrow.

Chen Man. So, the name of this cop—this *pig*—was Chen Man...

He Yu suddenly remembered picking up that phone call for Xie Qingcheng at Xie Xue's apartment. At the time, the caller ID displayed on the phone...he was pretty sure it'd been the same name.

Yes, that was the name. He Yu's icy expression cooled by several more degrees until the almond eyes beneath the brim of his cap practically frosted over.

He continued to silently observe the two people in front of him. He knew that Chen Man was somewhat close with Xie Qingcheng, but still, this degree of familiarity made him very uncomfortable.

The Many Faces of Malady was a collaborative film produced by Huzhou Medical School and Huzhou University to celebrate the anniversary of their founding. It was only being shown on campus, so the audience was composed solely of students from the two universities. What did it have to do with a pig who'd graduated from a police academy? Had Chen Man even contributed anything to the production? Was he the action director for the film, or had he provided police support on set? No. He'd done none of these things. So what had he come here for?

He Yu's mental state was quite twisted right now. On one hand, he refused to admit on pain of death that he was homosexual. He still thought that his desire for Xie Qingcheng was nothing more than a normal, physiological urge—that what he missed was the wild sexual entanglement, not Xie Qingcheng himself. But on the other hand, because of his masculine sense of possessiveness, he refused to allow others to touch something when he'd already taken a bite out of it. Even if he didn't want it anymore, no one else was worthy of touching it.

And so he observed Chen Man with ice in his eyes, like a wolf staring at a hyena that coveted its prey.

Chen Man felt the back of his neck prickling and instinctively raised a hand to touch there before turning to glance behind him.

"What's wrong?" asked Xie Qingcheng.

"It's nothing... I suddenly got goosebumps. Maybe the air conditioning is too strong," Chen Man said, sitting down next to Xie Qingcheng.

NO, HE'S NOT GREAT

The film itself started soon after. *The Many Faces of Malady* was made up of a series of several shorts that could stand alone as independent stories, but there was a hidden thread linking the characters and events of each individual narrative together at the end. It was two hours long, and all of He Yu's classmates were engrossed by it. Since the actors were all students from their own school, they inevitably ended up heckling each other during certain exciting scenes, and it was far noisier than an ordinary movie theater.

Meanwhile, He Yu barely watched the movie at all. All he did was sit in the back and stare at Xie Qingcheng. He had gone out of his way to pick a seat that wasn't directly behind Xie Qingcheng, but slightly to the side, so he could clearly see his face.

The flickering illumination of the screen veiled that sharply defined face in a layer of gauze. The light changed unpredictably, making Xie Qingcheng's features seem like treasure submerged in water, his taut skin emanating a soft glow.

He Yu's throat bobbed slightly as he swallowed. *He's not attractive at all,* he thought. Gazing at an apathetic man at such close quarters was as painful as self-flagellation. But his stare never faltered as he thoroughly flogged himself.

It was only when Xie Qingcheng frowned slightly at the screen that He Yu realized that the film had reached his own part. He didn't have many scenes, and his screen time was even shorter after editing.

On the screen, the gay couple played by He Yu and his xuezhang were talking.

"How much do you love me? How much will you give up for me?"

That was the scene that Xie Qingcheng had once helped him rehearse—a scene that involved a kiss.

Looking back on it now, both Xie Qingcheng and He Yu felt a bit strange. At the time, they'd been disgusted by just a kiss... But what about now, when the movie was released? The permissible and the forbidden—they'd already done it all.

He Yu watched as Xie Qingcheng lowered his lashes and looked away, as if the He Yu in the film reminded him of some uncomfortable memories. After a while, he straight up closed his eyes.

...It seemed that life had been rather hard on Xie Qingcheng as of late. His cheeks were slightly sunken, and there was some faint gray stubble on his chin, the consequence of less-than-meticulous shaving.

After he'd had his eyes closed for a while, his head began tipping slightly forward. He'd actually fallen asleep... Watching from behind, He Yu grew irritated at the sight. How could he fall asleep with all this racket?

About ten minutes later, Chen Man turned to his Xie-ge as though he wanted to discuss a scene with him. But when he looked over, he saw that Xie Qingcheng had his head down, already deeply asleep.

Chen Man quietly closed his mouth. The air conditioning in the theater was quite cold, and he was worried that it'd be too much for Xie Qingcheng when he'd only just recovered from his fever. His Xie-ge was such a strong person, yet his health had been steadily deteriorating for the past few years.

Maybe it was because of his excessive smoking or the undue stress of his work, but Xie Qingcheng had been coughing a lot recently. His eyesight wasn't as good as before, either. Xie Qingcheng used to have near-perfect vision, but lately, there'd even been a few times where Chen Man had seen him putting on glasses while reading or working on his computer.

Sighing, Chen Man gently removed his jacket and carefully tucked it around Xie Qingcheng's shoulders.

He Yu watched them with cold eyes. The longer he watched, the more displeased he became, increasingly furious about the encroachment on his territory.

But then Chen Man, gazing at Xie Qingcheng, couldn't resist doing something else—something which made He Yu's last nerve snap completely.

Cautiously, and with utmost care, Chen Man reached out and gently touched Xie Qingcheng's hand where it was lying on the theater seat's armrest.

Xie Qingcheng's fingertips twitched slightly in response. He seemed to have faintly sensed something, but he was just too exhausted to react. He'd endured so much torment these past few days...

He'd seen the freshly unearthed trail of clues about his parents' murder cut off right before his eyes.

He was subjected to an insane form of retribution by He Yu just as he began to entertain the notion of treating him as a true confidante.

He'd been dealing with the wild storm stirred up by the Qin Ciyan incident, which had lain undisturbed for years like so much silt.

He'd had his private information leaked, bright red paint splashed onto the walls of his house, his innocent neighbors implicated by association...

The silent eyes of the few friends and family he had gazed at him from under the cover of night, asking, *"Ge, can't you be honest, even to us?"*

He couldn't.

The weight of all these things crashing down on him was immense. Out of all the people in the whole wide world, he could confide in none of them. He was a silent secret-keeper. In the depths of the great abyss, he'd never cared if light would come.

Perhaps Xie Qingcheng was the only person alive who was strong enough to endure this turmoil, this pressure. He was indifferent and extremely calm. He no longer found it painful, nor did he feel wronged. He didn't even feel lonely.

In all this time, he'd never shed a single tear if he could possibly help it. Die-hard male chauvinists like him had very rigid views on gender—he believed that weakness belonged to women and only the most useless of men, that it couldn't exist in his own heart. He could barely even feel pain.

However, he was still made of flesh and blood, and if nothing else, he could still get tired. He truly was exhausted, so when Chen Man touched his hand, his only reaction was an instinctive twitch of his fingertips. He didn't wake up.

Chen Man had stopped watching the movie too. Instead, he gazed at Xie Qingcheng as all sorts of feelings welled up in his heart. The segment in *The Many Faces of Malady* featuring homosexual romance—the one that He Yu had acted in—had deeply moved Chen Man. He felt that the film had mirrored reality perfectly, that the feelings between people of the same sex truly were extremely difficult to express in words. He liked Xie Qingcheng, but he didn't dare say it aloud.

But in this moment, because Xie Qingcheng was fast asleep and because the movie had touched him, Chen Man felt a whisper of temptation. Bowing his head, he stared with rapt attention and bated breath as he covered the other man's hand with his own. Their fingers folded over each other as Chen Man's palm pressed against the back of Xie Qingcheng's hand.

This was something that He Yu had only ever done to Xie Qingcheng while in bed.

He Yu seemed to merge wholly into the darkness, with only the ghostly pallor of his skin still visible. He was wearing a mask, so no one could see most of his face, but his emotions felt like an overturned bucket of paint.

He didn't even want to spare Chen Man a glance. How laughable. What kind of garbage was this? What perversion! How had he missed the fact that this guy was a homosexual back in the cafeteria? How old was this police officer again? Twenty-something? Wasn't it a bit too kinky for him to like someone Xie Qingcheng's age? And they were both men. How disgusting...!

And what about Xie Qingcheng? Wasn't he usually more vigilant than this? Had he died in his sleep? Getting his hand groped and not even realizing it—what useless trash!

He Yu's mental state was as distorted as a Munch painting. He stared silently at Xie Qingcheng's sleeping face and the hand Chen Man was holding until he couldn't take it anymore.

He watched as Chen Man gazed, transfixed, at Xie Qingcheng, and then began to lean over, getting closer and closer to the sleeping man's face, which was cast in a faint blue glow under the light of the screen...

Wake up, you idiot! He Yu shouted in his head. He was overcome by rage—there was no way he could just sit there and watch. He picked up the iced lemon soda he had brought with him from his seat's armrest and upended it over Xie Qingcheng without the slightest hesitation.

Chen Man sat up straight at once, freezing in place, his face turning red, then white, then green. But Xie Qingcheng had no idea what had just happened. He had been sound asleep when a full bottle of soda was unceremoniously dumped over his head, chilling him to the bone.

Chen Man was a good-natured young man, but he wasn't so good-natured he could take something like this. He turned around and yelled, "What's wrong with you? What are you doing?!"

Still sitting behind them, with his hat pulled down low and his long legs crossed, He Yu replied in a neutral yet elegant tone, "My apologies, I lost my grip."

He spoke very quietly, and between the noise of the audience and the movie playing in the background, neither Xie Qingcheng nor Chen Man recognized him.

Chen Man frowned. "Look at him! He's soaked through!"

"...Forget it. It's fine." Xie Qingcheng was accustomed to keeping his cool. Since the student behind him hadn't done it on purpose, he saw no point in getting angry. But he really was soaked through. Chen Man was sitting next to him, but he was completely fine; every drop of the student's drink had fallen onto Xie Qingcheng.

Xie Qingcheng glanced down at his shirt and autumn jacket, both sopping wet and plastered to his body. He sighed and ducked down to speak with Chen Man. "I'll go backstage and ask Xie Xue where I can borrow a dryer. You stay here and watch the movie." With that, he left the theater.

He Yu watched Xie Qingcheng's silhouette fade into the darkness before finally disappearing into the emergency exit that was connected to the backstage area. He sat quietly for a moment. Then, as calmly as ever, he got up and followed him.

Xie Qingcheng borrowed the dressing room backstage.

If Huzhou University Theater had been putting on a play, this room would be bustling with people rushing back and forth. But they were showing a movie, so the dressing room was utterly deserted.

Xie Xue had been shocked when Xie Qingcheng asked her for the key. "Ge, how'd you get so wet?"

"...The student sitting behind me accidentally knocked over his drink," he explained. "It's not a big deal, but I need to borrow a hair dryer."

"Oh, okay, there's a bunch of hair dryers. The mounted ones in the changing rooms are the easiest to find—you can go take a look."

There were three changing cubicles in the dressing room, each with a hair dryer mounted on the wall. Huzhou University had been renovated a couple of years ago, and the president had overzealously installed a motion sensor light in each of the stalls—when Xie Qingcheng pulled open the curtain and walked in, the lamp lit up and illuminated the mirror inside with a brassy yellow glow.

He really did look wretched. Not only were his clothes wet, but his hair was soaked too. He drew the red velvet curtain closed and loosened the buttons of his waterlogged shirt.

The man in the mirror was very tall, with broad shoulders and a narrow waist, his wet shirt clinging to his slender figure. But he really had become haggard in recent days. With his buttons undone, it was clear that he had lost too much weight. His skin was so pale it was nearly translucent, as if his entire body had been drained of blood. Even the color of his lips seemed washed out.

There was a round stool in the changing room, for when people needed to sit or put on shoes, but Xie Qingcheng was a tightly wound man and preferred to stand. He simply stood there and began to blow-dry his short hair and damp shirt.

The dryer was so loud that he had no idea someone had walked into the dressing room—until the red velvet curtain was lifted aside, and the motion-sensing welcome light turned on once more.

Whipping his head around, Xie Qingcheng met He Yu's eyes.

"Xie Qingcheng," He Yu said softly.

He had already taken off his hat and mask, revealing a face as handsome as it was sinister. He was dressed very casually, in a long shirt and jeans. He was even wearing sneakers. Xie Qingcheng looked him over from head to toe, realization dawning—

"...It was you?!"

He Yu smiled, but it didn't reach his eyes. Crowding into the changing room, he grabbed Xie Qingcheng by the arm and shoved him against the mirror.

"It was me. It's just a shame that you realized too late."

64

BUT HE FELT VERY HOT

THE CHANGING ROOM was narrow and cramped, so squeezing in two adult men, both over 180 centimeters tall, made it much too crowded. It felt as though every hot breath they let out would be immediately inhaled by the other man.

After the previous round of misery he'd endured, how could Xie Qingcheng possibly be willing to stay in such a small, enclosed area with this pervert? Slapping He Yu's hand aside, he shot him a blistering glare and muttered, "Get out of my way."

He Yu released him and lowered his gaze, smiling faintly. "Why did you stop drying yourself? Go ahead. I'll just watch from here."

"Step aside."

"Why the rush? Look, your hair's still wet." He Yu reached out once more to brush his fingertips against the ends of Xie Qingcheng's dripping hair, only for Xie Qingcheng to shake him off.

He Yu ignored him—his lashes didn't even flutter before his fingertips slid down, sweeping over the gaping shirt and landing on the side of Xie Qingcheng's slim waist.

An electric, tingling thrill sparked from the pit of his stomach in a ripple of heat as he was engulfed by the outrageous memories of that night. He Yu gazed down at Xie Qingcheng's abdomen, the rims of his eyes flaming red as his voice dropped an octave. "You're wet here, too."

Xie Qingcheng was caught utterly off guard by He Yu's touch. He suddenly felt a flicker of fear.

But he was a coolheaded man who rarely lost his temper, as he considered it unseemly to throw screaming fits or make an unnecessary fuss. His voice remained low and merely sharpened like an unsheathed dagger that was about to slice into He Yu's neck.

"Step aside!"

"Mm. I'll step aside...so you can go find that pig?"

"Pig..." It took Xie Qingcheng a moment to realize that He Yu was talking about Chen Man. Such crudely derogatory language shouldn't come from the mouth of an educated man like He Yu—but he knew He Yu's elegance and refinement were only skin deep. In reality, he was just a beast. Xie Qingcheng narrowed his eyes. "You were staring at us the whole time?"

Us.

So the two of them were considered an "us," huh? He Yu felt another surge of cold rage.

He recalled everything he'd seen before: Chen Man draping his coat over Xie Qingcheng at the hospital, Chen Man calling him when something happened... What kind of ordinary guy would care for another man like that—a man who was his elder, no less?

He was blind not to have seen it sooner! To think that he'd actually shared a meal with the guy and enjoyed chatting with him!

With this wave of fury trapped in his heart, He Yu began to feel unbearably stuffy. He stared at Xie Qingcheng in silence for a good few seconds. "Xie Qingcheng, you really are an idiot," he said at last, his voice viciously cold. "That pig is just a pervert trying to take advantage of you. Getting so close to him, what exactly do you want him to do to you?"

Xie Qingcheng was also furious. Thinking that He Yu was just looking to pick a fight, he lashed back, "What is this bullshit? Don't project your own twisted thoughts onto other people."

The lava in He Yu's heart swelled as he narrowed his eyes, his expression unreadable. "Bullshit? If it weren't for me, he would've kissed you. You had no idea, you were just snoozing away, but I saw everything from behind you—"

"He Yu, are you insane?!" Xie Qingcheng was really pissed off now. "He would've kissed me? How old is he, even? There must be some limits to your delusions! You really think everyone is as screwed up as you?"

"You like him?"

Xie Qingcheng gritted out each word from between clenched teeth, "Are you aware that the word 'friends' exists in the modern Chinese dictionary?"

"Friends? What kind of friend would treat you so well? Asking for time off just to come watch a movie with you, worrying that you'll get cold and taking off his coat to keep you warm—can't you use your brain?" Xie Qingcheng didn't believe him at all, and it made He Yu so angry he felt like smoke was about to come from his ears. "He obviously wants you!"

"What the hell are you talking about?" Xie Qingcheng snapped, furious. "He's nothing like you."

"He's nothing like me? True, Officer Chen really is nothing like me. He's sunny and warm, clever and obedient—so you like him, don't you?"

"I have nothing to say to you." Sick of dealing with this lunatic, Xie Qingcheng tried to leave. But He Yu blocked his way, so the two of them began to tussle in the cramped space.

He Yu pinned this man down, the reason he hadn't gotten a good night's sleep in days, grunting at the force of his strikes but still taking each one head-on. He grabbed Xie Qingcheng's face and forced him to look at him. "If you don't like him, then stay away from him," he said darkly. "I told you, he's a creep!"

"Are you insane, He Yu? What business is it of yours who I'm friends with? Who the hell do you think you are?"

He Yu's face suddenly went blank, but the more expressionless he was, the more terrifying he became. His thoughts were unfathomable. He stared at Xie Qingcheng for a while before suddenly breaking into a smile. The curve of his mouth was chilly, touched by a hint of madness. "...You must've hit menopause. You're so forgetful."

He suddenly brandished his phone at Xie Qingcheng's face, pulling up the photograph that had accompanied him through so many nights of absurdity and shoving it right before the man's eyes.

Xie Qingcheng couldn't tell what it was at first, but when his eyes finally focused, he realized it was a picture of himself. It only showed the upper half of his body and his sleeping face, but it took him less than a second to recognize when it had been taken: the sight of the hickeys dotted over his collarbone and neck was enough for Xie Qingcheng to recall the intensity of He Yu's actions. The passionate desire on display seemed to leap out of the screen, making his ears redden. It was a photo from that night.

A photo taken after he and He Yu had spent the night together.

Xie Qingcheng's head seemed to buzz as a faint ringing filled his ears. A burst of extreme fury swept through his brain. His face blanched before reddening once more, a flush spreading from the corners of his eyes to the bases of his ears. He grabbed for the phone, but of course He Yu had been anticipating this; he outmaneuvered him and pinned him down firmly.

"...What the hell do you want?!" Xie Qingcheng looked as if he were about to grind his teeth to dust.

"At first, I only wanted it as a souvenir—" He Yu yanked on Xie Qingcheng's soft black hair, forcing him to look at the evidence of his crime on his phone. He stared, dark-eyed, at Xie Qingcheng's face for a long moment before he continued. "But now I can see that its real purpose is to cure you of your Alzheimer's."

Xie Qingcheng grit his teeth and said nothing.

"Didn't you forget who I was to you?" asked He Yu. "Didn't you forget everything that happened that night? But as soon as you saw this photo, you remembered who it was who made you feel so good that night, after such a long dry spell. It's more effective than any medicine."

Xie Qingcheng still didn't reply.

"Xie-ge, will you finally acknowledge me now?"

The youth's words and the image on the phone seared Xie Qingcheng's eyes red with anger. He had endured many things, but this was his first time dealing with something so base, so monstrous—even *he* had no idea what to do. He wanted to turn away, but He Yu wouldn't let him, yanking with pitiless brutality at Xie Qingcheng's hair and forcing him to meet his gaze. In the end, Xie Qingcheng simply closed his eyes, his lashes trembling faintly.

"He...Yu..."

"Mm. Moan some more, I like how it sounds."

Xie Qingcheng's eyes flew open, his expression extremely dangerous. "Are you gay?"

"No," He Yu replied instinctively.

"No? Then you should stop fucking acting like this! What more do you want? Even if I hurt you and upset you before, we should be even now. Why don't you get lost? Fuck off!"

As Xie Qingcheng spoke, ashen faced, he struck He Yu viciously in the chest. He no longer cared whether he hurt himself as he fought to tear himself out of He Yu's grip. He didn't even bother asking for the return of his clothes before he turned around and made to leave.

However, just as he touched the velvet curtain of the changing room, a hand shot out from behind him and drew the curtains tightly shut.

At that moment, having grown used to their presence, the motion-sensing light went out. The room plunged into pitch-black darkness, like the stygian lair of an evil dragon, filled only with the sound of He Yu's low, panting breaths. In the dark, his eyes flashed with a wolfish gleam as he moved closer to Xie Qingcheng, his hands slowly sliding down—

Click.

In the darkness, Xie Qingcheng heard the curtain fastener clicking shut. It was such a soft sound, but it sent goosebumps crawling up his spine.

"You think I don't want to end this?" He Yu narrowed his eyes. At that moment, the only light source was the circle of fairy lights inlaid around the mirror. Their dim, cool-colored glow glanced off the reflection of two people pressed far too close to each other.

Xie Qingcheng swallowed instinctively. He was pressed flush against the mirror's icy surface.

"He Yu, get out of my way."

He Yu did not get out of his way. "Xie Qingcheng, I'm telling you, I feel so hot... Did you know—I've been burning up all the time recently. It's like I have heatstroke." Perhaps because of the darkness and the atmosphere between them, he dropped his voice as well. It was low and searing, exactly as if he'd lost all sense of reason due to the heat. "What about you?"

Xie Qingcheng was silent.

"Xie Qingcheng, you don't feel hot at all?"

As he spoke, he suddenly grabbed Xie Qingcheng's waist to knead and caress it. He shoved him against the changing room mirror, crushing that wiry, half-bared torso between his palms and pressing him against his own upper body. The moment he touched Xie Qingcheng's scalding skin, He Yu couldn't help but groan low in his throat. It was as though his two weeks of erotic dreams had all come true, allowing this parched traveler on the brink of death to suddenly drink his fill. He didn't care if it was wrong or inappropriate anymore.

At times like these, it was only too ordinary for men to become overwhelmed by lust, at the mercy of their hormones—especially young men. For them, rationality was nothing more than dust in the wind.

In the pitch blackness, He Yu clutched at Xie Qingcheng as if he had gone mad. In that very moment, the possessiveness that Chen Man had incited and the lust that their previous carnal entanglement had kindled burned through all the fuses in his brain. He drew closer, dipping his head and nuzzling against the crook of Xie Qingcheng's neck. "Xie Qingcheng, it's so hot," he murmured. "I want you to cool me down."

In the grip of the late-autumn chill, how high must his blood have been boiling for him to feel so hot?

Amidst their chaotic entanglement, in the darkness of the changing room lit only by the LED lights encircling the mirror, He Yu's hands had already clamped stubbornly onto Xie Qingcheng's waist. With a crisp metallic click, the belt buckle came undone. Blood drained from Xie Qingcheng's face. In this moment, the nightmare that had wrested him from sleep and left him drenched in cold sweat for the past two weeks returned once more with a vengeance.

He grabbed He Yu's hand and viciously pinned it down. "Let go."

He Yu didn't let go. He only tugged stubbornly on Xie Qingcheng's belt, his eyes and every movement suffused with madness. "Jack me off," he muttered feverishly, again and again, like a threat. "Xie Qingcheng, jack me off."

"You think I'm running a fucking massage parlor here? Get the fuck out of my sight! Let go of me!"

"Xie Qingcheng..."

Xie Qingcheng grabbed He Yu by the wrist, playing an unseen game of tug-of-war with him as he bit out each of his words. "He Yu, I didn't drink any fucking wine today. Do you want to keep your fingers? If you don't, I'll break them one by fucking one. I'll say it one last time: let go!"

He Yu stared into his eyes. The two of them were so close they shared each breath, pupil nearly pressed to pupil. The fire in Xie Qingcheng's eyes burned so fiercely that He Yu was almost reduced to ash.

He Yu looked at him for a while and smiled. Then the smile slid off his face. He didn't let go. Instead, he dragged Xie Qingcheng to the wall with a blank expression on his face and threw him against it, disregarding the litany of curses the man let out as he pressed the full weight of his body against him.

Of course, Xie Qingcheng would never go down without a fight. Eyes practically sparking with anger, he spun around and swung at He Yu. In the cramped changing room, the two of them began to tear into each other like wild animals. A raging conflagration burned in both their chests, as if there was some deep-seated hatred between them, each and every blow landing with full strength. Such violence—

For Xie Qingcheng it was simple: he could finally unleash his long-suppressed wrath in this narrow stretch of no man's land. But He Yu's emotional state was a bit more complicated. He had been deeply affected by that initial encounter, and its aftermath had left him on edge for a long time. He was sure this sort of reaction wasn't right, but he found it impossible to shake the perverse hunger he had developed for Xie Qingcheng since that day.

He had no way to relieve it himself, yet he was still addicted, like an undercover narcotics agent who'd been hooked on drugs, hating himself as he sank further into ecstasy.

He was the one who'd been avoiding Xie Qingcheng like the plague, but now that he'd gotten a taste, he couldn't stop thinking about tangling with this man with all the hunger of someone desperately starving. As time went on, He Yu's craving grew more and more deadly—like a boy in the middle of a growth spurt, he could never eat his fill, could never get enough.

The corner of his lip was already bleeding from where Xie Qingcheng had hit him in the face, but the metallic taste only seemed sweet to him. With a crimson-streaked grin, he let out a delighted yet twisted laugh as he dragged Xie Qingcheng back by the hair, thwarting his attempts to escape. Enduring blow after blow that was strong enough to break his ribs, he locked the man in place and moved to kiss him.

During this fierce yet silent hand-to-hand battle, he felt a sense of joy at finally being able to vent the desires blocking up his heart. He even had a sudden revelation—after he fucked Xie Qingcheng that first time, why did he act like such a hypocrite and block him? He should have thought this through earlier. Then Xie Qingcheng would never have had the chance to contact Chen Man at all. Xie Qingcheng would have no choice but to wear himself out servicing

He Yu every day, getting taken in the office, on the sports fields at night, in the classrooms after school let out...

As for He Yu, he wouldn't have had to waste so many nights in meaningless conflict with himself...he wouldn't have had to punish himself for so long.

Perhaps it was because both men had sustained injuries, but at some point they had stopped fighting. Their scuffle had been fierce—He Yu's lip had been torn bloody, and Xie Qingcheng's wrists were covered in fingerprint bruises.

"I'll never appear before you again, okay?" Xie Qingcheng rasped hoarsely. "Now smash that phone to pieces! Stop disgusting the both of us!"

"No," He Yu said, his voice taking on a roguish quality that sounded almost coquettish. "I refuse."

The older man stared at him.

"Xie Qingcheng, all people can change."

"...What do you mean?" Xie Qingcheng replied, sensing that something was wrong.

"I mean that I've suddenly realized that we *can* continue on like this."

Xie Qingcheng's eyes widened. He had never seen He Yu's sickness act up in such a terrifying way before.

As he spoke, He Yu's gaze was obsessive, yet calm. It was as though he were stating some inevitable fact of life, his voice so indifferent it left no room for argument. "Look, I had a failed crush, remember? When someone with a failed crush has nothing else to rely on, it's very easy for them to become suicidal. You might as well look after me by keeping me company in bed. That way, this disease growing inside my heart won't push me to my death. And who knows? Maybe I'll be able to help cure your sexual frigidity.

It's a pretty good deal, right? You won't be losing out. And I'm still young, too—when you married Li Ruoqiu, you were both getting on in years, weren't you? It'll feel different with me. So why not give me a try?"

He pressed forward as he spoke. The searing heat of the young man's body made Xie Qingcheng break out in goose bumps, and the sensation of being forcibly touched made him want to retch. He Yu yanked him around, making him face the mirror.

"I'll waive the fee if it doesn't work."

Xie Qingcheng had never realized that this sort of play existed— He Yu truly was an extraordinary self-taught talent.

He forced the half-naked Xie Qingcheng to look at himself in the mirror. Then, from behind him, He Yu rubbed his hot, firm body against Xie Qingcheng's tailbone, sparking a current of fear straight to Xie Qingcheng's scalp even through his clothes.

This terrifying person pressed into him from behind. Even as the theater outside teemed with thousands of students, one of the feature film's actors was here in this pitch-dark, unoccupied changing room, forcing Xie Qingcheng to look at their bodies straining against each other in the preposterous madness reflected in the mirror.

"You fucking want money too?" he said in a trembling voice.

"If you're suffering financial difficulties, I can work pro bono."

He Yu had the time and leisure to joke around with him now. He held Xie Qingcheng in place by the waist and leaned forward to kiss his earlobe. Then he looked up at the deeply humiliated, incandescently furious man in the mirror and said, "But if I'm working pro bono...I'll have to ask for your cooperation. Doctor, let's cure each other, okay?"

With that, he forced Xie Qingcheng's face around and, brooking no refusal, kissed his thin lips. It had been nearly two weeks since

he last kissed those lips. Since then he'd avoided them like deadly poison while reliving the memories time and again in his dreams.

The figures of Xie Xue, Lü Zhishu, and Chen Man flashed before He Yu's eyes. He felt sincere joy—the joy of smashing each of those images into the ground. It was a joy gleaned from trampling all of them, enacting vengeance against them, hurting them.

Xie Qingcheng had bitten through his lip, but He Yu didn't care. It was just blood, right? It was his favorite scent of all.

Xie Qingcheng gritted his teeth. "You dare—"

"Mm. I wouldn't dare." He Yu laughed softly, then kissed Xie Qingcheng again with his fingers clasped around the man's neck. His voice muffled by the kiss, he murmured gently to Xie Qingcheng even as the other man was on the verge of snapping his neck. "How could I possibly dare to do something so untoward?"

The more he spoke, the more earnest he sounded.

"No transaction in this world can be forced. If you're unwilling, then of course that's fine too. But you see these photographs, Xie Qingcheng? They're just pictures of your sleeping face, they look pretty normal, but I wonder what Xie Xue would say if I sent them to her?"

Xie Qingcheng froze.

"If she happened to ask me how I managed to get a picture of you sleeping, why don't you tell me how I would answer her?"

"He Yu, you...!"

He Yu kissed Xie Qingcheng's earlobe, which had paled from shock, and chuckled softly. "When I'm going mad, I can say anything, I can do anything—you know that better than anyone."

Silently, his fingers slid down to rest on that ice-cold metal buckle once more. He felt Xie Qingcheng's waist tense up, and he once again grabbed He Yu's hand to stop him.

He Yu's smile faded, his eyes darkening. "Xie Qingcheng," he said dispassionately, "you'd better think things through. I'm no longer the He Yu you once knew. I find all of you unspeakably disgusting, so I could do anything right now. It's simple: do you want to seek pleasure with me, or do you want to bet on whether I'll tell Xie Xue about what we did together? I'll tell her everything. The slenderness of your waist, the number of moles on your shoulders... I'll send her your photos too. You won't have any way to explain yourself to her. So think things through."

Having said his piece, He Yu waited, calm and unruffled amid the chaos.

He waited and waited as Xie Qingcheng resisted and trembled. He waited for a long time—a long, long time—but in the end, Xie Qingcheng didn't make any further moves.

A cold smile finally spread across He Yu's overcast expression. He knew that he now held Xie Qingcheng's Achilles' heel in his hand. Given Xie Qingcheng's particular type of straight man cancer, there were times when he valued his masculine pride over his life.

After all, they were the only two people who knew about their private affairs. Once there had been a first time, a second couldn't be ruled out, if the conditions were right. If He Yu took the risk and used the events at the night club as his bargaining chip, Xie Qingcheng wouldn't dare do anything rash in the short term.

He knew that this would be Xie Qingcheng's choice. Languishing in the dark would always be preferable to public humiliation— especially being humiliated in front of his sister.

So with a smile quirking the corners of his mouth, He Yu reached one hand into Xie Qingcheng's gaping shirt and curved it around his waist, while sliding his other hand forward to gently cover Xie Qingcheng's own.

Clasping his large hand over Xie Qingcheng's fingertips, he manipulated the man's fingers into slowly pulling down the zipper of his slacks.

It was just a single action, but reflected in the mirror, it made it seem as if the very air within the changing room had been set aflame. Little by little, the temperature began to rise. With a click, the cold metal buckle on Xie Qingcheng's slacks snapped open.

The youth gently kissed the older man's nape, then sighed with satisfaction. Reaching up, he stroked over Xie Qingcheng's icy features with crooked fingers, inch by inch. Then he closed his eyes and retraced his path with the tip of his nose like a hound, intimate and adoring, yet with a hidden element of hair-raising coercion. "That's more like it," he said gently. "My dear Doctor Xie, you have to behave."

The dressing room was too small. There was only so much space. When He Yu forcibly yanked Xie Qingcheng's slacks down and reached inside, the temperature within seemed to melt the two of them into wet clay before melding them seamlessly back together.

He Yu turned slightly, fondling Xie Qingcheng through his underwear while he lavished sloppy kisses on his ear, taking his earlobe into his mouth and slowly tonguing at it. The lewd, slick sounds made a shiver run up Xie Qingcheng's spine.

He Yu had never liked men, but drunk on desire like this, his hunger far outweighed his distaste. He did feel some initial revulsion as he palmed the man's cock through the fabric, but at the sight of Xie Qingcheng's face flushing with extreme humiliation and embarrassment, that revulsion dissipated like smoke in the wind, evaporated by the heat of lust.

But as He Yu curled his hand around Xie Qingcheng's cock, he felt somewhat dissatisfied...because he'd jacked off way too many times while thinking of Xie Qingcheng in the last few days.

What he'd wanted at the start of all this was to see Xie Qingcheng fall into a pathetic state, but in the end, in his solitude, he was the one who ended up being the most pathetic of all.

He Yu felt that he'd been cheated. Xie Qingcheng, this divorcé, really was awful. Xie Qingcheng was experienced in the bedroom and had been with a woman before. He wasn't inexperienced like He Yu—he wasn't reliving that night with single-minded focus all the time, nor was he constantly thinking about it, constantly wanting it, the way He Yu did.

Xie Qingcheng didn't care at all, of course; he didn't want He Yu in the slightest.

This thought made He Yu feel even bleaker inside. He began to kiss and bite Xie Qingcheng's ear with renewed energy and greater force. His hands didn't remain idle either, as they swiftly removed Xie Qingcheng's underwear after some intimate groping.

Xie Qingcheng turned away immediately, but He Yu kept him pinned and forced him to face the mirror. "Don't move," he said softly, stroking him. "Look."

Xie Qingcheng's breath hitched. The reflection in the mirror was so ridiculously obscene; it completely exceeded his imagination. He Yu stood behind him, stroking Xie Qingcheng's largely unresponsive dick with one hand while the other gripped his jaw, forcing him to tilt his head back.

He Yu stared into the mirror as well, as though he was staring into all those unbearably absurd wet dreams from the past few nights. His canines peeked out slightly as he spoke, the tips of his teeth pressing gently against Xie Qingcheng's neck, again and again. "What do you think?"

"...He Yu...whatever you want to do, just do it. Stop coming up with new ways to mess around..." Xie Qingcheng already knew that resistance was useless, but although his eyes had already reddened with humiliation, he forced himself to stay calm as he spoke.

However, like a faint whiff of blood, the subtle tremor in his voice didn't go unnoticed by He Yu.

He Yu's hand moved from gripping his jaw to holding onto him from behind. He inhaled deeply against the side of Xie Qingcheng's neck as if he was smoking some addictive drug. Then, with his eyes half-lidded, he began to stroke Xie Qingcheng's chest lewdly and forcefully as he pulled him further into the circle of his arms.

A pair of eyes lifted to glance at the mirror. Those pupils were filled with a near-diabolical madness.

"You call this messing around?" he asked, throaty and dark. "This is called making love, Professor. You're already thirty-two and have been married before—do you really need me to teach you the meaning of this expression?"

Humiliated, Xie Qingcheng tried to turn his face away again, but He Yu shoved him back, pressing his entire body up against the mirror and forcing him to observe the lurid scene even more clearly.

He Yu's hand kept stroking up and down the man's cock, but how could Xie Qingcheng get any enjoyment out of this? No matter what he did, that delicately beautiful length didn't react at all.

It left him even more frustrated.

He was already unbearably hard, so hard that the front of his underwear was already slightly damp, but Xie Qingcheng truly had no reaction whatsoever. He Yu's eyes couldn't help but take on a sheen of anger. In the end, he decided to give up on taking care of Xie Qingcheng for now—did he really expect to cure him?

So what if Xie Qingcheng didn't respond? He only needed to get himself off.

Thus, somewhat angrily, he flipped Xie Qingcheng around, pressing his back against the ice-cold mirror as he stared into Xie Qingcheng's peach-blossom eyes up close.

"You really are frigid. When you haven't taken any aphrodisiacs, you can't even get it up."

Xie Qingcheng gnashed his teeth hatefully. "What kind of normal man would react to another man like this? You're just a fucking nutcase."

The word "nutcase" was taboo to He Yu. As soon as the word left his mouth, He Yu slapped him across the face and then roughly shoved him down.

"Get on your knees and unzip me with your teeth."

Forcing Xie Qingcheng to "make love" to him was already the last straw, but if He Yu wanted to sexually humiliate him even further due to a momentary impulse or a flash of anger, he'd better think again.

Xie Qingcheng staggered from his shove but managed to stay on his feet. "In your fucking dreams!" he snarled. His eyes flashed with cold blades of light. Staring into them, He Yu conceded that he really was a pervert—seeing Xie Qingcheng like this only made him even more excited.

He hadn't hit him too hard just now. It had just been a reflexive reaction when he was caught off guard by the word "nutcase," combined with his innate tendency toward sexual aggression. Now, as He Yu looked into Xie Qingcheng's eyes, he couldn't help reaching up to touch where he had just slapped him. Then he replaced his hand with his lips and kissed Xie Qingcheng gently on the cheek, again and again.

"You're acting up again," he murmured softly between kisses, "even though I just told you to behave."

Then he pressed his hands against Xie Qingcheng's shoulders, trying to shove the man to his knees.

But this had struck Xie Qingcheng's limit. Each and every one of Xie Qingcheng's lean muscles tensed to the fullest, and He Yu found it impossible to physically force him to lower his head.

He Yu sneered. "You really are a tough nut to crack... We're about to do it anyway, so what difference does this make? Didn't I just take care of you?"

"Take care of me?" Xie Qingcheng's eyes had gone red. "All I felt was disgust."

He Yu's mouth drifted from his cheek to lightly cover his lips, brushing against them over and over. "Mm... Then you can try something even more disgusting."

But he did stop trying to force Xie Qingcheng to kneel and use his mouth. The struggle was too demanding and would use up too much of his strength. There wasn't much point in wasting his time on it, so He Yu simply grabbed Xie Qingcheng's hand and pulled it down. With his large palm tightly enveloping the back of Xie Qingcheng's hand, he used Xie Qingcheng's fingers to undo his own zipper and remove his underwear. Then, he forced Xie Qingcheng's stiff hand to touch the terrifying length that sprang from his pants.

His cock was very hot, very large, and painfully swollen, with veins protruding menacingly along its surface and sticky liquid beginning to collect at the tip, and when he dragged Xie Qingcheng's hand down to touch that moist, hot length, Xie Qingcheng couldn't help but begin to tremble.

His mind was clear and his disposition calm, and he wouldn't make a sound even when he was gripped by terror. But the shaking of his body betrayed the truth.

Pleased by his reaction, He Yu kept a commanding grip on Xie Qingcheng's hand, allowing him no opportunity to hurt him, and leaned down to seek Xie Qingcheng's faintly trembling lips in another lingering, sloppy kiss. He licked and sucked as he deepened the kiss, his breath quickening as soft, wet noises filled the room.

Pressing Xie Qingcheng amorously against the mirror, he stroked and kissed him for a long while, only releasing him once the mirror had begun to fog up from the hot sweat dripping from their bodies.

He Yu was a mentally ill pervert; there was a hint of violent aggression even in his lingering, exploratory kisses. Xie Qingcheng was no weakling either, so after their kiss, both of their mouths were a bit raw. Xie Qingcheng was even bleeding slightly from the corner of his lip.

After a moment of silence, He Yu leaned in again to lick away that speck of blood with the soft tip of his tongue. Then, as if he was trying to steal away all the air in Xie Qingcheng's lungs, he pressed another heavy kiss against his lips.

Gripping Xie Qingcheng's wrist, He Yu forced the other man to stroke him off as he continued to entangle him in an open-mouthed kiss. Then he shifted past Xie Qingcheng's ear and trailed his lips down the side of his neck, biting down with his white teeth as if he wanted to suck his blood.

Abruptly, He Yu straightened up, his throat bobbing as he wrenched both of Xie Qingcheng's arms up over his head. With Xie Qingcheng's hands pinned in place, He Yu pressed closer and stared at him.

"You've got a talent for this. You're making me feel so good—look how hard I am."

As he spoke, he leaned into Xie Qingcheng and rutted forward, hard and sensual, his wet, searing length pressing against Xie Qingcheng's stomach and rubbing back and forth intimately.

"Can you feel it?" Grinding his dick against Xie Qingcheng's torso, He Yu whispered into his ear, "Soon, it'll be fucking into you, just as hard as it is right now."

Xie Qingcheng's eyes were already completely bloodshot, yet he no longer wanted to speak. He had mounted an intense struggle, but it turned out to be utterly futile. He might as well face He Yu's shamelessness as coldly as he could.

Eyes half-closed, He Yu nuzzled against Xie Qingcheng lightly, then flipped him around so that he was facing the mirror once more. As he stood behind Xie Qingcheng, the tips of He Yu's fingers played over his pale nipples. Then he kneaded at Xie Qingcheng's waist and hips with his large hands, every motion overflowing with sensual implication, as he rubbed the terrifyingly erect length that Xie Qingcheng had just stroked against the cleft of his ass—as if biding his time amid that softness.

"Professor Xie," He Yu called out softly, his hot breath brushing over Xie Qingcheng's skin. "I've always wanted to ask you..." His voice was low and throaty, as though carrying an electric current, intense enough to make gooseflesh rise. "That night, when I fucked you into coming—did it feel good? Did you think about it afterward?"

Silence.

"Did you?"

Still no response.

"Answer me."

It seemed He Yu had really touched a nerve. Xie Qingcheng abruptly turned to glare at him, hissing through gritted teeth, "What I think is that you're absolute trash. You have absolutely no idea what you're doing—how do you have the face to ask me something like that?"

Sure enough, He Yu's expression darkened. "As if you can talk. Were you any better when you started out with your ex-wife?"

"You really think everyone is just like you... He Yu, you...!"

Now that he'd asked the question, though, He Yu realized that he didn't actually want to hear Xie Qingcheng's answer. He didn't want to hear about how Xie Qingcheng had slept with a woman before—it made him feel extremely uncomfortable. Before Xie Qingcheng could say anything else, He Yu clamped his teeth down on the vein running along his neck. He licked at it delicately, then trailed kisses from the side of his neck to the back, finally stopping at the red mole at the nape of Xie Qingcheng's neck.

When he kissed that mole, a faint shiver ran through Xie Qingcheng's entire body, as if He Yu had bitten down on some soft vital point.

"Of course," said He Yu, "you can say what you want, but I fucked you until you were leaking that night... You were on your hands and knees underneath me, spilling all over the sheets... You've got a good memory, Professor; surely you didn't forget what happened. I can make you feel so good when I'm inside you—could Li Ruoqiu do that?"

Xie Qingcheng immediately flew into a rage. "The fuck she could! Could you be any more absurd?! She's a woman! Not some psycho like you..."

Xie Qingcheng continued to curse him out. Naturally, this was well within He Yu's expectations. But he didn't care. He didn't care about anything Xie Qingcheng said—he was too hungry, too desperate to once again hear the hoarse sounds he'd fucked out of Xie Qingcheng when he caught him off guard that night.

So he let him talk, resolving to show Xie Qingcheng that no one else, whether they were a man or a woman, could make him feel as good as he could.

Xie Qingcheng was too stiff and dispassionate—he had no desire to play around, and he wouldn't have known how to even if he had. The average woman wouldn't be able to get much out of sleeping with a man like this. Most women wanted overwhelming passion from their partner—if they couldn't sense any passion at all, they'd feel very frustrated.

But when someone like this was the one being subdued and encroached upon, the initiative fell into the other person's hands. He Yu wasn't a woman—he would play around with anything as long as it was exciting. He was the only one who could drag Xie Qingcheng down into the gaping chasm of desire.

He kissed Xie Qingcheng again and again, his lips hot and wet as they trailed over his skin—and as he kissed him, he started to nudge a fingertip into that hidden entrance that had been the object of his mortal fixation these past few days, working his way in bit by bit. He became a bit overeager once he had his finger pressed inside and thrust into him roughly and carelessly, mimicking the motions of intercourse as he stretched him open.

He was a fast learner with an excellent memory. He could remember all too clearly the things he hadn't done right the last time, as well as the things that had been especially arousing. He would adjust accordingly this time and put everything to use on Xie Qingcheng's body.

Though his movements were a bit hurried, he had smeared some hand cream from the dressing room's vanity onto his fingers. Thus, as he worked his way inside, that small opening went from being dry and tight to increasingly slick. The youth thrust into the man again and again until his fingers no longer encountered so much resistance.

By then, He Yu couldn't hold back anymore. Extracting his fingers, he pulled his zipper down all the way. With his dick in one hand, he pressed it to Xie Qingcheng's entrance, and with the other, he landed a slap on the full curve of his ass.

"Relax," he said, his voice growing even huskier, "I'm gonna fuck you now."

"You don't need to give me a fucking play-by-play..."

He Yu gave his waist another vicious pinch. "You don't need to be in such a hurry to snipe back at me, either. Let's see what you have to say when I start fucking you."

As he spoke, he palmed roughly at his own cock, achingly hard after being left wanting for so long, then pressed it against Xie Qingcheng's puckered hole and slowly pushed in.

He Yu gasped immediately, his dark pupils taking on a wet sheen; just getting the very tip inside was enough for his body to immediately recall that night's intense pleasure. He could feel Xie Qingcheng's entrance passionately drawing him in but also resisting him, unable to fight back as it was forced open, clenching and tightening. In an instant the ecstasy of fucking into that hole came back to him, the feeling that had threatened to drive him mad with obsession every time he remembered it.

He Yu panted with relish as he clutched Xie Qingcheng's waist with his other hand, pinning the man between himself and the mirror. The force of his grip and the overwhelming thrill made the veins in his forearm pop out.

Although the tendons in Xie Qingcheng's neck were protruding in discomfort, he clenched his jaw, refusing to make a sound even as sweat beaded on his forehead. Unlike this young student reliving his first time, Xie Qingcheng was the one being forcibly fucked, and on top of that, he was a grown man with a great sense of self-respect.

Even with just the tip inside, every muscle in his body tensed as his face flushed with humiliation, a blush staining his frost-pale skin. His hands strained against the mirror, sweat soaking him in a layer of amorous dampness like water from melting ice.

With the opening breached, He Yu kept slowly inching further inside. At first, because they were both very tense, he pressed in deeply yet slowly, the entire process stretched out like a slow-motion shot, reflected in the mirror in all of its fiery glory. But in the end, he was still too impatient. As soon as he was halfway in, he lost any sense of consideration; the eager young man couldn't resist any longer. He was about to die of thirst, about to go mad with it. He had gotten off to Xie Qingcheng's photos so many times, and the longer it had gone on, the more frantically he lusted after his body, enough that just rubbing against his blanket would leave him on the verge of coming. Now that Xie Qingcheng's hole had taken half of him in, the pleasure of being buried inside him was like a jolt of electricity. How could he possibly wait any longer? With a muted groan and a sudden violent thrust, he shoved his entire length inside.

This sudden invasion and the burst of pain that followed nearly had Xie Qingcheng breathing his last against the mirror. Although he wasn't caught off guard as fully as he had been that first time— back then, he'd let a yell escape his throat—his whole body still began to tremble.

He Yu was now fully seated. He held Xie Qingcheng tightly, his voice a hoarse rasp. "Ge, you're covered in sweat and so hot inside. You're squeezing me so tightly. So hot... So wet..."

Xie Qingcheng refused to let out a single sound. This searing invasion had torn a gash through his calm, his skin flushing crimson. It was like his nightmare reenacted, dragging him back into that night's filthy quagmire. But to He Yu, this was a reenactment of a wet dream. Pushing deep into that warm, tight, wet opening, he expelled a rough breath of delight, his black eyes burning with hot desire. He kissed Xie Qingcheng fiercely, from his neck, down to his collarbones, to the sides of his shoulders, on to his trembling shoulder blades, and took a deep whiff.

"Xie Qingcheng," he said hoarsely, "why does your body...suddenly smell so good?"

Xie Qingcheng's voice was even hoarser than He Yu's. "Smells good my ass," he whispered, eyes red. "Something's wrong with your nose..."

Now that he was inside Xie Qingcheng, He Yu didn't bother arguing. Instead, he kissed Xie Qingcheng again. "So good."

The parched man finally got his drink of water, feeling pleasure to the extreme as even his spine trembled from his second taste of this euphoria. Holding Xie Qingcheng, he began to thrust hard and deep.

When He Yu began to move, Xie Qingcheng truly couldn't take it anymore. Without the influence of the aphrodisiac, the humiliation of being invaded like this was impossible to ignore. Even more terrifyingly, He Yu had shown up in the heat of the moment this time, acting entirely on impulse: he wasn't in the habit of carrying condoms, so he had just stuck it in without any protective barrier whatsoever. This fact had occurred to He Yu, too, but it only made him even more excited. Like every eager young man getting his first taste, instinct drove him to push into those warm depths again and again, panting heavily as he thrust deep and hard.

The temperature in the changing room rose like a burning furnace, as if everything inside was about to melt away. Skin slapped against skin. He Yu sometimes quickened his pace and sometimes went slow. When he slowed down, he kept Xie Qingcheng pinned beneath him, pulling out entirely before viciously slamming back inside. But when he sped up, he fucked into Xie Qingcheng with rapid shallow thrusts, a feeling that left him breathless. Without withdrawing completely, he shoved himself deep inside immediately after pulling out the slightest bit, fucking Xie Qingcheng quickly, the pleasure building up maddeningly as it gathered within him.

Perhaps it was how long it'd been, or perhaps it was because there was no condom in the way, but the sensation of being tightly squeezed by that spasming channel became all the hotter and more thrilling. He Yu was all but losing his mind from how good it felt. His thrusts grew sharper and sharper as he fucked Xie Qingcheng faster and faster, driving deeper into him with single-minded ferocity and reducing the man to a quivering mess. One of his hands was still tightly stroking the older man's flat belly as if trying to see whether he could feel how deep he'd gone, how hard he was pushing through the thin layer of Xie Qingcheng's muscled abdomen.

"Fuck..." He Yu felt so good that he didn't even bother to maintain his usual calm, genteel veneer. Vulgar words spilled from his mouth, his Adam's apple bobbing erotically, as his cock drove continuously into Xie Qingcheng's body. The little bastard's entire face was shrouded with burning desire, truly insane from lack of release; he thrust so fast and so deep it seemed as if he wanted to fuck the man beneath him right to death.

How could it feel so good...? Why did fucking this man feel so good?

He Yu couldn't have stopped if he wanted to—Xie Qingcheng's hole felt so hot and so tight, wrapping around him, enticing him, sucking him in; it took him in so fully and tightly that he was on the verge of insanity.

But Professor Xie's eyes had gone scarlet from the assault. He was pinned to the mirror and thrust into with such feverish hunger, without any chance of escape. The sensation gave him the terrifying feeling that he was going to be fucked to the point of suffocation.

In the past, Xie Qingcheng had always been calm and collected when he slept with Li Ruoqiu, so much so that their encounters could even be described as polite. They had never behaved outrageously or wildly—it was as if they were simply performing the duty that a mutually respectful married couple had to fulfill. But now, to his horror, as a man over thirty years old, he was having sex with a university freshman inside a school changing room while thousands of students watched a movie in the theater before the stage.

The boy pushed into him deep and fast, brimming with lust, fervor, and a scalding impetuousness. All of it seeped through skin and bone, past where the two of them were stickily joined, sinking forcefully into his body.

"Professor Xie, you really...feel so good... So good..." As He Yu fucked him, his black eyes stared fixedly at their entwined figures reflected in the mirror.

With that first frantic craving somewhat sated by Xie Qingcheng's body, he came back to his senses a little. He panted out a breath, suddenly pulling out and gazing at Xie Qingcheng's face, which seemed almost sensual to his eyes. Then, his chest heaving, he grabbed a small stool, the only chair in the changing room, and sat down.

This time, He Yu faced the mirror himself as he pulled Xie Qingcheng toward him, stroking his own cock.

"Ride me," he said, the jut of his throat bobbing. His eyes gleamed with more than just lust—there was obsession in them, a madness that brooked no argument.

Xie Qingcheng was only human—his body couldn't handle being fucked so brutally for so long. No matter how strong he was, He Yu had made his torso go limp, to say nothing of the tremor in his legs. Until now, he had been enduring it through sheer willpower, but when He Yu yanked him over, he had no ability left to resist.

As He Yu dragged Xie Qingcheng closer to him, Xie Qingcheng caught sight of the terrifying shaft that had just been thrusting crazily inside him. His eyes were already red from humiliation—he immediately looked away. But He Yu grabbed the tie he'd tossed aside and wound it around Xie Qingcheng's neck, letting it hang down over his gaping shirt and bare chest. Then, with a yank on the tie, he pulled him down. "Sit," he told him again. "Fuck yourself on it."

Xie Qingcheng refused, shaking his head, still unwilling to make a sound. The only thing keeping him upright was the hand he had pressed to the mirror.

He Yu tipped his head back and said softly, "How am I going to treat your illness if you're so disobedient?"

Xie Qingcheng didn't answer.

He Yu continued, "It's already like this between us. We won't ever be able to settle the score. But I'd like it for you to feel good too."

Still, Xie Qingcheng shook his head. By this point, even the rims of his eyes had gone red, most likely due to the hurt born of his anger at the intense humiliation his masculinity had suffered.

He Yu stared at him for a while before he sighed, cursed softly, and wrapped his arms around Xie Qingcheng's waist. He hadn't actually been counting on Xie Qingcheng taking the initiative himself. He hauled him over and forced his legs to part around his own waist, then readjusted his position. With one hand on his own cock and one hand on Xie Qingcheng's waist, he guided him into place so that his slick entrance once again swallowed up his fiercely throbbing length, bit by bit.

The process was extremely arousing. As He Yu held Xie Qingcheng, he gazed over his shoulder into the mirror, where he could clearly see the way Xie Qingcheng's trembling body was taking him in and clenching around him in such a humiliating manner. As that wet, slick heat engulfed him once more, he first pressed in firmly with quick grinding motions, then thrust in and out unhurriedly, burying himself further, just like that, rubbing against a terrifyingly deep spot inside Xie Qingcheng's body.

"Ge, you're taking me in so deep..." He Yu stroked Xie Qingcheng's back, brushing his fingers over his beautiful shoulder blades. He moved his hips gently, grinding up with small thrusts. "Can you feel it?" When he again received no reply, he continued, "Do you want to see what you look like when you're being fucked down there?"

He Yu was a man of action. He didn't care how Xie Qingcheng replied; this depraved gentleman's question was merely an impulsive gesture of politeness.

He moved so that his back was to the mirror and Xie Qingcheng was facing it. From this angle, He Yu's body was blocking Xie Qingcheng's view of the place where their bodies joined together. But he could all too clearly see the way his legs were spread wide open, sitting in a boy's lap, bouncing up and down with each thrust. That was more than humiliating enough.

And from this position, He Yu could look up and see the face of the man sitting astride him. He could see just how Xie Qingcheng looked as he pressed into him slowly and deeply, shivering as he took it. Just like that, with the older man straddling his lap, he tilted his head back and thrust upward as he held him in his arms. In this position, even if Xie Qingcheng refused to move, gravity did the work for him, and He Yu was able to bury himself especially deeply into his body—so deep it felt as though he was about to pierce right through his belly.

After fucking into him with those small thrusts for a while, He Yu began to get impatient. Once again, his movements grew increasingly ferocious and ruthless. His hips slapped against Xie Qingcheng's ass with the sound of flesh striking flesh. For a while, the dressing room was filled with the noise of the two men's heavy panting and their bodies urgently colliding, alongside the filthy, wet sounds of their fucking.

Xie Qingcheng had never experienced this kind of stimulation before while sober, and he found it impossible to bear. Shuddering slightly from He Yu's violent thrusts, he abruptly raised a hand to brace himself against the mirror. There he was greeted with a close-up view of his own reflection: sitting astride a young man with his long legs forced open, enduring each ferocious thrust as his legs trembled to the rhythm of their movements.

He Yu panted deeply, thrusting in as deep and hard as he could, as if he wanted to take all of the desire he had bottled up for the last two weeks and concentrate it into this man's body.

At that moment, if anyone came into the dressing room, or even if they just passed by the door, they would definitely hear the sounds of their frantic lovemaking, of He Yu fucking into Xie Qingcheng. He Yu didn't seem to care if they were discovered, though—he had no intention of holding himself back as his thrusts became increasingly rash and forceful.

Anyone who walked by would see that shoe stool shaking beneath the red curtain of the dressing room and hear the muffled creaking noises of its wooden legs as they scraped against the floor.

The two men's legs tangled together over the trousers that had been thrown onto the floor. Xie Qingcheng's toes were curled taut, their paleness tinted with a blush of color, at once unnatural and erotic. The stool shook more and more fiercely as He Yu's motions jerked and rocked Xie Qingcheng's body on his lap with astonishing strength. He slapped Xie Qingcheng's ass over and over, squeezing lewdly at its plump fullness. The sounds that came from his throat were the low sighs of a male in the midst of his rut finally satisfying his desires. "So good... Ge, fucking you feels so good... You were made to get fucked, you know? You're so tight... Damn... You're sucking me in too tight. *Fuck!*"

He Yu almost never used such vulgar language, but when unleashing his bestial desire on Xie Qingcheng's body, he showed a side of himself that no one else had ever seen. He was overflowing with scalding desire, coarse, wild, and primal in the extreme.

But more mortifying than his words were his deep, searing, intoxicated thrusts. Each one was slick and sticky, filling the cramped changing room with wet noises as the prostate secretions mixing with Xie Qingcheng's intestinal fluid made the frenzied, scorching sex grow even wilder.

Xie Qingcheng had been fucked for a long time now—so long that his eyes had grown unfocused, so long that he thought he'd be trapped here and fucked until he suffocated and died. The air inside the changing room had become so hot and thick that he couldn't even catch his breath anymore...

And then—

"Xie-ge."

He Yu suddenly called out his name, very hoarsely, almost passionately.

He had heard his name called nearly the exact same way, just as full of anticipation, the first time Li Ruoqiu had slept with him...but He Yu wasn't the same. A woman would call out with a softly cajoling tone, as if begging for her partner's tenderness. But this youth's voice held an irrepressible impetuousness, an uncontrollable tide of desire—as if he was in the grip of some intense emotion that had him wanting to devour Xie Qingcheng whole.

His voice was soft, blazing, and pure, and yet it wouldn't give Xie Qingcheng any chance to take the initiative, much less allow him to escape. That voice seemed to be telling him that he was expected to take everything he was given.

"Xie-ge... I'm gonna..." He Yu panted urgently for a moment, his throat bobbing. Perhaps because it felt too good, so good his soul was about to leave his body, he didn't even finish his sentence. He just started fucking him even more frantically. Skin slapped against skin, and the stool shook violently. Veins popped on He Yu's arms as he tightened his grip on Xie Qingcheng, his skin flushing redder and his rapturous panting growing rougher to match.

Xie Qingcheng really couldn't take any more—he felt like he couldn't get any air. But as He Yu fucked him more and more urgently, faster and faster, his breathing ragged and the pulse in his neck throbbing, the expression he wore when he looked at Xie Qingcheng changed. As that thing inside him got even harder, more terrifyingly hot, Xie Qingcheng could sense it vividly—he could even feel it beginning to pulse as it fucked him. He was a man, too—he knew He Yu was about to come.

Xie Qingcheng had endured until now without crying out a single time. But now, the humiliation was too much. Grabbing He Yu's arms, he tried to struggle to his feet. "Don't... Don't come inside...

Pull... Pull out...!" he wailed. There was even a slight tremor in his voice, a surprising note of fear. "Not inside, He Yu... not inside..."

But to He Yu, that voice almost sounded pleading. It only served to incite his masculine sense of dominance and brutality even further. How could he possibly be willing to pull out? His response was only savage force. Brooking no argument, the youth pushed the man back down into his lap. Xie Qingcheng had risen slightly to his feet just now, and so forcibly shoving him back down actually plunged He Yu even deeper.

Xie Qingcheng couldn't help but let out a muffled groan as He Yu gasped roughly in pleasure. Then, making use of the momentum, He Yu simply picked him up entirely and rose to his feet, pressing Xie Qingcheng against the mirror with his entire body suspended in midair. His only points of support were the place where they were connected and the ice-cold mirror behind him.

This new position made Xie Qingcheng's eyes fly open. It was too terrifying... So deep, so hard... He Yu didn't pull all the way out at all; he only pulled back a bit before slamming back inside, fast and hard, the slap of his balls against Xie Qingcheng's skin blending with the wet sounds that had finally begun to emerge after their long coupling. The cock inside him was frighteningly hard and hot, moving in and out like a piston—

Listening to He Yu's rough panting, knowing full well this student was about to ruthlessly come inside him, Xie Qingcheng reached his limit. "He Yu!" he begged again, his voice quavering. "Don't... Don't...! No... Don't come... Pull out, pull out! Don't come inside... Ah... *Ahh*!!"

But even as Xie Qingcheng protested, He Yu kept holding onto him, panting with great urgency as he gave it to him deep and fierce, pulse after pulse, twitching as he came thickly inside him... Coating his deepest recesses, as if he wanted to fill him up completely and leave a mark that could never be wiped clean. Xie Qingcheng's hoarse moans propelled He Yu to even greater heights. He Yu pounded into him like his life depended on it, like he was trying to fuck him to death; he fucked shot after shot of thick fluid into him, fiercely thrusting until the entire wall panel of the changing room was shuddering violently.

Xie Qingcheng lost it on the spot; he had been fucked to the point of breaking down... His legs were spread wide apart, forced to wrap around the student's waist, his chest heaving with what could have been the gasps of a dying man... Between the extreme humiliation and the frightening sensations, tears began to drip involuntarily from the corners of his eyes...

He Yu's bulk pressed down onto Xie Qingcheng as he panted deeply from excitement and stimulation. "Ge, you're so good at sucking me in down there, it feels so good..."

Xie Qingcheng finally couldn't help but lose his senses and scream as he was vigorously filled with a stream of hot come. "Ah... *Ahh*...!"

He Yu had endured so much hunger and thirst, but now, at last, pulse after pulse of his cum shot fiercely and ceaselessly deep into Xie Qingcheng's body. It was so deep and so incredibly thick, the unfamiliar, horrifying feeling of it making Xie Qingcheng's entire body tremble uncontrollably. It was as if his entire person had been shattered to pieces by the reality he was facing in this moment; for all his resolute masculinity, there were tears of humiliation clinging to his eyelashes. His pale lips still kept hazily mumbling, "Don't come...inside... Don't come... Don't come... Ah..."

But it was already too late. He had indeed come inside...

Because of the male instinct to impregnate a sexual partner, even once he'd finished, He Yu kept subconsciously pushing deeper into Xie Qingcheng's body. With his hips pressed between Xie Qingcheng's thighs, he thrust inside and refused to pull out, forcing his still-throbbing cock deeper. It twitched again and again as it amorously plunged further in, spurting out the last bit of his cum before He Yu tenderly plugged all of it inside that wet, twitching little hole with his cock.

This was the first time He Yu had ever come inside another person's body. Before today, he never would have imagined that it would be with Xie Qingcheng...

That it would be a man... That it would be *Xie Qingcheng*...

He'd fucked him until he was so sloppy, pathetic, and miserable; he couldn't do anything but splay his legs and accept his role as the first person in whom He Yu had spent himself...

He Yu collected himself from within the throes of intense stimulation, staring calmly at Xie Qingcheng's face. He continued to fuck gently into Xie Qingcheng as he panted, gazing unblinkingly at the man in his arms, who was so drenched in sweat that it seemed like he'd just been dredged out of the water. All of a sudden, he couldn't hold back anymore—as some unfamiliar yet scalding emotion in his heart surged forth, he suddenly dipped his head and kissed Xie Qingcheng's panting, slightly parted mouth.

Such a thin, cold pair of lips—yet they felt so soft under his own. He Yu closed his eyes and angled his head as he kissed Xie Qingcheng, refusing to pull out down below even as he clung wetly to him further up. As He Yu kissed him, he leaned down, one hand slowly placing the delirious and broken-down Xie Qingcheng on that single cushioned stool, as his other hand slid down involuntarily to touch Xie Qingcheng's abdomen.

This sensation was seriously too strange... He Yu could feel his own heart trembling. He felt like something was different now. And not just within himself—it seemed that Xie Qingcheng's relationship with him had also changed.

This was the first time he'd actually come inside someone else's body. It seemed to mean something completely different from using protection.

In all his nineteen years... The first time he fucked someone and the first time he came inside someone had unexpectedly taken place during these few days and with this man.

He Yu kissed Xie Qingcheng for a long time before, at last, he slowly let go. Their lips had separated a little, but there was still a suggestive wetness staining the corners of their mouths.

"Ge..." Stroking Xie Qingcheng's abdomen, He Yu spoke with a dark and complicated expression. "I came inside... I came so much... Feels like I'm going to get you pregnant..."

This outrageously shameless statement made Xie Qingcheng's eyes gradually come into focus. He raised his hand to bring it down in a vicious yet trembling slap. "He Yu, you motherfucking—"

The blow didn't land. He Yu had grabbed his wrist as if he'd been expecting it. He didn't bother bickering with Xie Qingcheng this time, just allowed him to curse him out as he turned his face, closed his eyes, and pressed a soft kiss to that delicate tattoo.

"Ge, why don't you sit? I'll help you get dressed..."

65

AND WAS VERY EASY TO ANGER

THIS TIME, the idea had struck He Yu on the spot.

He had been truly, miserably starving, so he tormented Xie Qingcheng until he couldn't take it anymore. After eating his fill again, he helped Xie Qingcheng into his clothes, then hugged him and nuzzled against him for a while, kissing him again and again until the fire within him once again began to stir. If not for an interruption by a phone call from the school, asking him where he was and informing him that the awards ceremony following the film's showing was about to begin, there was a ten-thousand-percent chance he would have gone for another round.

Afterward, Xie Qingcheng was in an incredible amount of pain. The same feeling from more than ten days ago, a kind of dull ache that he couldn't put into words, pressed deep into his body once again like a brand. But this time, the queasy feeling in his body was even harder to bear. Last time, He Yu had at least taken protective measures, so there hadn't been any bone-deep discomfort after the fact; Xie Qingcheng only had to deal with the pain. It was nothing like now, when this feeling made even the act of walking drain his face of all color.

As Xie Qingcheng sat back in his seat, Chen Man let out a sigh. "Ge, where'd you go? What took you so long? You were gone for nearly an hour. I almost went to look for you."

Xie Qingcheng sat completely rigid, his back straight and tense. He refused to relax even slightly, much less allow Chen Man to see any of his discomfort. But he didn't want to say anything. His mind was on the verge of collapsing from the frenzied and illicit things the two of them had just done, completely heedless of consequences.

"It's fine," said Xie Qingcheng. After a moment's silence, he added apathetically, "Just keep watching the movie."

Chen Man nodded, but as his gaze swept over Xie Qingcheng's collar, he paused and raised his hand—

"What are you doing!"

Xie Qingcheng saw everyone as an enemy right now. Even though he didn't believe what He Yu had said about Chen Man being gay, he still instinctively grabbed Chen Man's wrist.

The strength of his grip was enough to frighten Chen Man. "Ge... There—there's a strand of hair on your collar."

Xie Qingcheng picked it off himself without saying a word. That strand of hair was slightly longer than his own—of course he knew whose it was. Suppressing the furious trembling of his fingertips, he tossed the hair away with a cold expression.

"Do you have a towelette?"

Chen Man did have one, so he dug it out and handed it to Xie Qingcheng.

Xie Qingcheng wiped his fingers clean one by one, like they had been contaminated by some virus that would cause his entire body to rot if it remained on his skin for too long. Holding back his intense disgust and revulsion, he set the used towelette aside and closed his eyes.

The movie was already almost over. Less than five minutes after Xie Qingcheng had returned to his seat, the end credits began to roll.

But the event wasn't over yet. Next came the awards ceremony.

By the second half of the semester, Huzhou University's various student rankings had already come out, and so at the end of this kind of major performance, there would usually be an awards ceremony. In addition to awards for producing the campus film, the names of the new student government chairs, scholarship winners, and top ten outstanding students would all be announced tonight.

Naturally, the students who would be winning these awards had been informed by their teachers in advance.

"The newly selected member of the student government's publicity committee is..."

As the names were read aloud one by one, each of the students walked onto the stage to accept their awards to the sound of the audience's applause.

"The new chairman of the student government, as selected by the school board, is He Yu from the Screenwriting and Directing class 1001. He Yu, please step up to the stage to receive your award from the university president."

Xie Qingcheng looked on blankly as the beast that had just ravaged him in the dressing room walked onto the stage. As required, he had changed backstage into Huzhou University's student uniform of a white dress shirt and loose slacks, and he looked dapper and refined as he shook the hand of the university president with a smile.

Foolish, love-struck girls and even some starry-eyed boys applauded loudly from the audience, craning their necks to get a better look at the distinguished face of the scholarly and altogether exemplary Young Master He.

"Our He Yu is a paragon of virtue and learning, modest and reserved. I hope that as the new chairman of student government, he will serve as an even more outstanding model for all of our students and dedicate himself even more fully to our university."

The president pinned the student association chairman's badge onto the chest of He Yu's uniform. Because He Yu was very tall and the president was a slightly stooped old man, He Yu bent down slightly, a picture of consideration and modesty. After the president finished conferring his award, He Yu smiled and leaned forward in a slight bow, the long curve of his eyelashes making his expression seem exceedingly gentle.

"He's so cute..."

"Such a gentleman..."

"He's well-mannered too..."

Fury blazed from Xie Qingcheng's chest to the rims of his eyes. He was a gentleman? Well-mannered? Cute? Then who was that in the dressing room just now? Was this the same person?

Onstage, He Yu was still being lavished with assorted commendations from the school council; they said he was "modest and courteous" and "with high standards of moral integrity" as he accepted trophy after trophy. Xie Qingcheng was the only one who knew that less than fifteen minutes before stepping onstage to receive all these awards, this smiling and refined young xueba at the center of the crowd's attention had been entangled backstage with a man thirteen years his senior.

The same mouth that had kissed Xie Qingcheng so fiercely and deeply was speaking such dignified words up on the stage right now, his voice gentle and elegant, winning round after round of applause. But what had that mouth been saying fifteen minutes ago?

He had been pressing kisses all over Xie Qingcheng's ear, pouring all sorts of unbearably shameful and corny sentiments into it. Coming out of his mouth, those flirtatious words became coarse and filthy.

Xie Qingcheng could still feel the lingering sensation—even the slightest movement aroused such torment from that hot stickiness that it made all the hairs on his body stand on end. It was so awful that he wanted to die.

Meanwhile, the culprit who had reduced him to this state was taking the microphone onstage and calmly beginning to deliver his speech, dressed in the most proper and serious of uniforms, with a badge signifying the school's highest approval pinned to his chest, the very picture of handsome refinement.

Xie Qingcheng looked at him with a grim expression.

Gradually, his eyes glazed over as he thought back to their conversation in the dressing room...

This time, he really had acquiesced to He Yu. But in the end, the reason for his compromise wasn't the photo itself. Rather, based on that photo, he had simply made the diagnosis that He Yu was both too ill and too difficult to deal with. He had imprinted on him in a completely abnormal way, like a baby bird.

Xie Qingcheng had a very clear understanding of his purpose in life. He needed to focus his energy on completing the mission that was hidden in his heart. There was no way any person or object could block his path. On that private, secret road, he would cut down anything he encountered, demon or deity. Other than death, no obstacle could stop him.

The kind of desire that He Yu had for him was just another stumbling block—a very troublesome one. So he would rather say yes to He Yu, dealing with him casually and perfunctorily by agreeing to continue this kind of relationship with him, even if he himself didn't have a modicum of interest. At least that way, He Yu wouldn't waste any more of his time.

Before, when Chen Man had realized that Xie Qingcheng was a frightening person, he was actually quite right. Xie Qingcheng was truly terrifying.

Chen Man had thought that he didn't fear death, that he seemed willing to die at any time. But what Chen Man hadn't realized was even more terrifying—Xie Qingcheng didn't see himself as a person at all.

It wasn't only Chen Man—even Xie Xue and Auntie Li had yet to discover that Xie Qingcheng only saw himself as a machine, a blade, a shield, a scabbard, as a bargaining chip that could be invested, as an offering that could slake an evil dragon's thirst for blood.

The only thing he never saw himself as was a living person.

This was precisely why Xie Qingcheng had willingly acquiesced to He Yu's demands—if this choice could direct He Yu's life back onto the right track and prevent him from harassing Xie Qingcheng more and stirring up any more trouble, then, seeing as things had already come to this point, he might as well let the younger man do whatever he pleased.

Someone who didn't see himself as a living person wouldn't take this kind of thing too seriously. Even though it was very stressful and irritating in a physical sense, in the grand scheme of things, it was worth basically nothing.

Xie Qingcheng was very frightening—he didn't need himself, and aside from Xie Xue, Chen Man, and Auntie Li, there was likely no one else in the world who needed him either.

In truth, there were times when Xie Qingcheng thought that now that Xie Xue and Chen Man had grown up and could look after Auntie Li, the three of them would be able to survive without him.

In other words, there was no one in the world who couldn't live without him.

And so Xie Qingcheng tore himself into countless pieces so that he could use his own flesh and bones to deal with any feral dogs or wicked dragons he encountered on the road. When he thought things through, it really was that simple. He didn't have the time to act out a cycle of proposition and rejection with He Yu every single day. Thus, in the end, he simply chose to use himself to deal with this crazy dragon, and then drag his own life back onto the right track once more. When it came to certain things, he really was heartless.

But the little beast was different. That little beast didn't think about it so much, and he had no idea that Xie Qingcheng was harboring such a terrifying state of mind when he agreed to continue that kind of relationship with him. After leaving the stage, he went to find Xie Qingcheng.

At that moment, he was in a terrific mood because Xie Qingcheng had finally said yes to him. After more than ten days, a genuine smile finally spread across his face for all to see. But who would've thought that when he stepped down from the stage and looked around, Xie Qingcheng had already left. The seats were empty—Chen Man was gone too.

He Yu stood rooted to the spot as the departing crowd surged around him, his smile fading into mournful stillness.

As soon as he returned to his dorm room, He Yu removed Xie Qingcheng from his blocklist.

He still disliked homosexuality, just as he disliked Xie Qingcheng, but he told himself that sex and love were two different things. Naturally, he could regard them separately. He felt that he could still be a straight man with a clear conscience.

Therefore, this time was different from the previous time at the club. That first time at the club, he'd blocked Xie Qingcheng as soon as he left—because he had been too naive.

This second time in the dressing room, he unblocked him in a hurry—because he'd suddenly found an excuse he could use to dispel his doubts.

That first time, when he had blocked Xie Qingcheng immediately after doing the deed without even batting an eye, he hadn't realized the severity of the problem. But afterward, his dreams were all filled with images of him fucking Xie Qingcheng. The young man's blood had been set aflame by the experience with no way of putting it out.

It was impossible to walk back from certain things once they'd happened.

After relapsing on the drug known as "Xie Qingcheng" in the dressing room, he was still riding the high even now, and it was a high so thrilling that even his illness seemed like it had been cured.

The straight man stared down at his phone screen. It was merely a WeChat profile picture, yet his pretty almond eyes were still slightly infatuated.

"Xie Qingcheng," he typed, *"why did you leave without saying anything?"*

When he read it over afterward, the tone seemed a bit harsh.

Usually, He Yu didn't really care about whether his tone made Xie Qingcheng uncomfortable or not. But when he thought about how good he'd felt just now, He Yu figured he couldn't leave him with too terrible an impression. Right now, he didn't want Xie Qingcheng to find him too annoying.

So he edited his message again. *"Xie-ge, what did you think about my treatment? Is there anything that I need to work on?"*

...Not appropriate. He knew with certainty that Xie Qingcheng wouldn't respond to him.

He Yu deleted his message again and pondered for a while, thinking that it was probably better to send a voice message in lieu of a text message. He and Xie Qingcheng were already in this kind of relationship now, so sending a voice message was the most appropriate course of action. It would also allow Xie Qingcheng to hear his actual tone, so he wouldn't misunderstand.

After thinking for a while, He Yu began to talk. Surprisingly, his voice was quite gentle, but it still sounded a bit choppy, like the first greeting a lover gave the morning after the wedding night—by doing his utmost to feign calmness, his sudden overt solemnity ended up making him sound even more unfamiliar.

"*Ahem*... Xie-ge..." He Yu hesitated for a long while after he pressed the voice message button, not knowing what to say. "Um... where are you? I'll pick you up in my car."

No, that was no good. He couldn't send a message like that. He hastily deleted it.

The one thing that Xie Qingcheng hated the most was when others tried to look after him. He was too paternalistic, so anything along the lines of "I'll help you," "I'll give you a ride," or "I'll take care of you" was taboo to him. When He Yu had offered to help him get dressed in the dressing room just now, Xie Qingcheng had angrily but weakly told him to scram, even though in the end, He Yu had insisted on buttoning his shirt for him. If He Yu said he wanted to drop him off, Xie Qingcheng would be furious.

He Yu mulled it over again, finally thinking things through. He had decided to continue this relationship with Xie Qingcheng, and he had just been thoroughly satisfied. Like any male who had found a mate, the little dragon was naturally feeling quite obedient, retracting his claws and hiding his fangs, his tone practically cajoling. "Xie-ge... That..."

He remembered that Xie Qingcheng was especially fond of winning over others and enjoyed very competitive activities—in other words, he was extremely manly. So, after thinking things over a second time, this dumbfuck straight man came up with an utterly preposterous method of winning Xie Qingcheng's favor—

"My family invested in a recreational property in the suburbs, and the outdoor facilities are very good. Why don't we go golfing tomorrow, or maybe... Ge, do you like horse racing? How about we go horseback riding together?"

He was a bit clueless when it came to homosexuality, so it hadn't occurred to him for a moment that there was no way Xie Qingcheng would be able to hit a golf ball so soon after the sex they'd just had. If anything, it was more likely that the ball would end up hitting him instead.

He even had the gall to fucking suggest horse racing...

Men and women were completely different. But he had no idea that his ge couldn't recover that quickly. He even told himself that this would be an excellent way of winning back Xie Qingcheng's favor, suited specifically to his tastes.

He really was as clueless as a man could be.

He sent the message. Then he let out a sigh and immediately tossed his phone aside. In nineteen years, he had never been so nervous about saying anything to anyone before. Even his palms were covered in a fine sheen of sweat.

Of course, he knew that there was a chance Xie Qingcheng wouldn't reply, so once he sent the message, he made sure to lock his phone screen and place it out of reach. He figured he'd look at it again in a couple of hours—who knew, maybe something unexpected might happen.

What he hadn't anticipated was the phone vibrating right away, while he was drinking some water with an air of feigned composure. At getting such an instantaneous response, he nearly dropped the cup.

"Cough cough cough..." Choking, he wiped away the water that had accidentally splashed onto his face. Suppressing the anticipation in his heart, he pretended to calmly and indifferently straighten out his shirt and took out a tissue to dab away the water. Only then did he succumb to temptation, picking up the phone and unlocking the screen.

What came into view was a bright red exclamation point that nearly blinded him. A message was appended below:

"'Godfather' has enabled friend verification. You are not yet one of his/her friends. Please first send a friend request—you will only be able to chat after the user accepts it. Send a friend request."

He Yu stared at his phone, dumbfounded.

In an instant, his expression went from exceedingly delighted to extremely pale, as if he had been thwacked on the back of his head with a golf club or kicked squarely in the chest by a horse.

X-Xie Qingcheng had deleted him? Xie Qingcheng had actually dared to delete him?!

For a moment, He Yu felt like he was being suffocated, like poisonous fumes of anger were coiling around his heart. He was so furious that the world began to spin before his eyes.

He Yu had merely blocked him—their chat logs were all still there, and he could reverse his decision any time he wanted. Why was Xie Qingcheng so trigger-happy that he'd delete He Yu—and all of their contact history—without leaving him the slightest bit of leeway?

How could he delete him...?!

He Yu became very impulsive when he lost his temper. He was usually calm and composed in all matters, but he had grown accustomed to being willful when it came to Xie Qingcheng. He immediately rushed out of his dormitory, jumped into his car, and floored it all the way to Moyu Alley.

Despite speeding the whole way there, he found himself at a loss as to what he wanted to say even as he was knocking on Xie Qingcheng's door. Maybe he simply ought to say nothing at all, but rather curse him out and then leave as soon as he was finished.

The door opened.

But the person who opened it was Chen Man.

A buzzing noise filled He Yu's head. His expression immediately became extremely unsightly.

As things stood, Chen Man was fully illuminated to He Yu's eyes, while He Yu himself remained in shadow. He Yu knew about Chen Man's sexual orientation, while Chen Man had no idea that He Yu had already slept with Xie Qingcheng. When Chen Man saw He Yu, he was every bit as friendly as the time they'd met in the dining hall.

Chen Man recognized him on sight. He smiled, and said, "It's you."

He Yu's expression was extremely bleak as he silently swept his gaze over Chen Man, but, faced with someone other than Xie Qingcheng, he still maintained his composure. "It's me."

"It's been so long since the last time we met, you…" Chen Man was halfway through launching into small talk before he finally noticed the hostility in He Yu's expression. He started in surprise, unsure of how he had managed to upset him. "Um, is there something…I can help you with?"

He Yu said mildly, "I'm looking for Xie Qingcheng."

"…Oh." Despite his misgivings, Chen Man turned around and called out for Xie Qingcheng. There was no response.

"Wait a moment, he's taking a shower and probably didn't hear. I'll go tell him you're here."

He Yu's expression became even stiffer, his complexion taking on a tinge of green.

Chen Man came back to the door a moment later with a subtle expression on his face. Previously, he had regarded He Yu with a smile, but this time, he carefully examined the face of this fellow youngster with obvious searching intent.

He Yu was always courteous to others, but he didn't show any friendliness whatsoever toward Chen Man, just glared at him menacingly out of the corner of his eye. "What're you looking at?"

For a moment, Chen Man didn't respond.

"Xie-ge doesn't want to see you," he said. The former lighthearted gentleness in his voice had disappeared. "He said you should leave."

He relayed this after some deliberation—Xie Qingcheng's specific words had been "Tell that little beast to scram."

But even so, He Yu's temper flared. "And if I don't leave?" he said in a coldly sinister voice.

Chen Man wasn't as shameless as he was. He immediately flushed with anger. "Wh-why are you being so unreasonable?"

"Tell him to come out."

"Xie-ge isn't willing to see you. You can't demand that..."

He Yu watched Chen Man's face and ears turn red as he argued, an intense pressure building in his chest. He thought again of how Chen Man had sneakily touched Xie Qingcheng's hand in the theater, and how he'd almost kissed Xie Qingcheng on the cheek. He wasn't decent or honorable at all—he was just a goddamn filthy-minded homosexual. He wanted to kick Chen Man in the chest—after all, even if he injured or killed him with that kick, he'd probably get little more than a slap on the wrist.

This thought became more and more vivid, and He Yu was all but ready to put it into action. However, at that very moment—

"Chen Man, you can head home."

Chen Man turned and looked back to see that Xie Qingcheng had already finished showering and walked out. He was draped in a bathrobe, the collar pulled up high so that it covered the red marks below in their entirety, water dripping from his sopping-wet hair as he looked at the two of them.

66

I COULDN'T HOLD BACK

EVEN THOUGH Chen Man had reservations, he would never dare to disobey Xie Qingcheng. He left.

Once he was gone, Xie Qingcheng walked to the doorway and stood before He Yu.

He Yu was still dressed in the Huzhou University uniform, adorned with his badge from the awards ceremony. Xie Qingcheng looked him over. "I really ought to congratulate you, Chairman of the student government."

He Yu looked at him in confused silence.

"What more do you want to say?"

What did he want to say?

He certainly couldn't behave like a scorned woman and demand an explanation for why Xie Qingcheng had deleted him. He racked his brains for suitable excuses to no avail.

When He Yu didn't respond, Xie Qingcheng slowly narrowed his eyes, examining him carefully.

The look in his eyes made He Yu feel at once annoyed and uneasy. Ever since he was young, whenever he lied to Xie Qingcheng or kept anything from him, Xie Qingcheng would always appraise him with this kind of gaze. He rarely received this kind of look from anyone else—this look that felt like an X-ray, piercing straight through him.

He Yu instinctively began to feel restless. He looked searchingly from Xie Qingcheng's face, to the collar of his bathrobe, to the beads of water dripping from his black hair.

Chen Man didn't know why Xie Qingcheng had gone to take a shower the moment he got home, but He Yu was well aware.

And because it was all too clear to him, he felt very uncomfortable—Xie Qingcheng had already said yes to him, so the two of them would have plenty more entanglements in the future. In that case, why was he in such a hurry to wash the marks he'd left from his body?

Not to mention, Xie Qingcheng had allowed Chen Man to come home with him. And there was also the fact that Xie Qingcheng was actually so...so relaxed and casual toward Chen Man that he didn't even hesitate to take a shower when Chen Man was in his house.

Xie Qingcheng didn't believe what He Yu had told him about Chen Man at all.

The name "Chen Man" suddenly became a necrotic ulcer eating away at He Yu's bones, giving rise to an overwhelming torment that tarnished the color of his eyes. "What about him? What was he doing here?"

This annoyed Xie Qingcheng. The only reason Chen Man had come back with him was because he had left some debriefing reports at Xie Qingcheng's place and was picking them up on his way home. His house was too small, so he was worried that in such close quarters, Chen Man would detect a scent that wasn't his own on his body, so he'd insisted on taking a shower straight away even though Chen Man was there. Plus, he didn't feel the need to have his guard up against Chen Man.

So why did it sound so unbearably filthy coming from He Yu's mouth?

A chill emanated from Xie Qingcheng's eyes. "What's your problem, He Yu? What does his coming here have to do with you?"

"How could it have nothing to do with me?"

"Who is he to me, and who are you to me?"

"I don't know who he is to you..." He Yu said after a moment of silence. "But as for who I am to you..." He Yu's expression grew extremely dark. His happiness from half an hour ago might as well have been from a previous lifetime, as the derangement that Xie Qingcheng knew all too well surfaced once again in his eyes. "Now that you've washed up, has your memory been scrubbed clean too? You agreed to me yourself—you literally just agreed."

Xie Qingcheng stared at He Yu, his eyes completely devoid of warmth, his gaze so piercing it seemed like no one could possibly challenge him.

After the first time he'd been with He Yu, Xie Qingcheng had been under great physical strain. However, he wasn't an invalid. Once he readjusted his attitude and stood back up, his indomitable sense of self was such that any injuries he sustained had practically no effect on him.

"Listen here, He Yu—I agreed to you, but that only went as far as things in bed. Outside of the bedroom, you don't matter. Right now, there's nothing between us at all."

As he spoke, his collar loosened slightly, revealing the skin beneath like a thin sheet of ice, with the kiss marks He Yu had left on his body a little over an hour ago like peach blossoms frozen beneath the surface. Gorgeous yet utterly frigid, completely devoid of life.

A water droplet fell, gliding along the curve of Xie Qingcheng's face to his jaw before sliding down the side of his neck. Unblinkingly, He Yu's eyes trailed that drop of water all the way down. It left a meandering track of wetness all the way to his clavicle...

Xie Qingcheng straightened out his bathrobe coldly, cutting off his advancing gaze.

He Yu lifted his eyes again, meeting those twin pools of frozen peach blossoms.

"If there's nothing else, you should leave. Just because you got a taste of something new doesn't mean you should keep chasing after it forever." Xie Qingcheng's every word and sentence stabbed into him. "That would make you no different from a beast. And it would make you seem..." He paused. "...very inexperienced."

He Yu's expression turned very ugly. On the one hand, he didn't want to admit to this man that he really was that lacking in experience; he'd even lied to Xie Qingcheng before, saying that it wasn't his first time, that Xie Qingcheng wasn't the best he'd had. But on the other hand, he knew that Xie Qingcheng had already seen through his bullshit. He had been so frustrated at the club, missing the mark until sweat soaked his brow and veins stood out at his temples, and yet despite wasting so much time, he still couldn't figure out how to put it in.

And Xie Qingcheng was no virgin—how could he possibly not have noticed that this youngster was just trying to repair his shattered ego?

He Yu stared at Xie Qingcheng's face, which was still covered in beads of water. He said indignantly, "This time, I didn't come to find you for that."

"How unusual," Xie Qingcheng replied. "Then why are you here?"

But at this point, it was even more impossible for He Yu to admit that he had come to find him because of a deleted contact—that would be even more embarrassing. And so, He Yu began blabbering at random.

"Because I'm sick." After a pause, He Yu continued insistently, "I'm sick, and I want you to treat me."

Still no response.

"Don't you remember? You used to be a doctor, Xie Qingcheng."

It would have been fine if he hadn't said anything, but the moment he brought this up, Xie Qingcheng became incandescently furious.

If he didn't remember that, he would've already made a clean break with He Yu and stayed as far away from him as possible. There was no way he'd still be dealing with this stupid mess. After a momentary silence, Xie Qingcheng braced a hand against the doorframe and narrowed his eyes. He'd finally lost some of his cool, revealing the exceedingly vicious face beneath the broken fragments of his ice-cold mask. "I remember that very clearly."

The fury he'd suppressed for too long suddenly rushed out in an instant. Xie Qingcheng abruptly grabbed He Yu's face, bracing his other elbow against the doorframe.

He kept his voice very low, but the strength behind each word was practically enough to forcibly tear the human-skin disguise from He Yu's beastly body and throw the bloody husk to the ground. "But I hope you also remember that I quit that job four years ago. If you're sick, it doesn't have anything to do with me." As he spoke into He Yu's ear, his low, throaty voice had a searing heat to it, but each sentence was coated with splinters of ice. "If you die, though, you can notify me in one of my dreams. If I'm in a good mood, I might go to your grave and light you a stick of incense. You animal."

He straightened up and patted He Yu on the cheek. "Now, get lost."

But before the sound of his voice could fade, his pupils suddenly contracted.

Catching him off guard, He Yu had fiercely bitten down on his fingertips, his mouth filling with blood—

"Xie Qingcheng." He Yu stared fixedly at Xie Qingcheng's face, the tip of his tongue sweeping over Xie Qingcheng's fingers.

Xie Qingcheng pulled his hand away with a grim expression, but He Yu unexpectedly caught his wrist in his grip.

He Yu glanced at the tattoo that kept on appearing in his wet dreams like some sort of curse, then licked his bloody lips before smacking them gratuitously, purely intending to disgust Xie Qingcheng. "Your blood tastes sweet."

Xie Qingcheng nearly slapped him, but he didn't want to attract the neighbors' attention by making a scene. He only said in a low voice, "Let go."

He Yu did no such thing—rather, he only tightened his grip. In their deadlock, he surreptitiously forced Xie Qingcheng's wrist upward.

He lowered his head, but his eyes drifted up. In the dim entryway of the old house, he stared closely at Xie Qingcheng's face.

It seemed as if He Yu intended to take all the burning resentment that he hadn't been able to relieve since his first time and ferociously force it into Xie Qingcheng's body. He lifted Xie Qingcheng's scholarly wrist, forcing him to reveal the tattoo along its inside, then bit down ruthlessly on the tender skin there as though injecting him with venom.

Xie Qingcheng's expression tensed. His aching hand had gone numb, but he couldn't make a sound. He could only stare fiercely back into He Yu's eyes in the darkness.

"Remember this, Xie Qingcheng." He Yu finally spoke, flinging Xie Qingcheng's arm aside. "You are my father's old friend, my personal physician, and also someone that I've fucked. To you, I have to be special. So in the future, don't let me hear you ask 'who are you to me' ever again."

Xie Qingcheng's blood seemed to have satisfied him, yet it also seemed to make him thirst for more.

"And one more thing—stay away from Chen Man," He Yu continued. "He's a disgusting homosexual. He definitely has dirty thoughts about you."

Xie Qingcheng stared fixedly at He Yu for a while, then said with incomparable disgust, "He Yu, you think you have the right to say that about someone else right now?"

"Why can't I say it?"

"Don't you feel like a hypocrite? Just who's the homosexual here? You're really telling me it's not you? What right do you have to talk about Chen Man? Just think about it, what right do you have?"

It was as if He Yu had been slapped across the face. His cheek twitched as he pursed his lips tightly, still stained with blood that had yet to dry. His face had gone extremely pale. He wanted to say to Xie Qingcheng, *It's not the same at all. I didn't fuck you because I like you, it was only because it felt good. Because I don't like you, it can't be considered attraction, and therefore, I'm not gay.*

But he had only just opened his mouth when Xie Qingcheng pushed him out the door. "Get out. Get the fuck out."

"No. You already agreed to continue—"

"That's right, I agreed. But now I'm tired, I need to rest, and the clock's run out on your nighttime session—got it? Don't take yourself too seriously."

"...What nighttime session?!" He Yu snapped. "We're both treating each other for—"

Xie Qingcheng's expression turned malicious. "Then today's course of treatment is over. I feel great right now, really great, so can you leave already, you charlatan?"

Then he made to close the door. He was just about to slam it shut right in He Yu's face, but He Yu stubbornly wedged himself against it.

"Xie Qingcheng, don't push me..."

Xie Qingcheng shoved at the door, wordlessly but with great force, pinching He Yu's fingers against the frame and leaving red marks. The old metal door had been in disrepair for years, and there were even some barbs and splinters at its edges. Over the course of their silent confrontation, the back of He Yu's hand was pierced through and began to bleed.

But he didn't seem to feel it as he looked at Xie Qingcheng.

He had used up all his patience in this struggle, and right now he was already on the verge of madness. All of his coaxing and persuading had been for nothing. Xie Qingcheng had refused him and cursed him in response, so what was he supposed to do?

He Yu could only take off his mask, revealing the ugly and scar-riddled face of an evil dragon beneath.

His voice was abnormally, hair-raisingly gentle. "Great. That's just great. That Officer Chen of yours—you really trust him, don't you?"

"At least he's more normal than you are," said Xie Qingcheng dangerously.

Suddenly, He Yu bent his arm and ruthlessly wedged open the door with his elbow. Then he reached up, pressing his still-bleeding fingers to Xie Qingcheng's chest.

He leaned in close to Xie Qingcheng and murmured in his ear. "That's fine. If you think I'm not normal, then so be it. At any rate, I'm already used to it. I heard all your heartfelt words in that video, and I've experienced your deception firsthand. I don't care what you think of me. After all, there's never been anyone who sincerely loved me, who regarded me as an equal..."

His tone of voice softened even further, as though transforming into silk threads, soft yet cool and about to wind around Xie Qingcheng's neck.

"I'm used to all of it."

He suddenly pushed hard, shoving Xie Qingcheng into the room. Both the metal and wooden doors banged shut behind them. He Yu very magnanimously even remembered to lock the door from the inside.

As he locked the door, he pinned Xie Qingcheng against it and kissed him as if venting his emotions.

Xie Qingcheng really hadn't expected him to have so much strength. How long had it been since their earlier entanglement?

"He Yu! You can't go crazy here! Xie Xue might come home..."

Even Xie Xue wouldn't work as a safeword for He Yu anymore. He only paused briefly before giving Xie Qingcheng his answer—he pressed Xie Qingcheng down onto his desk, scattering half-written manuscripts all over the floor.

Of all the people he could possibly mention, why would he bring up Xie Xue?

He Yu's eyes turned distant and cold as the scab over that wound on his heart ripped open and began to bleed once more. He nipped at the side of Xie Qingcheng's neck even more ferociously, as though urgently seeking some medicine that could staunch the bleeding.

Indeed, over the course of He Yu's life, Xie Qingcheng was like medicine that could always quell certain things, or like an ice-cold prosthesis that could fill some void. Before, Xie Qingcheng had filled in for the care he never received. Now, he could fill in for the love that he desired.

Xie Qingcheng wasn't at all like the partner he'd anticipated in the past, of course—he was male, and he wasn't gentle, nor did he treat him well. When He Yu was with him, it was like he had found someone who could only barely manage to patch up a leak, like a false tooth or a metal limb that replaced a lost arm—even though they weren't quite satisfactory, they could at least fill some of that dreadful emptiness.

It would always be better than nothing.

With those thoughts, in the darkness, He Yu said to Xie Qingcheng in a low voice, "She's busy, she won't come back. So keep me company."

His voice was calm, but he sounded like a complete madman, lonely and paranoid beyond belief, his response born of despair. It was as if he had gone mad, but also as if he was begging.

It was still light beyond the window. But He Yu said, "It's dark out, Xie Qingcheng. Don't chase me away. There's nowhere else for me to go."

67

HE'S GAY

WHEN THE DRAGON found himself without a home, he insisted on staying with the humans. He seemed to be pleading, and he wouldn't let go of Xie Qingcheng—as if he hadn't gotten enough of this novelty back in the dressing room and wanted another taste. The dragon had marked his person, but that person had turned around and immediately washed himself clean. The dragon thumped his tail, deeply satisfied; it was only natural that he wanted to mark him again.

A few hours later, Xie Qingcheng lay between the pillows and blankets, his vision blurry. Although he'd already reestablished his mental barriers and chosen to accept this, physically he still couldn't take going through the motions.

Not to mention, he was beginning to suspect that agreeing to this relationship with He Yu had been the wrong choice. Instead of eliminating an obstacle that wasted his time, he'd ended up wasting even more time dealing with this damn relationship. This little beast had way too much stamina!

He Yu lay next to him, lazily twirling his own slightly-longer black hair around his fingers. "Ge. How did I do?"

A young man's libido was practically boundless. If He Yu saw even the slightest trace of lust on Xie Qingcheng's face, it was like an electric shock shooting up from his tailbone, and his exhaustion was utterly forgotten. He seemed to have an endless supply of energy; he only wanted more and more.

Unlike Xie Qingcheng, who was sleeping with him just to get rid of him.

Xie Qingcheng's body was like a sedative to him. No matter how harshly Xie Qingcheng spoke or how stubborn his attitude was, as soon as He Yu slept with him, he would settle down and become very agreeable. With his mood relaxed, the argument they'd just had didn't seem to matter to him anymore. Chen Man didn't matter either. Chen Man would never get a taste, anyway—leave him to his cravings.

The way He Yu looked at Xie Qingcheng now was much gentler, a sort of naked gentleness. His usual aura of gloom was peeled away, and he seemed very pure, like a normal nineteen-year-old in a normal relationship.

It was just a pity that Xie Qingcheng wasn't looking at him. He Yu called out to him again. "Xie Qingcheng."

Xie Qingcheng didn't respond.

He Yu touched the corner of his lips. "Did it hurt?"

Xie Qingcheng still ignored him.

He Yu hugged his waist again, pressing kisses from his shoulder to his collarbone. "Did it feel good?"

Xie Qingcheng finally responded. "Can you piss off now?"

He Yu smiled. "I'm exhausted," he said shamelessly. "I worked so hard, but you won't even humor me? I want you to take a nap with me." He hugged Xie Qingcheng tightly, leaving no room for argument.

Xie Qingcheng stared coldly at the ceiling. After a long while, he said, "You're not disgusted by men at all now, huh?"

"I am disgusted by them."

Xie Qingcheng scoffed. "I really don't see the difference between what you're doing and what any gay man does."

He Yu's expression dimmed. He was silent for a long time. "This is different," he said at last.

"How is it different?"

The boy was obstinate, as if he wanted to prove something. "Well, I only do this with you."

Xie Qingcheng slowly rolled his eyes until his gaze landed on He Yu's face—but it was cold, colder than the frost edging the window. "It's not gay if you're only doing it with me? How fucking absurd can you be?"

He Yu's expression turned ugly. He seemed to know deep in his heart that he was wrong, that he was twisting logic, but still, he chose to ignore his self-reflection. "I don't like other men," he said. "I'm only willing to do it with you. I don't want anyone else." He insisted, "Xie Qingcheng, I don't like men."

"Are you blind? I'm a man."

"You're different. You're an exception."

For a moment, Xie Qingcheng fell silent. Then, with a tone that seemed to contain the shadow of a viciously cold blade, he asked, "And why is that?"

He Yu didn't have the answer. Could it be that he had a complex about losing his virginity? But he couldn't say that, of course. He was He "Definitely A Total Casanova" Yu. Instead, after a pause, he very casually said, "You're...attractive."

"Why, thank you—so if I slice up my face, we could put an end to this tedious game?"

He Yu wasn't expecting a response like that. Flinching, he sat up at once to stare down at him. "Xie Qingcheng!" But immediately after his shock, he cooled. He stared into Xie Qingcheng's eyes, recovering his usual calm. "No, you wouldn't."

"Why wouldn't I?"

"You value life. You always treat it with great importance."

Xie Qingcheng slowly closed his peach-blossom eyes, his Adam's apple bobbing. "Hate to break it to you, kid, but I don't value my own life at all."

He Yu's temper suddenly flared, as if something had struck him in the chest. He hissed in Xie Qingcheng's ear, "If you dare, I'll lock you up, cover your face, and torture you to death!"

Xie Qingcheng opened his eyes, gazing at He Yu coldly. "When did you start liking my face so much? You never found me attractive before."

He Yu couldn't answer. In the end, he only snapped at Xie Qingcheng, "It's...it's not like you'd go so far as to disfigure yourself just because of me. Am I really that important to you?"

Xie Qingcheng didn't respond. After a long while, his sneer seemed to flow over the still-warm bedding like glacial runoff. "That's true. Just how important are you really, He Yu?" There was a slight sigh in his voice.

He Yu felt inexplicably uncomfortable. He didn't like it when Xie Qingcheng called him "He Yu." It occurred to him that Xie Qingcheng hadn't called him "little devil" in a very long time—not since that night.

Thanks to that discomfort, He Yu found himself entangling with Xie Qingcheng once again. By the time he returned to his senses, it was already fully dark out.

In the evening, Chen Man called again. He was still a bit worried about the situation between He Yu and Xie Qingcheng and wanted to ask how things were.

Of course, Xie Qingcheng couldn't tell Chen Man the truth. "Everything's fine," he lied. "We had a misunderstanding before, but we've resolved it. Things are okay now."

Chen Man chatted with Xie Qingcheng for a little longer. He told him that, in a couple days, he wanted to come over to Xie Qingcheng's place to eat Yangzhou fried rice after work.

He Yu listened to their conversation with an air of indifference. After Xie Qingcheng hung up, he kissed his slightly cool lips—Chen Man could only listen to the words that came out of this mouth, but *he* could kiss and suck on these cold lips until they were hot and damp.

"Xie-ge." Afterward, he pulled away slightly from Xie Qingcheng, their breaths still somewhat irrepressibly rough. But Xie Qingcheng's eyes had already turned cold. He Yu stared into those cold eyes of his, then said, "Can you get up and make me some fried rice? And a bowl of porridge."

Un-fucking-believable, thought Xie Qingcheng.

That disturbance from Chen Man had left He Yu's eyes clouded over and hazy, yet the words he spoke were cutesy in tone as he tried to bargain for favorable treatment. "If you want me to leave, then I'll go once I've freeloaded a meal."

Whether it was an encounter between two people of the same sex or the opposite, it was exceedingly rare for someone who'd been indulging themselves all night long to demand that the person they'd just screwed get up and cook for them. A normal person would go to the kitchen to wash their hands and make some soup, or they'd have the hotel's room service deliver a meal. Even an ancient ruler showing favor to a maid would at least task the eunuchs with waiting on her after everything was over.

But He Yu was uniquely shameless.

And as for Xie Qingcheng? At first he'd wanted to curse He Yu out, but he was so exhausted and tired of that boy—it took energy to start an argument, and he couldn't even bring himself to muster the strength to look at him right now. On top of that, he didn't want He Yu to think that he'd screwed him so hard he'd lost all strength. He'd always considered himself a manly man, and he felt compelled to prove his strength to others.

Thus, in an effort to make He Yu clear off as quickly as possible, Xie Qingcheng silently rose to his feet and went to make the food, his expression so blank that it seemed as though nothing had happened.

His waist was very sore, and there were other parts of him that were also unspeakably uncomfortable, but he internalized the discomfort; the only thing He Yu could discern from his face was a profound impassivity. It was like ruins thoroughly plundered by an unsuccessful graverobber who dug and dug deep into the ground but failed to find any worthwhile treasures.

He Yu got dressed, stood up, and went to the kitchen to watch Xie Qingcheng. For some reason, his heart went from calm to restless, from restless to disappointed, and then from disappointed to bewildered. Leaning against the doorframe with a grim expression, he kept nagging Xie Qingcheng, perhaps trying to relieve the moodiness in his heart.

"Xie Qingcheng, don't use so much sesame oil."

"Xie Qingcheng, cut the green onions more finely."

"Xie Qingcheng, don't put the salt in so soon."

Of course, he received no response to any of this guidance. He Yu was deliberately nitpicking even though he didn't actually know how to cook. He thought that if he showed off his non-existent skills before this expert by giving him such nonsensical directions, Xie Qingcheng would turn around and scold him loudly like he had before—but he didn't.

Instead, Xie Qingcheng simply did whatever he said with a bland expression on his face, spurning him utterly, silently enduring his presence, and unfeelingly dismissing him.

This silence made He Yu even more distraught. At least in the past Xie Qingcheng had been willing to bicker with him.

In the end, he walked over and hugged Xie Qingcheng around the waist without warning. He turned his head to kiss Xie Qingcheng on the neck, then placed his hand on his wrist, forcing him to let go of the porridge ladle.

Xie Qingcheng ignored him at first, his peach-blossom eyes watching the blue flames dancing over the gas stove. But finally, probably because he was irritated with He Yu's clinginess, he spat out coldly without looking back, "Do you actually want food, or are you in heat?"

But the colder he was, the more enticing He Yu found him— it was as if even the smell of disinfectant had become a concentrated pheromone. Honestly, He Yu didn't like behaving so licentiously either; he had always conducted himself immaculately in front of others. Or rather, to be precise, before bedding Xie Qingcheng, he had always been very gentlemanly even behind the scenes and had never touched any girls.

Xie Qingcheng was like an elder leading him deeper into the Garden of Eden. Regardless of how things had begun, the end result was that Xie Qingcheng had been the one to let him in. Now that he'd entered, the boy suddenly grasped a new understanding, sparking the primitive desire etched into his bones. After that, he wanted to remain forever in this forbidden land full of animalistic desire, to keep entangling with the man who had taken him in that first time, savoring the thrill that to him still held a certain degree of novelty.

Lowering his eyes, He Yu kissed the back of Xie Qingcheng's neck. "Let the porridge simmer for a bit."

Between the chilly autumn day and the burning stove, it was much hotter inside than outside. The old-fashioned window had fogged over with a thin layer of white haze, ensuring that nothing could be seen from either side.

But suddenly, a hand slapped against the window pane. Paler than ice and snow, with slender and elegant bones, it seemed to spasm slightly where it strained against the glass. If one looked closer, that hand could be seen to tremble, again and again.

Then, a younger-looking hand clasped the first hand, intertwining their fingers tightly. This time, one didn't even have to look that closely to see the violent shaking of the window. It seemed to be on the verge of shattering.

It was at this very moment that a muffled noise came from inside. The two hands moved away from the window, leaving behind a clear mark. Before the steam could mist it over again, one could vaguely make out through that handprint how the man leaning over the counter had been flipped over to lie face up; one might even be able to glimpse the messiness of his black hair and the straight lines of his broad shoulder blades. Look up even further, and for a moment the passionate, heated face of a young man standing before the kitchen counter would be visible.

When it devoured the human offering on the stone bed, did the lonely dragon have such a fervent and besotted look on its face, too?

The answer went unspoken, just as the cold wind and fog that heralded the approach of winter quickly misted over the clear mark on the window. Through the dense condensation it was impossible to see what was happening inside, and both men kept their voices low and muffled, making sure no one could hear anything they said...

In the end, only the soft sound of a choked moan escaped from a small crack in the window, its timbre changing slightly as it melted into the wind.

Through the blurred window, black shadows swayed—a head of black hair, a pale back like white jade, and an ill-fated entangled relationship, as one figure seemed to pick up the other. The wicked dragon lowered its head and kissed the human's shoulder with its scarred snout.

It was too hot inside, the aftermath of passion melting into a hot spring, soaking into the pair of sweat-soaked men.

"Don't cook for Chen Man anymore." He Yu was still panting slightly, as wild as a beast, a little willful and a little on edge. "I don't like him. He's a disgusting homo." Somehow he still had the face to say that—he was still immersed in that gentle softness, yet he had the nerve to disparage someone else for being gay.

Xie Qingcheng pushed him away as soon as the deed was done, cooling down with astonishing speed. His chest still heaved slightly, but the eyes that peered out from under his damp fringe were already cold, so frosty that it could strike a chill into the hearts of others.

Finally, he lifted the corners of his lips. "Back up ten thousand steps, He Yu," he said, with near perfect composure. "Even if he's gay, he's still better than you. Even if he's gay, he's never shown such relentless interest in me as you."

He paused before continuing, his voice piercingly mocking. Every single word was calm, but they cut through He Yu like a knife. "You really are a card-carrying heterosexual."

68

I'M NOT GAY

THE CARD-CARRYING heterosexual forgot to remove himself from Xie Qingcheng's block list.

He'd seen Xie Qingcheng several more times since then, but whenever he did, all he wanted was to cling to him and hug him some more. Then he'd suddenly remember after getting home, *Aiya, I forgot to add him on WeChat again.*

To tell the truth, He Yu could have easily used black-market technology to add himself back to his contacts. But he felt that the meaning behind getting Xie Qingcheng to add him again would be lost if he did. And Xie Qingcheng's current attitude toward him was making him feel a bit uncomfortable too. He almost never scolded him anymore—he treated sleeping with He Yu in a strictly business-like manner, as if he was going to work or dealing with a client, and then ignored him.

In other words, he very rarely paid him any attention.

At first, He Yu was obsessed with sex, but as time passed, this discomfort and frustration gradually began to take over. He didn't know where the old Xie Qingcheng had gone, but he wanted to dig out a sliver of that old version, the person who had taken care of him and scolded him. Even if it was a just lie, that poison would nevertheless quench his thirst.

But Xie Qingcheng didn't do any of that. Xie Qingcheng didn't deceive He Yu anymore, but he didn't give a damn about He Yu anymore either.

And so, over time, both the young man's heart and his lust went unsatisfied; although it seemed like he had a man who treated him with sincerity, it also felt like he had nothing at all.

Their muddled relationship dragged on for a while, just like that.

At the end of the school year, Professor Xie was reinstated.

Winter had arrived, and more than two months had passed since the broadcasting tower incident. As the Qin Ciyan dispute slowly faded, the school quietly invited Xie Qingcheng back to his lectern. One night, after his self-study period, He Yu slung his book bag over his shoulder and rode his new bicycle through the light snow from one campus to the other, stopping at the door of the medical school's faculty dorm.

This was the first time that He Yu had gone looking for Xie Qingcheng since his reinstatement.

Being reinstated was a good thing, so He Yu thought Xie Qingcheng's mood ought to be a little better. He ran up the stairs two at a time, his breath puffing out in warm clouds as he twirled his keys around his fingers.

"Xie Qingcheng," he called out.

Xie Qingcheng wasn't there, but a female teacher happened to be coming down the stairs.

"You're looking for Professor Xie?" She looked He Yu up and down as he stood in front of Xie Qingcheng's door, mistaking him for a xueba from their school seeking guidance from an honorable teacher, reverent and eager to learn. "You should check the library," she said. "This lousy dorm's heating system isn't very good in the winter, so he might be prepping for class there instead."

So off He Yu went.

It was only early winter, but outside, snow had already begun to drift down from the lead-gray skies. Winter in Jiangnan was going to be exceptionally long and cold this year.

There were a lot of people in the study area. He Yu kept looking until he reached a remote corner of the third floor next to the window, where he caught a glimpse of Professor Xie's elegant profile. Xie Qingcheng had lost a bit of weight recently, perhaps because he was getting older and didn't exercise much, and he was always exhausting himself staying up to do endless amounts of research. It was very strange—why did he always have so many papers to draft, revise, and organize?

Xie Qingcheng's health was getting worse and worse. As He Yu drew closer, he could see that Xie Qingcheng kept coughing lightly the entire time. There was a thermos bottle on the table, and after a particularly hard bout of coughing, Xie Qingcheng went to pour himself a cup of warm water. When he tipped the thermos, though, he found that there was no more water left. He didn't feel like getting up, so he unhappily capped the bottle again, picked up his pen, and started writing something in his notebook.

The tip of the pen scratched across the paper, only to pause a moment later as a disposable cup of hot water was placed before him.

He raised his head to meet He Yu's almond eyes. The boy had fetched some water for him from the library's water dispenser, then he pulled a chair over and sat down in front of him.

Xie Qingcheng's expression was cold. He immediately began to organize his books and laptop to leave, but He Yu put a hand down on his laptop. "Where are you going?" He Yu asked. "There's nowhere else to sit."

Xie Qingcheng's first thought had been to return to his dormitory, but now that he considered it, the library would probably be safer—this lunatic would be much less likely to go wild in here. Wouldn't he be walking into a trap of his own making if he went back?

With a dark expression, he sat back down.

Today, He Yu was wearing a white cashmere winter coat and carrying a canvas messenger bag. His sharp jawline and thin, slightly roguish lips were hidden behind a warm, thick scarf that only revealed his puppy-like almond eyes. He seemed no different from any other cultured, knowledgeable xueba at Huzhou Medical School, and his wide forehead, dark eyes, and straight, high nose made him appear even more likable. He looked very gentle.

But Xie Qingcheng knew it was a complete and total facade. This young man had an illness that had rotted down into his bones and couldn't be excised. He'd even ended up unleashing his madness onto Xie Qingcheng's body.

"Xie Qingcheng, I've been meaning to ask you since last time." He Yu sat calmly, playing with his pen, completely unaware of Xie Qingcheng's distaste. "Why are you wearing glasses?"

"Obviously it's because I've gone blind from all the disgusting things I've had to look at lately."

He Yu was unconcerned. Smiling, he asked, "How nearsighted are you?"

Xie Qingcheng ignored him, lowering his head to write his notes. But, unexpectedly, the young man reached over with one hand, took off the glasses that were sitting on his nose, and held the lenses before his own eyes.

"Wow, that's making me really dizzy. Why are these so strong? Your eyesight used to be pretty good."

Xie Qingcheng snatched his glasses away and jammed them back onto his face. "What does that have to do with you?"

But He Yu knew Xie Qingcheng wasn't one to hold back when it came to using his eyes.

Every day, he had to read thick books filled with difficult content written in microscopic text, the kind of thing ordinary people couldn't read more than three lines of before they'd find themselves drifting off into blissful slumber.

He Yu couldn't understand why someone of Xie Qingcheng's academic standing, someone who had been so exceptional at such a young age, still did so much research. It was like he was racing against time. Others might have assumed that Xie Qingcheng was simply born with a passionate interest in medicine, that he was the kind of person who'd die if he went a single day without doing medical research. However, He Yu knew that originally, Xie Qingcheng's dream hadn't been to become an excellent doctor.

There was no reason for him to be so obsessed with medicine. Then, could it be...

"Do you really like teaching?"

Xie Qingcheng didn't even lift his head. "I like money."

He was looking at a list of formulas. He probably thought that the formulas were much nicer to look at than He Yu. So he likely didn't intend to pay any attention to He Yu from this point on.

Silence was mandatory in the library, so He Yu couldn't talk to Xie Qingcheng for long without the medical students studying nearby complaining. He stopped talking, took out a copy of *Save the Cat!* from his bag, and idly flipped through it. He was beginning to wonder why he, a proper student at Huzhou University's Faculty of Fine Arts, was wasting time at Huzhou Medical School's austere library.

He looked up and, off to the side, caught a glimpse of Xie Qingcheng's phone.

He Yu picked up the phone, watching Xie Qingcheng the entire time to see if he'd react. But Xie Qingcheng was completely engrossed in writing his lessons and didn't even notice that He Yu had seized his cell phone.

He Yu found himself wondering, *If I kissed him now, would he even notice?*

As that thought crossed his mind, his heart stirred slightly. But they were surrounded by students, and he wasn't so overtly insane that he'd do anything in public. He extinguished that little flame.

He unlocked Xie Qingcheng's phone. This time, he remembered to add himself back on WeChat.

The password was very simple—all he had to do was enter "12345." Once the screen was unlocked, He Yu went into the WeChat app on his own phone and scanned his QR code with Xie Qingcheng's phone to add himself again.

When he'd finished, he saw that Xie Qingcheng still hadn't noticed and felt slightly disappointed. He really wanted to make Xie Qingcheng lose his temper with him. That angry version of Xie Qingcheng wouldn't be as maddeningly elusive as the one sitting in front of him... After thinking for a bit, he changed his nickname in Xie Qingcheng's phone: "World's Most Handsome and Experienced Lover."

Save.

After exiting the menu and taking another look, he realized that he wasn't the first in the address book. He even came after Chen Man. He thought it over some more, and then edited his nickname again.

"Ah, World's Most Handsome and Experienced Lover."

Seeing himself at the top of the As, he felt deeply satisfied.

With that done, he took his own phone and sent Xie Qingcheng a sticker he'd made when he was bored. This sticker sure was something else—he'd taken the photo he snapped of Xie Qingcheng's sleeping face in the club and photoshopped it into a selfie of himself with his head against a pillow. He felt that these two pictures looked very good together—it was quite a harmonious composition. He'd even added a floating transparent jellyfish as a special effect and a crass "Good Morning" as text.

Ding.

The sound of the message notification caught Xie Qingcheng's attention. When he noticed He Yu had his phone, he snatched it back with a scowl. "What are you doing?"

He Yu didn't say anything, just looked at Xie Qingcheng from the corner of his eye as he snatched his phone out of He Yu's hand. With a sense of great satisfaction, he watched Xie Qingcheng's face go from white to green when he saw his new nickname and the sticker. Although Xie Qingcheng had seen this photo before, he was still shocked to see such an idiotic image photoshopped into a sticker and paired with such a stupid nickname.

"He Yu!" His tone was murderous.

He Yu was delighted. "Professor, please be mindful of where we are. Focus on your reading. I'll keep quiet and play with my phone." Then, under Xie Qingcheng's sharp glare, he calmly picked up his phone, turned it sideways, and started fighting zombies.

Xie Qingcheng's face was ashen as he deleted the fucking idiotic sticker. With that taken care of, he swiftly rose to his feet and began gathering his books to leave.

He Yu extended a long leg beneath the table and nudged him lightly. "Where are you going? Sit down."

Xie Qingcheng just ignored him.

He Yu's next words were even softer. "Or would you rather go home?"

Xie Qingcheng looked like he was on the verge of exploding, but in the end, he weighed the consequences, gritted his teeth, and sat back down. However, he wasn't in the mood to read anymore, so he closed his laptop heavily and turned to look out the window.

The first flakes of snow were floating down like wisps of cotton, a beautiful sight—but like He Yu, their beauty hid their bone-chilling nature.

Meanwhile, He Yu kept playing his game.

After beating two rounds, he was about to chatter away at Xie Qingcheng some more when two female medical school students hesitantly approached their table. However, they hadn't come to ask the professor a question, but rather—

"E-excuse me, are you He Yu?"

"What is it?"

On meeting his gaze, the two girls turned red like boiled shrimps.

"We...we saw the *Many Faces of Malady* campus film, and we think you're very handsome, so we wanted to ask you, if we could..."

"If we could get your autograph."

"Can you sign my notebook?"

"I was hoping you could sign my backpack..."

He Yu paused for a moment before finally looking over at Xie Qingcheng with a smile. "Professor Xie, could you lend me a pen?"

"I have a pen, I have a pen!" one of the girls exclaimed hurriedly.

"I have one too! Do you want a ballpoint pen or a gel pen?"

But He Yu merely narrowed his eyes at Xie Qingcheng, a smile unfolding on his thin lips, which made him seem at once self-satisfied and gentle. "I want a fountain pen."

Very few people carried a fountain pen around these days, but Xie Qingcheng had one right by his hand.

The two girls weren't Xie Qingcheng's students, but because he was well-known throughout the medical school, they recognized him. They spoke up hesitantly. "Professor Xie, could we..."

"B-borrow your pen?" The more daring of the two girls finished her friend's sentence.

Xie Qingcheng met He Yu's eyes in silence. He'd been about to say no, but on realizing that this would only require him to waste even more words on He Yu, he finally said in an indifferent tone, "Sure. Go ahead."

"Thank you! Thank you!" The overjoyed girls took the distinguished professor's pen and deferentially handed it to He Yu.

Seeing the way all the life seemed to drain out of Xie Qingcheng again, He Yu's smile faded. He wanted to deliberately provoke Xie Qingcheng, so after taking the pen, he handed it back with a shadowy look in his eyes. "Professor Xie, could you dip the ink for me? Get a good amount—make sure it's not too dry."

Xie Qingcheng didn't react right away. He Yu thought he would definitely refuse this time.

But to his surprise, Xie Qingcheng just shot him a cold glance, then expressionlessly unscrewed the ink bottle, dipped the pen into the blue ink, and tossed it at He Yu. "Take it."

His attitude was indifferent and uncaring. He Yu's heart felt even stuffier. The boy didn't have even a hint of a smile on his face anymore. He took the pen, his finger grazing past Xie Qingcheng's. "Thank you."

Once they'd received He Yu's signature, the girls clutched them to their chests like they'd obtained priceless treasures. The two friends exchanged an excited look before mustering up their courage again—

"Then—"

"Then can we add your WeChat?"

Although Xie Qingcheng wasn't paying them any attention, he wasn't deaf, so he still heard every word of their conversation. He assumed that, given He Yu's excessively polite facade, he would certainly agree to the girls' small request. But rather than nodding, He Yu politely rejected them instead.

The girls were a little disappointed, but they cheered up when they looked down at the autographs they held in their arms. The two of them thanked He Yu and left in high spirits.

Xie Qingcheng didn't even look up as he worked on his paper.

"Why did you reject them?"

At this simple question, He Yu perked up like a reanimated little dragon, his invisible tail wagging to and fro. "Ah, and why would I agree?"

"You take pleasure in those kinds of things."

"You only look at the surface." He Yu paused, then added, "I only add people who spark joy."

"Then delete me too," Xie Qingcheng said mildly.

He Yu stared at him for a while. Then he unlocked his phone, opened the messaging app, and...under Xie Qingcheng's unwavering stare, he boldly pinned Xie Qingcheng to the top.

Xie Qingcheng stared at him.

Actually, it was quite necessary for He Yu to pin Xie Qingcheng to the top, because he liked to go and find him when he had nothing better to do. Of course, since Xie Qingcheng basically ignored him, there wasn't much the two of them could talk about; but no matter how dissatisfied and unhappy that made He Yu, whenever they met, they'd just do the deed to solve the problem.

It was just a pity that Xie Qingcheng was apathetic to sex. Xie Qingcheng didn't need He Yu to solve any problems for him—

he simply went through the motions and allowed the young man to practice on him.

Although He Yu didn't receive many responses from Xie Qingcheng outside the bedroom, there were plenty of ways he could force Xie Qingcheng to acknowledge him in bed. With his nimble xueba mind, he used every trick he could find, and as a young man, he had so much stamina that Xie Qingcheng sometimes feared that he was going to be fucked to death.

Xie Qingcheng had never experienced such debauchery.

He knew it was inevitable for a teenager who had just had his first taste of sex like He Yu to be voracious for more. However, given his own low sex drive, he really couldn't empathize. Eventually, Xie Qingcheng couldn't hold back his curiosity any longer. He looked it up.

He checked some discussion forums online, searching for what was considered normal for boys nowadays—in other words, to figure out when he would be able to do his own work in peace. But what he ultimately saw nearly gave him a mental breakdown.

> *Boys around 20, 3–5 times a week.*

> *For those with high libidos, 8 times in 10 days isn't too much either.*

> *If we don't go wild now, when are we supposed to? My girlfriend and I think even just once a day is too little.*

Even an exceedingly moderate old doctor of Chinese medicine replied pensively, "If a relationship has already been established, then it is essential for a twenty-year-old boy to do it twice a week."

Xie Qingcheng hadn't been deliberately avoiding He Yu at first, but after this research, he began to hide from him in earnest. He was busy at work and blunt in his efforts to avoid He Yu, so He Yu would sometimes go five or six days without getting the chance to meet with him alone.

Now, on top of always being denied psychological comfort, physical satisfaction eluded the youth as well. Consequently, every time he managed to get Xie Qingcheng in his clutches, He Yu lashed out in retaliation, tormenting him over and over again, as if the two of them didn't need to do anything other than this. He didn't consider the deed to be done until Xie Qingcheng passed out from exhaustion.

After he pinned Xie Qingcheng to the top of his contacts in the library, He Yu's hunger seemed to intensify. Sometimes, Xie Qingcheng would even receive voice messages from him in the middle of the night. Sometimes He Yu talked, but other times he did not. Usually, on the occasions when he didn't talk, all that could be heard on the line was the sound of low, muffled panting.

"Doctor, do you think I'm sick?"

Silence.

"I feel so uncomfortable."

Still silence.

"Doctor Xie, can you take a look at me?"

That night, Xie Qingcheng hadn't gone to bed yet; he was still in the middle of organizing his files. He Yu was annoying him, so he said, "Being gay isn't a sickness as long as you don't come looking for me."

The breathing on the other end of the phone cooled down. Then, after a long silence, He Yu said, "Xie Qingcheng, I'm not gay. I only want you."

"Right. Gays don't act like you do."

"Turn on your camera and let me see you," said He Yu.

"Are you aware that it's two in the morning Beijing time right now?"

The person on the other end fell momentarily silent. "Are you aware that at two in the morning Beijing time," he replied in a low yet fiery voice, "I can't fall asleep because I keep thinking about how much I want to fuck you?"

There was no reply.

"Xie Qingcheng, can I come to your dorm? I'm being blue-balled to death over here."

Remembering the messages he saw on the internet, Xie Qingcheng looked at the date on his phone. A normal twenty-year-old boy with a sexual partner would usually need to do it at least twice a week. He Yu didn't even get close to that amount. It had already been nearly ten days since He Yu had last gotten the chance to be alone with him. The boy was so pent up he was about to lose it.

Great, bring it on—it would be great if He Yu lost his mind; that would fix all of Xie Qingcheng's problems.

"If that's the case, my recommendation is that you'd be better off finding yourself a girlfriend," Xie Qingcheng said, "or perhaps a boyfriend. Don't..."

Before he could finish speaking, a box popped up on his screen. The image was very blurry and dark—it was the male student dorm at Huzhou University. The curtains were drawn around a single bed.

At first, Xie Qingcheng didn't recognize the shape that appeared on his screen. He took a closer look—and immediately felt as though the hand holding his phone had been stung.

The image wobbled as the camera panned upward and He Yu's eyes appeared. They were misted over, searingly hot, but with an undeniable gloom about them.

Despite his initial shock, Xie Qingcheng had a lot of experience keeping calm. After a moment of silence, he said, "I hope that you use your black-market technology for something of greater value than this."

"A single minute of a spring night is worth a thousand gold," said He Yu. "Don't you think that's something of value?"

Xie Qingcheng sighed and wearily lifted his hand to rub his forehead. "Spring my ass."

As he spoke, he set his phone face-down on top of the thick medical files, stood up, and walked into the bathroom, leaving He Yu to his own devices. He didn't realize that cursing He Yu out while they were outside the bedroom, with that slight edge of anger and hint of long-absent human emotion, had finally allowed He Yu's heart a modicum of relief.

Silver dust fell from the vast sky like so much fragmented jade, and with this kind of intimate back-and-forth tussling, the year drew to a close. The last day of the semester arrived.

The first years were still busy taking their final exams as, one by one, the fourth years packed their suitcases and towed them home.

Among the cars that had come to pick up the children, there was a military-style jeep that was particularly eye-catching. The car was majestic, the brand was preeminent, and most importantly, the officer leaning against the car was unbelievably handsome.

Dressed in uniform with boots and a pair of sunglasses, this officer was a highly ranked colonel. Beneath his towering nose was a pair of thin, narrow lips curved in a smile as refreshing as a mountain spring; strong-willed and dashing.

"Fuck." Passersby stopped to look back. "So handsome. Whose car is that? Whose relative is he?"

69

I ASKED HIM OUT
TO A MOVIE

"**A**RE YOU DUMB? Just look at the bottom half of his face and you can tell—he looks exactly like Wei Dongheng... He must be from the Wei family..."

"I heard that a while ago, when he was at the dorm, Wei Dongheng got into a huge argument with his family. Apparently he's not gonna come back to school for the second semester of his fourth year because his dad's making him head up northwest."

"Why the northwest?"

"I'm not sure... But isn't his father a senior official over in the western theater? He probably thought his prodigal son was embarrassing him, so he's taking him over there to put him in his place."

"How is a guy like Wei Dongheng okay with that...?"

The students murmured to each other as they passed the military jeep.

"Er-ge."[4]

"Oh, you're here." The officer turned his head, grinning.

Wei Dongheng stood before him, his expression cold.

"You sure are something else—I told you to meet me at three o'clock sharp, but it's already a quarter past four and you've only just made it out. If you were in my unit, I'd toss you into the mountains

---

4   Term of address for the second-eldest brother in a family.

and make you do a fifteen-klick ruck march. I guess I could let you off easy seeing as you're my little brother, but you'd have to give me at least ten klicks."

Wei Dongheng seemed to be in a terrible mood. "Don't try to discipline me with that stuff," he retorted.

"Aiyo, little brat, I wouldn't dare discipline you. I'm hardly qualified." The middle brother shook with laughter. "About that—when you get back, Dad's gonna discipline you himself. Lucky you."

"Don't mention that old fart to me."

"Fine, I won't." The middle brother seemed quite happy. He had been on military duty for a long time and was very excited to be out and about in the world, especially at this arts school full of beautiful women; he couldn't help but act like a fool. "Hey, I wanna ask you something."

"What do you want?!" Wei Dongheng couldn't stand the greasy way his brother was suddenly getting in his face, so he pressed a hand to his head and shoved him away.

His brother winked. "Where's your pretty little girlfriend?"

Wei Dongheng glared at his brother silently.

"That's why you took so long to show up, right? Because you were saying goodbye to someone? Why didn't you just bring her over and let your ge take a good look at her? Why so cold?"

"'Take a good look' my ass! As if you deserve to see her!" Wei Dongheng's voice was rough with anger as he shrugged off his backpack and swung it straight at his brother's face.

His brother couldn't hold himself back anymore. He dissolved into howling laughter on the spot. "Fucking hell, little bro, serves you right—you cried, didn't you? One look at your eyes and I can tell that you've been crying. Ah, but seriously, why don't you call her over? We can take her out for dinner before we leave, otherwise you won't see her for at least half a year once you're gone..."

"It's not like I'm serving in the army! I'm gonna be Commander Wei's fucking laborer—I can come back whenever I want!"

His brother clicked his tongue. "Hard to say."

"Oh, fuck off!"

"You're really not gonna let me meet your little beauty?"

"Fuck *off*!"

At that very moment, in one of Huzhou University's deserted multimedia classrooms, Xie Xue was wiping her tears and collecting herself. Then she walked out alone and locked the door behind her.

No exams had been scheduled in this building—it was empty and lifeless. She stood dazedly in the hallway for a long time, watching that silver-haired boy get into the military jeep. The vehicle rumbled off flashily into the distance, quickly disappearing from sight at the end of the avenue.

She couldn't stop her tears from falling once more, but as she lifted her hand and looked at the new ring sitting on her finger, she tried her best to calm herself down.

It was fine... It was only half a year...

After spacing out for a while longer, she walked out of the building with her bag slung over her shoulder. She looked as if her soul had left her body. To her great surprise, out on the spacious lawn next to the teaching building, she saw two people she never would have expected to see.

At first Xie Xue didn't react—she was too sad. But a few seconds later, she suddenly realized something wasn't right.

Was that He Yu and...her brother?

The sight of them together was so strange that it completely dislodged Xie Xue from the depths of her sorrow. She rubbed her eyes to make sure she wasn't seeing things—didn't they have that huge falling out?

Why did they just come out of an empty classroom together? And they were even bickering back and forth in such a familiar way...

"Go away."

"I'll give you a ride."

"Leave."

"I—"

"Are you leaving or not?"

Xie Qingcheng spoke coldly and without feeling the entire time; after they turned a corner, he abruptly pushed He Yu away. Between his severe expression, his piercing glare, and his unrelenting tone, he left no room for discussion.

At being pushed so fiercely, a slight chill surfaced on He Yu's face. He stood in place and watched Xie Qingcheng just like that, as Xie Qingcheng walked away without a backward glance, and as his figure disappeared beyond the stairs.

When he turned around at last, he happened to catch sight of Xie Xue, who hadn't managed to hide in time. At that moment, He Yu's expression became very strange, as if he had been caught red-handed doing something that he shouldn't have been doing.

"What are you doing here?" he asked warily.

It was the first time the two of them had faced each other since their quarrel. They'd crossed paths before this, but those encounters had been limited to the classroom.

Xie Xue was already in a bad mood, so this beast delivering himself to her doorstep presented the perfect opportunity for her to vent her feelings. "I should be the one asking you that," she said sternly. "What are you doing here instead of taking your exams? What were you doing with my brother just now?"

"...We weren't doing anything."

"Liar!" Xie Xue cried fiercely. "He wouldn't come to a deserted place like this with you for no good reason. Are you bullying him again?"

"Me, bullying him." He Yu sighed. "Jiejie, you really think I can bully him? If you were watching just now, you must have seen his attitude—*I'm* the one who's being bossed around all the time."

Xie Xue hesitated.

Although the scene just now was bizarre, she'd heard their conversation—it was true that her brother's attitude had been worse. And compared to that time when she had eavesdropped on them in the parking lot, He Yu seemed much gentler. In the parking lot, he'd mocked and humiliated Xie Qingcheng, but this time, Xie Qingcheng had been the one scolding He Yu, who had simply listened without saying anything aggressive in reply.

Xie Xue's tense expression relaxed somewhat. "Th-that's true." She shot He Yu another glare. "I suppose you wouldn't dare—why aren't you taking your exam?"

"It was easy, so I handed it in early."

Xie Xue blinked.

"Laoshi, surely you wouldn't go so far as to take issue with me handing my exam in early."

"You handed it in early so that you could come see my brother?" Xie Xue stared warily at He Yu. Like a cat, she thought she could smell something fishy.

"I was nearly done, and I happened to see him walk by outside."

"So the two of you have stopped fighting?"

"...Mm."

"That's more like it," Xie Xue muttered. "You were a real asshole back then. After something like that happened to him, you went and cursed him out like all those strangers..."

"About that," He Yu said mildly. "I don't think I said anything wrong."

Xie Xue's temper had only just started to calm down, and now it flared up again. "What did you say?"

"You saw the video from the broadcasting tower. Those things came out of his own mouth—with all the facts laid out like that, and given that he was a doctor, it's reasonable that he would be criticized."

"He Yu! You haven't changed at all, huh?" Xie Xue flew into a rage. "Acting so scholarly while you say such beastly words! He spent so many years with you—don't you know the kind of person he is? Don't you... Don't you trust or understand him at all?"

"How did I not trust him?" He Yu replied. "I used to trust him very, very much."

There was more he could say, of course...

I'm not like you—you're all normal people, so there are many things you've never experienced. You don't know how painful it is for me to live amongst you. When you heard the things that Xie Qingcheng said, you might not have taken them to heart.

But for me, those words stabbed into my ears and drilled into my heart. And that's to say nothing of those chat logs, and his lies about his contract... You don't know about these things, so of course you can choose to believe him without bearing any grudges. I can't do that.

But he kept those thoughts to himself. All he said was, "But the truth is the truth."

"But what you saw, what you heard—was that definitely the truth?" Xie Xue shouted. "My brother's the only one who knows what actually happened! It's true! He did quit his job back then, and he did leave the hospital not long after Qin Ciyan died, but do you think he was happy about it? When he got back home after resigning from the hospital, my saozi asked him what he was planning to do afterward. If you'd seen the look in his eyes—He Yu, if you'd seen the look in his eyes back then, you'd never say he ran away from his worries! The things he said—none of them were true! He didn't run away because he was scared!"

Xie Xue's voice had gone hoarse from her overwhelming indignation. "His eyes wouldn't lie—back then, his eyes were filled with pain, not fear..." By the time she finished speaking, her voice had taken on a sobbing tone.

Perhaps she had wanted to say this to everyone, but she knew that hardly anyone would believe her. So now that she had run into He Yu, the sadness she had kept bottled up for so long finally overflowed.

She lowered her head, furiously wiping at her eyes with her hands, wiping away the tears that she'd been shedding for Wei Dongheng and were now falling again for Xie Qingcheng. "My... My brother isn't a deserter...!" she wailed.

My brother isn't a deserter.

When Xie Xue said this, she was already overwhelmed with sobs.

He wasn't a deserter? Then why did he leave?

After the end of term, He Yu spent many days at home with the words that Xie Xue had blurted out through her tears echoing through his mind in every idle moment.

Once again, he sank into his thoughts, pondering over a problem that had already tormented him for far too long.

Xie Xue's words had touched a nerve. Every time He Yu remembered the messages he'd seen, it was like some kind of torture, cutting deep into his bones. But with the slightest glimmer of light, he found himself drawn, once again, like a moth to a flame. He wanted to touch the truth, even if it burned him to ashes.

In the midst of this self-inflicted torment, He Yu thought about those messages again and again. Those messages, those pieces of evidence, all pointed to Xie Qingcheng's weakness, to his retreat. What hidden motives could there possibly be?

"If you'd seen the look in his eyes back then," Xie Xue had said, *"you'd never say he ran away from his worries."*

This directly contradicted all the evidence He Yu had seen. The way he saw it, after leaving the hospital, Xie Qingcheng should have been happy, even overjoyed—he should have rejoiced over the fact that he had escaped from danger with his life intact and could henceforth lead a peaceful, contented existence.

But Xie Xue said that his eyes had been filled with pain.

Could Xie Xue have been seeing things? Could Xie Xue have been just like him in the past, looking at Xie Qingcheng through a beauty filter and trusting him too deeply, letting herself be deceived by his outer appearance? He Yu didn't know. But her words were like a heavy rock that had landed in his chest, sending ripples through his heart even though it had already frozen to ice.

He Yu suddenly longed to know Xie Qingcheng's true state of mind back then—the state of mind that he had revealed to Xie Xue. But there was no way Xie Qingcheng would be willing to talk to him about this now. All He Yu could do was toss and turn in his restlessness, thinking about that conversation—wondering if Xie Qingcheng...might still be hiding something.

If he was, then was he hiding something good? Or bad? How many more secrets were hidden in the sunless depths of that man's flesh-bound heart?

He Yu was mired deep in his thoughts, his imagination running wild, when a woman's voice sounded from beyond his bedroom door.

"He Yu."

He Yu started in surprise, then he realized that it was his mother.

Executive Lü was a woman of many responsibilities, but lately she had been spending quite a bit of time at the old residence in Huzhou. She had said before that she wanted to keep He Yu company, but he hadn't taken it seriously, treating her words as empty promises. But it turned out she really did stay this time. In fact, not only did she stay, she even washed her hands to personally make soup, and wanted to have heart-to-heart chats with her eldest son.

It made He Yu very uncomfortable. But still, he opened the door and looked down at that corpulent woman. "Mom, what is it?"

"I just... You're always locking yourself up in your room, so I was a bit worried." Lü Zhishu tilted her face, trying to look past He Yu into his room with its tightly drawn curtains.

He Yu calmly shifted to the side, blocking the view through the door. "I've always been like this. You don't need to worry about it."

"I'm just concerned about you... I made a reservation at a restaurant tonight. Their red-braised pork belly is amazing—sometimes ordinary dishes are the hardest to make well, so when they are made well, they're rare delicacies to be enjoyed. Do you want to—"

"I'm busy tonight. I'm going out."

Lü Zhishu's smile stiffened slightly, but she quickly pasted that trace of a grin back onto her fleshy face before it slipped away. Her cheeks trembled slightly as a pitiable expression showed through her false mask. "He Yu, I've been home for so long now, yet you still won't keep me company or talk with me..."

"...Next time," He Yu said. "Next time for sure."

He couldn't get used to this kind of unctuous tenderness—he felt like a vegetarian who had suddenly swallowed a mouthful of quivering, fatty meat. It didn't hurt or tickle when it caught in his throat, but he was disgusted by its greasiness.

Under Lü Zhishu's complicated gaze, He Yu put on his jacket and left the house.

He drove around aimlessly, without a destination in mind—but, probably because he was constantly thinking of Xie Qingcheng these days, when he finally returned to his senses, he found that he'd already reached the neighborhood of Moyu Alley.

Seeing as he was already there, He Yu decided he might as well park the car along the curb. At that moment, he noticed two people walking, one behind the other, out of a small restaurant nearby, the snow crunching beneath their feet—it was Xie Xue and Xie Qingcheng.

He Yu had originally planned on getting out of the car and heading over to Xie Qingcheng's house. However, Xie Xue's presence would be very inconvenient. He retrieved his phone from its mount in the car and, after a moment of contemplation, decided to send Xie Qingcheng a message instead.

He didn't know what to say, but after catching a glimpse of all the promotional posters for the latest New Year's films covering the street, he lowered his lashes and typed out a message asking if Xie Qingcheng wanted to see a movie with him.

Xie Qingcheng didn't respond.

He Yu sent another message. *"My car is parked on the street right outside your house."*

Xie Qingcheng responded, *"I'm not home."*

"Then who was it who went to eat spicy stir-fry with Xie Xue just now?"

No reply.

"Come out. I won't do anything else today, I only want to watch this movie, why are you avoiding me."

"We don't have anything else to do with one another."

He Yu started to lose his temper.

"Xie Qingcheng, are you saying that we can only see each other if we're hooking up? Fine, if you want to do it in the movie theater, I'm more than happy to oblige."

After writing these words, He Yu added another message. *"If you refuse to see me, then I'll just have to come to you. You can figure out how to explain things to Xie Xue yourself."*

He knew that this was an old and thoroughly unreasonable tactic, but it was very effective for dealing with Xie Qingcheng. Xie Qingcheng was a very clearheaded person, so if he had to choose between watching a movie with He Yu and arousing Xie Xue's suspicion, he'd inevitably go for the first option.

As expected, Xie Qingcheng walked out a short while later. Even though his expression was extremely unsightly, he got into He Yu's car. He slammed the door shut with a loud bang, treating this perfectly agreeable luxury car's door like it belonged on a taxi.

But He Yu didn't get angry. He said with a smile, "Where to, sir?"

Xie Qingcheng had absolutely no desire to banter with him. He said coldly, "Didn't you want me to watch a movie with you?"

"Which movie theater?"

"That's your fucking prerogative."

At that very moment, on a small island in international waters...

After spending some time contentedly sunbathing, the wanted fugitive Jiang Liping walked back toward the villa.

As she reached the front door, she ran into a woman with a face creased with wrinkles. This woman was sitting in a wheelchair and looked to be in a poor mental state, hanging on to life by a thread. She was like a flower on the verge of wilting, completely lacking in vitality.

When she heard her walking over, the woman opened her eyes slightly and looked at her young, lovely face for a while with something like longing. She shifted her gaze to the distant ocean horizon. "Ah, I'm running out of time."

Jiang Liping's footsteps came to a stop as she made a very respectful bow to the old woman. "Anthony's still out there looking for the data logs of the First Emperor for you on Executive Duan's orders," she said in a gentle, soothing voice. "He'll definitely find it."

"It's too late," the woman said. Her voice sounded like it was coming from an old muffled stereo system. "The First Emperor... It's just a legend, after all. It may be the most comprehensive simulation of the effects of RN-13 in humans, but it's still only a dataset. It's too late to study it now; it'll be impossible for me to recover and return to how I used to be."

Jiang Liping paused. "It's not too late, there's still hope... Executive Duan is thinking of a way. Please don't be so sad."

"Sad?" The woman sneered. "I'm not sad. There might not be a way to prevent me from dying, but even if we don't have the First Emperor's data, we have plenty of techniques to keep me alive... It's just that..." She paused, shooting her a menacing look, her expression sullen. "I don't want to keep living that way. Do you understand? I loathe men."

Jiang Liping blinked, at a loss.

"Why am I telling you this?" The old lady stared fixedly at her for a few seconds before looking away. "You're just a dog slobbering all over Huang Zhilong. I have no idea what's so great about him for you to be so besotted."

Jiang Liping forced a smile.

"Speaking of which, isn't your Huang Zhilong's new movie about to start playing in theaters?"

"Mm."

"So what are you planning to do?"

"I'll find a way to get back into the country and lie low in the company's safe house. There's some company business that only I can take care of properly—Executive Huang needs me."

The old woman snorted. "You sure are devoted." When Jiang Liping didn't reply, the old woman went back to watching the ocean. "How many more weeks do we have left...? If they still can't find the First Emperor's data, I'll need to have surgery. That boy's corpse is still fresh, but if we delay much longer, it won't be so useful anymore."

Jiang Liping still didn't reply.

"If you're heading back, go find that old shoemaker in Huzhou and bring me a pair of red high heels in that boy's size," the old woman said. "Like the kind in those old Hong Kong movies, the style you often wear. Back in my day, that style was very fashionable..."

Jiang Liping lowered her eyes. "Yes, Madam."

70

And Kissed Him in a Bar

I N A CERTAIN THEATER in Huzhou, the opening fanfare sounded, and the film began to play.

With a click, the film reel started turning, the screen lit up, and the story began to unfold before the eyes of the audience...

It was winter break, so the shows in theaters were all seasonally appropriate winter or New Year's films. Most of them featured star-studded casts and exquisite CGI, each and every frame as beautiful as a queen of the night flower in full bloom. With popular new celebrities showing skin and veteran actors propping up the production, you could smell the acrid scent of burning money directly through the movie screen.

As for the plot of the one they chose, it was astonishingly, scalp-numbingly bad.

He Yu had been watching attentively at first, but by the time the female lead killed her adoptive parents for the male lead without even stopping to think, he couldn't stand it anymore.

And it was clear he wasn't the only one.

The couple sitting to his left had started indulging in a very public display of affection, paying no attention to anything beyond their own dark corner—not even the blood splashing on the screen. The two of them seemed to be under the impression that they were keeping their voices down as they made out and bantered flirtatiously back and forth, but their neighbors could hear everything they said.

"Baby, kiss me again."

"Mwah!"

"One more time."

"You're sooo annoying."

"Just one more time."

"No way, pay attention to the movie."

"Be good, just kiss me one more time. If you don't kiss me then I'm gonna kiss you, okay?"

Truth be told, if it wasn't for the people flirting next to him, He Yu would have probably been doing some truly beastly things to Xie Qingcheng right now. But their behavior had made him lose all interest—listening to all the fuss this dumb couple was making, he ended up feeling quite calm. He expressionlessly picked up his soda, bit down on the straw, and indifferently took a sip.

But the more those two kissed, the more saccharine they became. He Yu endured it for a while, but he finally couldn't bear it anymore. Taking advantage of a flash of light on the screen, he took a glance at that disgusting couple.

That glance nearly blinded him.

This couple that was all over each other weren't a man and a woman at all—though one had a rather high and somewhat androgynous voice, it was very obvious that both of them had Adam's apples and that...they were...gay...

Utterly hypocritical homophobe He Yu's soda nearly went down the wrong pipe, sending him into a violent coughing fit.

Xie Qingcheng had been watching this awful movie with his face propped against one hand, but he jumped in his seat when He Yu suddenly started coughing next to him. "What's wrong?"

He Yu coughed. "... It's nothing..." He pursed his lips somewhat unwillingly, then said under his breath, "There are two gay guys sitting next to me."

Xie Qingcheng glanced over to He Yu's left. This pair of lovebirds were still treating the movie theater like a motel, making out so passionately it looked like they were about to go all the way right then and there.

Xie Qingcheng said nothing.

With the actual movie being unwatchably bad and these two audience members basically livestreaming gay porn next to them, there was nothing here worth looking at. Xie Qingcheng wanted to leave—he didn't want to waste a hundred and twenty minutes of his life like this. But just as he was about to say this to He Yu, it seemed the couple beside them got a little too worked up. Unable to hold themselves back anymore, the taller of the two dragged the other man to his feet and the two of them stooped to leave.

"Sorry, coming through."

Leaving the theater after making out so heatedly—it was obvious where they were going.

After a moment of silence, He Yu said, "... Do you still want to watch this?"

Xie Qingcheng tossed his paper towel into the trash bag. "I had no intention of watching this from the start. You're the one who wanted to come."

"Then let's go."

The two of them stood up simultaneously, bending over at their waists as they said to their neighbors, "Sorry, excuse us."

An older husband and wife were sitting next to them. The gay couple that had just left had been kissing so intensely, and this husband and wife had overheard everything and were likewise well aware of what those men had left the theater to do.

When the gay couple was leaving, there'd been a shower scene featuring a trendy young celebrity on screen. The wife was a fan of this young idol and, having had her view blocked at such a key moment, was already in a bad mood. It just so happened that the scene that was playing now, as He Yu and Xie Qingcheng got up to leave, was one where that trendy young celebrity had stripped off his shirt to patch up a wound. Xie Qingcheng was very tall, so even though he bent down, he still blocked the lady from admiring her little heartthrob's pecs.

The lady lost it—she was sitting through this dud of a movie solely for the eye candy, but now she had been interrupted twice in a row. She had a hair-trigger temper to begin with; she couldn't restrain herself any longer and yelled in a voice loud enough for the entire movie theater to hear: "Can you gays be a little less obnoxious? Getting each other so riled up that you're leaving one after another to find a room—could you be any more annoying?!"

The whole place fell silent.

Then, a few seconds later, everyone burst into raucous laughter.

He Yu and Xie Qingcheng hadn't expected something like this to happen. Xie Qingcheng said coldly, "You're mistaken, please move."

"You're *not* gay?" The lady felt her whole ticket had gone to waste now that she'd missed the chance to ogle her idol's body, so she pointed behind Xie Qingcheng at He Yu and cried shrilly, "You were kissing so intensely just now! Do you think I couldn't hear you?"

"If you have hearing problems, then you should see a professional," Xie Qingcheng replied. "That was the people sitting next to us; they've already left."

The lady set her hands on her hips. "Blaming others now, huh? You have the guts to do it, but not to own up to it? I'm embarrassed just talking to you! Disgusting homosexual freaks!"

The other audience members began to look over at them. This drama was much more interesting than the terrible movie.

Xie Qingcheng usually wouldn't be bothered by this kind of thing—he didn't care if other people called him a homosexual. But now, it was true that his relationship with He Yu wasn't innocent in the least. This was Xie Qingcheng's weakness. That woman had pricked him where it hurt, and his complexion flickered between green and white as he said balefully, "I already said that we don't have that kind of relationship."

He Yu knew that trying to explain would only create more of a mess, that giving more details would only implicate them further, so he pushed lightly at the small of Xie Qingcheng's back and said in a low voice, "Forget it, let's go."

"What're you poking me for?" Xie Qingcheng said coldly. "There's nothing between us."

"Oh, so you'll do it with a guy, but you won't admit to it? Just looking at men like you grosses me out. You gays should all just go to hell."

Normally, Xie Qingcheng would never lose his temper over something like this, but all the anger he'd been holding back these past few days surged out at once. "Watch your mouth!" he said harshly.

He Yu pulled at him, unusually serious. "Forget it!"

Realizing that Xie Qingcheng was legitimately angry, the shrew of a woman shrank back in fear, but when she saw that He Yu wasn't willing to stir up more trouble over this, she toughened back up.

"What're you gonna do?" she screeched. "Hit me? You were the ones disrupting us ordinary people's viewing experience with your PDA! What a pain in the ass! The movie theater shouldn't even be admitting you freaks! Have these seats been disinfected? For fuck's sake, don't let innocent people catch AIDS!"

"Xie Qingcheng, let's go."

"Let go of me!" Xie Qingcheng turned around to glare at He Yu, who was tugging on his sleeve. "What're you pulling at me for!"

He Yu sighed. The thought crossed his mind that maybe he should just leave Xie Qingcheng and go. But as he glimpsed a young man sitting behind them furtively raising his phone to record, he frowned. As if acting completely on instinct, he took off his jacket and draped it over Xie Qingcheng's head, hiding his face from view.

Even he himself was rather baffled as to why he did this. He really wasn't much of a benevolent person—when they were about to be filmed against their will and splashed all over social media, shouldn't he be covering his own face instead?

Why should he care about someone else's fate...

Xie Qingcheng had no idea what was going on. "He Yu, what are you doing!" he snarled.

He Yu held him in place. "Don't move, someone's recording us."

The woman rolled her eyes at them. "So intimate, yet you say you're not gay?" she said scathingly. "What's the point of pretending? Damn queers."

Xie Qingcheng reached up to pull off the jacket, but He Yu promptly grabbed his wrist and dragged him away without any further explanation.

Even after the two of them had left the dark movie theater and sat down in the small 24-hour bar downstairs, Xie Qingcheng was still worked up.

"Why didn't you let me speak?"

He Yu ordered two drinks and sat down across from Xie Qingcheng, folding his arms. "What's the point of arguing with someone like her? You wouldn't even recognize each other once you left the theater. Besides, I saw the guy behind us taking a video on his phone. Do you want this to become something much bigger?"

Xie Qingcheng fell silent for a while, then he irritably drew out a cigarette and lit it. But just as he brought it to his pale lips and was about to take a drag, He Yu snatched it straight out of his mouth and stubbed it out.

"You're not allowed to smoke. I hate secondhand smoke."

Xie Qingcheng slammed the lighter down on the table and ran a hand through his hair, pulling it into disarray, before turning toward He Yu and cursing. "Fucking hell, why am I wasting my time with you? Why the fuck did you ask me to come out here for no reason? Is it because you have no one else to hang out with?"

He Yu didn't reply at first. After a while, he said, "That's right."

Xie Qingcheng stared.

"I have no one else to hang out with. When I want to relax and talk to someone without having to wear a mask, you're the only person I can ask. Did you only just realize that?"

Xie Qingcheng looked away again. They were sitting by the window of the bar. The dark winter night had already descended over the Huzhou skyline. Heavy clouds gathered overhead, and icy rain began to fall.

Raindrops pitter-pattered against the window, smearing the neon lights outside into a rainbow blur. The colors were brilliant yet also gleamingly wet, drop after drop of rainwater finally coalescing into rivulets and streaming down like tears.

The bartender brought over their drinks.

After downing a gulp, Xie Qingcheng lowered his voice, gritted his teeth, and finally let out some of the emotions he'd been suppressing for so long. "What exactly do you even want—aren't you tired of this yet? When can we put an end to this senseless, unnatural relationship that we shouldn't even be having in the first place?"

"...I don't know."

Xie Qingcheng's anger started to build. "You haven't had enough yet?"

He Yu took a sip of his own drink. As he set his cup down, the question that had been lingering on his mind for days, the one he'd never been able to resolve, finally tumbled out of his mouth. "Xie Qingcheng, if you're going to ask me questions like this, there's actually something I want to ask you too. If you tell me the truth, then I'll do the same and answer your question."

"Go ahead," said Xie Qingcheng bluntly.

"Back then, why did you suddenly resign as my doctor?"

Even though Xie Qingcheng usually kept himself calm, and even though he no longer harbored much sentiment toward He Yu, he couldn't help but fly into a rage. His head snapped up, and he fixed He Yu with an extremely vicious glare. "You've already asked me this fucking question so many times!"

"But," He Yu said, "there probably isn't a single person who's been able to get the complete truth out of you, is there? Xie Qingcheng, I just want to know what kind of truth you're still hiding in your heart."

"He Yu...don't assume you're special just because we've slept together a handful of times. I don't give a damn about our physical relationship—it's true that I can't beat you at that game—but when it comes to anything beyond that, you've no right to come to me asking for answers!"

He Yu had expected this response. In fact, if Xie Qingcheng had really told him the truth, it would probably mean that Hell was about to freeze over. So he didn't get angry. He lowered his lashes, his gaze sweeping back and forth over Xie Qingcheng's lips. "Does that tongue of yours only soften up when it's being kissed in bed?"

Xie Qingcheng grabbed his cup to toss its contents into He Yu's face, but He Yu seized him by the wrist. "You shouldn't use the same tricks too many times. They'll stop working."

Xie Qingcheng yanked his wrist fiercely out of his grip. For an instant, a sliver of his tattoo peeked out, pale as smoke, but it was immediately covered up by his long sleeve again. "I'm leaving. You can drink by yourself."

"Don't go." He Yu blocked his way.

"What more do you want? You saw your movie. As for what you want to know, there's nothing more I can tell you," Xie Qingcheng said. "If I say it's the truth, then it's the truth. Now, get out of the way."

When they stared at each other, all that was reflected in He Yu's eyes was Xie Qingcheng. Yet in Xie Qingcheng's own eyes, He Yu could see the warm lamplight, the flying snow, the raucous crowd at the bar...

The only thing missing was himself.

Fury suddenly sparked to life in his chest, making all the things he had never planned on saying to Xie Qingcheng burn their way out of his throat—

"Are you sure what you told me is really the truth? Don't you feel guilty saying such things, Xie Qingcheng?"

Xie Qingcheng was completely unmoved. "What guilt is there to feel with a beast like you?"

He Yu pressed the man between his body and the bar. Xie Qingcheng was a tall, well-built man, but He Yu could trap and confine him. He Yu's voice suddenly became very soft. "Then let me ask you this—back then, what was the actual duration of the contract you signed with my dad?"

The light in Xie Qingcheng's eyes flickered—nearly imperceptibly, but He Yu still caught it.

"Back then, you specifically told me it was seven years," He Yu said. "You said that it had run out normally, and you didn't plan on renewing it—that it was a perfectly normal way for a relationship between two people to end. You told me to get over it." He Yu's eyelashes trembled beneath the dim light of the bar as his voice dropped lower than the beating of the drum. "If I'm a beast, then what are you? A despicable liar?"

As he searched for the most cutting words he could use on Xie Qingcheng, he stared unblinkingly at Xie Qingcheng's face, taking in every detail. When he'd exposed Xie Qingcheng's lies, the man had lost his composure for no more than a second before his features returned to their usual rigidly cold, steadfast appearance... Xie Qingcheng really was *too* calm, so calm that it seemed he didn't even plan on arguing anymore.

"You found out."

"Yes, I found out."

"He Jiwei told you."

"I don't need him to tell me," He Yu said. "Perhaps you haven't realized it yet, Doctor Xie, but I'm no longer that poor little devil who tried to use his allowance to keep you, only to be told I might as well save it to buy a slice of *cake*."

Xie Qingcheng said nothing.

"Thanks to your guidance, I've learned many things. I have plenty of ways to look into anything I want from the past."

Xie Qingcheng finally turned his gaze back onto He Yu's face— and He Yu saw the shadow of his own features reflected in his pupils. It gave him an indescribable sense of excitement.

"Correct," Xie Qingcheng finally said. "I lied to you about that. It was ten years, not seven. But so what? What kind of society do you think we live in? Did you imagine I was your family's indentured servant, that I wasn't allowed to leave ahead of time if I wanted to?"

"What are you saying?" He Yu asked. "I wouldn't dare. Didn't you already leave ahead of time?"

"Then what do you want to do about it now?"

"Doctor Xie, you're a very smart man. You know I wouldn't bring up old grudges for no good reason."

"Whatever nonsense it is you're waiting to say, just say it."

The bar's revolving laser lights spun over to them, their dazzling brilliance flitting across Xie Qingcheng's eyes and forehead. He Yu gazed at him, gazed at that untouchable alpine blossom that he couldn't afford to buy, that beguiling yet ephemeral mirage that he couldn't manage to hold in his hands. Then, he very quietly said two words: "Three years. Stay with me for another three years. Just like before."

Xie Qingcheng looked at him like he thought he'd gone mad. "You want me to go back to being your personal physician?"

"Yes."

"What time is it? You ought to wash up and go to bed."

"Xie Qingcheng." He Yu was very persistent. "I can give you everything my dad gave you back then. I've saved up a lot of money."

"Save it for your future wife."

With a single sentence, He Yu's expression darkened completely.

Save it to buy a slice of cake.

Save it for your future wife.

Five years ago and in the present, whether He Yu offered his childhood allowance or the money he'd earned, Xie Qingcheng's extremely rational attitude was always so patronizing. It was almost like he was mocking him.

"I have no such plans," said He Yu furiously.

"Then what plans do you have? To keep sleeping with me? For how long? If one year isn't enough, then three years, five years?" Xie Qingcheng's eyes were ruthless. "Aren't you sick of it yet, you good-for-nothing homosexual?"

"Stop talking such nonsense!" He Yu hissed. "I'm not a homosexual!"

"True, you probably aren't. It wouldn't do for an animal like you to embarrass the homosexual community."

He Yu stared at his infuriatingly calm features. Xie Qingcheng's emotions weren't as visible on his face as they had been when he was mistaken for a gay man in the theater.

Perhaps He Yu's brain had short-circuited, but he somehow came up with a crazy idea. He didn't care how ugly Xie Qingcheng's words were, he merely asked him one last time: "Do you agree or not?"

"Agree to what?"

"To come be my doctor again. To stay with me."

Xie Qingcheng's patience had run out. "I think it's about time you woke up," he said. Rolling his eyes, he turned to leave.

He Yu slammed him against the polished black granite of the bar. His temper had been under much better control since he and Xie Qingcheng started sleeping together, but now his eyes were a little ferocious and a little hazed over. "Fine...fine. Then I'll just have to find a way to show you the true meaning of humiliation."

A hint of fear flickered over Xie Qingcheng's face. Their altercation had gotten a little loud just now, and several of the people around them were looking in their direction. Tensing, he asked quietly, "What are you doing?"

He didn't know how else He Yu could possibly embarrass him. Even the insults hurled at him during the incident with the broadcasting tower and Qin Ciyan had left him unbothered, so what could—

Before Xie Qingcheng could finish his thought, He Yu had already grasped his tattooed wrist and, with the disco ball flashing overhead, pressed him against the bar. Then, in front of the many unmarried men and women out here enjoying the nightlife, he suddenly lowered his head—

And heavily, almost roughly, kissed him.

71

As If I'd Gone Mad

Xie Qingcheng felt a massive rumbling explosion go off in his head.

It was like something had shattered deafeningly or detonated violently, bursting into flames. His eyes flew wide open as the string of rationality in his mind instantly snapped. He couldn't begin to accept that He Yu could do something like this.

He Yu hated it when people called him gay. When he was in middle school, a male classmate had confessed to him with a bouquet of roses, and he'd reacted so badly that he broke the boy's shin. But in that moment, in front of a crowd, under the wine-red lights, before the stares of the patrons, the waitstaff, the bartender... Right in front of everyone, he was kissing him.

Xie Qingcheng was an exceptionally coolheaded person, but this truly exceeded the limits of what he could bear. His face was burning from the overwhelming shock.

And yet, as if he'd gone mad, He Yu was roughly kissing him on the mouth, their lips intertwining, sucking adamantly and plundering his mouth with his wet tongue. Xie Qingcheng was still numb from shock; he didn't have any of He Yu's technique or his shamelessness. In the midst of this intense, fervent kiss, soft, wet noises emerged in the brief moments their lips and tongues parted and then met again. Xie Qingcheng tried to seize the opportunity to turn his face away, but He Yu grabbed him by the hair and yanked him back, drawing him into an even deeper and more forceful kiss.

For a moment, his every breath was filled with the young man's scent. There was too much desire and heat in this kiss—in all his life, Xie Qingcheng had never shared such an intense kiss with anyone before, and certainly not in public.

And that was to say nothing of how he was the one *being* kissed. Or that the person kissing him was a student—a male student.

When Xie Qingcheng came to his senses, he was so furious that he shook from head to toe. His eyes had turned scorching red in an instant.

But how would the people around them see things?

This wasn't the same crowd as the audience in the movie theater. They were more open-minded and more interested in watching the excitement—and at that moment, they were already beginning to clap, one after another, laughing as they took in this spectacle.

"Nice!"

There was even some rascal who whistled at them and called out, "Gentlemen, there's a love hotel upstairs! When you're done putting on a show for us, you guys can finish your business up there!"

As a self-respecting man, how could Xie Qingcheng put up with such a blow to his pride? But the moment he began to struggle, He Yu pulled away slightly and, with his lips barely a centimeter from Xie Qingcheng's own and still slick from their entanglement, laughed softly at a volume only Xie Qingcheng could hear.

"Ge, I'm just scaring you," he murmured. "This isn't actually that bad—stuff like this is pretty normal in a bar." He nuzzled him gently. "We're just courting attention here, but if you keep causing a scene, we'll look like a joke. Do you want to give people something to laugh at? I have no shame, though, so it's all up to you."

It was dim in the bar, and beneath the laser lights flashing all the colors of the rainbow, the onlookers couldn't tell how ashen Xie Qingcheng's face was.

He Yu gently nosed against him again. "But if you agree to come back and stay by my side, then I'll let you off right away."

"I just want you to die."

There was a gleam of slightly inhuman madness in He Yu's eyes, but he still smiled as usual...although there was something frightening in this smile, and a little petulant. "Oh...then I might as well continue. Let's go all the way right here."

If Xie Qingcheng's face had been ashen before, now it was completely white—deathly white.

With He Yu's abnormal mind, his way of thinking was different from normal people's. Now that he had given himself up to despair, there was no knowing when he might suddenly decide that the line he would never cross was now just a pile of worthless weeds to trample over. In the past, Xie Qingcheng had only needed to take a single look at He Yu's beautiful almond eyes to know when he was joking, when he was hesitating, when he was being sincere. But now, as he looked at the pair of eyes before him, he couldn't see anything clearly despite their closeness. Those eyes seemed to be shrouded in a layer of mist, leaving him no chance of ever again recognizing that little devil he once knew so well.

He Yu was truly insane. His hands had even begun to fumble with his buttons already.

The crowd became even rowdier, banging on their tables and chairs, with some people even going so far as to take out their phones to snap pictures.

However, there was one aspect of He Yu that was still somewhat human—he didn't care whether he was photographed, but he used his free hand to completely cover the upper half of Xie Qingcheng's face, from his forehead to the tip of his nose, revealing only a pair of thin, slightly panting lips and an upraised jaw.

Seeing the way he was frozen in place, He Yu finally said with a smile, "Xie Qingcheng, come back."

If Xie Qingcheng were to ask himself in earnest, he would say that he had never really been afraid of anything. But right at that moment, He Yu had truly struck fear into his heart.

He was insane.

Was this person still a member of their society? Did he have any rationality left?

Covering Xie Qingcheng's eyes, He Yu kissed him on the lips again. Xie Qingcheng didn't want to be kissed like this, so he abruptly stopped speaking, allowing He Yu to press passionate kisses to his cold, unfeeling lips.

Clearly, He Yu had kissed Xie Qingcheng into silence, but the boy closed his eyes and nuzzled against the side of his neck as he said, "Ge, if you won't answer me, then I'll take that as a yes."

He had asked the question with his eyes closed, but he opened them abruptly when he finished speaking, peering into Xie Qingcheng's eyes, staring at the face half-covered by his ten fingers. He stared at those thin lips. It seemed like the moment those lips parted, before the word "no" could be voiced, he was going to capture them roughly in another kiss.

He detested homosexuality and resented being called gay just as much: even he didn't know why he would do something like this so readily, without hesitation, just for the sake of winning back Xie Qingcheng's company. Why would he behave like this?

Xie Qingcheng's whole body had frozen from head to toe, numb and unfeeling. He had been gripping the wooden bar behind his back so tightly that a frightening crack had formed in the wood.

For a split second, he truly wished to kill He Yu.

However, he still managed to control the impulse.

Throughout their protracted deadlock, He Yu still hadn't received a clear refusal from Xie Qingcheng—this was because Xie Qingcheng's head was spinning with anger; he had never encountered such a deranged situation before. For the first time in his life, he found himself at a complete loss for how to deal with a problem.

But to He Yu, this amounted to a tacit agreement.

With an air of satisfaction, he finally let go of Xie Qingcheng, adopting a victorious posture and smiling as he pulled him into his arms to prevent the crowd from taking pictures of Xie Qingcheng's face. His eyes were dangerously cold on the surface, but deep down, they were filled with unbridled delight.

The youth's expression was unhinged, but his movements were extremely gentle as he lifted his fingers and softly caressed the edge of the man's ear, paying no mind to the coldness and stiffness of the body in his embrace. He rocked gently back and forth as he held him by the bar's dance floor, like a boy who had finally managed to buy the slice of cake he had yearned for for so long.

Dipping his head, he whispered into Xie Qingcheng's ear, "Ge, you're being so good for me. You've agreed, so I'll stop making things difficult for you. As long as you listen to me, I can still be your little devil."

He Yu's voice was so tender it made one's blood run cold. Xie Qingcheng could say nothing.

"This time, you need to look after me properly. You can't lie to me again, okay?"

The bar was never lacking in liveliness—once everyone finished watching what was happening on one side, something else would attract their interest to the other side. When He Yu and Xie Qingcheng stopped kissing, the crowd's attention gradually shifted elsewhere.

When He Yu let go of him, Xie Qingcheng looked as though he had already lost all desire to speak further. For someone so overly calm, perhaps even something this intensely upsetting only left behind an aftertaste of numbness.

Even though hardly anyone had their phones raised anymore, He Yu was still very territorial by nature. He didn't care if people took photos of his own face, but he didn't want them to turn their cameras on someone he had touched, someone he had slept with. Although he acted like a beast in every other regard, he was very conscientious about keeping Xie Qingcheng's face hidden the entire time.

That was why he removed his baseball cap and put it on Xie Qingcheng, pulling the brim down low. His mood seemed to have improved a great deal.

"Wait for me here," he said to Xie Qingcheng.

Xie Qingcheng looked at him with an expression so cold that it didn't seem to belong to a living person. He Yu smiled, completely oblivious. Then he leaned forward and said something to the employee behind the bar, who nodded.

Occasionally, customers at the bar would come up to the stage and fight for the DJ's job. People did this for various reasons—they wanted to express their love or try to seduce someone, or they were bored, or there were even some teenage boys who simply loved being the center of attention and wanted to show off.

He Yu had no intention of figuring out exactly what his own underlying motivation was. All he knew was that he had the sudden urge to do this, so he went and did it.

After speaking with the leader of the house band, he walked on stage and took the proffered guitar. Under the stark white spotlight, He Yu lowered his lashes and played a song that Xie Qingcheng had never heard before. The lyrics were in English, and its melody unfolded with a charming lilt. The boy played the song with nimble fingers, smiling at the audience below as he strummed the strings, his canines peeking out when he turned his face to the side.

He looked relaxed and refined as he played this song that was entirely unfamiliar to Xie Qingcheng.

As he sang the melody in a gentle voice, the boy on stage seemed to glance back carelessly, his gaze landing on Xie Qingcheng's face where it was half-hidden in the darkness. For a while, He Yu watched Xie Qingcheng from afar. Even though Xie Qingcheng wasn't looking at him, he felt immensely satisfied.

As he neared the end, he lowered his head to concentrate on playing a particular section, before finally putting the guitar down. Looking up at the spotlight illuminating him, he slowly closed his eyes.

Flecks of dust floated through the beam of light, unable to fall just yet. As people in the audience began to clap, He Yu felt very comfortable—much more comfortable than he'd ever felt before, when he was being an uptight and perfectly behaved model youth.

He thought—whatever he wanted in the future, he needed to seize it directly for himself.

And if someone refused to give it to him, he would just have to demand it regardless.

He had been too restrained and gentle before, and for what? All the praise and approval he had received was essentially useless. All of his hard work had landed him in such a wretched state, and he still had nothing at all for himself.

Now, as long as he didn't care about his image, he could obtain anything he wanted.

He could grasp it tightly in his hands.

It was just too bad that this sense of satisfaction wouldn't last long.

A few days later, He Yu had everything prepared—he'd even personally cleaned up the guest room that Xie Qingcheng had lived in before. Feeling very satisfied and pleased that Xie Qingcheng would definitely be staying here again, he happily called the man himself to ask when he would be coming.

However, the smile he pressed against the receiver gradually withered away to become frost frozen over the corners of his lips.

What he received was a thorough and well-considered refusal. As he listened to Xie Qingcheng's ice-cold voice through the phone, there was even a smudge of dust on his face from all the cleaning that he'd yet to away.

Xie Qingcheng's words were unequivocal:

It was impossible.

He Yu was about to mention the photo, but Xie Qingcheng beat him to the punch. Before he could even open his mouth, Xie Qingcheng said bluntly, "Send it. If you want to send it, then just fucking send it. But if you dare to send it to Xie Xue, then there's no need for us to ever see each other again, and that goes for hooking up as well. So consider your options wisely."

He Yu's excitement dissipated in an instant, leaving behind only a wretched face covered in grime.

Xie Qingcheng's meaning was very clear—it was a compromise where he would stop resisting He Yu's advances in bed. Xie Qingcheng had already resigned himself to having his physical energy worn down by their hook-ups, but it affected him no further than that. Xie Qingcheng was already very indifferent toward this, so He Yu couldn't use it to hurt him, much less obtain anything from him in return.

So it turned out that, in the end, He Yu was the wretched one.

He had lost sight of himself, while Xie Qingcheng had not.

After the psychological stress from the first time they slept together had faded, hooking up no longer dealt much of a shock to Xie Qingcheng anymore. Having adjusted his mindset, there were times when he could regard He Yu as a prostitute delivered to his doorstep. Even though he had no need for that kind of service— and a typical prostitute wouldn't provide that kind of service—this mindset allowed him to regain the sense of authority to which he was accustomed.

But he couldn't go back to being He Yu's personal physician.

That was a matter of social status and employment. If he said yes, he would lose both body and mind to He Yu. Not to mention, it would be a waste of his valuable time. And so, he refused.

It had to be said—Xie Qingcheng was much more adept at manipulating He Yu than the other way around.

Xie Qingcheng was right; throughout their lustful entanglements, though Xie Qingcheng appeared to be the one losing out, the person who had truly lost himself was He Yu.

Xie Qingcheng remained that indifferent, unfeeling Doctor Xie.

After receiving the other man's clear refusal, He Yu was very gloomy. It was as if he had been pulled out of a warm April day full of spring blossoms and tossed into a bone-piercingly cold winter.

His heart had originally been full of hope, even overflowing with confidence, as he sat up perfectly straight and waited for the person who had abandoned him five years ago to come back. But what he'd received was a loud, resoundingly clear slap to the face.

Once again, his dream had been shattered.

He Yu had no choice but to stay home, swallowing pill after pill.

Sudden mood swings between sadness and joy were liable to cause illness, and so, unsurprisingly, he fell ill.

Each outbreak of psychological Ebola was more severe than the last. He Yu felt colder than ice, but his body temperature topped forty degrees Celsius; when he opened his eyes, it felt like even his retinas were burning.

He lay in bed and sent a message to Xie Qingcheng.

I'm sick, I'm sick.

I'm sick, Xie Qingcheng.

I'm sick, Doctor Xie.

There was no reply.

Perhaps Xie Qingcheng thought he was lying, or perhaps he just didn't care if He Yu died. Whatever the case, he never gave He Yu an answer, and as He Yu waited for days on end, his illness steadily worsened.

He Yu didn't care—personal physicians came and went, one after another, all of them failing to alleviate his symptoms. In the end, he decided to simply stop letting these people keep disturbing him. At least that way he wouldn't have to make such an effort to restrain his urge to hurt them.

He shut himself in his room and took one of the books on the rare diseases of the world down from his shelf to read. In that book, there was an entry that had left a very deep impression on him about a condition called "ossification disease."

It detailed the case of a seemingly normal little boy from another country who had accidentally broken a bone playing sports when he was six years old. The doctor conducted a routine surgery to treat it, but after the surgery, not only did the little boy's leg fail to heal, but it became increasingly swollen as additional bony growths began to form around the site of trauma.

In the interest of restoring him to health, the boy endured more than thirty major and minor surgical procedures in total before the doctors finally made the shocking discovery that this boy's muscle tissue was abnormal. Whenever he received an external injury, the boy's body would mount an intense self-protective response and begin to produce new bone growth in an effort to stave off external harm.

"It's similar to ALS, but even more terrifying." Xie Qingcheng had explained the case to him long ago. "He couldn't be allowed to get hit by anything, not even the slightest bump. In most cases, if a person collides with something, they'll form a minor bruise, but for him, new bone grew wherever he was struck. Gradually, the patient's entire body would be sealed up by bone until he was completely immobilized."

The boy featured in this case file had endured a long illness, slowly watching his own flesh harden into bone. Finally, when he was in his thirties, his painful life came to an end.

"Because of his ossification disease, his doctors couldn't treat him through surgery, nor could he undergo any diagnostic procedures that gave him even the smallest of injuries—he couldn't even have his blood drawn," Xie Qingcheng had said to the boy, who was completely engrossed in the story. "Therefore, before he died, he had a wish—he hoped that doctors would be able to better study his disease, so that if there were unlucky patients with the same condition as him in the future, they could be treated successfully and live a life completely different from his own. He chose to donate his body to science. His skeleton is still displayed in a museum today."

There was a photograph in the book of a twisted skeleton standing peacefully in a clear display cabinet, with his name and dates of birth and death written below. In addition, there was the sentence, "At the time of his death, seventy percent of his body had been ossified."

But He Yu's attention was drawn to another photograph of a display cabinet next to the boy's skeleton. Inside was a similar skeleton with a smaller build, nearly all its ribs fused together into a single, terrifying mass.

"That was a different girl," Xie Qingcheng said, noticing what he was looking at. "The spread of information was slow at the time, and they weren't from the same country. He didn't know that while he was enduring a loneliness that no one could understand, there was actually another girl across the sea who was suffering from the same disease. It wasn't until after his death that this girl learned that there had been another person in the world who could have empathized with her suffering. Still, this girl was very optimistic; she didn't give up on life because of her ossification disease. She was interested in fashion and designed many outfits that allowed her to participate in various activities... After she died, she made the same choice he did, and afterward, their skeletons were displayed next to each other in a medical museum. They never met when they were alive, but perhaps, after their deaths, they can support and comfort each other—that was the museum director's vision."

With that, Xie Qingcheng had closed the book. He Yu was feverish and tired, but he still remembered what Xie Qingcheng said next: "Perhaps there's someone out there who's suffering from the same illness as you, but you just don't know about them. Perhaps that person is striving their hardest to live, but you just aren't aware of it. He Yu, you mustn't lose to them."

Dazed from fever, the young He Yu had felt bloodthirsty, but all the strength in his body was gone. Swaddled in a heavy blanket, he'd squinted fuzzily up at Xie Qingcheng's face. "Then, after I die, will there be someone displayed next to me in a museum?"

"I'm afraid your bones wouldn't have any exhibition value," Xie Qingcheng said, "so I recommend that you first think about how to live on as best you can."

But what was the point of living on?

There were people who lived for money or power, for fame and fortune, for family and love. But none of these things seemed to have anything to do with He Yu now: either they had abandoned him, or he had no interest in them at all.

He Yu fiddled idly with a utility knife. He had taken a medicine that he knew would be particularly effective, but it had yet to kick in. Sitting next to the window, he watched as the servants bustled about below, but before long he found that he couldn't stop thinking about slitting their throats one by one, so he looked away.

His hand trembled, his pupils contracting to tiny dots, but his face remained completely expressionless.

He pushed out the blade, pressing it to his wrist. Just as he had before, he took all the hurt he wanted to inflict on others and shifted it onto his own body.

The knife scars and the traces from his tattoo were already very faint. With his head tilted to the side, he stared for a while, gripping the blade, and then very lazily began to cut—

N-o-t-h-i-n-g...

The sound of the tattoo artist's voice seemed to ring in his ears once more. "This is quite long, so it will hurt a lot. Would you like to find something else?"

"It's fine. I want this one."

Nothing of him that doth fade,
But doth suffer a sea-change
Into something rich and strange.

He gazed steadily as the letters appeared one by one, lines of blood trickling out like strands of spider silk. Perhaps this was what Xie Qingcheng wanted to see, he thought. His karmic retribution.

If he died right now, Xie Qingcheng would probably set off a string of firecrackers to celebrate as soon as he found out...

The youth sat silently on the windowsill on the second floor of the villa. The fiery brilliance of the sprawling sunset dazzled his eyes until he could barely keep them open anymore. In a deep, absent-minded daze, his body swayed back and forth, and then...

It was as if he had suddenly become very light. The evening wind carried an age-old tenderness as it blew past his face.

He tipped forward and tumbled down...

Thud!

"Young Master! The Young Master fell off the building!"

"Oh my god! Help!"

"Quick, call an ambulance! Call an ambulance right now!"

72

I WAS INDEED A MADMAN

WHEN HE WAS EIGHT, the door opened. "Good morning, Doctor Xie. My dad asked me to come greet you in hopes that we can chat more."

He was pretending to be well-behaved, but he was actually a little confused. So he just stood in the doorway of the room, covered in etchings of summer hydrangeas, and bowed to the young medical student sitting at the desk.

That doctor turned around and indifferently looked him up and down. "Come in and take a seat, then."

And then, when he was ten: he ran through the long corridor, the results of a particular lab test in his hand. "Doctor Xie, Doctor Xie."

With a push from the boy, the door opened again.

Xie Qingcheng was standing next to the window frame reading *Ode to the Nightingale*. He frowned at the racket the boy was raising, and in the sunlight and patterned shadow, Xie Qingcheng said to him, "How many times have I told you to knock before entering?"

"My levels are almost normal this time! I'm getting better!" He couldn't hold back his excitement, sweat from his run beading on his face. "Look, Doctor, look."

"If you keep getting excited like this, you'll regress." Xie Qingcheng shut the poetry anthology, and though his expression was indifferent, he still beckoned toward him casually. "Come in, then. Let me see."

And then, when he was fourteen—

It was dark and overcast outside. He stood in front of that heavy door for a very long time. And then, he knocked.

The door to the room opened once again.

The youth noticed at a glance that the room had become very chilly. Xie Qingcheng had already finished packing up his things. The answer to his question was already self-evident. But still, like a dying patient who refused to accept his fate and hoped to live just a little longer, he asked, "What my mother said—is it true?"

The empty closet, the clean surface of the desk, the luggage in the corner of the room— all these inanimate objects answered him silently.

But he only looked at Xie Qingcheng. Stubbornly, obstinately, filled with dignity and yet pathetic in the extreme, he asked once again, "Is what she said true?"

Xie Qingcheng had an ironed coat draped over his arm. He sighed. "Come in. We'll talk after you come in."

And finally, again when he was fourteen—

He Yu went overseas not long after Xie Qingcheng departed. Before he left, he arrived at the guest room's closed door all alone. The boy's hair was a little messy, wispy strands hanging in his eyes.

He stood in silence, head bowed, for a very long time. Finally, he lifted his hand and knocked on Xie Qingcheng's door.

Again and again.

The door creaked open.

Heart swelling, He Yu gazed inside expectantly, but there was nothing there—a gust of wind had blown the door open.

The room was dark inside, like an empty, rotting tomb, like an illusion that had gone cold.

He entered. The only proof that Xie Qingcheng had once been there was the book on rare diseases of the world he'd left behind for He Yu, placed on the table next to the window. He opened it in a daze to see Xie Qingcheng's handwriting in light blue fountain pen on the title page. Stately and straight, one could see the man's upright figure through his penmanship.

To He Yu:

Little devil, there will come a day when you walk out of the shadows in your heart on your own.

I hope I can trust in that.

From Xie Qingcheng

The young man lifted his hand and caressed those stern words, as if trying to glean some residual gentleness that could allow them to part on good terms and eventually forget about each other.

However, He Yu never admitted that, later on, in many of his dreams—whether on the banks of the Thames or the sandy beaches of Sicily, during foggy Danish nights or brilliantly hot Spanish summers—he dreamed of returning to the residence in Huzhou, to that secluded, carpeted corridor.

He dreamed of that dark wooden door, engraved with its infinite summer flowers.

And he dreamed of knocking, again and again, helplessly, desperately, every single time—until the clock struck midnight, and from within his dream of self-salvation, that heavy door opened from inside once more.

Xie Qingcheng stood in the room, his expression indifferent yet so reliable, just like how he had always been whenever He Yu needed him as a child, like the world's best older brother, the strongest man, the doctor that he most hated to leave—

The man looked down at him as if nothing at all had happened.

He only tilted his head slightly. "Ah, little devil," he said, just like before. "It's you. Come in. Have a seat."

"Come in, have a seat."

"Little devil..."

But recently, everything had changed. Nowadays, even when He Yu opened the door in his dreams, the room was empty.

He would never be able to return to the corridor from the time before he'd turned fourteen; the door full of light wouldn't open for him.

His heart hurt so much...

And thus, He Yu woke up with a start—

He found himself in his own bed. There was gauze wrapped around his forehead, and more tying him down at the wrists and ankles. The curtains of the room were drawn, and the smart speaker was playing the news.

"The serial murders at Huzhou University that shocked the whole country... The police have revealed...that the murders were motivated by revenge. The police have found evidence that Lu Yuzhu, one of the suspects in this case, purchased hacking equipment. She was the secretary of the Qingli County Party Committee and was the first girl from her area to attend university. She majored in computer information security, and the police suspect that..."

The sound was sporadic because of the weak bluetooth signal.

"The other suspect, Jiang Liping, is currently on the run... The two of them had adulterous relations with the victim... Perhaps... Cheng Kang Psychiatric... they were inspired by Jiang Lanpei's murder and wanted to create a horror similar to the rumored 'revenge of Jiang Lanpei's ghost'... but that doesn't rule out the possibility of a deeper connection between these two individuals and Jiang Lanpei's case..."

The radio continued, discussing Jiang Liping's escape.

He Yu lay there and let his heartbeat gradually calm down. The door in his dreams faded away.

He remembered that he had accidentally fallen from the second floor.

He didn't move. Didn't react at all.

He was still alive...but it wasn't much of a happy surprise. He just lay there in a daze, listening vaguely. There were a lot of follow-up reports about that incident, since bizarre homicide cases made for the best clickbait, providing a rich spawning ground for wacky explanations and theories.

He Yu had been following this incident closely before, but at this moment, when he woke from his slumber and heard what was on the radio, he only numbly thought—

What did it have to do with him?

Nothing in this world had anything to do with him.

Suddenly, a voice came from his bedside. "He Yu, you're awake?"

He Yu moved his head, only now realizing that Lü Zhishu was there.

She'd returned and was sitting next to his bed, deeply worried. Seeing him open his eyes, she hurriedly said, "You—"

There were a few seconds of silence.

He Yu opened his mouth, voice hoarse from having just woken up. "I know what happened." He looked somewhat surprised at her presence, but he numbly continued, "I told you to leave me alone. Why are you always in Huzhou?"

The warm mother-and-son reunion Lü Zhishu had imagined failed to materialize. There were no tears of gratitude for her bedside companionship. She hadn't been expecting him to act like this the moment he woke up and couldn't help but freeze. "H-how can you talk to your mother like that?"

"How do you want me to speak to you? Should I use formal speech the entire time? I'm not in the mood for that right now. Don't you know I'm sick? I act polite with you guys, but it's all fake. This is my true self. Can't handle it? If you can't handle it, then go back to Yanzhou and find He Li. Stop hanging around here all the time."

Lü Zhishu flew into a rage. She was wearing a black see-through lace dress today, and when He Yu made her shake with rage, her ample figure made her look like a chubby, quivering spider. "I know that I neglected you in the past, but there's no need to...there's no need to..."

"I would like you to keep neglecting me." He Yu's eyes were cold. "I'm already used to it, understand? Please leave."

Lü Zhishu wanted to say something, but He Yu's eyes had become rather terrifying.

"Leave."

She stumbled, but still left as he asked.

He Jiwei had returned as well. Lü Zhishu ran into him in the living room as she was descending the stairs.

He really hadn't expected to be greeted with the sight of his wife weeping angry tears over his son. It'd been a long time since Lü Zhishu showed such weakness in front of him.

She came down the stairs, took a seat on the sofa, pulled out a couple tissues, and wiped her tears, turning her head away without looking at He Jiwei.

"...You two had a fight?" He Jiwei asked.

"He just woke up. I wanted to have a proper conversation about finding him another personal physician... I've noticed he's been taking too much medicine lately, and you know as well as I do that if the medicine becomes ineffective, there'll be no way to keep his mental state under control." Lü Zhishu sniffed but kept her face turned away, staring at the corner of the tea table instead as though harboring some sort of deep grudge. "I meant well, I was just concerned about him. I'm his mother—how could I possibly try to hurt him?"

He Jiwei said nothing.

"But he wouldn't listen, and he was so hostile to me." Lü Zhishu took a couple more tissues, blowing her nose noisily. She hadn't been like this when she was younger. "Old He, help me convince him." Lü Zhishu's tears began to fall again. "I feel so wronged... I-I sacrificed so much for his sake, and he doesn't even know it. I became what I am now for his sake... Do you know how much it hurts for him to treat me like this? I just feel so wronged."

As she spoke, she buried her face into her short, chubby palms.

"I'm a mother too..."

The He family dynamic was extremely odd, warped, and strange. They didn't have the vibe of a normal family whatsoever.

He Jiwei looked at Lü Zhishu for a moment. "Why don't I go up and talk to him," he said with a grim expression.

And so, He Jiwei went upstairs to He Yu's bedroom.

Father and son rarely saw each other, and with the dark-haired youth sick in bed, it felt as though they were about to act out a scene where the father choked back words of self-blame with tears in his eyes. However—

Slap!

The flat of a palm cracked resoundingly across He Yu's face.

He Jiwei was different from Lü Zhishu. Normally, he was stern and reasonable, but right now he really couldn't hold himself back anymore. He approached the boy and immediately began berating him sharply. "He Yu—so you've learned how to seek death, have you?"

He Yu took the full force of the slap, but there wasn't the slightest flicker of emotion on his face or in his eyes as his face jerked to the side from the force of the strike. When he turned back, there was a faint trace of blood at the corner of his mouth.

He showed a bloody smile. "My goodness, why're you back too? It's not like I need both of your honorable presences at my funeral yet."

"What the hell are you talking about?!"

"Why are you backing away?"

He Jiwei said nothing.

He Yu's gaze was aimed at He Jiwei's leather shoes. The moment the youth had smiled his sinister smile, he saw He Jiwei involuntarily take a step back.

He waved his hand slightly, looking up at the ceiling once more. Still smiling lightly, he said, "Don't be afraid. Haven't you tied me up nice and tight?"

There were many restraints on He Yu's bed. He Jiwei and Lü Zhishu could lie about his disorder to everyone but themselves. Even though He Yu had never cruelly hurt any people or animals in public, almost every doctor he'd seen had determined his violent tendencies to be on par with those of murderous psychopaths.

He Jiwei's jowls quivered. "It's for your own good," he said after a long pause.

He Yu shifted casually within his bonds. "Thank you very much." He smiled.

"...When did your illness get this bad? Why didn't you say anything?"

"Well, *apparently*, I'm a psycho," He Yu replied carelessly. "What did you expect me to say?"

"He Yu, if you carry on like this, you'll have to be forcibly institutionalized." He Jiwei lowered his voice, a complicated look in his eyes. "Do you want to lose your freedom? Do you want to be caged like an animal in a zoo? Your mother and I have helped you hide your condition for so long, just so you could try to live like a normal—"

"Just so the *He family* could try to live like a normal family, to grow and flourish." He Yu gazed up at the ceiling, smiling softly.

As though his vocal cords had been severed, He Jiwei instantly fell silent.

"Rather than someday becoming the subject of other people's idle gossip—did you know, the eldest son of the He family, that virtuous, talented boy who looks so bright and beautiful, is actually a madman? It was hidden very well—who knew the He family was so rotten? They're in the pharmaceutical business, but they can't even cure their own illnesses."

He turned his head. His limbs had been bound, but he seemed seized by a gentle mirth, resulting in an aura that was nothing short of terrifying. "Isn't that right? Dad?"

He Jiwei's face had gone pale. His expression was furious, but all the same, his fury seemed to ultimately reveal a hint of remorse for his treatment of He Yu.

He Yu couldn't see it; his eyes were empty.

"When I was born and you found out I was sick, you should have killed me right then," he said. "Why'd you bother keeping me? All of you spend your days on tenterhooks, while I spend mine like a walking corpse. This really is a case of completely pointless mutual torment."

"He Yu..."

"You should go. I'm not used to you being here, so it'll make me even crazier. If it gets out, I'll probably ruin all your reputations."

He Jiwei seemed to want to say something comforting, but the interactions he'd had with his eldest son were pitifully few. He was high in status and very powerful, so he was accustomed to giving commands. For someone like him, tenderness was a far greater challenge than strength.

In the end, he said nothing.

On the bed, He Yu turned his face away, unwilling to look at his old man. The room fell terrifyingly silent. And in this silence, He Jiwei's expression slowly changed from fury to remorse, from remorse to sorrow, until finally, that sorrow returned to calm.

He started regretting the slap he'd given He Yu right upon entering. In that moment, he'd truly lost control of himself.

He knew that He Yu had fallen, even though it hadn't been from a particularly great height. He saw how far He Yu had pushed Lü Zhishu. In that moment, his exhaustion and fury, his fear and anxiety—those had been his most genuine feelings, enveloping his hand and whipping it involuntarily across He Yu's face. Even though he'd never really kept He Yu company in the past, he hadn't ever hit him, either. This was the first time.

No matter how indifferently he treated He Yu, they were still father and son. Seeing that He Yu had deteriorated so far without saying a word, it would be a lie to say he wasn't angry.

He couldn't bear it anymore.

Pulling up a chair, he sat down at He Yu's bedside.

The father silently bowed his head as if he didn't want to speak to him. All he did was look at He Yu's injuries, and then—

Click.

A soft sound.

He Jiwei undid his restraints.

He Yu opened his eyes.

He Jiwei didn't speak for a long time. Father and son faced each other, the silence heavy.

It'd been a long time since He Jiwei first stepped into this bedroom. He looked around in silence, his gaze finally falling on He Yu's empty nightstand.

Resolutely, he began to speak; his tone was terribly weary, but not as stern and unreasonable as before. "He Yu. I remember that there used to be a photo of the three of us on your nightstand. That picture was taken when you were four, when we went to Yellowstone…"

He Yu spoke up now as well. His tone was still very cold, but at least he answered him.

"I threw that picture away ten years ago."

In that moment, the exquisitely furnished villa room seemed as cold as a glacial cave.

He Jiwei sighed, reaching for a smoke.

"I don't like secondhand smoke," said He Yu. "If you want to smoke, please go outside."

He Jiwei coughed, lowering the cigarette in embarrassment. "I'm not so bad I can't go without; I won't smoke. As for what happened just now…it was my fault. I got too worked up. He Yu, why don't I keep you company for a while?"

If this had happened ten years ago, He Yu would've softened.

If it were fifteen years ago, He Yu might've even cried.

But now, it was too late. A thick callus had already grown over He Yu's heart, and this hint of slight tenderness only made him feel as if the peace beneath that callus had been disturbed. He couldn't feel any positive emotions.

He Jiwei was silent for a long time. "I know that you've resented us deeply these past few years," he said at last. "It's true that ever since your little brother was born, we've spent far too little time with you. I don't want to defend myself in any way; what's wrong is wrong. Our neglect of you is an undeniable fact."

The father fiddled with his unlit cigarette, speaking softly.

"That's not neglect," He Yu said blandly. "The word 'loathing' might be more appropriate."

He Jiwei's hand shook slightly.

He too realized that He Yu had become more vicious. The He Yu of the past would never have spoken to him so plainly. Even if he were dissatisfied, he would still maintain the most basic courtesies.

He Jiwei stared down at the thick wool blanket covering the bed. After a long while, he said, "He Yu, she doesn't loathe you. She loathes her own past."

The room was very quiet; one could hear the ticking of the clock.

Time ticked by, second by second, minute by minute. He Jiwei twisted the cigarette between his fingers as he mounted a final struggle with himself—or perhaps it was better to say that he'd already decided to have this conversation with He Yu, but now that he was sitting in this unfamiliar room, he didn't know where to start.

He thought it over in silence.

After a while, he sighed deeply and began to speak. "He Yu, there are some things that we've never told you about. You were too young—you weren't even an adult, and I was worried that you'd feel even worse if we told you. This is an extremely painful wound to your mother. It would be impossible for her to pry it open herself and invite your touch. But I feel that—recently, I've felt it more and more strongly—that the time has come to tell you. Perhaps, once you've heard me out, you might not want to abandon yourself so deeply to despair. Perhaps...perhaps you might even understand her a little bit."

He Yu suddenly sat up from the bed. "I already understand enough—"

"Hear me out," said He Jiwei. "I rarely talk to you alone like this. This time, I ask you to please listen to me patiently, and then, if you feel any dissatisfaction or resentment, you can unleash it all at me. All right? You're my son, but all this time, I've kept things from you. And because of that, I've made you sacrifice far too much."

A long silence followed. In the end, He Yu lay back down under the covers, covering his eyes with his arm, as if not looking at He Jiwei would help him be a little more rational.

Finally, he said coldly, "Speak. I'm listening."

73

WHY DID I BECOME
A MADMAN?

"IF ONLY YOU STILL HAD that photograph that used to be on your nightstand," He Jiwei said once He Yu had calmed down. There was a faint sigh in his voice. "I don't know if you still remember that picture—it's one of the few photographs that remain from when your mother was young. When you were four, she still resembled her youthful self... She doesn't like seeing what she looked like before we got married, so she's gotten rid of almost all our old photos. But from that group photo, you should be able to tell that she was very beautiful back when she was in her twenties—even though her appearance had already begun to change by that point, the lines of her face still had that same elegance."

At this point, He Jiwei's eyes subconsciously took on a touch of deep emotion, but it was the kind of sentiment that floated up from the past for the bygone beauty of a lover, like an old photograph that had already begun to yellow.

He closed his eyes for a moment and sighed before opening them again. Fixing his gaze on the carpet, he continued his story in a low voice. "I don't know if you've ever wondered how your mother became how she is today. The corporate lifestyle is very exhausting, and its demands can cause formerly graceful people to gain weight. But that isn't an inevitability—as you've seen over the years, I haven't changed all that much.

"The first time I saw her, she was wearing a long red dress and had such a genuine smile. She was so beautiful, with a pair of bright, clear almond eyes, exactly the same as yours. She was extremely kindhearted as well, and not so competitive. She loved to look after animals, garden, and read—Back then, anyone who saw her sincerely liked her. Compared to now..." The lament in He Jiwei's voice grew stronger as he pressed his hands together and touched his fingertips to his brow. "She really was completely different. Back then, there were many people pursuing her, but in the end, she picked me. And shortly after we got married, she became pregnant with you.

"But the good times didn't last.

"As you know, our family's primary business is biopharmaceuticals. At that time, your mother worried that I had too much on my plate, so she would go into the lab, monitor the equipment, and help me with various tasks. I could never figure out what went wrong, how that careless error happened during the procedure...but when your mother was pregnant with you, she came into contact with a virus that leaked out of the lab. All the protective measures were very rigorous, and no similar incident had ever occurred before."

Even though He Jiwei had closed his eyes as he spoke of this, his suffering was evident in the deep furrow between his brows.

"At that point, she was already several months into her pregnancy. Our family's personal physicians said that she needed to receive treatment—a treatment that would have definitely led to the death of the fetus, so they wanted to induce early labor. But she refused. Her health wasn't very good, and before she became pregnant, the doctor had told her that it would likely be very difficult for her to conceive a second time. She was incredibly excited about you because she thought she wouldn't be able to have another child. And for those few months, she had been looking forward to your birth with so much hope, she even spent more time speaking to you than to me. So when they wanted to force you out of her body and sentence you to death, she refused.

"No one saw you as a living person—they all saw you as a mere embryo, nothing more than a seed. But because she shared her blood and flesh with you every second of every day, she loved you deeply before your heart had even formed. She said you were the best gift the heavens could have granted her, so from very early on, she'd already given you the name He Yu: Yu as in *to give*.

"We all pleaded with her for a long time, including me—I'm sorry." He Jiwei continued, "I'll admit that at the time, I loved her more than I loved you. I didn't want anything to happen to her, so I kept asking her to have the abortion—I thought that it would be fine to be childless, or to adopt. I just didn't want to lose her.

"But no matter what, she refused to yield. She might have seemed very agreeable, but as soon as she made up her mind about something, nothing could move her. Every time she would cry and say that we couldn't hurt He Yu. She said she could feel that you were afraid, that she was the only person who could protect you—she believed that it was all her fault, that it was only because of her carelessness that the accidental contamination occurred."

That girl's hoarse sobs—the sobs of a woman, a mother, a wife— seemed to ring in his ears once again—

"Don't kill him... I can feel him... That's my son..."

"Don't touch him... Please don't touch him... Hurt me instead, you can do anything, it was my fault, I hurt him, I want him to live... He's still so small... Please don't kill him, please..."

He Jiwei hadn't recalled these excruciatingly painful memories in detail in a very long time. He spent a long moment stifling his emotions again before he was calm enough to continue his story.

"Back then, her mind was on the verge of total breakdown. It was very hard to imagine what would have happened if we forced her to have the abortion. I suspect that she wouldn't have been able to handle it—if you died, she would have lost the will to live. Every mother is different, and she's a woman with very strong maternal tendencies—she couldn't possibly accept it if her mistake resulted in your death. Never mind the fact that there was a good chance she'd never be able to be a mom in the future.

"She would cry all day long, and she was so thin that she lost her figure. Her fear and anxiety made her mentally unstable, and that was to say nothing of how her organs began to fail because of the virus. She ran away from home several times... She thought that we would try to kill you while she was sleeping. She wanted to make it to the nine-month mark; that way no one could stop her from having you."

He Jiwei let out another long sigh. "There really was no other way... If she continued on like that, she would have tortured herself to death. So after the last time I found her and took her home, I sought out a researcher in my lab. I asked him if there was any way to address the virus's harmful effects on her body while protecting you at the same time, so that you could survive the last month safely. In the end, they gave me a drug: RN-13.

"It was a cell-regenerative drug synthesized in the lab that had the ability to completely repair damaged cells."

He Yu lost his temper, sure that He Jiwei was making this up. "How can there possibly be anything in the world that can repair cells in their entirety!"

"There is. He Yu, calm down. It exists," He Jiwei said. "But what you said is correct—RN-13 cannot actually repair cells completely. It was still at a very early stage of research, with a long road ahead. But according to the later First Emperor data..."

"Who's the First Emperor?" demanded He Yu.

"You've seen *Resident Evil*—do you remember the Red Queen? The First Emperor is like the Red Queen—it's not an actual person. No living person could endure the torment of a full course of treatment with RN-13. The First Emperor is a digital simulation of a human undergoing cell regeneration. And what they call the First Emperor data is the computational output indicating the extent to which such a human could repair themself in response to different kinds of diseases.

"I can't give you too many specifics, but RN-13 was our best hope at the time. So even though it was very risky—we had yet to carry out clinical trials, so it was an entirely prohibited drug—we still used it. Among all of the terrible possibilities, this was the only one with a chance of saving you both.

"... I'll admit that I was careless back then," He Jiwei said, "but I didn't have a choice. Pregnancy anxiety, paranoid delusions, clinical depression... With all these conditions piled on top of each other, her mental state was complete chaos. Rather than see her torment herself to death...I chose to take the gamble."

The curtain fluttered lightly, as if heaving a sigh for the events of the past.

"RN-13 did indeed defeat the virus in her body, and it regenerated her damaged cells at an astonishing rate. Her mood settled down, and she gave birth to you at last. But RN-13 wasn't a fully developed drug at the time. It was too ambitious—the problem of cell regeneration is the biggest challenge in human disease. With the limitations of modern medicine, it's completely impossible—the First Emperor is only an idealized projection. It was true that this drug had powerful regenerative capabilities, to the point that it could even reverse organ damage, thus allowing the patient to recover.

But its side effects also became apparent in both your and your mother's bodies.

"Even though the pharmacist prescribed a very small dosage and administered it in a very cautious way, the side effects were impossible to avoid. Your mother began to develop abnormalities in her hormone levels, and her appearance began to change... She didn't look as nice anymore." It seemed like even now, He Jiwei found it very difficult to use the word "ugly" to describe his wife, even though it was a truth evident to anyone with eyes.

But he couldn't say it out loud. That was his wife, the girl who picked him out of a crowd of admirers—he could still remember how lovely she was.

"She also began to lose her figure," He Jiwei said with difficulty. "When you were four, it was still possible to barely make out a shadow of her past self, unlike now."

Anyone who looked at her now would only see how she resembled a greedy, fleshy spider.

For a beauty to lose their looks during the prime of their life was actually a very cruel and painful thing. Lü Zhishu hadn't noticed it at first, but slowly, she began to realize—it was a type of "organ failure" with respect to social status.

A lovely face could bring you endless kindness and convenience. Ever since she was young, she'd been accustomed to being the target of envious, adoring, and admiring gazes. People were always friendly to her; she didn't know what it was like to live in another woman's world.

In the beginning, she had still been immersed in the joy of becoming a mother and didn't notice how her reflection in the mirror had begun to resemble a melting popsicle. But later on...

"I'm sorry, but this seat is taken."

"No, I'm afraid we can't make an exception."

"Auntie, this dress is too small for you. Why don't I get you a more suitable one?"

Suddenly, when she walked out into the world, everything seemed unfamiliar. No one tried to win her favor anymore, and men didn't blush at her acknowledgment when they spoke to her. People called her "auntie," and pretty young girls laughed behind her back at her flabby body and drooping figure.

She felt extremely anxious, like a cat that didn't know how to walk because its whiskers had been cut.

What hurt her even more deeply was that each time an old friend saw her present self for the first time, a look of astonishment appeared in their eyes—regardless of whether they tried to hide it, those expressions were still so sharp, piercing into her until she was a bloody mess.

She became more and more depressed, losing her temper and smashing things...

One day, He Jiwei came home to discover that she had set a fire in the courtyard. The servants were all standing nearby, not knowing what to do, watching as she took all of the clothes, shoes, and photographs from when she was a girl...and fed them to the flames.

She turned around with a smile, her drooping cheeks quivering slightly as she revealed a slightly sinister elation.

She had left her old self fully in the past.

This was a woman who had emerged from her cocoon, fully transformed.

"Your mom changed," He Jiwei said. "Slowly, she changed more and more... Never mind you, even I had trouble recognizing her at times. She loved you, but she was too afraid of seeing her past self in you—of being reminded of those days she could never return to. She did all she could to forget about those things.

"She didn't like small animals or gardening anymore. She even left my side and became completely independent. She built a business by herself and earned her own living. Once she made a name for herself in society, the respectful way people treated her vaguely reminded her of how everyone used to regard her with kindness back when she was young and beautiful."

He Jiwei's voice grew somewhat sentimental. "He Yu, she's really quite pitiable. You shouldn't blame her too much. She simply has no way to face you properly. Even I feel exceptionally guilty—that's why I go along with what she wants most of the time. It's not that she only likes He Li—it's just that He Li is more like her current self, so she can avoid thinking about the darkest period of her life.

"Your illness...was also the result of RN-13. She's felt very guilty about it all this time. Every time you have a flare-up, it's a kind of torture for her too. Even now, she's still living with that pain—sometimes, when she's sleeping, I'll even hear her say..."

He Jiwei paused.

It might have just been the lighting in the room, but his eyes seemed rather wet.

He Yu had been listening numbly for a long time. Now, he asked softly, "What does she say?"

He Jiwei bowed his head, looking like a puppet with cut strings. "She says that it's her fault."

The woman would murmur in her sleep:

"It's mama's fault."

"Mama couldn't protect you."

He Jiwei's voice had gotten hoarse. He cleared his throat, but his voice remained thick. "After she says that, she smiles in her dream; she almost looks crazed... I believe that she's never been able to free herself from what happened."

"Especially after she gave birth to He Li, when she found out she could still get pregnant with a second child...I don't know if she had any regrets, but she did become harsher. There were many times when even I couldn't communicate with her properly. It seemed like she no longer wanted to believe in anyone other than herself.

"Nowadays, no one can understand your mother's inner thoughts. But, He Yu, I can be certain of one thing." He Jiwei turned his head and looked at the young man who'd been lying in bed quietly this entire time.

"...She once laid her life on the line to love you. Even if... Even if she's unrecognizable now...I think that in the deepest part of her heart, some of the love that she once had for you is still there."

He Jiwei's eyes had actually gone red, and not because of the light. After so many years, this was the first time he'd ever peeled off this scab to show someone else the wound.

"So, no matter what...I think...you ought to be...a little kinder to her... When she wants to express concern for you again, she has to step on the knives of the past to walk toward you. He Yu, since she was once the only one who wanted you to survive at the expense of her own life"—He Jiwei's raspy voice lowered even further—"could you treat her a little better...?"

He Yu did not respond.

After some time, He Jiwei thought he saw a gleaming trace of wetness slide from beneath the arm that He Yu had been using to shield his face. It was hard to say whether it was his imagination, as that glimmer of wetness soon melted into the hair at his temples, where it disappeared without a trace.

As for He Yu, he turned so that he was no longer lying face up but had his back facing him.

"You can leave," he said quietly. "I'd like some time alone to calm down, okay?"

The drug known as RN-13 was the primary cause of psychological Ebola.

When He Jiwei had used it, he was in desperate straits. Furthermore, the foreign drug manufacturers he worked with weren't following the rules. It seemed that they had taken this drug from a research facility in the United States, so they couldn't tell him everything about it. That was why He Jiwei hadn't been fully informed that people who took RN-13 would develop psychological disturbances.

By the time he found out about the case files of previous test subjects who had been afflicted with similar disorders, it was already too late.

Lü Zhishu didn't become ill, but her disposition and appearance both changed abruptly—in the end, it wasn't all that different from developing a mental illness. He Yu, on the other hand, wasn't so lucky: he became psychological Ebola's Case #4.

When He Jiwei discovered his son's symptoms, he confronted that foreign drug company. However, the company had undergone internal restructuring, and power had changed hands. The original CEO had been ruthlessly killed, and the new leader was almost entirely unfamiliar with this incident, so he had no desire to help.

He Jiwei never collaborated with or contacted that foreign drug company ever again. But the reality of what had happened could not be changed.

He Yu lay in bed for a long time. With the heavy curtains closed, it was hard to tell if it was day or night. There was only the sound of the grandfather clock that had been echoing through the quiet room the entire time.

Tick tock, tick tock.

He Yu didn't know how much time had passed when he finally stood up. He walked over to his bookshelf and drew out an old photograph from a tattered copy of *One Hundred Years of Solitude.*

The photograph had been taken in front of a geyser at Yellowstone National Park; it was from the only trip he and his parents had taken as a family of three. He was still very small in the picture, and a young He Jiwei was carrying him in his arms. Next to him was a woman of medium build whose face still held traces of graceful beauty. She was smiling, with dark curled hair that fell to her shoulders; she was wearing a black lace dress and a bucket hat as she pressed close to her husband's side.

He stroked the face of the woman in the picture...

A long, long time later, He Yu slowly closed his eyes.

As Lü Zhishu prepared breakfast in the Western-style kitchen the next day, she looked up to see that, in an unprecedented first, He Yu had come downstairs to the dining table.

Even though the age of print media had long since passed, He Jiwei was still in the habit of reading the newspaper cover-to-cover as he drank green tea in the morning. He looked at He Yu over the top of his paper. "You're up early."

When she heard this, Lü Zhishu turned around. Seeing that the son she had tried in vain to win over for so long was actually willing to eat breakfast with them this morning, she lost her grip on the frying pan and nearly dropped it on the floor.

He Yu's expression was as indifferent as ever, but she still saw this as a huge step in the right direction.

"He Yu, what would you like to drink?" she asked. "Coffee? Tea?"

"Anything's fine, thank you," He Yu replied calmly.

After they finished breakfast, Lü Zhishu could keenly sense the signals He Yu was giving off—Rome wasn't built in a day, so there was no way to build closeness so quickly. But at the very least, he was no longer completely walled off.

He was trying to reach out to them. Lü Zhishu felt very heartened.

"Ah, He Yu..."

"Hmm?"

"I've found a new doctor for you. He's very young, so he should be easy for you to talk to. You haven't been doing very well these past few days—what do you think about letting him treat you?"

A new doctor, huh...

He Yu didn't know why, but he thought of the first time he met Xie Qingcheng, when he came to their house with a bouquet of hydrangeas.

Closing his eyes, he fell silent for a long while.

Then, finally, he quietly said, "It's up to you."

74

WHY ARE YOU LEAVING AGAIN?

THE PERSONAL PHYSICIAN came. Just as Lü Zhishu had said, he was a youthful doctor with handsome features and a lithe physique. He went by the English name of Anthony. Doctor Anthony had a very good temperament and a great attitude, and he gave off an inexplicable sense of familiarity. But He Yu couldn't even remember his name, let alone his features; he was just like an irrelevant punctuation mark.

This irrelevant punctuation mark began treating He Yu with hypnotherapy.

"Young Master He, please lie down and relax, follow me and take three deep breaths in... Think about some of the happiest events in your past."

"What if I don't have any?"

After a moment of stunned silence, the doctor said, "Then think about the things that you wish would happen."

He Yu closed his eyes and began to think.

What did he wish for...?

Perhaps he wished that he'd never been born.

Perhaps he wished, for himself and Lü Zhishu, that neither of them had been affected by the medicine—that they could both be normal.

Or perhaps...

"When I was born and you found out I was sick, you should have killed me right then!"

He closed his eyes under the physician's hypnosis, his mind slowly returning to a few days earlier...

He dreamed of what had happened when he woke after his fall.

He was arguing with He Jiwei. *"All of you spend your days on tenterhooks, while I spend mine like a walking corpse. This really is a case of completely pointless mutual torment."*

"He Yu..."

"You should go. I'm not used to you being here, so it'll make me even crazier. If it gets out, I'll probably ruin all your reputations."

The conversation was identical to the one that had happened in reality.

But, under the effects of Anthony's hypnosis, the storyline gradually began to change—

In real life, He Jiwei had gone on to tell He Yu about the secret of RN-13. But in this dream, He Jiwei opened his mouth, and just as he was about to speak, someone knocked on the door.

He Jiwei seemed to let out a sigh of relief. "Come in."

"Mr. He, Doctor Xie is here. He's waiting downstairs."

That's right.

He Yu lay dumbfounded. As it turned out, he still subconsciously hoped that Xie Qingcheng would return.

He yearned for it so much, but he also feared it so much that his hypnotized dreaming self actually froze the moment he heard. He wanted to get up, but the restraints held him fast, the metal buckles clattering.

"I don't need a doctor. Who told you to bring him here?" The more the youth yearned for him, the more afraid he was, struggling like an evil dragon trying to escape its shackles. A mad glint shone in his eyes, and even the servant who'd come to deliver the message couldn't help but shrink back in fear. "Send him away!"

"You think it was easy getting him here?!" He Jiwei snapped. "If it wasn't for the fact that he heard about you jumping off a building and nearly getting yourself killed, he wouldn't even bother sparing you a glance!"

He Yu grew even more humiliated and furiously anxious at this. "Then have him wait till I'm dead so he can come visit me at my grave!"

He Jiwei raised his hand again. "If you mention dying again, I'll..."

He Yu gazed at him coldly, those almond eyes unblinking as he stared fixedly into He Jiwei's face.

He Jiwei's hand shook, then lowered. He sighed deeply and pushed the door open to leave. The final glimpse He Yu saw of his eyes seemed to be immeasurably disappointed and incomparably worried, but also unspeakably exhausted.

"Send Doctor Xie in," he told the servant. "I still have a very busy day ahead of me... I'll miss my flight if I'm late, so I'll be off now."

For a moment, He Yu grew so hateful and furious that he slammed a fist into the side of the bed, making the buckles of his restraints clatter. Unfortunately, he couldn't turn in place, nor could he bring the covers up over his face; in the end, all he could do was shut his eyes tightly and tense up his entire body.

It was as if he didn't want to be humiliated like this in front of Xie Qingcheng, not even in a dream.

Not at all.

But both He Jiwei and the servant had left, and no matter how much he resisted or refused, no matter how restless with hate he was, he still heard those familiar footsteps draw closer.

And then, they came to a stop by his bedside.

He trembled, shivering from too much yearning.

Even if it was hypnosis, even if it was just a dream, He Yu felt as though he could still smell a hint of Xie Qingcheng's scent: the chilly scent of disinfectant that brought to mind thoughts of surgical scalpels, syringes, and the clinical white of hospital sickrooms. He'd found the scent cold whenever he smelled it in the past, but now, for some reason, it felt warm.

That man lowered his head without saying a single word, as if he didn't want to say a single word. He only looked at He Yu's injuries and then—

Click.

A soft sound.

Xie Qingcheng had undone his restraints.

The He Yu within the dream went still, as if suddenly fully satisfied, while the He Yu outside of the dream closed his eyes, and tears welled up beneath his lashes. As it turned out, in the depths of his sickness-induced agony, this was what he'd always been hoping for.

He hoped for Xie Qingcheng to personally undo his restraints with his own hands.

He hoped that Xie Qingcheng would know he was truly sick, that Xie Qingcheng would *believe* he was truly sick, that Xie Qingcheng could return to his side.

"Very good..." Doctor Anthony observed his condition and continued to guide his hypnosis. His voice was so soft, it was almost beguiling. "Very good. Whatever it is that you're dreaming of, keep going... You need to believe that you'll be able to find your own way out..."

However, that very phrase...seemed to hit a nerve. He Yu's dreamscape flickered.

The way out?

What did that mean?

He thought of the real Xie Qingcheng's icy gaze, thought of Xie Qingcheng rejecting him: *"We have to part. Sooner or later, you'll have to depend on yourself to walk out of the shadows in your heart."*

"I'm not your bridge, He Yu. Neither is Xie Xue."

"He Yu..."

He Yu.

Each syllable was a bone-piercing shard of ice.

He Yu suddenly fell back into the dream—he was still lying in bed, and Xie Qingcheng was still the one who had undone his restraints, but his surroundings had become very dark. Xie Qingcheng's expression was just as dark, as if he had been veiled by a cool-toned filter.

He dreamed of Xie Qingcheng's pale lips opening and closing. He knew Xie Qingcheng wanted to tell him the reason why he came back, but he could vaguely sense that that reason would bring him incomparable pain.

He wanted to flee from this dreamscape, immediately.

But it was futile.

In the dream, Xie Qingcheng spoke decisively, enunciating each word with clear emphasis, and he had nowhere to hide. "Although I would truly prefer it if you were dead, I will oversee your recuperation this time. But don't misunderstand—I've come only because of your father's generous compensation." Xie Qingcheng's voice was extremely cold and utterly emotionless. "That compensation is more than you can afford. It's enough that after this, I won't ever have to see you again."

Inside the dream, He Yu felt like he had been stabbed, like Xie Qingcheng had ruthlessly slapped him across the face—he was so injured, so hurt. Outside the dream, He Yu's breathing quickened, his brows knitting tightly together. He wanted to break out of this dreamscape, but the dream was also the demon inside his heart that he had no choice but to defeat.

Under his personal physician's hypnosis, He Yu sank even deeper into his internal world.

As he continued dreaming, he once again saw that dusty guest room door.

In this dream, Xie Qingcheng had come back and was once again living in the room that He Yu had meticulously tidied up.

But under hypnosis, the Xie Qingcheng who had come back because of He Yu's fall was extremely indifferent. He didn't seem to care about He Yu at all—every day, after he finished recording He Yu's vital signs, he tossed him a syringe and watched as he injected it; he couldn't even be bothered to personally administer his medicine.

At first, He Yu didn't say anything. Perhaps out of his laughable sense of self-respect, he acted like nothing had happened, silently giving himself the injections that Xie Qingcheng handed him and then passing the syringes back for disposal. They didn't exchange any words throughout the entire process, as if they were in a silent movie.

But in time, this silence made He Yu's heart feel increasingly uneasy, and gradually, he stopped wanting to cooperate.

The dream kept the cycle going, on and on.

Finally, after Xie Qingcheng examined him as usual and passed him a syringe, He Yu sat up in the Windsor chair in his bedroom, but he didn't take it.

"Doctor Xie," he suddenly asked, in a voice that was very calm yet verged on the brink of despair, "have you ever thought about how I might take these needles and use them for something else?"

Xie Qingcheng didn't pay much attention to He Yu's expression. "Well, it doesn't seem like you're *that* desperate to die," he said.

"Is that so? You really get me, don't you?" He Yu smiled mockingly, and then suddenly raised the syringe and stabbed himself without batting an eye—not into a vein, but rather a random spot—injecting the medicine—

The color drained out of Xie Qingcheng's face immediately. He stepped forward at once, but it was already too late—that patch of He Yu's skin quickly turned black and blue, swelling up alarmingly.

"But honestly, I'm not so desperate to live either," He Yu said mildly. Any ordinary person would already be grimacing with pain, but there wasn't the slightest ripple of emotion on his face. It was as though that needle had gone into the body of someone completely irrelevant to him.

His pitch-black eyes gazed steadily, unblinking, at Xie Qingcheng's ashen face as he pulled out the needle. Only a small amount of fluid remained inside the syringe—the rest had all gone into the contusion beneath He Yu's skin, which was becoming more and more unsightly.

He Yu paid it no mind. He handed the syringe back to Xie Qingcheng and said with deliberate emphasis, "Here. You do it."

Xie Qingcheng's face had gone white, as though startled by this madman's actions.

"It needs to be you, Xie Qingcheng," He Yu insisted. His tone seemed somewhat menacing, but upon closer examination, his words also concealed a faintly indistinct grief. "Otherwise, I won't take a single shot today. You came for the money, so you need to work for that money. You've got to do a good job."

Xie Qingcheng snapped out of his daze and closed his eyes. "Don't force me to tie you up."

"Nah, go ahead," He Yu said dispassionately. "Do what my parents do—tie me up. It's not like that's beyond you."

In the dream, it seemed like He Yu had given Xie Qingcheng a headache.

"He Yu, what exactly do you want?"

What exactly did he want?

He honestly didn't know either.

He had realized that he genuinely had a problem—he cared deeply for Xie Qingcheng, and his feelings just kept growing.

When he couldn't see Xie Qingcheng, he felt very restless. Even when he did see him, he still couldn't seem to calm down. Xie Qingcheng had become a sharp thorn in his heart—whether it was pulled out or left where it was, it would still cause a lethal amount of discomfort.

But he shouldn't be like this.

He detested homosexuality, there was no way he could get tangled up with a man—but he found that whenever his thoughts wandered, he remembered what Xie Qingcheng looked like in bed. At first, he'd only thought about Xie Qingcheng's body, but then he even began to long for Xie Qingcheng's emotional responses—

It was unbearable.

He always felt like he couldn't breathe, the anxiety a heavy weight in his chest.

In the dream, the two of them were caught in a deadlock. Finally, He Yu said to Xie Qingcheng, "Did you know that I never wanted to be like this before? Xie Qingcheng, you watched me grow up. You know what I was like before... I persevered for nineteen years, all for the sake of that so-called 'calm' everyone kept telling me about. But I can't keep it up anymore.

"My parents made me pretend to be normal so that I wouldn't be thrown in the loony bin. The only reason they dared to do this was because I never broke the law or bent the rules. I really did live just like a normal person—even though it was disgusting and exhausting, even though I could never say a word about my suffering or my sickness. Even though I had to constantly study all the emotions on the faces of the people around me to give them a satisfactory response. But I was able to do it.

"For nineteen years, a person who belonged in an insane asylum lived amongst normal people in society. A person who should've been locked up in a cage walked free. I was constantly worried that if I revealed how deranged I was, I'd go from being envied and admired to being yelled at and beaten up. None of my friendships were genuine because no one knew what I was really like—they only ever encountered the mask I wore. Who could I talk to honestly? Before, I thought that at least your sister, Xie Xue, was different from everybody else. But it turns out, I was naive. I'm sick, Xie Qingcheng."

By this point, he had begun to smile, but his expression was pained and dangerously unhinged, a genuinely terrifying sight. Jabbing at his own heart, he said, "I'm fucking sick! After learning the truth about me, who would be willing to treat me the same way they used to? I have to live my entire life behind the mask of a normal person—even a prisoner's sentence has a time limit, but how long is the sentence of my illness going to be?"

By the end, his voice was shaking.

"It's been nineteen years, Xie Qingcheng. Why did you save me? Before you, none of my doctors found a way to slow down the progression of my illness. You're the one who gave me hope, only to push me back into the abyss—so why did you save me? Why did you lie to me? You hate me, don't you, Xie Qingcheng—well, did you know that I hate you too?! Since the day you left, I've hated you so fucking much!"

He Yu practically never swore, but right now, within this hypnotic dream, he lost control of himself. Chaos had been brewing in his heart for too long, and he couldn't stop it from rushing into his blood, his heart, his limbs, his bones.

In the dream, he raged against Xie Qingcheng, like a real nineteen-year-old boy—without logic, without rhyme or reason, without careful consideration, he irrationally and impetuously poured out all of the words that had been smothered in his throat.

He cursed and cursed, the rims of his eyes red.

"I really hate you, Xie Qingcheng," he said. "Now that you hate me too, tell me, wouldn't it be great if you'd never bothered to help me in the first place and just left me to die? If it weren't for this illness, if it weren't for meeting you, we'd both have one less enemy in our lives, and we wouldn't have suffered so much. You and I wouldn't loathe each other so deeply."

In his dream, Xie Qingcheng didn't say anything as he looked at him with complicated eyes. Then, after a long silence, he turned around.

"...I'll have the assistant give you the injection."

"Why don't you do it yourself, Xie Qingcheng?! Are you scared of me?" He Yu's eyes were full of rage, but his voice was terrifyingly calm. "Or is it that you don't want to dirty yourself by touching me?"

"You can think whatever you want," Xie Qingcheng said. "But there was one thing you said that was correct, He Yu: if it weren't for this illness, if it weren't for meeting you, we'd both have one less enemy in our lives, and we wouldn't have suffered so much. Now, please get your emotions under control. Otherwise, I'll have no choice but to restrain you."

"Fine. Then you'd better tie me up as quickly as possible. Tie me up right away!" He Yu tilted his head back and smiled, his eyes red and his voice distant. "If you don't, sooner or later you'll regret it."

Xie Qingcheng didn't pay him any further attention. He turned around, pushed open the door, and left.

The moment Xie Qingcheng walked out of the door in the hypnotic dreamscape, He Yu's chest heaved violently where he lay on the treatment chair in the real world, like he was a fragile creature on the verge of death. As that door opened and closed again, he knew that even within his dream, Xie Qingcheng wasn't willing to stay any longer.

His departure seemed to pull the last breath of life out of He Yu's chest.

He Yu startled awake, his eyes opening wide as he panted raggedly. A trail of tears seeped out of the edge of his eyes.

Anthony the personal physician was watching him from beside the chair. He calmly poured out a glass of water and handed him some pills, as well as a tissue. "There's something—or someone— that's causing excruciating torment in your heart."

He Yu said nothing.

"Take the medicine," Doctor Anthony said. "At the very least, you've seen the cause behind this flare-up. And now that you've found the cause, you can think about how to overcome it."

The doctor patted the sweat-soaked young man on the shoulder. "Today's treatment is over. Young Master He, please try to keep yourself under control. Don't think about that matter—or that person—any longer. Make sure you rest properly."

75

XIE QINGCHENG, ANSWER ME

WITH THE HYPNOTHERAPY administered by his new personal physician, this latest flare-up of He Yu's disease finally passed, and his wounds slowly began to heal.

In the dreamscape of hypnosis, Xie Qingcheng's silhouette began to fade—and in his dreams, He Yu returned to that long, secluded corridor less and less frequently.

He took a lot of medicine and underwent treatment many times. After about two weeks, He Yu finally returned to normal.

That day, He Yu and his family sent Anthony the personal physician off together. Lü Zhishu thanked the doctor profusely, and He Yu also shook his hand.

"Thank you."

The young Doctor Anthony smiled. "Remember to keep adjusting your attitude. The most important thing is for you to slowly but completely break free of the inner demon hiding in the deepest part of your heart."

Presently, that inner demon was Xie Qingcheng.

He Yu gave him a faint smile and nodded.

"Thank you, Doctor, I will."

Anthony got in the private car that had been called for him. The engine started, and the car drove away.

The private physician sat in the cozy back seat, turned on his phone, tapped into the photo gallery, and looked down at it with a blank expression on his face. Light fell through the leaves of the trees outside, spilling into the car window and slanting across the screen of his phone.

Shown there was…a picture of Xie Qingcheng.

Anthony switched off his phone, his face reflected in the now-dark screen. And a pair of peach-blossom eyes seemed to overlap with where Xie Qingcheng's eyes had been in the picture moments ago…

Suddenly, the phone buzzed. He tapped on the incoming message.

Duan: How did it go?

Anthony thought for a moment, then responded.

He should have a decent impression of me. I'll be seeing him again in the future.

Duan: Good.

Anthony exited out of the chat window, then sent a message to He Yu.

Young Master He, keep gradually adjusting your mindset. If you ever need me, you can call me any time. From now on, I'll be your personal physician, so I'll do everything I can to accompany you and take care of you.

He Yu received this message as he was walking past the villa's lawn.

He stood on the grass where he had met Xie Qingcheng for the first time and read Anthony's message with his head lowered. He did not speak for a long, long time.

Lü Zhishu asked, "What is it?"

"Nothing," He Yu said. Looking up, his gaze landed on a nearby corridor.

Many years ago, he had met Xie Qingcheng for the first time right here. Xie Qingcheng had said to him—

Nice to meet you. I'll probably be the one treating your illness in the future.

He Yu stared at the place from which Xie Qingcheng's figure had disappeared long ago. He fell silent for a moment. "It's nothing, I just suddenly remembered someone."

Lü Zhishu wanted to ask more, but He Yu didn't want to talk. She could only hesitantly try to sound him out.

"How was Doctor Anthony?"

"He's great." For some reason, a cruel desire for retaliation arose in He Yu's heart, even if this "retaliation" didn't seem like it would affect anyone at all. "He's the best. Much better than Doctor Xie. Why didn't you find such a good doctor earlier?"

Lü Zhishu seemed to let out a sigh of relief. She laughed. "Excellent, I'm glad you like him."

Lowering his lashes, He Yu looked down at his phone again, but he didn't reply to the Good Doctor Anthony's message.

He exited the app and opened his photo gallery, which consisted almost entirely of "Bad Doctor" Xie Qingcheng's photographs. There were so many it seemed obsessive.

Feeling as though his sense of dignity had been stung, He Yu looked away and closed his eyes.

Winter had arrived.

The endless hydrangeas had finally reached the end of their flowering cycle.

A few days later, Lü Zhishu went to see He Yu in the library with a tray of pastries and hot tea. On that particular afternoon, he was reading a copy of the ancient Egyptian *Book of the Dead* with annotations by Jin Shoufu. She knocked on the door, then entered at his invitation.

"He Yu, you don't have other plans for the rest of winter break, right?"

"No, why?"

"Oh, listen—I found a production internship for you. Aren't you studying screenwriting and directing? A colleague of mine is a producer, and his company is about to begin shooting for a project. I got a copy of the script and a synopsis of the project for you—you should read it over. The scale is much bigger than that little web-series you did last time; I think you could learn quite a lot from it. I thought it might be good for you to join the production team and experience it for yourself..."

Lü Zhishu was practically sucking up to He Yu, but eventually, because she couldn't read any emotions from He Yu's face, she started getting a bit nervous.

"Of course, if you don't want to, or if you have other plans, just pretend I didn't say anything..."

He Yu stared at Lü Zhishu's obviously tense expression. It was incredibly...difficult to get used to.

It was already very hard for him to grasp what "parental love" was. He knew about Lü Zhishu's past now, but knowing was one thing and understanding was another. It was actually extremely awkward for him to face Lü Zhishu's suddenly reawakened care.

But that old photo from Yellowstone National Park surged up before his eyes like the geysers in the background of the picture. While it still disconcerted him, he was nevertheless trying his hardest to accept this affection so late in coming.

"Thanks, Mom," he said. "I'll think about it."

Lü Zhishu gave him a sheepish smile. She seemed to want to continue chatting, but coaxing vegetation to grow once again over long-barren, salted earth was no easy task, especially with more than a decade's worth of emptiness yawning between them. She couldn't come up with any good topics of conversation, so she just patted He Yu on the shoulder, her greasy face flushing red. "Then go ahead and read. I won't keep bothering you."

She had already emailed him all the movie information.

He Yu clicked on the email and started reading. It was a patriotic film with very grand and lofty ideals about public security workers ardently pursuing justice for the common people. The leads were a policeman, a public prosecutor, and a lawyer.

Everyone had their own sense of aesthetics. In He Yu's case, he preferred the somewhat convoluted kind of art films about fringe communities that challenged one's moral compass and posed questions about the complexity of the human soul. He wasn't at all interested in unsophisticated, morally idealistic movies. But he understood Lü Zhishu's intentions. Participating in a mainstream patriotic film production like this would provide him with many benefits in the industry—especially if he intended to continue down this path domestically, instead of moving to France or England or Italy to become an art film director.

He looked at the filming schedule. He would only be required to join the production for part of the filming. Lü Zhishu stated clearly in her email that she had already spoken to the producer and arranged for him to work as an assistant to the director. Frankly, it was an opportunity for him to loaf around while gilding his resumé and studying—his role was exceedingly minor, and he would be able to return to school at the start of the new term.

He sat in front of his computer and thought for a long time.

He thought about what He Jiwei had said to him, and Lü Zhishu's pitiable face when she had tried to endear herself to him just now.

After that, he thought about the message from his "new doctor" Anthony.

Then, he thought about his "old doctor" Xie Qingcheng—

It had been over two weeks, but Xie Qingcheng had never contacted him of his own accord.

In truth, He Yu had always needed to take the initiative between the two of them. If He Yu didn't actively look for him, Xie Qingcheng would probably never send He Yu a single message between the Qin dynasty and the year 20,000.

Now that He Yu's condition had improved, he was starting to wonder if he might have gone a bit too crazy this time.

Of course he didn't like men—he might even say that the bodies of his own sex disgusted him—but since his first bite of the forbidden fruit had been with Xie Qingcheng, he'd gotten addicted and began entangling with him day after day.

He didn't mind being ignored by Xie Qingcheng once, but having been rejected so many times, an uncertainty began to grow in his heart...

What was he doing?

Did it really have to be this guy?

He turned on his phone and looked at their chat history. The last message he had sent to Xie Qingcheng was still from before his accidental fall: *I'm sick, I'm sick.*

I'm sick, Doctor Xie.

But Xie Qingcheng thought he was lying. Xie Qingcheng paid him no mind.

He Yu suddenly felt more awake. Once again, he felt a strong desire to quit the drug that was Xie Qingcheng.

He remembered how last time, when he had needed a distraction from his feelings, he had gone to Hangshi to fill in for a role.

A huge, lavish production like this one was bound to be even busier, so perhaps he could completely forget about that man—the demon in his heart.

So the next day, He Yu told Lü Zhishu that he would accept the position that she had arranged for him.

Lü Zhishu was clearly very happy about this, but faced with her enthusiasm, He Yu had the strange feeling that she was about to stick out a long, toad-like tongue and lick his cheek, leaving behind a sticky trail of saliva. However, he quickly thought that he shouldn't think that kind of thing. After all, he was the reason why Lü Zhishu had become like this.

"Baby." She hugged him, tiptoeing on stubby, bucket-like legs, and patted him on the back. "You've never let me down."

After she let him go, Lü Zhishu immediately contacted her business partners and arranged for He Yu to continue his studies on the film production team.

January...

The shooting of *The Trial* was about to begin.

A chauffeur picked up He Yu and Lü Zhishu and brought them to the film studio complex.

It wasn't convenient for her to stay for long, so she would be returning home the same evening, but given her jam-packed business schedule, it was completely unprecedented for Executive Lü to personally accompany her elder son to a project site.

"Executive Huang, aiya, Executive Huang, you look great! Congratulations on an auspicious start to the filming of *The Trial*." By the time Lü Zhishu's car reached the front entrance of the cast and crew's hotel, the director Huang Zhilong was already waiting in the main lobby.

Huang Zhilong was a physically robust middle-aged man with an imposing and rugged air. He was in his late fifties and had two children. Although he was going gray at the temples, he was not lacking in energy or vigor—he was still very dashing in his suit and had a glint in his eyes that was rare even among younger people. He seemed quite proper and upright and even wore a string of prayer beads on his wrist.

He Yu was somewhat aware of who he was—Huang Zhilong was a very well-known director in the industry, and also the head of an international entertainment company that accepted and eliminated countless trainees each year. He was constantly surrounded by beautiful young women, but it was said that he was still in love with his long-deceased wife, and he rarely appeared in the tabloids.

Huang Zhilong was very courteous to Lü Zhishu, smiling as he shook her hand. She greeted him enthusiastically, then introduced He Yu. "I'll have to humbly request that Executive Huang look after and guide my son."

"Surely you speak in jest, Executive Lü—how can you place so much trust in me? Your son is such an outstanding and handsome young man. It's this old man's honor to get the chance to work with a youngster of his caliber."

This whole production was completely different from the dinky little web series in Hangshi. *The Trial*'s extravagance overshadowed the web series ten thousand times over in every way possible. Of course, the cast and crew were likewise much more difficult to parse, and their conversations were a hundred thousand times more cunning.

He Yu was used to it, so didn't mind it all that much, but ever since he'd learned about what Lü Zhishu was like when she was young, when he saw her slickly conniving ways now and the unctuous smiles sprouting up on her face like mushrooms after the rain, he felt rather conflicted.

After they finished having dinner with the producers, Lü Zhishu climbed tipsily into her car. He Yu was still very clear-headed, so he politely allowed his elders to leave first before heading back to the hotel in Huang Zhilong's car.

"Ah, Xiao-He, how old are you?" asked Huang Zhilong.

"Almost twenty."

Huang Zhilong smiled. "So young... I've met your little brother before, such a cute boy—you both have your strengths, and I like you both very much. Executive Lü and Executive He are very fortunate."

When he heard the director bring up He Li, He Yu was very aware of the meaning behind his words. "Executive Huang, have you known my mother for a long time?"

"Oh." Huang Zhilong smiled. "It's been so many years now, I can't even remember how long it's been. Executive Lü is an old friend. So there's no need to be shy while you're here—if there's anything that you want to learn or try, just let me know." He blinked at him. "But there's one thing I have to tell you up front—you need to keep your distance from my girls, ha ha ha."

"Is Executive Huang worried that they'll get so sick of me they run away?" He Yu asked with a bland smile.

"Please, you're so handsome—I'm afraid you'll get sick of *them*, and then your mom will take it out on me." The alcohol had gone to Huang Zhilong's head, and he was more relaxed now. "They're just bit players, they're hardly good enough for you."

"Surely Executive Huang is joking."

Huang Zhilong had yet to finish. "I'm completely serious. It's not just the little girls, you should stay away from the boys too. Boys these days, you never know." Finally, Huang Zhilong propped his face up in his hand and sighed with a smile. "Ah, seems I've drunk a bit too much today."

"In that case, Executive Huang should head back and get some rest," He Yu said politely.

"Yes, yes." He waved his hand. "Xiao-He, I told Assistant Zhang to arrange a room for you. I don't trust any of these actors or actresses— if anything happens, I won't be able to explain it to your mother—so I got you a room near where our technical consultants are staying." Huang Zhilong took a sip of bottled water and added, "As you know, our movie is a collaboration with each branch of the public security authorities. We need to cover all the bases, so we definitely need their people to help guide us."

"Mm."

"The people staying over there are all the police officers, lawyers, and other professionals we've invited to fill the minor parts in our production... Ah, they certainly won't be as easy on the eyes as the actors, but I can breathe easy if you're staying with them, and I won't have to worry about explaining anything to Executive Lü."

...So this whole time, He Yu realized, Huang Zhilong had been worried he'd sleep around with pretty girls.

He Yu couldn't be bothered to waste more words on Executive Huang. Upon arriving at the hotel, he followed the director into the elevator and very courteously sent him off to his floor, then went to find his own room according to the room card he'd been given by Assistant Zhang.

The elevator door opened on the seventh floor with a *ding*.

He Yu stepped onto the thick carpet and walked out.

It was already quite late, and the corridor was very quiet. It would have been a sublimely peaceful night if only he hadn't run into a certain someone in the hallway—Xie Qingcheng.

Something collapsed with a rumbling boom inside He Yu's head. Never had he imagined that Xie Qingcheng—after refusing to be his personal physician, ignoring him on WeChat, and seeming to all but evaporate from the world—would be standing next to an open window further down this hallway, calmly smoking a cigarette.

Neither of them had anticipated that they would cross paths here, and both were extremely shocked to meet face-to-face like this without warning.

It wasn't until the lit end of the cigarette burned down to Xie Qingcheng's fingers, singeing his fingertips, that he snapped out of it, his surprised expression easing back to its usual coldness. He stood ramrod-straight next to the open window just like that, watching He Yu, his lips tightly pursed and not saying a word.

The two of them remained at an impasse for a long while. In the end, it was He Yu who broke the silence.

"What...what are you doing here."

Xie Qingcheng exhaled a mouthful of smoke, glancing wordlessly at He Yu for a moment with a cold, hard gaze. Then he turned around and began to walk away.

All of He Yu's hypnotherapy treatments seemed to go out the window the instant he saw this man again—his blood seemed to heat to a boil, so scalding hot that it burned the rims of his eyes until they turned red. He reached out and grabbed him. "Xie Qingcheng, you—"

At that very moment, the door to the closest room opened as Chen Man walked out with Xie Qingcheng's phone in hand. "Ge, Xie Xue's looking for you. You should call her back soon."

He Yu immediately felt a chill run through his boiling blood, cooling it to its freezing point.

He narrowed his eyes. The rims were still red, but the scorching fire had already turned into ice-cold rust.

For so many days, his parents had told him to accept his new doctor. And his new doctor had told him to forget the person from his past.

Even Xie Qingcheng had told him, with his silence, that a clean break would be the best ending for both of them. It was as though the entire world had been telling him, *let go of Xie Qingcheng, let him walk out of your world. It will be good for not only you, but him as well.*

Everyone had been urging him to give up, but he was the only one who kept on stubbornly persisting—no matter how the hypnosis tried, it couldn't wipe away Xie Qingcheng's shadow. Even He Yu didn't know why.

He obviously hated this man.

He obviously resented him for abandoning and deceiving him.

But he persisted, unable to forget.

Until that moment, when he saw that Xie Qingcheng was actually staying in the same room as Chen Man. His own persistence suddenly seemed laughable, pathetic.

He Yu felt like all his breath had been stabbed out of him. All of Anthony's treatments instantly became useless. Very, very slowly, he asked Xie Qingcheng, "He brought you here? You've been with him this whole time?"

Xie Qingcheng turned his face away to look outside at the street, then tapped the ash off his cigarette in silence.

The raging fire He Yu had been suppressing in his heart suddenly surged forth. Cold light flashed in his eyes as he glared at Xie Qingcheng, who was still leaning against the windowsill.

"I'm asking you a question! You've been living with him this whole time?"

76

NICE GOING, YOUNG MASTER CHEN

H E YU'S EXPRESSION had turned very unsightly. He looked like he was on the verge of having another flare-up.

It had taken his new doctor over ten days to stabilize his emotional state, yet it had taken his "old doctor" only a split second to obliterate his rationality.

He pinned Xie Qingcheng with an unwavering glare.

Xie Qingcheng didn't back down, however, as he faced him coldly. At last, with his cigarette in hand, Xie Qingcheng gave him a calm look and spoke.

"He Yu. You better get this straight." Ash drifted down with a tap of his slender finger. "No matter who I'm with, it has nothing to do with you."

He Yu was silent. At this moment, he found himself thinking of Xie Xue, for some reason. He had liked Xie Xue, but she only saw him as an ordinary friend. Later on, an unlikely turn of events had led to him sleeping with Xie Qingcheng, but in hindsight, he was the one who had fallen into an impenetrable mist, while Xie Qingcheng had firmly regained the upper hand.

He'd been so sure that he'd successfully torn Xie Qingcheng open and swallowed him whole. But it turned out he'd actually swallowed a handful of snow that would never thaw, a mouthful of ice that would never melt. He'd gulped it eagerly down into his belly, but that ice was impossible to digest. Instead, it froze his organs until they ached and made all the blood in his body run cold.

Was he doomed to fall at the hands of someone with the name Xie?

The tension in the air was so thick one could cut it with a knife.

In the end, it was Chen Man who broke the silence.

"Um...hello again." Though Officer Chen had been caught off guard, he still recognized He Yu. "Are you providing technical guidance for the production too?"

He Yu didn't bother answering him. He just leveled a cold, hateful, stubborn stare at Xie Qingcheng.

Xie Qingcheng turned his head. "Chen Man, you've come just in time. He's had too much to drink and reeks of alcohol. Please take him back to his room. Don't let him go on a drunken rampage out here."

The only reason He Yu smelled like alcohol was because the air at the banquet had been saturated with it. He'd hardly had anything to drink himself. But Chen Man believed it—what sober person would dare to speak to his Xie-ge like this? "Let me help you back. Where's your room card?"

He Yu shoved Chen Man away at once, glaring at him as though he intended to pierce straight through his body with his eyes. "Xie Qingcheng, you know that I'm not going on some kind of drunken rampage. I'm asking you a question."

His eyes looked calm and his voice sounded steady, but it was impossible not to notice the flames of fury raging in his heart. He Yu was beyond furious.

He could accept Xie Qingcheng showing up at any place and time—after all, it wasn't as though Xie Qingcheng was special to him; he didn't even like him. But he couldn't accept him being with Chen Man.

How could Xie Qingcheng possibly be living with him?

And over the past few days...he had endured so much suffering. His mind had been a muddled mess, and he had even fallen from a building—if he'd fallen from a higher floor, he might have even died, just like that.

And the entire time, Xie Qingcheng had been off gallivanting with Chen Man.

He really didn't want to mention his fall to Xie Qingcheng—that would be too feeble, too pathetic. He Yu was a very prideful person, and now that he was aware of Xie Qingcheng's attitude toward him, he didn't want to try to use his accident to win sympathy that Xie Qingcheng would inevitably refuse to give him. He would rather Xie Qingcheng never find out about his fall; would rather pretend that nothing had happened.

But that didn't mean he didn't care what Xie Qingcheng had been up to all this time.

This Chen Man—just what kind of a creep was this guy? Back in the school theater, He Yu had watched with his own eyes as Chen Man took Xie Qingcheng's hand and attempted to kiss him on the cheek while he was sleeping. He had warned Xie Qingcheng about it on multiple occasions. Why wouldn't Xie Qingcheng believe him...?

If he hadn't run into them today, if he hadn't coincidentally joined the same production, just how long were Chen Man and Xie Qingcheng going to live together? And what were they going to do together?

While he was at home, miserable and suffering, refusing to forget Xie Qingcheng to the very end, while he wretchedly awaited the slightest reaction or reply, when even a simple "Mm" would have sufficed...

What were the two of them doing in that room?!

Possibility after awful possibility flashed through He Yu's head, each and every one of them like a sharp-clawed fairy tearing apart flesh and bone, digging out the violence inside him.

As the stare he leveled at Xie Qingcheng grew increasingly terrifying, Xie Qingcheng narrowed his eyes—he could sense He Yu's abnormal and completely irrational state of mind.

"Xie Qingcheng," He Yu said darkly, "I'm sure you remember what I told you. Would you like me to remind you within earshot of this Officer Chen?"

Xie Qingcheng's expression flickered minutely.

He didn't know the kind of agonizing torment He Yu had recently endured; he didn't know that He Yu had truly fallen ill, much less that he had fallen from a building. But looking at him now, he could tell that the young man's edges were even more jagged than he remembered.

Truth be told, Xie Qingcheng couldn't tell what He Yu's limits were now.

In the past, He Yu still had some firm boundaries. For instance, Xie Qingcheng never would have believed he'd kiss another man at a public bar. But He Yu was no longer playing by the usual rules. Judging from He Yu's expression, it seemed like he really didn't give a damn about saying such shameless things out loud.

Chen Man could also tell that the atmosphere between them was a bit off. However, his imagination wasn't so wild that he would ever suspect He Yu had fucked Xie Qingcheng before. He could only tell that they had some conflict between them that they couldn't discuss in front of others, so he stood to the side and didn't interrupt.

"Come to my room," He Yu said. "I need to talk to you."

Xie Qingcheng pinched out his cigarette. "I have nothing to say to you."

"Don't push me."

"Let's get something straight—right now, *you're* the one pushing *me*."

"...I want you to come with me," said He Yu menacingly. "To my room."

"And if I don't go?"

"Then just wait and see what I'll do." He Yu's eyes were bloodshot. "Try me."

"Try you?" Xie Qingcheng narrowed his eyes. "Okay. I'm trying, right now."

"Xie Qingcheng—"

"What do you want?" Perhaps He Yu had been too aggressive, and he'd embarrassed Xie Qingcheng in front of Chen Man—whatever it was, Xie Qingcheng abruptly lost his temper. "Are you done? He Yu, I'm telling you, if you have something you want to say, then say it. If you have something you want to do, then do it! Right here. Don't think I'm afraid of you."

The rage in Xie Qingcheng's eyes burned so fiercely that He Yu actually found himself recovering a bit of his rationality.

—Or, no, perhaps it wasn't because Xie Qingcheng had gotten angry, but because there was something other than anger in Xie Qingcheng's eyes that made He Yu very uncomfortable. There was something there that could puncture He Yu's sense of dignity. That feeling—that Xie Qingcheng was looking at him like he was trash that needed to be taken out—allowed He Yu to slightly restrain his darker impulses.

The confrontation dragged on. Xie Qingcheng's gaze cut into He Yu like a keen blade as he stared him down. Finally, with deliberate emphasis, he said, "If there's nothing more you want to say, then please go back to your room. *Go.*"

The oppressive atmosphere between them was overwhelming. Chen Man watched silently as he stood to the side with his back to the wall. He honestly had no idea why these two would suddenly have such a falling out—hadn't the newspaper reports said that this boy had been shot after following Xie Qingcheng into the archives? If the trajectory of that bullet had veered just slightly off to the side, He Yu probably would have died then and there.

Given Xie Qingcheng's personality, Chen Man had assumed he would take this youth under his wing, no matter what—that he would treat him well and protect him. Xie Qingcheng had always been someone who repaid his debts of gratitude.

What could He Yu have possibly done to make Xie Qingcheng's attitude toward him take such an abrupt 180-degree turn?

He Yu still wasn't leaving—it was as though his feet were rooted to the ground—but he didn't step forward either. He just stared closely at Xie Qingcheng's face, completely silent. His expression was ruthless and obstinate, but for some reason, it also seemed like he had experienced some tremendous grievance—his eyes gleamed with an ominous light, yet they also gradually reddened.

Just as he was about to unleash the grievance and agony that had been lodged in his throat for so long...

"Ha ha ha, all right, all right!"

The door to a nearby room suddenly swung open. Light spilled over the hallway carpet as an endearingly chubby man walked out, bidding goodbye to the person inside with a smile on his face.

"In that case, we'll handle the situation like this for now. I'll have to trouble Attorney Zhang to speak with the male lead about this issue again tomorrow. Aiya, my apologies for disturbing you so late at night, but the schedule's so tight, there really was no other way... There's no need to see me out. Please stay put, Attorney Zhang, and get some rest."

The chubby man had a full sleeve tattoo featuring, of all things, Hello Kitty. His sudden appearance dragged the men standing in the corridor out of their own turbulent emotions. All three of them snapped back to their senses at once.

This Hello Kitty's name was Hu Yi, and he was the screenwriter and a producer on *The Trial*.

Hu Yi had been born to a relatively high-status family. His parents were both generals who had worked in the General Political Department's performing troupe[5] in their youth, where they met and fell in love. Hu Yi had followed in his parents' line of business, and both his abilities and connections were extraordinary.

Even with his many privileges, Hu Yi was a decent fellow. He was extremely forthright; his status, fame, and fortune never consumed his heart, and no matter what he did, he never crossed the line. He was unlike the greedy, crazed, lying backstabbers that made up the majority of shitty capitalists—anyone unlucky enough to be tricked by such people once would be screwed out of the clothes on their back and unwilling to work with them again. But it was precisely because Hu Yi never bullied the weak that people from all walks of life were willing to work with him, and he forged long-term collaborations with many of them.

As soon as Hu-laoshi saw this array of people in the hallway, he slapped his forehead and flashed them a friendly grin. "Aiyo! Young Master He! Young Master Chen!"

He Yu froze for a moment. It was perfectly fine for Hello Kitty to call him "Young Master He," but "Young Master Chen"...? His head snapped around, and he looked at Chen Man as if truly seeing him for the first time.

---

5   The General Political Department's official army choir. Their repertoire includes music, dance, theater, opera, and comedy.

Hu Yi was still rambling on. "Ah, Young Master He, I'm sure Executive Huang must've already told you. I found an error in the logic of this legal scene—it's very urgent, so I was just talking about it with Attorney Zhang. That was why I didn't make it to your welcome dinner tonight. Young Master He, you look so upset—you aren't angry about my absence, are you?"

"Hu-laoshi is surely joking," He Yu replied absentmindedly as he looked Chen Man up and down.

At that, Hu Yi began to laugh. "Ha ha ha ha ha, as long as you're not upset with me. Hey, Young Master He, I had no idea that you were acquainted with Young Master Chen."

Young Master Chen... He said it again. So it wasn't a mistake.

But wasn't this guy just a random police officer? Why in the world would Hello Kitty add a "Young Master" to his surname? Hu Yi wasn't some blind idiot, either—he wouldn't have gotten the wrong person or started calling random people "Young Master."

He Yu suddenly remembered that the first time he met Chen Man in the dining hall, he'd thought the man looked vaguely familiar, but he couldn't recall where he'd seen him before. Could it be...?

"...Looks like you guys don't know each other very well?" Hu Yi's eyes swept over the scene, noticing the sense of distance between them. His face broke out into a smile. "In that case, come now, let me introduce you—Young Master Chen, this is He Yu, the son of Executive He Jiwei and Executive Lü Zhishu."

Then he patted Chen Man on the shoulder and turned around to say to He Yu, "Young Master He, this is my childhood friend."

Chen Man felt a bit awkward. Hello Kitty was acting way too familiar with him. This laoshi couldn't really be considered his childhood friend—they had merely known each other since they were young.

As it turned out, Chen Man's mother was the third daughter of a certain senior party official.

Back in the day, this distinguished young lady had turned her entire house upside down when she declared her intention to marry Chen Man's father. Her family refused to allow it under any circumstances; they said she was insane, that running off to be a widower's second wife was tantamount to becoming his concubine. She furiously and resolutely cut ties with her family, eloped, moved to Huzhou, and had a child.

No matter how the senior party official's family resisted, there was nothing they could do—what was done was done, and it wasn't like they could send the baby back to where it had come from. In the end, the Chen family accepted the marriage, but relations had already soured. Aside from a period of illness when he was young, when he'd stayed at a hospital in Yanzhou, Chen Man hardly ever saw his maternal grandparents.

But still, Chen Man was different from his elder half-brother Chen Lisheng.

Half of his blood was still that of a young master, after all, and as the party official grew older, his heart grew softer. Though his daughter refused to speak to them, the old man began to miss his grandson, who'd had a difficult childhood and never had the opportunity to be spoiled by his grandma and grandpa. When the old man's will was finalized last year, the document stated that Chen Man was to receive the same share of the inheritance as any other ordinary grandson, and not one cent less. In his remorse, the old man had even left Chen Man an additional house in Yanzhou as well.

Chen Man's status wasn't lower than He Yu's at all. The two of them were roughly of the same social class.

The only reason Chen Man was participating in this production was because the old party official thought it would be a good opportunity for his grandson—who had received very few benefits through him—to gain some firsthand experience. Thus, he had made a phone call and arranged to have Chen Man serve as one of the consultants.

"How magnificent it will be to see your name in the credits— taking part in this film will be a great experience, and meaningful too."

Chen Man hadn't wanted to go at first. But Xie Qingcheng had been going through a difficult time lately, so Chen Man had thought it would be good for him to find some peace and quiet and forget his worries by working as part of this production team. He'd said he wanted to unwind with Xie Qingcheng, so the two of them had both joined the production of The Trial.

"Ah, that's right! Young Master He, Young Master Chen, you two have met before, right?" After he'd introduced them, Hu Yi suddenly slapped himself on the head as though he'd just remembered something. "I remember now—you guys were very young, and I was there too, at that big party in Yanzhou. Didn't we play hide-and-seek together? With a bunch of little kids..."

As he spoke, Chen Man and He Yu looked at each other, recognition dawning in their eyes as they both remembered—no wonder he looked so familiar!

They had actually met once when they were kids... It had been at a gathering of many notable and important people, and the children were all playing together. Chen Man and He Yu had been the captains of the two teams, so they'd both left an impression on the other...

He Yu slowly narrowed his eyes.

"So it's you."

He was suddenly on high alert. A palpable chill seemed to emanate from his tall figure.

He turned back toward Xie Qingcheng, who was standing beside the window, and shot him a meaningful look, his eyes gleaming with a calm yet chilly light. Though he seemed collected on the surface, the undercurrent of sinister intent was stronger than ever.

If Chen Man had been an ordinary person, just an ordinary little policeman, He Yu might not have cared so much. But as it turned out, despite flying under the radar so modestly, he came from three generations of wealth!

He Yu bit his lip. He felt as though fangs had grown from his mouth, aching to snap Xie Qingcheng's neck with a single bite and drag him back into his lair. It didn't matter if he ended up covered in blood—he had underestimated Xie Qingcheng.

No wonder Xie Qingcheng could ignore him so easily. No wonder Xie Qingcheng didn't want him, didn't reply to him, didn't pay him the slightest bit of attention.

It must have been nice, leaning against a great big tree and cooling off in its shade.

He Yu's blood ran cold. As a despicable, sickly burden, what was he worth compared to this obedient Chen Man, who was not only a normal, healthy person, but also a young master who'd spoken not a word of his true identity?

He Yu looked at them in silence for a while, barely noticing that he had bitten through his lip. Then, his thin lips spread into a cruel, bloody sneer like the blossoming of an evil flower. "Ah, I see that Doctor Xie has found himself a much better job as Young Master Chen's personal physician."

He forcibly restrained all his chaotic emotions; when he looked at Chen Man again, he appeared completely indifferent, even displaying a hint of masochistic ridicule. "How does Young Master Chen find his services?"

77

NICE GOING, CUZ

CHEN MAN COULD TELL his tone was hostile, but he had no idea why. "You're mistaken, Xie-ge isn't my personal physician," he said, frowning slightly. "He's always been my friend."

He Yu smiled, his eyes cold as ice. He didn't speak a word in response.

Chen Man continued looking at him in confusion. "If I remember correctly, you're Xie-ge's friend as well."

He Yu's smile became even more gently refined.

In truth, he was racked by torment and desperately wanted to drag Xie Qingcheng over, shove him against the wall, and vindictively kiss him before Chen Man's very eyes—to defile Xie Qingcheng as everyone watched.

However, wounded by how Xie Qingcheng had treated him, his pride didn't allow him to act that way in the presence of others.

In fact, he seemed exceedingly indifferent. He spoke with slight disdain. "Surely you're joking. He and I merely have a working relationship."

With Hu Yi present, there was no way for the three of them to say much more, so they all returned to their rooms with their own thoughts weighing on their minds.

However, upon reaching his room, He Yu could contain himself no longer.

He sat on the sofa for a while, spacing out, but he still couldn't cast off the gloom in his heart. In the end, he went downstairs and bought himself a pack of smokes—Marlboro, the brand that Xie Qingcheng had been smoking recently.

Standing by the road, He Yu held his cigarette in a slender hand and slowly finished smoking it in its entirety, his comportment graceful yet twisted as his eyes flickered in the lit end's glow.

Upon returning to the hotel, he contacted the production assistant, intending to switch his room to the one next door to Chen Man and Xie Qingcheng. "As it turns out, my room is too close to the generators. I can't sleep."

The assistant didn't dare to be remiss, and promptly helped He-laoban switch rooms with no fuss at all. However, He Yu still found this to be inadequate. He looked over the room's layout, then hauled the bed across the floor and shoved it up against the wall that he shared with Xie Qingcheng's room. Then he collapsed on the bed and closed his eyes, giving in to his darker emotions as he bit and gnawed at his own body. Some time later, he finally picked up his cell phone and gave Xie Qingcheng a call.

The hotel's soundproofing wasn't great. Lying against the wall, He Yu could vaguely make out the sound of Xie Qingcheng's phone ringing incessantly in the neighboring room. It was even accompanied by Chen Man's voice: "Ge, your phone!"

Then he heard Xie Qingcheng's voice. It was a bit distant, but very cold and calm. He Yu couldn't quite tell what he said. But it was evident that in the end, he didn't answer the call.

He didn't answer, so He Yu tried again.

"Ge, he's calling again."

Still, Xie Qingcheng did not answer.

After the third call, He Yu finally heard Xie Qingcheng's footsteps draw closer. This time, the call went through.

He Yu was just about to speak, but Xie Qingcheng simply muted his phone's speaker so he didn't need to listen to He Yu's voice, then tossed the cell phone right next to the television.

"Yesterday, Municipal Party Secretary X visited a nursing home in X District to pay a call to the lonely senior citizens in the area..."

He Yu was at a loss for words. It seemed Xie Qingcheng intended to make him listen to an entire night's worth of news, in hopes that the light of justice emanating from the late-night newscast could rinse clean the unspeakable filth caked on his soul.

But even with the unpleasant newscast droning into his ears, He Yu didn't hang up. Because he could hear Xie Qingcheng and Chen Man's conversation.

"Ge, why don't I go and talk to him. Giving him the silent treatment like this isn't really..."

"There's no need."

"What happened with you two? Weren't you on good terms before?"

"You should go and wash up, Chen Man." Xie Qingcheng didn't respond to his question. "Go to bed. You have to supervise a scene set in the police department tomorrow."

Young Master Chen was truly too well-behaved—He Yu heard how he didn't even try to protest, merely sitting silently for a while before rising to his feet with a rustling noise and closing the bathroom door behind him.

He Yu lay on his bed and listened quietly, his hair tickling his brow. Although he didn't usually leave his bangs down, his dark hair was very soft; if he didn't comb it carefully, some fine strands at his temples always fell over his forehead.

The newscast continued to play, and Xie Qingcheng likewise continued in silence.

Still, He Yu did not hang up.

He stared up at the ceiling as the news headlines blaring out of his earbuds shifted from the municipal party secretary's visit with aging empty-nesters to a story about some neighborhood's pet dog learning how to hold a basket in its mouth and going out to help its owner buy groceries.

He listened without uttering a word.

He Yu couldn't describe what he was feeling right now. There had always been a heavy mass blocking up his heart. Now that he knew the truth about Chen Man's social status, now that he knew what Xie Qingcheng had been doing in recent days and who he had been with, it was as though that heavy mass had grown twisted, plantlike roots that stabbed into the deepest reaches of his heart and veins.

He didn't know why he cared so much. Just who was Xie Qingcheng anyway? Nothing more than a fucktoy. He was only seeking a temporary novelty. He'd grow tired of it eventually, once he'd had his fill.

But even so, he couldn't bring himself to hang up the phone.

"Gujing genuine distilled spirits, the finest authentic wine..."

The other end of the line started playing commercials.

He Yu heard Xie Qingcheng get off the bed, walk closer, and then pick up the phone he had set next to the television.

A brief silence.

Perhaps Xie Qingcheng hadn't expected He Yu to wait so patiently and listen to the news for so long; when he saw that the line was still open, he truly did go quiet for a long while. No other noise came from the phone.

NICE GOING, CUZ 267

Then, He Yu heard Xie Qingcheng speak.

"What exactly are you trying to do?"

He Yu didn't know how to answer.

Gazing up at the ceiling with overcast eyes, he picked up his cell phone and brought it to his lips.

"Xie Qingcheng," he said, "There's no way that an ugly old man like you—divorced, poor, boring, and in bad health—could possibly catch the eye of a grandson of a founding party member like him. If you want to be with him, you're a fool."

He didn't know which twisted corner of his heart had fomented such jealous words, nor did he know whether Xie Qingcheng had heard what he said, whether he'd unmuted his call.

But in the end, Xie Qingcheng just hung up. When He Yu dialed the number again, his phone had been turned off.

Despite a long time spent tossing and turning, He Yu couldn't fall asleep. Resting his head on his hands, he stared at the ceiling with his almond eyes as vehicles sped past the window at irregular intervals, their lights mechanically cutting into the shadows as they swam across the ceiling like whales.

Meanwhile, he was like a whale fall, a giant carcass sinking deep into the sea.

He felt as though his heart had already begun to rot. It wasn't like that time in Hangzhou, when he could still feel pain. His entire body was cold. He's gone numb.

The dark night gradually fell silent.

A pair of girls passed through the corridor on the seventh floor, walking right past He Yu's door. Lying awake in his room, He Yu could hear them talking.

"The event today was a lot of fun..."

"Yeah... Hey, what's that?"

There was a glass cabinet, over two meters tall, at the end of the hotel corridor. But it didn't quite look like a piece of furniture—more like a giant pill capsule. The light in the corridor was dim, and there were a bunch of indistinct shadows inside the cabinet. To these girls who'd just come back late at night, it looked like a human figure.

"Ah...!"

"This is..."

"Th-there's a *body*!"

"There's a body in the glass cabinet!"

Their cries jolted He Yu out of his gloom. Climbing out of bed, he opened the door and went outside.

The two girls were pale with fright. Seeing a tall young man show up, they stumbled over to He Yu's side, pointing behind them as they ran. "Th-there's a body over there! In the cabinet!"

Perhaps their screams had been too loud; not long after, the door to He Yu's neighboring room also flew open. Xie Qingcheng walked out.

He Yu met the eyes of the man he had been spam-calling a few hours earlier for just a moment, then Xie Qingcheng looked away.

Chen Man also ran out of the room. "What's going on? What happened?"

"I-inside that cabinet," one of the girls stuttered out. "Standing... standing right there...there's a person...completely motionless... They must be dead..." She was so terrified that her face had gone chalky white. Like her friend, she quickly became incoherent beyond words.

"I'll go take a look," said Xie Qingcheng.

He walked over. He Yu had wanted to follow him, but Chen Man beat him to the punch. Once Chen Man had already gone, He Yu found himself reluctant to follow, and he ended up standing there with his arms crossed, a dark expression on his face.

Once Xie Qingcheng got closer, realization dawned.

He turned back to the girls. "It's fine, it's just a prop."

"Ah...?"

"It's a prop for *The Trial*. We'll be using it in a few days for filming." Xie Qingcheng cast the beam of his cell phone's flashlight over the contents of the cabinet.

Just as he said, under the bright light of the cell phone, the girls could clearly see that the thing standing inside the cabinet was just a lifelike rubber dummy. Even as the girls let out a sigh of relief, they found themselves somewhat torn between laughter and annoyance. "Who would leave a prop like that in a place like this?"

"Right? What a dick."

"The eighth floor's reserved for makeup, costuming, and props," said Chen Man, "so it might be a sample that they brought along and just left here for the time being."

Patting themselves on their chests in lingering fear, the girls finally left.

Xie Qingcheng examined the dummy in the glass cabinet. It made him a bit uncomfortable... Perhaps it was the uncanny valley effect—the dummy was a bit too lifelike, to the point of inspiring terror.

He looked away and walked back to his room.

When he turned around to close the door behind him, he saw that He Yu had already returned to his own room next door. It seemed like he didn't want to say even a single extra word to him in Chen Man's presence. He Yu locked his door with a *click*.

Xie Qingcheng had only just begun to relax when, less than a minute later, his cell phone suddenly buzzed. It was a text message from He Yu.

Xie Qingcheng, I'm warning you one last time: he is gay. Not to mention, you two are such a bad match. You're divorced and he's barely in his twenties. You have no money or status, while his grandfather is Political Commissar Wang. It's a terrible match no matter how you look at it. Why in the world would he like you? Be careful you don't end up swindled to hell and back. It's time to wake up.

That young man seriously had issues. Xie Qingcheng deleted his message, entered his room, and shut the door.

Neither of them had noticed that a figure stood in the shadows of the stairway behind the glass cabinet. Hidden in the darkness was a frightful-looking man wearing a black raincoat and boots, holding a knife half-concealed beneath the raincoat...

"You guys got off easy this time," he muttered to himself ominously. "I was planning on making my move tonight. If the higher-ups hadn't switched my target to a much bigger fish all of a sudden..."

Chuckling softly, he slowly sheathed his knife.

"Whatever—looks like I won't be 'fishing' tonight."

The first day of shooting for *The Trial* had a rather rocky start. There were mishaps in a number of different areas, and issues arose with the actors' performances. The film's creative team consisted entirely of established artists who took their craft very seriously and refused to lower their standards, and after several rounds of polishing, the sky had already gone dark as they ran over the shoot's scheduled end time.

"Looks like it's gonna be a late night tonight," a production assistant sighed from atop a box of lighting equipment.

The winter night was chilly, so the director ordered a case of hot beverages to be sent over to the production team. All the crew members taking their breaks swarmed around it to grab a drink— even if they didn't drink it, it could at least warm their hands up a bit.

He Yu was shadowing the director. He'd been staring at the monitors so intently his eyes hurt; if nothing else, it helped divert some of his attention.

It was only after they finished shooting one of the major highlights of the film that He Yu finally made his way over to the case of drinks, by which point nearly all that remained were fruit teas. He didn't like fruit tea, so he leaned down and rummaged around for a good while until he finally dug out a cup of hot chocolate. At that very moment, however, a hand calmly reached over and snatched that cup of hot chocolate from right under his nose.

He Yu looked up. The sky was dim and dreary, forecasting snow, and there were no lights in this area, so it took a while for his eyes to adjust before he recognized who it was.

He found himself face-to-face with Xie Qingcheng.

Both of them fell into an awkward silence.

Xie Qingcheng was working with Group B next door today. The reason Groups A and B were both working at the same set was because the highly ambitious creatives behind the film had unexpectedly scheduled a large-scale scene on the very first day of the shoot. As a result, a chaotic jumble of actors, consultants, body doubles, and extras were all present for the opening day of filming.

Xie Qingcheng hadn't recognized He Yu until now—otherwise, he probably wouldn't have come over at all. After a long beat of silence, he lowered his head, picked up the hot chocolate alongside a cup of fruit tea, and turned to leave.

It was a good thing he left. Having spotted Xie Qingcheng on his own, He Yu could feel a rather deranged impulse rearing its head. His mental illness made him want to take advantage of the fact that Xie Qingcheng was alone to drag the man into his lair and tear him to pieces.

He wanted to chain this offering to a bed of stone and force the human to listen to his every word, lest he snap his arms and legs off. This was a dragon's evil instinct.

Xie Qingcheng had once occupied the dragon's bed, and so even if he became a skeleton, it was imperative that he rot in He Yu's territory. Not even his bones could be stained by another's touch.

He Yu closed his eyes to calm himself, suppressing the fantasy that had sprung up at a completely inopportune time. Fruit tea in hand, he returned to the soundstage with a somber expression on his face.

The soundstage was warmer than outside, but his heart was even colder than before...

That was because he'd learned that the technical consultation crew had required Xie Qingcheng and Chen Man to move from Group B to watch Group A's shoot. And as for the hot chocolate that he had yielded to Xie Qingcheng just now, Xie Qingcheng had already passed it to Chen Man, who was waiting for the camera to move to the correct position for the second take.

Xie Qingcheng hadn't done this on purpose, nor had He Yu told him this was the drink he had just dug up for himself, yet He Yu still felt a sense of displeasure course through his whole body.

Sitting on a plastic chair with a chilly look on his face, he asked the assistant for an old announcement flyer. He thought it over for a moment, bowed his head and wrote a few words, then folded the notice into a paper airplane.

The paper airplane soared straight through the air toward Xie Qingcheng's back, landing on his shoulder.

Xie Qingcheng turned around to see He Yu sitting in a plastic chair less than twenty meters away with his cheek propped up against his hand and his long legs crossed, his posture lazy and his gaze indifferent.

The moment their eyes met, that boy whose beauty bordered on effeminacy merely raised an eyebrow provocatively and then rolled his eyes, turning away with a lax expression on his face.

Xie Qingcheng picked up the paper airplane, on which a handful of words could be read. He unfolded the old flyer to see the ugly, nearly illegible scrawl that He Yu had written in his lousy mood.

Does it taste good? Are the two of you enjoying your drinks together?

When Xie Qingcheng finished reading, the look in his eyes was even colder than usual. Right before He Yu's eyes, he folded the notice in half, tore it down the middle, and tossed it straight into the garbage bin.

He Yu didn't make a sound.

He'd anticipated that Xie Qingcheng would react like this, but he'd still insisted on doing it anyway just so he could see Xie Qingcheng's face, which was chillier than the weather outside. When Xie Qingcheng turned back around to speak with Chen Man, it was like his expression had frozen over in a blizzard.

As He Yu stared at Xie Qingcheng, his eyes weren't pure at all. Rather, they burned hotter and more blatant than the lover's desire that was currently being portrayed on camera by an award-winning actor. At once coldly gloomy and searingly hot, it was as though something was slowly simmering over a tiny flame in his heart, gradually heating up to a boil. He turned his face to the side, the jut of his throat bobbing silently as he swallowed.

Xie Qingcheng walked into a break tent to sit down, and He Yu immediately came up with an excuse for the director and left to follow Xie Qingcheng into the tent. When Xie Qingcheng looked up and caught sight of him entering, the already coldly detached expression in his eyes cooled several more degrees, sheening with frost.

He Yu felt a surge of annoyance as soon as he entered the tent. He'd wanted to find a chance to speak with Xie Qingcheng alone; he hadn't expected that a small crowd of resting crew members would all be sitting around the makeshift plastic table inside the tent.

"Are there any more seats?"

"There's a stool over here." Seeing a handsome young man come in—and the director's assistant to boot—one of the crew members stood up at once. She grabbed a plastic stool from the corner, wiped it off, and handed it to He Yu.

"Thank you."

The crew member blushed. But she might as well have blushed for a blind man, because He Yu merely took the stool and sat down across from Xie Qingcheng.

Everyone was seated around a long table, which was piled high with miscellaneous items. There were even several crew members shoveling takeout into their mouths.

He Yu liked cleanliness, so he wouldn't usually want to stay in such a messy place for very long. But sitting right across from Xie Qingcheng, his eyes didn't take in a single speck of dust—all he could see was Xie Qingcheng's face as he looked down and fiddled with his phone.

Xie Qingcheng seemed to have decided to pointedly avoid looking at him, as if he would much rather stare down at his phone screen than spare He Yu half a glance.

He Yu looked him over. In this moment, all those thoughts— "I need to quit this person," "I won't get addicted to Xie Qingcheng again," "Xie Qingcheng is an ugly, poor, divorced, chain-smoking old man"—disappeared from his mind. So many people's breaths mixed together in the air, but it seemed like he could only smell the cool scent of disinfectant on Xie Qingcheng's body.

That was a scent he lusted for deeply.

As He Yu stared at him, his gaze became less and less innocent. If that gaze could materialize into touch, He Yu might have already unbuttoned Xie Qingcheng's suit.

It was unfortunate that a human's gaze was always honest. It was unsophisticated and candid, oblivious to self-concealment, and could not become an accomplice to the inner self. Furthermore, it was completely incapable of committing offenses such as stripping off someone's clothes.

In the past, He Yu had never thought that he would want something like this. Before, he'd always felt rather indifferent toward people, and he looked down on the other highborn sons in his circle who lost themselves to alcohol and the pleasures of the body. He had never realized that carnal desire could make a person so helpless to stop.

Since Xie Qingcheng wouldn't look at him, he bowed his head and sent him a message.

Doctor Xie. Are you pretending you can't see me?

Xie Qingcheng's phone vibrated.

He'd clearly seen the message.

He Yu waited.

But Xie Qingcheng didn't reply.

The weeds in his heart started sprouting in a riot of overgrown greenery. The more Xie Qingcheng ignored him, the stronger the oppressive feeling in his heart became, and the more liable he was to do something unhinged.

He Yu was truly audacious—in this crowded place, he even dared to send Xie Qingcheng some of those "good morning" couple photos that he'd photoshopped.

This time, He Yu saw Xie Qingcheng's knuckles turn white as his hand tightened around his phone. The lines on his face tensed up in tandem, his entire body emanating the aura of an ice-cold, dangerously sharp blade.

This reaction soothed the shadowy perversion in He Yu's heart a little. Extending a long leg, he slowly nudged Xie Qingcheng's foot under the table, again and again.

Xie Qingcheng finally looked up. His eyes were extremely cutting, but even though his expression was unsightly, he was still unexpectedly calm—he didn't want to lose his temper with He Yu. After all, what use was there in getting angry with an animal?

He gazed indifferently back at He Yu as if he were staring at a beast in rut.

Under that stare, He Yu inexplicably remembered that after he'd forced Xie Qingcheng into an unbearably wretched state, he had once said to him:

"Don't you know the biggest difference between humans and animals? Humans can control themselves."

Xie Qingcheng hadn't said anything, yet He Yu felt he could read these words in his eyes once more.

For some reason, he suddenly felt a wave of intense resentment— He'd had self-control before, but Xie Qingcheng was the one who had torn it to shreds. Shouldn't he shoulder the blame? When Xie Qingcheng's face had gone slack on his pillow, how was he any different from a female beast that had been deeply marked and lost all sense of reason? How could he have the face to look at him so indifferently?

Xie Qingcheng tried to move his foot away, only for He Yu's leg to emphatically block his way.

Both of them paused for a moment.

Everyone sitting at the table was very relaxed. Whether they were chatting, eating, or browsing their phones, each person minded their own business. No one noticed the turbulent undercurrent on their end, or the surreptitious entanglement beneath the table.

He Yu stared deeply into Xie Qingcheng's eyes, as if he wanted his gaze to burrow into the man's pupils... Even he was confused as to why this man could drive him to this.

A fierce vindictiveness suddenly rose within him.

He looked down and typed:

Since when were Doctor Xie's legs so strong? They weren't like this when we were together before—were you just pretending you had no strength left because you actually liked how I treated you?

Oh yeah, Xie-ge, does Young Master Chen know that we've slept together before? Does he know what you looked like when we were doing it?

The more he typed, the more outrageous his words became.

If those high-level Huzhou University administrators who had given He Yu all those awards knew that the boy they'd selected as one of the "top ten outstanding male students," "chairman of the student government," "model first-year student," "scholarship recipient of distinguished learning and virtues," who had received endless compliments and medals, was able to compose such vulgar messages, Their Esteemed Elderlinesses' eyeglasses would probably shatter into a million pieces in their shock.

The moment I saw that Chen Man, I could tell he doesn't suit you at all. If you're with him because of his status, then you might as well forget about it. Be good and come with me—just tell me if there's anything that you want. Anything he can give you, I can give you too.

A dull *smack*.

Xie Qingcheng slammed his phone heavily onto the table, so hard that everyone around them froze and turned to stare at him.

Xie Qingcheng hadn't planned on making a fuss in public, but he was simply so furious he hadn't been able to hold himself back.

However, he didn't want to put on a show for their onlookers right now either, so in the end he just stared wordlessly at He Yu for a few seconds with the utmost self-restraint and chilliness, then got up to leave.

Just then, the curtain of the tent rose and fell again as another person walked in. Xie Qingcheng's eyes flickered briefly.

He Yu was sitting with his back to the entrance, but seeing Xie Qingcheng's expression, he guessed that Chen Man had likewise walked in to take a break.

He had absolutely no desire to see Young Master Chen right now, to the point that he wished he could get his hands on a dimensionality reduction eraser[6] and completely wipe Chen Man's existence from this world.

So he didn't look back.

Not until the other man's voice rang out. "...So you're here too, Doctor Xie."

It was the low, husky voice of an adult man, one who also gave off the scent of disinfectant.

He Yu finally turned around to see a meticulously dressed man standing at the entrance. He looked around thirty-five or thirty-six years old. He had his hands in his pockets, his attitude steady and his expression gentle.

The man's gaze shifted to land on He Yu's face.

He raised his brows slightly. "So many familiar faces in this production. It really is a big one—Cousin, you're here as well?"

Xie Qingcheng had merely been surprised to see this man at first, but now, upon hearing him call He Yu "Cousin," even the highly composed doctor couldn't conceal a look of shock.

---

6   Online slang derived from the "dimensionality reduction" weapon from Liu Cixin's novel The Three-Body Problem; typically used to describe a cheap trick to defeat an enemy.

Back when Xie Qingcheng had come down with a fever after being tormented by He Yu for an entire night, this man was the one who had treated him in overnight urgent care—he was the director of Huzhou First Hospital's emergency department.

And he also happened to be He Yu's older cousin.

They were distant cousins, and because they weren't very closely related by blood, their families didn't see each other often. He Jiwei's relationship with his family's elders was quite stiff, so they only saw each other once in a while at large family gatherings. They were utterly indifferent to each other, their relationship even more superficial than that of random neighbors; He Yu hadn't even known that this cousin was a doctor at Huzhou First Hospital.

Since He Yu didn't know, of course Xie Qingcheng wouldn't know either.

Huzhou First Hospital was very big, so its staff members weren't necessarily all familiar with one another. The director wasn't particularly close to Xie Qingcheng, as they'd only consulted together and seen each other at medical conferences a handful of times.

However, despite their scant interactions, Xie Qingcheng had always found him relatively agreeable. He never could've imagined that this emergency department director was actually He Yu's distant cousin...

78

I TOOK ON A SEX SCENE

THE EMERGENCY DEPARTMENT director was on set to give guidance on parts of the movie set in a hospital emergency room. However, there weren't many scenes that required his direct oversight, so he'd be returning to the hospital in a few days' time.

Now that his elder cousin had appeared, He Yu couldn't blow him off, no matter how distant their relationship was.

At the same time, an actor needed to ask Xie Qingcheng about something related to his field—an assistant ran over to request his presence, so Xie Qingcheng left.

He Yu left the tent with his cousin to walk around the area.

The director also smoked and smelled faintly of disinfectant, but for some reason he didn't smell like Xie Qingcheng—He Yu found his scent unpleasantly sharp.

"You know Xie Qingcheng too," the director said—a statement rather than a question.

"Someone in the family told you?"

The director took a drag of his cigarette. "No. I read it in the papers. The reports about what happened at Huzhou University were very detailed. When those old videos were dug up, most people thought he had been discredited for good. Yet you're still so close to him?"

He Yu didn't respond to the director's question, but he realized something: if his cousin worked at Huzhou First Hospital, he might know some concrete details about what had happened back then.

"Were you there?" He Yu asked. "When the two videos were filmed?"

"You sure asked the right person. I was."

"Then, at the time..."

"It was exactly the same as what you saw in the videos; he wasn't misrepresented. What did you think? That the videos were edited?" The director arched a brow, shooting He Yu a mocking glance.

The two of them walked shoulder to shoulder.

After a while, the director added, "That said, I for one feel that Xie Qingcheng is much too elusive. It's like he's always been hiding some secret, something he doesn't want people to know about."

"... Is that what you think?"

"Mm-hm. People are often psychologically tense when they have something weighing on their mind. He's exceptionally calm and self-disciplined for all 365 days of the year—not a second goes by when he isn't on full alert. That's a textbook example of someone with a heavy mental load." The director flicked away some cigarette ash. "But if you really want to know, you should just ask him. Surely the difficulties you faced together at the Huzhou broadcasting tower brought you closer."

It would've been fine if he hadn't mentioned that issue, but the moment he did, He Yu's eyes darkened once more.

"What, he won't even tell *you*?" asked the director.

"No," He Yu replied. "We're not that close."

Thanks to his conversation with the director, by the time they wrapped for the day, He Yu's state of mind was truly dismal.

He didn't return to the hotel in the film director's car. The tent they'd used today wasn't all that far from their rooms to begin with, so he just stayed with the emergency department director. The two cousins took a leisurely stroll back.

He Yu never expected to spot Xie Qingcheng and Chen Man sharing a midnight snack as they passed a collection of night market stalls along the way.

Evidently, the director noticed as well.

Sitting at that greasy little night market stall, Xie Qingcheng was truly too eye-catching. With his cold, aloof aura and ramrod-straight posture, it was very difficult for him to disappear into a crowd. It seemed like he wanted to smoke a cigarette, but Chen Man was trying to persuade him against it, even going so far as to grab his lighter from him. Ignoring him, Xie Qingcheng got up and went over to the next table to ask a man with a sleeve tattoo for a light, who lit the end with a *click*.

Chen Man could only return his lighter.

"I've seen that guy before," said the director. "He's a cop."

"He's a cop who doesn't have a single badge on his shoulders," He Yu corrected him.

The director stared at them for a bit. "I *thought* he looked famil-iar last time I saw him... He's the grandson of Yanzhou's Political Commissar Wang, isn't he?"

Though Chen Man didn't usually mention his background, he was still the grandson of a founding party member and similar to him in status, a thought that had made He Yu uncomfortable every time it had crossed his mind over the last few days.

The director wasn't done yet, though. He continued blandly, "Are they a couple?"

He Yu turned toward him with a blank expression. "A couple of what?"

The director raised his eyebrow. "What other kinds of couples are there?"

"...Why do you ask?"

"Last time I was on call in the ER, Xie Qingcheng came in with a fever. This cop was the one who accompanied him. Nurse Zhou said there was another time when this Young Master Chen watched over him while he received an IV drip." Despite their veneer of propriety, these doctors were unexpectedly gossipy. "They didn't admit it, but I even saw hickeys on Xie Qingcheng last time. The way that little cop kept at it until his lover had a high fever and had to go to the hospital...I suspect that even though he looks well-behaved, he's probably a violent maniac."

The violent maniac listened expressionlessly without speaking a single word. But his heart simmered with displeasure. *He* was the one who left those kiss marks—they were evidence of how fervently they'd fucked. What the hell did they have to do with Chen Man?

After bidding his cousin goodbye and returning to the hotel, He Yu's bloodthirsty and irascible desire only intensified.

As the elevator doors opened, he walked toward his room, hoping to avoid encountering any living souls so that his desire for violent conflict wouldn't have the opportunity to rear its head. However, as he approached his room, he just so happened to see that the door to Xie Qingcheng's room was open. There was a push cart standing just outside the door—likely because Xie Qingcheng had called housekeeping and asked them to come and clean the bathtub.

He Yu was very familiar with Xie Qingcheng's fondness for baths. Back when Xie Qingcheng had stayed at his house, on extremely busy work days, he would usually take a hot bath in the evening to unwind after spending the entire day on edge.

As expected, when he tilted his head slightly to the side, he could see a housekeeping attendant scrubbing away in the bathroom.

He Yu paused.

He knew that Xie Qingcheng and Chen Man had yet to become involved physically. Xie Qingcheng simply didn't believe that Chen Man was gay, so never mind cleaning the bathtub, even a change of bedsheets wouldn't necessarily mean that they'd engaged in any filthy activities together.

Well. Xie Qingcheng might not be filthy, but Chen Man was way too much of a sleaze. Chen Man had tried to steal a kiss from Xie Qingcheng, He Yu thought with cold detachment.

He Yu felt that if you were truly a man, you ought to kiss him openly and without any tricks. If worse came to worst, you'd get slapped in the face and cursed out. But in the end? Chen Man didn't dare.

Even amongst gays, He Yu thought darkly to himself, this Young Master Chen was a useless piece of trash.

But he still felt very uncomfortable. When he thought about how Xie Qingcheng would be bathing in this very room with Chen Man right outside, he felt uncomfortable from head to toe.

To prevent his mood from deteriorating even further, He Yu looked away, fully intending to head back to his own room. But as he turned his head, he caught sight of the two beds inside their room.

Both of the beds were very neatly made, but even so, it was very easy to tell which one belonged to Chen Man. That was because Chen Man had tossed a PSP and a police uniform onto his bed.

Chen Man's bed was the one pressed to the wall...

Ashen faced, the very first thing He Yu did upon returning to his own room and slamming the door shut was to roll up his sleeves and move his bed, which he had spent considerable effort in shoving against the wall the night before, back into its original place. He absolutely refused to be so close to Young Master Chen.

Unbearably moody, He Yu heard the housekeeping attendant next door prepare to leave. Who knew what exactly he was thinking—perhaps he'd suffered a brain spasm—but he went and called the attendant over.

"Is there something I can do for you, sir?"

With an outwardly calm expression, He Yu said, "Could I trouble you to help me clean my bathtub as well? Thank you."

Once the housekeeping attendant left, just like Xie Qingcheng, He Yu took a bath. He lay in the tub, savoring the warm pressure of the water, as if it could fill the gaping cavity inside his chest.

He hadn't turned on the bathroom lights. Closing his eyes in the darkness, he lay there for a long time, the warm water rippling quietly around him.

Chen Man's identity.

His cousin's words. Xie Qingcheng's receding figure, cold and forbidding...

"It's like he's always been hiding some secret..."

"People are tense when they have something weighing on their mind."

"He won't even tell you?"

"Surely the difficulties you faced together at the Huzhou broadcasting tower brought you closer."

"Are they a couple?"

"I even saw hickeys on Xie Qingcheng last time..."

He Yu's breathing grew heavier and heavier as an ache tore into his heart and thoroughly extinguished whatever thoughts he'd once had about trying to quit the drug that was Xie Qingcheng. He resented him, had endless contempt for him, but in the end, he couldn't resist the rampant lust of youth.

It was even more difficult to suppress than the violent bloodlust stemming from his illness. He could still control his impulse to hurt people, but he couldn't restrain his ruthless desire to possess Xie Qingcheng.

He was unable to pry a single honest word out of Xie Qingcheng's deceptive, lying mouth; Xie Qingcheng simply refused to tell him anything. But at least in bed, when Xie Qingcheng was dazed from his ministrations, the expressions on his face were honest, just as the emotions within his grasp were completely unadulterated and true.

He doubted that Xie Qingcheng had ever acted like this with Li Ruoqiu. If that was true, then the only person in the world who had ever seen Xie Qingcheng in such a state was He Yu himself.

This thought finally gave him a bit of relief from the pressure of his physical and mental strain.

But after clearing his mind, changing into fresh clothes, and walking out of the bathroom, He Yu glanced at his reflection and found himself thinking that the lonely boy standing in the mirror with water dripping from the ends of his hair seemed pretty pathetic.

"He-laoshi, are you there?"

Just as he finished blow-drying his hair, someone knocked on the door. These days, many people had the habit of calling those they didn't know well "laoshi."

He Yu opened the door to see Executive Huang's assistant standing outside.

"What is it?"

"Oh, it's just a few things." The assistant pushed her glasses up—she was still very nervous around He Yu. "Here's the script and the schedule for the next few days. There's also this—the list of characters with just a handful of lines and scenes. Executive Huang said that they were originally planning on finding some experienced extras to play these parts—he was wondering if you might be interested in picking a role to try out."

Because the executive producer Mr. Huang Zhilong was paying him special attention, and because his mother, Lü Zhishu, had called Executive Huang and implored him again and again to give He Yu opportunities to gain different types of practical experience...

In addition to He Yu's daily routine of shadowing the director, Executive Huang had also arranged a cameo role for him.

He Yu took the thick stack of papers. "Thank you for your hard work."

That evening, He Yu lay alone on his bed and spent a long time reading the script. Executive Huang's assistant had very considerately highlighted the cameo scenes in different colors and even made a table of contents, so looking through it wasn't tedious at all.

After he'd finished reading everything, He Yu sent a message to Huang Zhilong with all of his usual politeness, thanking Executive Huang for going out of his way to look after him.

Then he told him which cameo role he was interested in taking.

The moment Executive Huang saw the character's name, he was struck dumb. He'd thought that role would be the first one He Yu crossed off the list.

You're not joking with me, are you, Xiao-He?

I'm serious.

The slightly rumpled bed was covered in papers. In the end, He Yu had circled and selected one of the cameo roles that had been marked on the schedule for the day after tomorrow. Next to that character's name, there was a line of shocking scarlet words spelling out a highlighted reminder:

This role is featured in a sex scene.

Meanwhile, clearly written in the notes column of the schedule:

A psychiatrist will serve as the technical consultant for this scene. The expert for this day: Xie Qingcheng.

79

YOU WATCHED ME PUT ON A PERFORMANCE

XIE QINGCHENG AND HE YU sat facing each other inside the small temporary rest tent.

Chances were good that Executive Huang was secretly over the moon that He Yu had taken on this thorny role, one that had caused the production team no small measure of grief.

This kind of role had very little screen time and was nothing more than a minor walk-on part, but its difficulty was astronomical. Plus, it included a significant sex scene, which made it automatically objectionable to a lot of people. When the casting director tried to enlist students from the film school, most of them refused. While they could recruit someone from among the extras, the results would likely be extremely cringeworthy. Not to mention, the screenwriter had described the character as being "a handsome crime boss with a gently refined appearance and noble bearing"—where could they possibly find a minor supporting actor fitting these requirements in such a short amount of time? It was an extremely irksome problem.

When He Yu said that he'd do it, it was akin to the sky bestowing sweet rain after a long drought. How could Executive Huang not burn incense and thank Executive Lü profusely?

A lot of detailed work went into filming a sex scene. Prior to the beginning of the shoot, everything had to be discussed in very clear terms—To strip or not to strip? How to go about stripping?

Where should the discarded articles of clothing go? What kinds of emotions should the actors portray? Should they be passionate? Teasing? Urgent? Restrained? Highly experienced and completely in control? Inexperienced and completely ignorant of what to do? All of these things had to be hashed out in concrete terms before the cameras began to roll.

Before the shoot began, the director especially sought out He Yu to communicate all of this to him. After their chat, the director's eyes practically welled up with tears. Where did Executive Huang find such a lifesaver?

He Yu had virtually no conditions and accepted all the requirements that the director cautiously brought up with perfect cooperation. He said that he was studying what went on behind the cameras and understood the difficulties that directors faced very well, especially the pride of craftsmanship that arose when the director sought to execute their work with perfection.

The only condition he raised was that he wanted a long one-on-one chat with the scene's psychiatric specialist, Xie Qingcheng.

"As you know, I don't have any experience." He Yu spoke with extreme humility, as if he'd morphed the words "Pure and Kind of Heart" into clothing and draped them over himself. "I'm very anxious about causing trouble for everyone, so I want to ask Professor Xie to give me some pointers about this scene beforehand."

He seemed so pure that he was too embarrassed to even say the words "sex scene." Everyone felt that they were seriously burdening Young Master He with this. Look at what a virtuous child he was— he was basically sacrificing the sanctity of his body for art. Since the child had such a minor request, how could the director refuse? He immediately asked Xie Qingcheng to come over and give him private psychological guidance.

This was an outdoor scene that involved a crime boss having an affair with his nemesis's wife.

It was an affair that was doomed to fail, as that woman did like the young, handsome man, but she was already the mother of three children and wife to a seriously ill husband; she couldn't abandon her family. She gradually calmed down from the honeymoon phase of the affair, and so, despite her heartache, she intended to break up with her lover. But the man refused: he parked the car at the deserted outskirts of town and fucked her.

Through it all, the crime boss and his illicit paramour both loved each other deeply, but thanks to all the conflicting and complicated dynamics at play, that love had become thoroughly twisted.

The crime boss had been a psychiatrist before returning to his home country to take over his father's turf, so he was very skilled at enticing women with words. Thus, she went from rejection to reciprocation, then ultimately ended up completely limp in her lover's arms. However, she was unable to endure the double torment of the pain and joy growing vigorously in her heart, and she chose to take her own life shortly after returning home.

The winter wind was very strong, so the production crew had set up several temporary tents near the abandoned road. He Yu and Xie Qingcheng were inside one of those very tents, with a thick, heavy curtain hanging over the door. Since everyone knew they were talking business, no one came in.

Xie Qingcheng smoked as the rain poured outside. Winter nights in the mountains were incredibly cold, and the evening's chill rendered his face so bloodless that the flickering glow of his cigarette was the brightest spot of color on his body.

"How does Professor Xie think such a mentally deranged sex scene ought to be performed?"

Xie Qingcheng's face was completely devoid of expression. "No idea."

He Yu smiled as he suddenly took the cigarette from Xie Qingcheng's hands, holding it between his slender fingers. Then he dipped his head, moving in to kiss Xie Qingcheng on the lips.

Xie Qingcheng's hand shot up to grab him by the wrist. "Have some self-respect."

"What do you mean? You're the one who refuses to teach me, so I'll just have to teach myself using your body."

Xie Qingcheng flung his hand away.

"This role was made for you." Xie Qingcheng shot He Yu a cold glance from across the faintly flickering kerosene lamp. "You don't need me to teach you. When it comes to this type of beastly behavior, a psychiatrist like me would be no better than any armchair psychologist. Unlike you, He Yu—you've had firsthand experience."

Xie Qingcheng's words were cutting. He Yu gazed quietly at him for a while before bringing the cigarette he'd snatched from Xie Qingcheng to his mouth. Slowly, maintaining unflinching eye contact, he bit the moistened filter. He even went so far as to press the tip of his tongue against the place where Xie Qingcheng's mouth had been and lick across the surface. He took a deep drag.

As he exhaled the smoke, he pulled the cigarette away and brought it back to Xie Qingcheng's lips. Lowering his gaze, he said, "Since you've put it that way, I'll just have to accept it without reservation. By the way...this cigarette smells awful. Are you going to keep smoking it?"

Of course Xie Qingcheng wouldn't smoke a cigarette that had been in He Yu's mouth. Under He Yu's keen gaze, he took the cigarette and stubbed it out on the table with a hiss, right next to He Yu's hand.

He Yu made no reply, nor did he look away from Xie Qingcheng. After a moment of silence, his gaze stroked over Xie Qingcheng's pale, tobacco-laced lips as he whispered, "Xie Qingcheng, are you really so determined to avoid me? Too bad, because you can't.

"To be honest, I didn't plan on getting any advice from you on a madman's mindset during a sex scene. But I have to be alone with you for a while before the shoot, and then during the scene, I'll need to have you in my sight the whole time. That's the only way I'll be able to perform to the best of my ability.

"There's nothing that can help me get into character better than your face. Whenever I look at you, Doctor Xie, I think of what we did all those nights—how you trembled and shook, how enthusiastically you moved your hips, how alluring you looked when you cursed at me in your rage..."

Xie Qingcheng looked up, gazing at him without the slightest bit of warmth in his eyes. Under normal circumstances, someone as calm as Xie Qingcheng would not become enraged so easily.

He Yu had just been putting on a show of "I Am a Pure and Innocent Virgin Who Is Eager to Learn" for the director, yet now, he was prattling on arrogantly like some kind of animal. However, Xie Qingcheng's only reaction was to lift his eyes and say—

"Why don't you take some fever-reducing medicine? If you show up to the set like this, I can't help but worry for the actress who's partnering with you for this scene."

Although his mouth said "worry," his eyes were filled only with cold ridicule.

He Yu fell silent in an instant. A few beats later, he looked over at Xie Qingcheng with dark, icy eyes. "So *now* you care about me. Back then, when I sent you all those messages, I thought that even if I ended up dying from my illness, perhaps you wouldn't give me a single word in response."

"Is there something wrong with your ears?" Xie Qingcheng replied, his voice glacial. "I'm worrying about your co-star, not you."

He Yu truly wanted to slap Xie Qingcheng across the face, then let him know that he was on the verge of being frustrated and tormented to death. Fucking hell, yet there Xie Qingcheng was, still making sneering quips.

But what use was there in slapping him?

Back at the club, he'd kicked Xie Qingcheng so hard in the chest that he couldn't even get up for a long time. And still, Xie Qingcheng had just looked at him with that calm, unyielding gaze.

What could a slap solve? What could it salvage?

And so He Yu only grinned with a bit of sinister roguishness and pressed closer. "Then why don't *you* help me reduce my fever?"

Xie Qingcheng glanced at his watch. "There's fifteen minutes until filming starts. Given your prowess, there's probably time for three rounds. So it's not completely impossible."

He Yu's expression darkened, his features shifting as he clenched his jaw. Xie Qingcheng really was trying to infuriate him to death with that calm demeanor of his.

"You're talking all sorts of nonsense today," he spat. "It's been so long since I've been alone with you that you've even forgotten about how last time, you couldn't handle it and straight up passed out. Doctor Xie is so forgetful in his middle-age, looks like I'd better work on reinforcing your memories."

Xie Qingcheng adjusted his watch and replied coolly, "I'm afraid you won't have many opportunities to do so in the coming days. Have fun with work."

With that, he rose to leave.

He Yu wanted to stop him, but he thought that might make him seem a little too pathetic. His fingertips twitched slightly as he resisted the impulse.

He stood in the depths of the tent, staring hard at the man's silhouette. "Xie Qingcheng, did you know? I really want to film a sex scene with you. I'll be thinking of your face during the scene, so make sure you get a good look from the director's monitor—no matter who I'm acting with, the partner I'm thinking about will always be you."

Xie Qingcheng stood before the insulated curtain that he'd lifted partway to finish listening to He Yu's spiel, then he made his clinical diagnosis: "If it gets over forty degrees, you should go see your cousin for urgent care. Don't give yourself brain damage."

Then he left without a backward glance, leaving He Yu alone with an unfathomable expression on his face in the tent that still held a faint trace of his tobacco scent.

The greatest skill this beast named He Yu possessed was the fact that he could talk dirty one moment, without batting an eye, then change his tune in the next moment and put on a perfect show of gentility and refinement to interact with outsiders.

Xie Qingcheng did have to watch He Yu's performance through the monitor in the creative director's tent.

Before filming began, He Yu went to check in with the screenwriters. It was well lit here, putting his face on full display. The stylist had done his makeup in a soft and refined style, and his lips curved in a gently meaningful smile when he shot a glance in Xie Qingcheng's direction.

He really did seem shy and embarrassed to be shooting his first-ever sex scene.

"Relax," said Executive Huang.

Hu Yi laughed. "Ha ha ha ha, Young Master He, we'll be clearing the area in a short while and you won't be undressing too much, so don't worry."

He Yu thanked them all in turn, but when he got to Xie Qingcheng, he suddenly came to a stop.

He stared fixedly at him. Then, as everyone looked on, he said to Xie Qingcheng with perfect courtesy, "Doctor Xie, thank you very much for your guidance earlier. I hope that my performance will not let you down."

Only Xie Qingcheng and He Yu knew how many sordid secrets, like clandestine messages transmitted in Morse code, were hidden within those courteous words. Xie Qingcheng couldn't say much in front of all these people. Cigarette in hand, he stood there with his back ramrod-straight, dark eyes gazing calmly at He Yu.

"I'll be waiting with bated breath."

He Yu glanced down, a smile at the corners of his lips, as he turned to the side. Then, with an assistant holding an umbrella behind him, he brushed past Xie Qingcheng and walked onto the finished set.

It was easy for a sex scene to feel awkward, so the director had cleared out the area and told everyone who wasn't directly involved to leave. Next to the car, in the pouring rain, the director clutched the screenplay in his hand and went over the scene one last time with He Yu and his scene partner. Then, after giving the two actors some words of encouragement, he turned off his microphone and had them climb into the car where they were going to perform, leaving them to get comfortable with each other for a while.

The production team had gone through considerable effort to hire this actress. Although she was a C-lister, her combination of looks and experience made her the best candidate the production staff could find.

The woman she was playing planned on breaking up with her lover during their final secret rendezvous.

That day, her character had been sitting in the hotel in a strappy red nightgown, her hair still mussed, when she suddenly said that she wanted to take a drive and get a breath of fresh air. She got into the man's car and the two of them drove in wordless silence for a long time before she finally told him her thoughts. The man slammed on the brakes, and then the car sex scene would ensue.

Although the actress had played many types of characters before and had a wealth of experience, this was her first time acting in a sex scene. She was quite nervous and couldn't look He Yu in the eye as she sat in the passenger's seat and fiddled with her hair. However, as she twirled the strands in her fingers, she remembered that He Yu was so much younger than her—still a student, even—and that, as his senior, she should at least try to look after him.

So she cleared her throat, made an effort to calm herself down, and began to make small talk.

"Hey kid, are you nervous?"

He Yu smiled. "I'm all right. About the same as you."

"It's okay, just pretend the camera isn't there. Don't worry too much."

"Thank you."

Seeing that the younger man wasn't all that tense, the actress also relaxed slightly. She finally found the courage to meet He Yu's eyes. "Have you ever had a girlfriend?"

Although He Yu seemed like a very friendly person, his aura of distant propriety was quite apparent as well. He smiled and didn't respond.

The actress chattered on anyway. "A friend once told me that if you've been in a relationship before, if you really can't get into the scene, you can close your eyes and try to think of your lover."

He Yu said very gently, "Okay. Thank you."

The actress blinked, blushing slightly.

The time they'd been given passed very quickly. The two of them chatted about nothing of consequence for a little longer, then the director called for the official start of the first take.

The beginning of the scene was focused on the actress's monologue. She had no problems with this section and put on a passionate performance—as she spoke, she began to weep, and was crying so hard by the end that her words were completely choked with sobs.

Falling rain drummed against the windows as He Yu pulled up the handbrake and coldly turned toward her. "Are you finished?"

"Let me out of the car. I want to leave."

She unbuckled her seatbelt and went to open the door, but He Yu locked it without a word and pulled her back. "You really hate me this much? Do you really have to treat me in this way?"

The actress cried, "I'm a mother! I have a husband and children, and my husband is your rival—do you know how painful these past few days have been for me? Can't you spare me, and spare yourself too?"

"You don't love your husband at all," said He Yu. "Your marriage was a mistake from the very beginning—that much should be clear to you."

The woman didn't listen to him. She wept as she kept trying to pry open the car door, saying quietly, "I have to go back."

"If you insist on leaving, I'll have him killed at once, but if you stay with me, I'll allow him to linger at death's door for a while longer. You better sit down—if you dare get out of this car and go back to him, I'll run you over right here and now."

Startled and angry, the actress stared into her lover's face in disbelief, as if she was seeing him clearly for the first time. "Why... why are you doing this? You're a complete madman!"

"Cut!" The director interrupted them. "Qianqian, your emotions here aren't right."

Qianqian was the name of her character—the director usually called the actors by their characters' names to help them immerse themselves in the role.

The actress slowly pulled herself back to reality, wiped her tears, and obediently listened to the director's feedback with an open mind. Unfortunately, the director was a pedantic and showy intellectual with a heavy Fujian accent, while the actress was a northerner. It took quite a bit of effort for them to communicate, like a chicken trying to hold a conversation with a duck.

In the end, He Yu got the gist of what the director meant. "Let me," he said. He turned to the actress. "Jie, did you have any issues with your lines?"

"I didn't."

"You see," He Yu said very patiently, "The screenplay says you're very confused and hurt, but at your core, you're a strong-willed and clever person. When you mentioned breaking up, my reaction wasn't outside your expectations. Even though you were a bit shocked that I said something as extreme as 'if you leave, I'll kill you,' you've seen me kill many people before and are perfectly aware of how ruthless I am, so your degree of shock actually shouldn't be that high."

"B-but just now, that's exactly how I tried to play it," the actress said.

Perhaps the issue lay in how northerners and southerners tended to display a different level of intensity in their personalities. After thinking it over, He Yu spoke briefly to the director through his microphone. Then he said to the actress, "Wait here for a moment. I'm going to the tent to ask about the specifics."

The actress chimed in, "Then I'll also—"

"Just sit." He Yu closed the car door for her. Even though she had an assistant to help her, the rain was currently too heavy and her nightdress was too long and unwieldy—it'd be a nuisance if she got mud on it. "I'll go," he said.

He Yu returned to the director's tent. The creative director and his crew were all sitting in front of the screens. Xie Qingcheng was in the furthest corner, his expression unreadable.

He Yu glanced at Xie Qingcheng, but it wasn't the time for flirting. Quickly turning his attention to the director and Hu Yi, he spent some time discussing something with them in hushed whispers.

All three of them worked behind the scenes and were attuned to nuances in language, so the discussion wasn't frustrating in the least. He Yu wrapped up their talk quickly and was about to return to the set, but his hand hadn't even touched the insulated curtain when someone lifted that curtain from the outside and stepped in.

It was Chen Man, who was with Group B today at a nearby location.

Having run into He Yu, Young Master Chen shot him a smile while He Yu indifferently sized him up, his gaze finally landing on the takeout caddy of warm drinks that he was carrying.

"Xie-ge's stomach isn't all that good and it's way too cold out here, so I bought some warm milk. We're wrapping things up over there." Chen Man was impatient by nature while He Yu was silent, so Chen Man ended up explaining the situation like a rapid-firing machine gun. Then he turned and walked, with a slightly bent back, to Xie Qingcheng's side.

"Ge, here—to help you warm up."

He Yu turned to glance at them. Xie Qingcheng also seemed surprised by Chen Man's arrival, but he couldn't resist the allure of warm drinks and took the paper cup that Chen Man handed him.

"The straws are here," said Chen Man quietly. "How much longer do you guys have..."

"We've just started. You can head back on your own."

"It's okay, I'll wait for you."

Even though he spoke in a low voice, He Yu heard everything with perfect clarity.

There was a soft rustling noise. He Yu had suddenly dropped the insulated curtain, no longer intending to leave. He turned back to the director and said something softly into his ear with his eyes lowered.

The director was a bit surprised. "Are you sure? I deliberately cleared out the area."

"The lighting crew is still there," He Yu said calmly. "So a few more doesn't matter. You have to look at the screens so you can't leave, but Professor Xie and the others should watch on site. That way, if a problem arises, we can make adjustments faster and have better outcomes."

Their savior was genuinely thinking of the quality of the performance—the director was greatly moved. He agreed to the request, and thus got up and turned around, pointing out the individuals that He Yu had requested to go and watch the scene onsite.

"Hu-laoshi, Xiao-Zhang, Professor Xie, head over to the set with He Yu for a bit."

Xie Qingcheng raised his head, his gaze moving past Chen Man and landing on where He Yu was busy putting on airs. He Yu actually seemed fairly indifferent. He didn't look at Xie Qingcheng at all, even though his expression seemed to give off a hint of malice.

...Yes, he was making it very clear that he wouldn't allow Chen Man and Xie Qingcheng to sit together.

Assistant Zhang and Hu-laoshi had already risen to their feet, and finally, Xie Qingcheng straightened up as well.

Xie Qingcheng had already sensed He Yu's provocative demeanor—he knew he was deliberately making trouble for him. He didn't want to involve Chen Man, and more importantly, he didn't want He Yu to say anything inflammatory in front of Chen Man. He turned to the man and, barely moving his lips, said, "You should just head back."

And then, bringing up the rear, he followed He Yu, who didn't even spare him a backward glance, to the site of the outdoor sex scene.

80

You Heard Me Share Our Secrets

THE RAIN WAS POURING down at the outdoor shooting location. The crew had set up a tarp for people to stand under to avoid being rained on. Luckily, not many people were still on set, so it wasn't that crowded.

He Yu got back into the car and relayed the results of their discussion to the actress. "We deleted part of a line."

"Which one?"

He pointed at the script in her hand. "This one."

The actress read the line out loud. "Why...why are you doing this? You're a complete madman!"

"Right, you only need to say the last sentence," He Yu said. "There shouldn't be too many emotional ups and downs, and your voice should be a bit softer. Change the surprise to despondency—you've failed to communicate with your lover, and he can't understand your suffering. Give it a try."

The actress mulled over the line, mumbling under her breath. Then she looked at He Yu and said softly, "You're a complete madman..."

He Yu nodded, and spoke through his microphone: "Director, let's try it again."

This take was much smoother—it still wasn't an eighty- or ninety-point performance, but the two of them carried out the emotionally charged conversation to an acceptable standard, at least.

The actress was taken aback. After the director called for another cut, she asked He Yu, "How did you know that approaching it this way would work? Have you acted in this kind of scene before?"

"I haven't."

"So then how..."

"I've met someone with this kind of attitude before."

He Yu paused, casting his gaze slightly to the side to land on Xie Qingcheng, who was standing behind the light reflector. Xie Qingcheng's face was completely devoid of expression, as if he hadn't even watched the performance. His head was lowered as he fiddled with his phone—chances are he was texting Chen Man.

He Yu withdrew his gaze, his gloominess intensifying.

After regrouping briefly, they began to work on the second part of the scene.

This part was the sex scene.

This car sex scene was to be filmed in one continuous shot. After being firmly rejected by Ai Qianqian again, He Yu's character would be furious, and the two of them would begin to struggle. Under his provocation, Ai Qianqian lost control of her emotions, and in the midst of their pushing and shoving, He Yu would find himself unable to restrain the violent and possessive urges in his heart—he would lean down, press her against the passenger's seat, and forcibly kiss her. The kiss would then intensify, escalating into the car sex scene.

The performance began.

"You have no idea who you're messing with." Before the camera, He Yu lifted his almond eyes with an air of malice. "I can have you and leave you whenever I want. What do you think you are to me?"

The young man's acting was raw and inexperienced, but with a predatory expression on his face, his aura was just right. He leaned over and fixed his gaze on her, his lips opening and closing.

"Ai Qianqian, there's nothing you haven't done with me. How ridiculous of you to pull this chaste maiden act now."

"Shut up."

The actress adopted the mood He Yu had described to her—she remained even-keeled, suppressing her anger and expressing mostly calm and hurt. This kind of mood was just right—it drew He Yu into the scene.

He Yu looked down and smiled. "I'm deigning to show interest in a married woman with three kids—you're being way too ungrateful."

"Stop talking..."

"You know perfectly well that you can't go back to how it used to be with your husband. I've already defiled you."

"This is my final decision. No matter what happens...I won't regret it..."

"Do you even have the right to make this choice?" The wind and rain gusted ominously as He Yu's eyes darkened, surging with a turbulent undercurrent. Then, before the woman could respond—

With a cigarette held between his fingers, he pressed his hand against the back of the seat and lowered it before suddenly leaning down and kissing her roughly. The actress's eyes flew wide open...

"Cut!" The director's voice blared through the microphone, "Um, Qianqian, the feeling still isn't quite right. Let's discuss it some more."

This director was insanely nitpicky. He Yu let go of the actress and gave her some time to speak with the director. Then he turned his face to the side, lifting that pair of beautiful almond eyes still tinged with his character's crazed darkness to shoot Xie Qingcheng another subtle glance.

Xie Qingcheng still wasn't looking at him.

The lines in the movie were so sordid, portraying such a twisted love. He Yu's lover in this scene was also married, and their relationship was just as messy. When he was acting, though his eyes were fixed on the actress, his mind was filled with the way Xie Qingcheng looked in bed.

But it seemed like Xie Qingcheng was completely unwilling to acknowledge this, not even willing to spare He Yu half a glance. All the time and energy he'd spent on his performance had been in vain, as he hadn't been able to provoke a single ripple of emotion in that man's heart.

He Yu was feeling unwell.

The actress was still talking to the director, so he went ahead and got out of the car, slamming the door shut behind him. He stuck his hands in his pockets as he stepped out into the downpour, the expression on his face somewhere between his own and the young crime boss he was playing. His aura was like a soft sword or a whip—it might not appear too rigid or cold, but anyone could tell that if he hardened his heart, the results would be lethally bloody.

Everyone watching became a little uneasy.

He ducked beneath the rain tarp and gave Hu Yi a courteous nod.

Hu-laoshi said, "Does Young Master He have any other questions?"

With everyone looking on, He Yu smiled and said, "I'm a little uncertain of the correct mindset I should have, so I'm looking to chat with Professor Xie."

There were too many people here, but the rain was also coming down too hard—if it wasn't for the rain, he would have definitely found an excuse to pull Xie Qingcheng into the cover of the nearby reeds that were as tall as a man, and fiercely kiss his ice-cold lips to unleash the resentment blazing in his heart—how dare he not watch him?

But now, there was nothing he could do—if he pulled someone into that bank of reeds in the pouring rain right in front of everyone, he might as well have borrowed a loudspeaker and yelled, "Hello everybody, I'd like to announce that I'm having a fling with this person."

He could only stand before Xie Qingcheng beneath this tarp, surrounded by people and the anxious pitter-pattering of unceasing rain, and stare into his eyes as he asked him with gentle poise, "Professor Xie, what do you think, did I get the feeling right in my performance just now?"

There was an awkward silence. Everyone around Xie Qingcheng knew that he hadn't been watching the scene at all.

Xie Qingcheng had a very strong sense of responsibility—he provided very thorough guidance on all the other scenes he'd been assigned to supervise, never missing the smallest details of their performances.

The others thought that perhaps Xie Qingcheng had something keeping him busy today, so he needed to be on his phone when He Yu was performing—what a stroke of bad luck, that Young Master He went over to personally ask him about his acting!

How would he respond?

Xie Qingcheng lifted his lashes and looked at He Yu calmly. "I didn't watch your performance."

Everybody was speechless. How blunt of him.

He Yu smiled and lowered his head. "Professor Xie, the director asked you to guide me—is this how you intend to guide me?"

"During our previous conversation, the feelings you described were all correct, so I didn't think it was necessary," Xie Qingcheng said. "I don't think there's any further need for me to continue standing here."

He Yu's smile disappeared. He stared at Xie Qingcheng fixedly with his pitch-black almond eyes. "Please continue standing here. I won't have confidence if you're not here. Regardless of who may be waiting for you tonight, please ask them to head back first. You should be watching me," He Yu added menacingly. "I told you before—I can only immerse myself in this role if you're standing here."

What he wanted to say was, "*No matter who I'm acting out a sex scene with, the person I'll be thinking of fucking will always be you.*" With all the people around them right now, he couldn't say that, but how could Xie Qingcheng possibly miss the meaning behind his words?

Xie Qingcheng watched He Yu bite his lip in silence after he finished speaking, his sharp canines peeking out and unsheathing a sinister cunning that, due to the angle, went unseen by everyone else.

Even though this conversation seemed to be overstepping some emotional boundaries, after giving it some thought, the listeners concluded that Xie Qingcheng must have mentioned something to He Yu when they were psychoanalyzing these characters, and now He Yu needed Xie Qingcheng to be present in order to remember what had been said and express the right mood. They didn't give it any further thought.

The director's lackey Xiao-Zhang figured it was something like that, so he reminded Xie Qingcheng to stop looking at his phone and pay careful attention to He Yu's performance to check for anything that needed to be corrected.

They started the scene from the top once again.

When He Yu returned to the car, the actress seemed to be in a rather helpless state. She and the director still weren't on the same wavelength.

This whole time, the director had been trying to show her where she was missing the mark in this sex scene. "You need to think about what exactly you're trying to express here."

The actress was nervous to begin with, working with such a big-shot director. Seeing that he was getting angry, she felt even more at a loss. "I...I need to express surprise."

She only dared to say what was written in the script.

Upon returning and seeing her state of distress, He Yu thought for a bit and said, "Jie, try turning your head away. This goes for when we're acting out the sex scene later on too, but you should be resisting me with everything you've got. Don't worry about me, you can even bite me if you want." He paused, then added, "But your resistance isn't completely out of hatred—in your heart, you actually love this man very much, do you understand?"

He once again encouraged her not to be nervous.

The director gave the two of them some time to settle into the right mood and discuss the details of the performance. When the cameras started rolling again, the director reaped an unexpected harvest. Perhaps because He Yu was studying screenwriting and directing, he was far more astute, daring, and uninhibited than most actors his age who only had experience in front of the camera. After receiving some advice and guidance, the actress's performance also gradually moved onto the right track. Quarreling, weeping—bit by bit, the atmosphere heated up.

He Yu's menacing voice emerged unhurriedly from the microphone as he advanced on his quarry step by step. Under his coercion, the actress went from willfully coolheaded to indignant, and then from indignant to hurt. Their conversation stirred up a formless maelstrom in the air, slowly pulling in the gazes of all the staff members whose thoughts had initially been elsewhere.

Xie Qingcheng was also watching indifferently from a corner.

Never mind He Yu specifically coming over to tell him to stop playing with his phone—the atmosphere right now was much too arresting, and with everyone around him so captivated, it would seem very strange if he made a point to look away. From his angle, he couldn't see He Yu himself, but the video camera's small screen was visible. The youth's profile on the display was like a dark cloud descending from the skies above, pressing the actress into a corner until she had nowhere left to go.

When He Yu lowered his head, the actress abruptly turned away, only for him to grab her by the jaw and force her face back toward him even more viciously.

The woman closed her eyes in pain and let out a muffled groan, but He Yu didn't take notice as he braced his hand against the seat. The cigarette between his fingers had burned all the way down to the end, but he pinched it out without blinking, as if he didn't feel the searing pain at all. Then, looking at the actress's face that he had forcibly turned toward himself, he leaned down and kissed her again.

The hormonal tension nearly pierced through the screen.

It was utterly silent on set, as if the air itself had started to congeal. He Yu controlled himself very well as he kissed the actress—with only their lips coming into contact, it wasn't actually a French kiss, but he kept shifting positions as if he were pressing in deeper, making it look like an extremely intimate entanglement to the onlookers. A heavy sense of passion emanated from the screen.

The microphones picked up the actress's feeble, anguished voice— it was difficult to tell if the emotion in her voice was a performance, or if there was some real feeling in it...

Many of the crew members' faces turned red as they watched. The screenwriter and the director exchanged a knowing look—

they couldn't have hoped for a better atmosphere to make the audience's hearts race. Although the actors' clothes were merely disheveled rather than fully removed, the flames had been sufficiently stoked.

By the time He Yu let go of the actress at the end of the scene, her eyes were glazed over and her reddened mouth fell slightly open. As she lay back against the leather seat, it was as though her body had turned to softened clay.

But just as the director was about to yell "cut," unable to stand watching any longer, she remembered who and where she was. Although her body was still trembling, she suddenly tensed up, and the look in her eyes immediately turned despairing and ice-cold.

In those eyes, which still held some residual desire, there appeared a mournful sadness, accompanied by some of the actress's own genuine panic at how late she'd caught her mistake. On the monitors, it seemed reasonable to think that her panic belonged to the character.

Looking at the actress's beautiful, tearful eyes through the lens, the director thought—seeing as they'd already filmed it to this point and could definitely use some of the footage, and given that it was very difficult to perform such an emotionally heavy scene in a single continuous shot, he might as well let them continue. He stopped himself from calling "cut."

The actress slowly regained her bearings and gazed at He Yu in humiliation.

"If you treat me like this, I'll hate you to death."

He Yu was acting according to the script—at this point, his character's anger was supposed to pass while his sense of reason returned. Seeing the person he liked with that kind of expression on her face, his heart was to suddenly ache with unexpected regret.

At a loss for what to do with himself, he tried to wipe her tears, but she slapped his hand away.

He Yu let his hand fall. "...I'm sorry. Don't hate me."

"Okay, cut! That's all for this take. Adjust the camera positions—actors, take a break. We'll start the second take shortly."

Each scene needed to be filmed from many different angles, so they were never actually finished after only one take—even if the footage was usable, they would record a few more takes to make the editing process easier. In a little while, they would have to do it again.

He Yu got up and took a tissue from an assistant, which he passed to the actress. He'd controlled himself very well. Even though there were some emotions he couldn't completely suppress, they stemmed from his personal experience and had nothing to do with the actress. He had immersed himself completely in the absurd things he and Xie Qingcheng had done together.

He really wanted to see what kind of reaction Xie Qingcheng would have this time. After pulling on a shirt, he walked under the tarp—

Only to find a rather infuriating result.

Xie Qingcheng had indeed watched him, but at that moment, he was smoking in the corner with a bland expression on his face, as though He Yu's performance hadn't affected him in the least.

How could he be so unmoved?

How could he *still* be so unmoved?!

He Yu didn't care what the other crew members thought, but he could sense the emotional reactions from them, men and women alike; they were restless, embarrassed, anxious, or flustered, and some didn't dare meet his eyes.

A large part of why he had thrown himself into this kiss scene was because he wanted to act it out for Xie Qingcheng to see. Everyone else was affected—only he had no reaction at all.

Professor Xie smoked his cigarette, every exhale blurring his outline like the changeable moods of an April day. He seemed like a celestial being, impossible to make out, hidden within the clouds and mist.

He Yu's fury had more or less reached its peak. Since Xie Qingcheng didn't spare him a single glance, he simply grabbed a tissue to wipe his mouth and remained silent with a grim expression on his face. He typically had an approachable air and gently beautiful looks, but acting the part of a youthful, deranged crime boss allowed him to behave more like his real self. Right now, with the excuse of getting into character, he could write the words "I'm sick, stay away from me" all over his face without reservation.

The people around him didn't dare to speak, or even approach.

An assistant passed him water with bated breath, and he lifted his head to drink it, but he didn't feel all that thirsty. He just rinsed out his mouth and then sat down on a plastic chair, reading the script for the upcoming scenes with a gloomy aura.

People hadn't shaken off the atmosphere of the scene; apart from the sound of the rain, it was so silent one could hear a pin drop. He Yu kept loudly flipping through the script. Suddenly, with a surge of uncontrollable malice, he slammed the book shut.

"Can you stop smoking?"

That furious reprimand came out of nowhere, causing everyone to flinch with fright.

The only people smoking were the director's special assistant Xiao-Zhang, and Xie Qingcheng. Xiao-Zhang had smoked before, but He Yu hadn't said a thing, enduring it as best he could. Any clever mind could immediately tell the target of his dissatisfaction.

Several people turned to look at Xie Qingcheng.

Xie Qingcheng didn't want to waste breath on him. Sometimes, a calm reply could be more effective than getting angry, so he stubbed out his cigarette, paused, and replied blandly to He Yu.

"My apologies."

He Yu whipped his head back around and continued reading the script, never looking at him again.

In this atmosphere, more crushingly oppressive than the pressure of the abyssal sea, the cameras were quickly set up in their new positions. Xiao-Zhang let out a sigh of relief. "All right, come back everyone, we're moving on to the second take."

And so, the second take began.

This one was more intense than the previous take. Due to the brutally primal atmosphere that emanated from the drama, entrapping the actress deep within its mire, she acted well above her usual level and gave a deeply moving performance.

Meanwhile, as He Yu kissed her before the camera, though his feigned movements were just as well-executed as before, he seemed even more infatuated than in the previous take. It was as if he'd made up his mind that regardless of whether that person was watching, he was going to act as gut-wrenchingly as possible.

In the latter half of the scene, they broke apart, panting heavily. The actress clutched at his clothes, twin tear-tracks streaming down from the outer corners of her eyes.

"I..." She choked with emotion. "I..."

Her final line in this scene was "If you treat me like this, I'll hate you to death." But her heart had melted from the kiss. She kept swallowing, the words catching awkwardly in her throat as she repeated "I" a number of times, unable to finish.

Furious, the director sighed alongside all the others watching the monitors, slapping the table. It seemed there was no way to continue, so he might as well call "cut."

But just at that very moment, He Yu suddenly picked up the scene from the line she'd dropped, acting out a response that was filled with hatred and fury, yet tinged with panic and timidity. He looked down at her with a completely different gaze than before. "That's fine," he said in despair and passion, like an obstinate moth flinging itself into an open flame, cold yet deranged. "Then from now on, just loathe me, despise me, and hate me."

Xie Qingcheng was standing close by beneath the tarp, where not even the pouring rain outside could drown out He Yu's voice. So he heard those words. Xie Qingcheng, who had stayed calm through the entire evening, finally froze upon hearing He Yu say those words out loud.

The first night they had plunged into the abyss, He Yu had bent down and said something similar into his ear.

Shock and fury engulfed his entire body like wildfire. He Yu was airing out a closely guarded secret that only the two of them knew in front of so many people.

Xie Qingcheng stared at the monitor.

The eyes of the youth on the screen were ruthless, stained with the madness of someone who cared nothing for the consequences of their actions, just as he had been that absurd night Xie Qingcheng sought to bury deep into the recesses of his memories.

He Yu was still going. As if he had made up his mind to take Xie Qingcheng down with him, he repeated another line he'd said on that night of madness.

"All this time, there's never been anyone who loved me for real. At least in the future, there'll be someone who hates me passionately. That would be good too."

Silence fell over the set.

These altered lines were truly shocking, the depth of their emotion utterly terrifying. The director stared in a daze for a long time before suddenly breaking into applause.

"Excellent! Cut!"

He Yu took a moment to gather himself. Slanting his gaze to the side, he stared into the camera with a piercing expression in his eyes, as though trying to stab through the lens into a certain observer's heart.

The scene soon wrapped up. Exceedingly pleased with this bit of improvisation, Hu Yi slung an arm around He Yu's shoulders with a smile and proceeded to subject him to a nonstop stream of chatter.

Now that he was finished with his performance, He Yu's face reverted to its usual impassive appearance. Lifting his long eyelashes, he returned to the director's tent. As he carefully observed the results of the day's shoot before the monitors, he casually swept his gaze over the crew members standing present.

Then, he paused, his eyes darkening.

Xie Qingcheng was gone.

He scanned the entire tent, but there was no sign of Xie Qingcheng's silhouette. At some point in time, he had left, disappearing into the downpour.

81

I KISSED YOU IN THE RAIN

XIE QINGCHENG had left directly from the film set; he hadn't even returned to the director's tent.

Luckily, this was already the final take of the night. After he watched his performance from the monitors and spent some time speaking to the director, He Yu began to gather his things to leave. It was at this very moment, however, that Chen Man appeared at his side.

It turned out that Chen Man had ended up staying. Seeing that everyone had returned except for Xie Qingcheng, who had disappeared without a trace, he rushed over to ask He Yu, "Have you seen Xie-ge?"

When He Yu didn't respond, Chen Man repeated his question, his voice taking on a somewhat anxious quality.

He Yu looked up slowly as he pulled the zipper of his backpack closed. "Can't you just call him? Why are you asking me?"

"His phone's dead. He asked to borrow my charger earlier, but I didn't get the chance to give it to him..." But before Chen Man could finish speaking, he was struck by the shards of ice in the youth's eyes and abruptly fell silent.

He Yu flashed a smile that was sweet yet menacing. "You're the one who lost him, so why are you asking me? Officer Chen, aren't you much closer to him than I am?"

With that, his smile swiftly disappeared; his shifting moods were truly abnormal. He slung his backpack over one shoulder and walked away with his hands shoved in his pockets.

If He Yu had to guess, Xie Qingcheng had probably taken a quiet side path and wouldn't have gotten very far. Therefore, after climbing into the production team's hired van, he instructed the driver to take the byway back.

It rarely rained so heavily during the winter. The downpour had blurred the windows of the car, but He Yu could still easily recognize the figure a short distance away. Just as he'd expected. He instructed the driver to pursue him.

The driver couldn't quite make sense of He Yu's erratic moods, but from a glance at him in the rearview mirror, he thought He Yu seemed fairly unconcerned. *He-laoban must consider this man an eyesore,* the lackey thought, and so he floored the gas pedal, deliberately speeding through a large puddle of water and splattering Xie Qingcheng's whole body in muck.

Xie Qingcheng stopped in his tracks. With his hands still stuck in his pockets, he turned around, his handsome face ashen and his once-crisp windbreaker dripping with muddy water.

Warm air gusted over him as the hired van's automatic door slowly slid open, but when he saw who was inside, the warmth only served to make Xie Qingcheng's cold face frost over with an even thicker layer of ice.

"Do you find this amusing, He Yu?" Every word he spat out was like a blade of ice. "Are you a child?!"

He Yu sat inside the stopped van. Although he was being cursed out, he felt a twisted thrill from the bottom of his heart. The reason Xie Qingcheng was in such a wretched state—the reason he was so angry, the reason for this extreme reaction—it was all because of him.

Chen Man was a fool. Whether he brought him milk tea or offered him kindness and warmth, Xie Qingcheng would always respond with bland indifference. Those seven years of He Yu's life served as a testament to this. It was no use treating someone like Xie Qingcheng well; treating him with gentleness was even more of a waste. The man had no heart—no matter how you tried to warm him up, he would never thaw.

The only way to force that lofty gaze to land on you was through cruelty and humiliation.

He Yu felt that his own methods were much better—no one could obtain Xie Qingcheng's love, but at least he had managed to obtain Xie Qingcheng's hatred.

It failed to occur to He Yu that his preoccupation with Xie Qingcheng's love wasn't normal in the first place. With an indolent expression on his gently beautiful face, he crossed his long legs, sat lazily back in his seat with his fingers interlaced, and looked over Xie Qingcheng's face as he stood in the torrential downpour.

"Professor Xie, it's raining so heavily," he said. "How could you leave without an umbrella? Please get in the car. I'll give you a ride back to the hotel."

"Fuck off."

He Yu kept smiling. "You still have such a fiery temper even when you're soaked through. I wonder who provoked you so?"

Xie Qingcheng obviously couldn't say that it had been He Yu's lines that had provoked him—the driver was still listening eagerly from the front of the car.

Seeing him completely soaked through, cold and seething with hatred, satisfied some deep desire in He Yu's heart. He picked up a black umbrella with a carbon-fiber handle from the seat and stuck his hand out of the car. The umbrella opened with a *swoosh*, and the sound of the rain grew louder as raindrops fell in an agitated stutter over the umbrella's surface.

He remained sitting inside the van, but he leaned over as he handed the umbrella to Xie Qingcheng. "If you don't want to get in the car, you can have this."

After a moment's consideration, he extended his long legs, pressing one foot against the outer edge of the car and leaving the other dangling as he bent down even further to press his lips against Xie Qingcheng's ear. He murmured in a voice that only Xie Qingcheng could hear, "Ge, do you really hate me so much?"

Xie Qingcheng was normally a highly unruffled person, but no matter how calm he was, there was no way he could stand the open-yet-veiled provocation of He Yu sharing their conversations from that night in the club's private room for all to hear. Not to mention, He Yu's words now carried the same blistering undertone of mockery. Unable to bear it any longer, Xie Qingcheng lashed out and delivered a vicious slap across He Yu's face.

The driver flinched at the sharp sound but did not dare turn his head.

He Yu's face jerked slightly to the side from the force of the blow. After a moment, he slowly turned back to Xie Qingcheng.

The sudden slap had Xie Qingcheng's full strength behind it, and several fingerprint bruises immediately surfaced in its wake on He Yu's pale cheek, but He Yu didn't care. Instead, he grabbed Xie Qingcheng by the wrist, slowly rubbing against the tattoo hidden beneath the layer of cloth.

Then he bared his snowy-white teeth in a smile. "It hurts so much." He bent even lower, as though he wanted to shove Xie Qingcheng down. "My right cheek's over here, would you like to hit that too?"

Xie Qingcheng gritted his teeth. "I see you're unafraid of pain, but surely you're not so far gone that you've completely lost your sense of shame."

"Why should I feel shame?" Pulling away, He Yu suddenly tilted the umbrella he had been holding over their heads to the side. The torrential rain splashed over the ground, soaking through the arm and leg that He Yu had extended out of the car, and pouring over Xie Qingcheng.

He Yu held the black umbrella steadily aloft at a slant, using it to block the driver's line of sight.

"I think the way we are right now is pretty great," he said.

With no further warning, he yanked Xie Qingcheng closer by the wrist. Under the cover of the heavy downpour, there was hardly any distance between them as they stared at each other. He Yu's gaze stroked over Xie Qingcheng's dark, rain-drenched brows and thick lashes again and again, the expression in his eyes so intense it seemed like he wanted to press the line of his sight into Xie Qingcheng's blood, flesh, and marrow.

The molten lava in his heart had been bubbling for a long time. Under the flimsy barrier of the black umbrella's thin fabric, he suddenly dipped his head—

As the heavy rain poured down, he captured Xie Qingcheng's lips in a kiss.

Finally, he was kissing him again.

The moment their lips met, a buzzing sound echoed through He Yu's mind. It was as if an electric shock had passed through his entire body; he felt nearly numb with pleasure.

He hadn't planned on kissing Xie Qingcheng here—his body had reacted on instinct—but as he kissed him wetly, he came to the unexpected realization that this kiss was completely different from the ones he'd shared with the actress when he'd acted out his sex scene. He'd thought that he had done quite well at acting out that scene, but now he could see how incredibly ignorant he had been. A deep, depraved kiss, a passionate outpouring of emotions—how could it possibly be as he had portrayed it? There was no way that a man who was overcome by lust and cloaked in despair would be able to do what he'd done in that scene and finish things off so easily.

A kiss like this was a fuse, burning away at his rationality. He hated Xie Qingcheng so much he wanted to step out of the car at once, shove him into the narrow, mud-covered alley, and crush his flesh to pieces—to pound him to death in the frantically falling rain.

And yet, at the same time, he pitied him so much he wanted to drag him into the car without a care for anything else, take his shivering body into his arms, strip him of his drenched clothes, and press his own scalding heat to his icy chill so that he could warm him up properly—from the inside out.

That was what it felt like to stifle one's emotions for so long.

He hadn't fully grasped this feeling back when he'd been acting out his sex scene with that actress. In the end, his performance had been utterly fake.

A warm mouth sucked on thin, chilly lips, the sweet wetness of rainwater mixing into their kiss. Thankfully the rain was very loud, and with the large umbrella blocking his view, the driver couldn't see anything—but Xie Qingcheng couldn't move. He was unspeakably shocked and furious, but he couldn't move. After all, He Yu was holding the umbrella—the little bastard could let go any time he wished.

He couldn't make a sound, either. If the driver found out that they were kissing behind the umbrella in this great downpour, the only person he'd be embarrassing would be himself. Xie Qingcheng's only option was to bite down hard on He Yu's lip, hoping to hurt him enough he'd let go. But all that got him was the heavy taste of blood—and a deeper entanglement as He Yu sucked at his lips even more intensely. He Yu kissed him too deeply, as though he wanted to drain all of Xie Qingcheng's breath from his lungs, as though he was trying to steal away his life.

Xie Qingcheng wasn't sure how much time had passed by the time the kiss finally ended. His face was very calm, but his fingertips trembled slightly. If he'd had a knife on hand, he might have sliced through this crazed dragon's throat.

He Yu, meanwhile, stared at Xie Qingcheng, his eyes shining with water as if they'd been moistened by the storm. His bottom lip dripped with fresh blood.

He let go of Xie Qingcheng's wrist, but lifted his fingers to run them slowly over the man's face: his pitch-black brows and eyes, the handsome lines of his profile. Crooking his fingers, he swept them over the high bridge of the man's nose, then lingered over the thin lips that were stained dark red by his kisses.

He pressed his knuckles against Xie Qingcheng's mouth as Xie Qingcheng said to him in an utterly frigid voice, "Are you done?"

He Yu could feel the tepid heat of his breath as he spoke—oh, was there really still warmth in this man's body? He stared at Xie Qingcheng in silence for a moment, gathering his emotions into some semblance of order until the only thing remaining in his eyes was mockery.

"You see?" he said, so, so softly. "Why should I feel any shame when you're the one who's afraid of being discovered by the driver, the one who refuses to admit to our rotten affair? None of this matters to me. I don't care about any of it."

Xie Qingcheng's lips were still stained with blood, yet his eyes were cold as ice. "…If you're done with your ridiculous rampage, you can leave."

He couldn't have been colder. He was no longer even willing to say something as emotional as "Fuck off."

He Yu didn't reply, only moved his hand away from Xie Qingcheng's mouth. His knuckles were still stained with the blood from Xie Qingcheng's lips. But he lifted his hand, leaned down slightly, and looked up at him through his lashes before gently kissing the redness on his own fingers.

Xie Qingcheng was at a loss for words. As he kissed the blood, He Yu's unwavering, unblinking gaze never left his eyes.

"Xie Qingcheng, I'm not used to getting any affection from ordinary people, so even your hatred and blood can bring me joy."

With that, he straightened up, returned the umbrella to its position over Xie Qingcheng's head, and passed him the handle.

Instead of taking it, Xie Qingcheng knocked it to the ground, sending up a spray of water.

"He Yu, do you know where you're sick? It's not your head." Under the falling rain, Xie Qingcheng leveled him with a frigid stare. "It's your heart. You're sick in the heart. You take blood for medicine and hatred as treatment—if you carry on like this, no one will be able to save you. Take a good look at yourself right now. You're pursuing your own fucking destruction—you're lowering yourself to something less than a beast. I'm disappointed in you. I feel like all the time and effort I spent on you in the past was a complete waste of my time. That time was actually very valuable to me, but now I feel like I might as well have fed it to a dog."

When Xie Qingcheng finished speaking, he walked away without a backward glance, taking a narrow pedestrian pathway that was impossible to follow by car.

He Yu licked his lips, his almond eyes dark. He slowly sat back down inside the car, using a handkerchief taken from within the vehicle to slowly wipe at his dripping hair.

The driver could see through the rearview mirror that his lips were bright red, seemingly covered in blood. Even though he didn't know how the blood had gotten there, he was still terrified.

"He-laoban," the driver said quietly, "um...are we leaving now?"

That was the only question he dared ask. Some stones were better left unturned.

"Of course." He Yu smiled, tossing the handkerchief away with a casual flick of his hand as his indifferent eyes turned eerily dark. He looked like a deranged madman, but somehow, he still sounded perfectly courteous, utterly refined, and completely polite as he said, "Please take me back to the hotel, thank you."

The driver shuddered. The heating was on inside the car, but for a moment, he felt a hair-raising chill, a shock that sent sweat beading all over his back.

When he returned to the hotel, He Yu examined himself in the mirror.

The blood on his lip had already dried into a dark scab. He touched it gently, thinking about everything that had just transpired.

Xie Qingcheng said he took blood as medicine and hatred for treatment.

How ridiculous. As if he wanted to be like this.

Was love an option for him? Was true medicine? Was there a bridge that could lead him back toward regular society?

Xie Qingcheng had even said that the time and effort he'd spent on him was very valuable, that he now felt like he'd fed it to a dog... He really didn't need to be so polite. In all likelihood, in the depths of his mind, Xie Qingcheng probably thought he'd done worse than feed his efforts to a dog. At least a dog would still seek their master's affection. Xie Qingcheng should've cursed him out as an ungrateful wolf biting the hand that fed him.

Really, he could have spoken much more viciously.

At any rate, He Yu didn't care anymore. He'd long since stopped caring.

When Xie Qingcheng left him. When that video was played on the broadcasting tower. When Xie Qingcheng said the lives of the mentally ill were unworthy of mention, when He Yu told him again and again that he'd fallen ill but never received a word in response.

By then, he'd already stopped caring.

In fact, he felt that if they continued to torment each other like this until they died, that would be a perfectly good conclusion.

But what He Yu couldn't escape was the fact that when he'd kissed Xie Qingcheng earlier, he'd been acting entirely on his own inexplicable physical impulse.

This wasn't the same as the time he kissed him in the bar—that had been a kiss with some goal in mind, as at the time, he'd wanted to force Xie Qingcheng into agreeing to his request beneath the watchful eyes of the crowd.

But earlier, that kiss hidden behind the umbrella?

It seemed completely meaningless, an action born of the heart. It didn't seem like something a normal man would do.

Still, he forcibly assuaged his pathetic dignity, telling himself that this was perfectly rational—that it was just the same as fucking

Xie Qingcheng. The only reason he kissed Xie Qingcheng was to make him suffer. There was no love whatsoever in an action like that.

He lay in bed, mulling it over again and again, only to discover that he couldn't manage to calm down, that there was no way he could fall asleep.

He Yu swore quietly and rose to go to the bathroom, slamming the frosted glass door closed.

In the steaming heat of the shower, he thunked his forehead against the icy tile. The lights were off in the bathroom, so his clearly defined profile was shrouded in darkness. The water from the showerhead pounded against his back, splashing all over his flesh-and-blood body.

He closed his eyes, thinking, *Seriously, what the hell?*

He Yu needed to maintain calm for his own good, but since the broadcasting tower incident, his flare-ups had been so frequent and long-lasting that his sickness had begun to worsen. Under normal circumstances, a little bit of conflict and provocation like what had happened today wouldn't affect him too much, but He Yu still had a flare-up.

After cooling off in the shower, he managed to calm himself down, but even at midnight, his sickness was still pouring violently out.

As the number on the thermometer approached thirty-nine, the urge to see bloodshed and the craving for destruction within him began to surge higher and higher. He Yu took a handful of pills and just barely managed to make it through the latter half of the night.

As dawn broke after a sleepless night, He Yu finally heard faint sounds of movement coming from next door.

He dug out his phone and glanced at the schedule. It said that it was Chen Man's last day providing guidance on set, so the scenes that required his oversight would end today.

Shooting for his first scene began quite early; the schedule said that they'd be departing at six in the morning. The noise was probably from Chen Man.

He Yu turned over in his blankets and swiped further down on his phone to see that Xie Qingcheng needed to stay on set until just before the new year. Which was to say, after today, the ambient percentage of Chen Man PM2.5 in the air would fall to zero. Chen Man would be gone. The only person left next door would be Xie Qingcheng.

At this realization, like a desert blessed by rainfall, He Yu's state of mind showed a sudden improvement after an entire night's worth of torment at the hands of his psychological Ebola.

Or rather it would have, if not for what he heard Xie Qingcheng saying through the wall.

82

AND RAN INTO SOMEONE FROM THE PAST

"IT'S FINE, I'll see you off," Xie Qingcheng said.

"Ge, you should sleep some more," Chen Man told him. "You hardly got any sleep last night."

"Enough nonsense, let's go. I'm not doing anything today, so I can rest when I get back." Xie Qingcheng paused. "Where's your suitcase?"

"In the wardrobe."

"Do you need to bring it with you? Or will you come back to get it in the afternoon?"

"I'm not coming back. I'm leaving directly from the set after the shoot. My mom said my grandpa's coming to Huzhou tonight."

"Okay," Xie Qingcheng said. "I'll hold on to it for you. Let's go."

The door opened and closed again. The sound of two sets of footsteps, along with the faint scraping of the suitcase's wheels, gradually faded into the distance.

He Yu suddenly sat up in bed, his hair disheveled.

He hadn't misheard—Xie Qingcheng was accompanying Chen Man to Group B.

Yesterday Chen Man had come to see Xie Qingcheng, and today Xie Qingcheng was sending him off. That goddamn homosexual Chen Man had to go and disgust him one last time before he left.

He Yu's desire to stay in bed and play dead vanished immediately. Even though he was still burning with fever, violently bloodthirsty urges blazing through his heart, he decided to get up and leave his room. He wanted to go to the set too.

The last scene where Chen Man was providing technical guidance was set at a police academy. It featured a large ensemble of a few hundred extras who all required supervision, and it was being filmed on-site at the nearby campus of an actual police academy.

By the time He Yu had freshened up and arrived on set, the first rays of dawn were already peeking over the horizon. They had just finished filming one section, and while the crew was blocking out the scene with one group of extras, the others were resting.

It was so crowded that He Yu didn't see Xie Qingcheng at first. He had to look around the whole area before he discovered the man standing with Chen Man under a white plum blossom tree. Xie Qingcheng stood with his back facing him, saying something to Chen Man beneath the dawning sky full of rosy clouds.

He Yu was far enough away that he could only hear faint snatches of their conversation.

"... It'll be fine, ge—it's just a performance, and they won't film your face."

Xie Qingcheng was saying something, but He Yu couldn't hear him clearly.

Chen Man's smile grew brighter. "Just think of it as humoring me—as a gift for wrapping up my part in the film?"

This time, Xie Qingcheng's voice was audible. "You're not an actor, so why would you need a wrap gift?"

What sort of wrap gift had Chen Man asked for?

As He Yu walked closer, it all became very clear. At that very moment, Xie Qingcheng also happened to turn around—He Yu was no longer faced with that straight-backed silhouette, but instead those handsome features.

He couldn't help but stop in his tracks: Xie Qingcheng was wearing a police uniform.

His cap was pulled a bit low, hiding his dark, distant eyes in the shadows beneath its brim, while the silver-buckled belt pulled in the crisp line of his waist. This navy-blue winter uniform made his figure look exceptionally tall and slender, sharpening his cold, austere aura until it was utterly solemn and severe. As he turned around beneath the white plum blossom tree, it was impossible to say whether it was the flowers or the man that had been more thoroughly chilled by the cold.

The wind rose, stirring up a flurry of plum petals that drifted down and dusted over Xie Qingcheng's uniform like pure white snow. As he glanced to the side and caught sight of He Yu, he started slightly in surprise before raising his hand to straighten his hat and looking briskly away from He Yu once more.

He really didn't want to see him.

He Yu hardly needed to rack his brain to understand why Xie Qingcheng was dressed up like this. Although the actors needed to go through makeup and costuming ahead of time, it was actually very simple to make them look like modern police academy students. It didn't require much effort at all—especially for someone like Xie Qingcheng, who looked good in anything and was ready for the part with just a change of clothes. He had come to keep Chen Man company, but he felt awkward just standing by the side doing nothing, so he'd agreed to be an extra in the scene as a small favor to Chen Man. He was just filling in a spot in the crowd for a wide-angle shot, so his face wouldn't be clearly seen.

If he'd been asked to play any other minor role, Xie Qingcheng might not have agreed, but this navy-blue uniform was the cherished childhood dream that he'd ultimately abandoned. He could at least

take advantage of the chance to wear the full outfit in this production as a way to indulge his old ambition.

He Yu had gotten used to seeing him in his doctor's clothes, which made him look very scholarly—though his figure in the snow-white coat was ice-cold, it nevertheless emanated a somewhat pure and holy aura. He never could have imagined that a police uniform would suit Xie Qingcheng even more.

He was so upright—whether it was the epaulets, the belt, the silver buttons, or the dark navy formal dress blues, they all matched his aura of competence perfectly. The police uniform was much more formfitting than a doctor's, revealing the beautiful, clean lines of his broad shoulders and long legs. His whole figure was like a frosty dagger on a winter's night, sharp and frigid, with moonlight glancing off its icy blade.

He Yu's mental illness had given him a high fever, but he was already used to such high temperatures; it couldn't affect him all that much. But at that moment, it felt as though all the blood in his body had caught fire.

Xie Qingcheng had put on this uniform at Chen Man's request. He was wearing it for Chen Man to see. If He Yu hadn't followed them here, he wouldn't have been able to witness this magnificent view.

The thought gnawed away at He Yu's heart. Even though Xie Qingcheng clearly had "keep your nonsense away from me" written all over his face, He Yu still made his way over.

"Xie Qingcheng," he said.

Chen Man turned his head, and the smile on his face stiffened as soon as he caught sight of him. "Can I help you with something?"

He Yu didn't bother to look at Young Master Chen at all. He stopped just one step shy of Xie Qingcheng to gaze at the man before him through lowered lashes.

Then he lifted his hand...

Slap.

Xie Qingcheng grabbed his wrist.

Dressed in solemn navy blue, Xie Qingcheng's aura seemed even more cutting than usual. Staring at He Yu, he repeated Chen Man's question: "Can I help you with something?"

He Yu calmly allowed him to hold his wrist in his grasp. He was sick, burning up from head to toe. He was sure that Xie Qingcheng could feel it when he grabbed his wrist.

They stared at each other, just like that.

He Yu had no idea how solid Xie Qingcheng's heart had been frozen—the heat from his illness and fever was being transmitted straight into Xie Qingcheng's chest, but the doctor didn't ask him anything.

He waited for a long time, but Xie Qingcheng still didn't ask anything at all. The only words he said to him were the same as Chen Man's.

"Can I help you with something?"

The cool, subtle fragrance of white plum blossoms wafted over them.

Finally, He Yu smiled faintly and said, in a voice full of both arrogance and resignation, "It's fine. It's nothing." He threw off Xie Qingcheng's hand and plucked a cold plum blossom off of his epaulet. "I just saw a flower fall onto your shoulder."

Then he turned and walked away, still holding the plum blossom between his fingers. As though he'd forgotten to throw it away, he ended up slipping it into his pocket.

The shoot for this large ensemble scene was very long. He Yu had shown up unexpectedly, but when the creative director caught sight of him, he immediately arranged for him to sit down in the tent.

Thanks to his flare-up, He Yu was feeling very bloodthirsty. Making him sit in a crowd right now would be like throwing a vampire into a group of living people, so he automatically refused the offer.

He wouldn't be able to see Xie Qingcheng in the crowd during this shoot anyway, so after giving it some thought, he decided to leave and head over to the set in the same police academy where Group A was filming a fight scene featuring explosives.

This proved to be the right choice. Although Group A's shoot today didn't feature many people or use an extensive set, the contents of the scene were extremely bloody and thrilling.

The protagonists had been cut off by their pursuers and surrounded. Guns were fired and blades were drawn, and blood splattered everywhere. There were even several extreme close-up shots where the cameraman had moved in too far and the fake blood splashed directly onto the camera lens, mottling the brutal tableau like a blood-soaked starry sky.

Looking at these scenes was like a sedative for He Yu. With his symptoms alleviated somewhat, when the director yelled "cut" and the cameras returned to their original positions, he simply rose and headed over to the set for a walk. Even though the bright red staining the ground was fake, just looking at it soothed his heart.

As he idly strolled through the set, He Yu inadvertently caught sight of an extra—a woman whose hair had gone mostly white. She wore a floral cotton quilted jacket and played a member of the crowd who was trying to flee during the chaos. When He Yu's gaze fell on her, he lingered briefly on her face. For some reason, this woman seemed somewhat familiar.

But there were plenty of people in the world who looked similar to each other, so He Yu didn't pay it much mind and calmly looked away.

But a few seconds later, He Yu abruptly froze—a memory suddenly surfaced in his mind, polished to a bright shine.

He immediately turned back and stared closely at that woman's face. There was no mistaking it.

A long time had passed—she seemed older and more desperate, with wrinkles corroding her face and muddling her features—but He Yu still recognized her.

He had watched the broadcasting tower's video of Xie Qingcheng on repeat so many times. Of course he recognized her. Of all people, this woman was the patient who had gotten into a heated dispute with Xie Qingcheng in that video!

Most extras spent their breaks listlessly lying around. This woman was no different. She didn't have much of an education, but she enjoyed acting, so after she'd escaped her unhappy marriage and left her hometown nearly three decades ago, she had never returned. Back when she'd just arrived in the city, she had still been full of passion, hoping to one day achieve fame and become a household name. However, not everyone was destined to become a leading actor, and she had spent her entire life as a bit player.

Her only moment in the limelight had been in the aftermath of the broadcasting tower incident, when the viral video featuring her quarrel with that doctor had spread wildly across the internet.

She couldn't read and didn't really browse the web, and as someone who grew up in the countryside, she still carried an air of rustic simplicity, so she wasn't so insane as to try to use that video to develop a following. However, she was still eager to share with those around her, telling them, "Have you seen that video? The person arguing with the doctor was me..." If someone asked her for more details, she would explain in her thick rural accent, "Back then, I was very scared...but..."

She had a heavy accent and her storytelling was very disorganized, so when people heard her opening words, a lot of them would be reluctant to listen to the rest. More often than not, even those who listened to her story through to the end had trouble making sense of what she was trying to say. Before long, people's initial curiosity turned to indifference.

Recently, the other bit players that she knew had all taken to calling her Auntie Xianglin.[7] They often teased her, "Auntie Xianglin, what happened back then? What did you go to see the doctor for?"

"It's not that simple—" At first, she had anxiously tried to explain herself. But eventually she came to realize that no one believed her, and that they were all just making fun of her. So she would only smile, the wrinkles on her face filling with an awkward flush as she stammered to a halt.

"She really is like Auntie Xianglin when she gets embarrassed," people would muse.

She knew very well that things could get very tiring on a production set with all these repeated takes, so she was currently sitting in a shady spot in the hallway, taking advantage of the time it took for the cameras to return to their positions. Never mind whether the floor was dirty or not—it was much more important to conserve her energy.

Suddenly, to her surprise, someone addressed her with a quiet, "Hello."

Startled, she looked back to see He Yu's face. From his face alone, she could see that he belonged to a completely different class in the hierarchy of this production.

Years of struggling to get by had caused her to develop a pitiable instinct—as her sense of self-esteem had grown numb, her conditioned reaction to seeing people of influence led her to hastily rise

---

7   A character from Lu Xun's short story The New Year's Sacrifice (祝福), who often repeats the story of her own life.

in a panicked fluster and apologize profusely. "Ah, I'm so sorry, I'll leave right away."

She thought that she had blocked his path, or that the place where she was lying had somehow interrupted a shot.

But He Yu asked her to stop. "Please wait."

Even more alarmed, the woman stared anxiously up at him. Until he said, "If I may—are you the patient who was humiliated by Doctor Xie in that video from the broadcasting tower incident?"

She paused for a moment.

"Are you?"

She stared at him blankly for a long time before she recovered her senses. "I am...and you are...?"

After a few beats of silence, He Yu smiled. "There's a café just outside the police academy—could I buy you a cup of coffee? I'd like to ask you a few questions."

They had missed the morning rush, and it was very quiet inside the café.

He Yu picked a table in the farthest corner. The server who came to take their order looked at the odd-looking pair with an air of bewilderment: an unkempt old lady with a humble but frightened face, and an immaculately dressed, handsome young man. They didn't seem to be a mother with her son, but they didn't look like a wealthy lady and her gigolo either.

"Are the two of you together?" the server asked hesitantly.

The awkwardness made the old woman's wrinkles deepen even further. Combined with the flush on her face, she looked like a dried out, purple-skinned walnut.

He Yu cast the server a coldly indifferent glance. "Yes. Two cups of coffee, please."

The domineering aura of He Yu's gaze was much too powerful. Immediately cowed, the server didn't dare look at them or ask any further questions, and he carried two piping hot cups of coffee over in no time at all.

By this point, the woman had gotten He Yu to explain why he'd approached her. "Um... I can't say much," she said anxiously. "I promised that doctor..."

"That's fine." He Yu handed her the sugar bowl and smiled gently. "I'll listen to everything you have to say—however much you want to say, or however much you're able to."

The woman licked her lips as though desperately thirsty.

She bowed her head, thinking for a long while. Recently, she'd been going on about that video to anyone and everyone she met, but she had never actually said anything that she was supposed to keep secret. She had no idea why that doctor had asked her to act the way she did, but she'd accepted his money, so she ought to follow his requests and do her job accordingly.

She might not have been the sharpest tool in the box, but she could tell that the youth sitting before her was different from the bit-part actors she was used to. He wasn't here to listen to a funny story in passing; he genuinely cared about what had happened.

Therefore, she didn't even know where to begin. She nervously picked up her coffee and took a sip, only to find that it was too bitter, nearly choking it back up.

"*Cough cough cough...*"

"Auntie, here. Use this to wipe it up." He Yu handed her a napkin.

Even the woman's ears had gone red. "I'm sorry..."

"No, it's my fault for being inconsiderate. You don't like coffee, do you?" He Yu called the server back over and exchanged her coffee for a cup of hot tea.

The whole time, he never tried to rush her, so she slowly began to relax just a bit. She thought things over carefully. Faced with someone who genuinely wanted to listen, she felt unexpectedly hesitant.

"...To be honest...I can't tell you anything. I don't know what exactly he was trying to do, either...but he asked me to keep it a secret."

"That's fine. In that case, why don't I ask you some questions? All you have to do is nod or shake your head. If you can't do either of those things, then just treat this as me buying you a drink. You don't have to take it that seriously—is that okay?"

The woman rubbed her feet together anxiously under the table.

It was exceptionally easy dealing with this kind of honest, simple woman. "Auntie," said He Yu, "just now you said that that doctor asked you to 'keep it a secret,' but in that video, the two of you were arguing—can I take this to mean that your argument was faked?"

The woman froze.

"According to some recent discussions online, the day you appeared outside his department, your behavior was very suspicious. Apparently, you registered for an appointment with the gynecology department, but you kept wandering around the psychiatry department, which aroused the suspicions of the doctor on call. He saw that not only did you have the wrong registration number, but that your number had already expired, yet you still hadn't visited the gynecology department and insisted on hanging around his office door. Therefore, he thought that you must have some mental health issues and called the security guards to come take you away—and that's when the two of you had your altercation." He Yu gazed at her through the steam rising from his coffee. "At the time, were you really mentally ill?"

When all was said and done, the woman was an honest person, so she quickly waved her hand. "I wasn't. I'm not ill."

"Then why did you go to the hospital and sit in front of his consulting room?"

She didn't reply.

"Were you plotting a medical disturbance?"[8]

Of course he knew that she wasn't, but the woman began to panic. She said, "I-I've never done anything immoral. I might be poor, but I wouldn't cause trouble for doctors who are treating patients."

He Yu stared at her. "Auntie, you don't seem to resent him at all, even though he spoke to you so unreasonably back then and called security to take you away. But your reaction right now is that you can't say much because you need to keep a secret for him."

She fell silent.

"You're really not very good at lying," said He Yu calmly.

The woman's face turned even redder as she gazed at him in embarrassment.

"You're an actress, so could I be so bold as to make a guess?" he asked.

The woman didn't say anything, her head hanging low, as if she wanted to bury it in her chest. But even in this ostrich-like posture, she couldn't evade He Yu's soft voice.

"Would I be correct in guessing that Doctor Xie invited you to work with him toward some sort of goal—that he specifically had you wait outside his consulting room to act out a charade that the two of you had discussed beforehand? He didn't tell you anything about the goal he had in mind—he simply told you not to tell anyone the truth. You took the money, did as you were told, and then left according to his instructions. Many years later, when you had nearly forgotten about this event entirely, the video from

---

8   Medical disturbance, or yi nao (医闹), refers to the widespread phenomenon of premeditated violence against medical personnel, usually on behalf of dissatisfied patients or their families.

the broadcasting tower murder case suddenly went viral, and you remembered this job that you took long ago.

"Auntie, is that what happened?"

The woman's eyes were wide from shock. With every sentence He Yu said, her eyes grew larger and larger, until they finally looked like they were on the verge of bulging out. "T-this...you...how could you...how...?"

She wanted to say, *How could you understand everything so clearly?* But she was so astonished that she couldn't finish her sentence.

But He Yu didn't need her to say anything else. His expression had turned very grim, and his eyes grew extremely dark.

He'd already gotten the answer he was looking for from her face.

83

ARE YOU SICK TOO?

WHEN HE YU RETURNED to Group B's film set, his heart was pounding and burning in his chest.

He thought of what his cousin had said, and then of the expression the old woman had revealed. It was like Xie Qingcheng was wearing layer upon layer of clothes—whenever he stripped off one shirt, there was always another one underneath. He was like an intangible fog, and after all this time, He Yu still couldn't touch him to tell whether his blood was hot or cold, whether his skin was icy or warm.

The only thing that He Yu knew for sure was that Xie Qingcheng was still keeping secrets from him. From everyone.

But why was he doing this?

What else did He Yu not know?

Group B was currently in the middle of a break. When he got back, He Yu saw Chen Man speaking to the director alone. There was no one else around him. He Yu looked away and frantically searched for any sign of Xie Qingcheng.

Then he saw him—smoking next to the flowerbed on the police academy's drill grounds.

He Yu descended the steps, walked halfway across the field, and grabbed Xie Qingcheng's arm as he approached him.

"Come with me."

Xie Qingcheng snapped out of his daze. Rage flashed in his eyes for a split second when he saw it was He Yu—but he quickly suppressed it, as if he thought that being angry with someone like He Yu was a waste of energy.

"What is it you want? Are you trying to haunt me like some kind of ghost?"

He Yu didn't respond as he dragged him into an empty classroom in a nearby teaching building. He pushed Xie Qingcheng in first before he followed, slamming the door shut behind them.

He didn't turn around, he kept his eyes fixed on Xie Qingcheng— but he reached behind his back and locked the door with a *clack*.

Xie Qingcheng stood before him, wearing the formal winter police uniform. He looked extremely dashing and upright, just tempting someone to rip off his uniform and kiss him.

He Yu had always been very smart, but the CPU of that smart brain of his was about to collapse under the weight of his complicated feelings for Xie Qingcheng. With everyone else, whether it was his cousin or the woman from the video, he handled them with skillful ease and an almost relaxed air. It was only when faced with Xie Qingcheng that he felt like he'd been electrocuted. His thought process was completely numb.

Those cold eyes bored into him. "He Yu, you're still not done?"

Originally, He Yu had planned to immediately ask him about the matter with the old woman. But now that he'd locked the door, now that he was breathing in Xie Qingcheng's scent, it was as if he had suddenly been struck in the head. His bloodthirsty desire surged, along with his youthful urges. As He Yu looked at this man who was hiding too much, the restless hatred in his heart swelled forth in a deluge.

He almost didn't have the time to interrogate him; in the single moment that he gazed at him with his eyes rimmed red, he wanted to curse him out, wanted to tear him apart, wanted to cut him open and dissect him. There were so many crazy emotions washing through him that he felt like he was about to burst.

He found himself unexpectedly unable to speak, with no choice but to seek immediate release. He Yu took two steps forward, moving for the first time since he'd found himself alone with Xie Qingcheng—

Wrapping a hand around the back of Xie Qingcheng's head, he shoved the man's entire body against the lectern, turned his head to one side, and vengefully bit into his neck.

Xie Qingcheng let out a low, muffled grunt at the unexpected pain. The soft sound sent sparks flying up He Yu's spine as the sweet, coppery taste of blood rushed into his mouth.

The dragon sucked at the blood of his sacrifice. It was hot and sweet—so much more stimulating than the fake blood that had splattered onto the camera lens. Sharp teeth bit into the human's neck and refused to let go. Wave after wave of warmth gushed out of Xie Qingcheng's broken skin; He Yu couldn't help but let out a low sigh of satisfaction as he swallowed the warm blood, his Adam's apple bobbing.

Just like that, the restless emotion that had been driving him to the edge of madness mere moments ago was put to rest through this bloody encounter.

The unending fever from his condition was making He Yu's entire body burn up, and when he pressed himself against Xie Qingcheng, it felt as though he could sear the older man's flesh and blood through their clothes. Xie Qingcheng wanted to break free, but He Yu wouldn't relinquish his grip; instead he pushed the man in the neatly pressed uniform against the lectern, knocking down some police academy teaching materials and promotional brochures in the process.

"Get off... He Yu, I'm telling you to get off me. Let go."

He Yu found his mouth way too annoying, so he lifted his thin, bloodstained lips from Xie Qingcheng's neck to press an almost savage kiss to his lips, sealing away that cold, mood-spoiling voice of his.

He Yu entangled with him desperately. He'd never realized that kissing could be such a pleasurable activity, that it could soothe the ordinary animal desires of youth and calm psychological Ebola's bloodlust at the same time.

Xie Qingcheng could see that speaking to him properly was no use, so he bit him back viciously instead. This kiss was far more brutal and blood-soaked than any they'd shared before. Perhaps Xie Qingcheng had really angered He Yu this time—or perhaps He Yu had truly stopped caring, as Xie Qingcheng had never bitten him this hard before, but He Yu still refused to back off. Either way, in the end, it was Xie Qingcheng who came off worse. With his lack of libido, he had never experienced such a searing, frenzied kiss before. It was the first time such a large amount of He Yu's blood had filled his mouth, spilling deeply into his throat, the heavy taste so unbearable it made him want to choke. He began gasping for air.

It was only then that He Yu let him go. His bright red lips were wet, smeared with both Xie Qingcheng's blood and his own. They had each gotten a thorough taste of the other's blood.

"I really want to fucking kill you, just like this," He Yu said as he bore down on Xie Qingcheng's body, his hands clamped around Xie Qingcheng's wrists, prohibiting any movement. But finally, he straightened up slightly, pulling away just a fraction so that he could take a clearer look at Xie Qingcheng in his disheveled uniform.

"Seriously," he said, with extreme hatred, resentment, and agitation, "that's exactly what I want to do right now—because that might be the only way to get a word of truth out of your lying mouth. Am I right?"

Xie Qingcheng could finally breathe. His chest heaved fiercely as he gasped. His navy-blue jacket had been torn open as they tangled, revealing the light blue police uniform dress shirt underneath. He Yu wanted to unfasten the uniform's silver belt buckle, so one of the hands he was pinning Xie Qingcheng with went slack.

How could Xie Qingcheng possibly allow He Yu to run rampant like this? The moment He Yu loosened his grip, he immediately turned the tables with a burst of strength, slamming He Yu fiercely against the desk before slapping him in the face with full force.

"You fucking animal!"

A red mark appeared on his cheek immediately, but He Yu only felt pleasure, not pain. He was abnormal to begin with, and his illness only served to intensify his brutal nature. Such a violent release of emotion only brought him mental and physical delight.

"Curse me out some more," he said.

Xie Qingcheng grabbed him by the hair and yanked him up, shoving him into the blackboard before kicking him ruthlessly and knocking him to the ground. Tables and chairs toppled over behind him with a resounding crash.

"I called you an animal." Panting, he tugged his navy-blue necktie with its silver clasp straight before refastening the buttons of his jacket one by one, his bloodshot eyes sharp as a blade and piercing as an awl as he stared at He Yu.

He Yu didn't get up. He slowly wiped at the blood smearing the corner of his mouth and cheek, and only straightened up slightly. It was as though the mess of tables and chairs behind him had become his throne; he leaned against the mass of upended furniture, just like that, and lifted those unfathomable almond eyes to carefully look Xie Qingcheng up and down with a coldly sinister air.

Then, pressing his tongue to the back of his teeth, he laughed. He tilted his head back and laughed for a long, long time. The scent of blood saturated every breath he took, yet he felt an indescribable pleasure, a pleasure that stemmed from his pathology being satisfied.

"You know that I'm in the middle of a flare-up, right, Xie Qingcheng?"

Xie Qingcheng looked at him in silence.

"The sicker I become, the less I care what you do. Even if you stabbed me through the heart with a knife right now, I'd just feel happy—incredibly happy—because it wouldn't hurt, but you'd owe me for the rest of your life. You'd never be able to act innocent and pure ever again." He Yu panted, his eyes ruthlessly predatory as they bored into that man. "You really are too good at disguising yourself, Xie Qingcheng."

Xie Qingcheng still didn't reply.

"You're wreathed in layer upon layer of disguises, like a cocoon within a cocoon—let me ask you, which of those layers is actually real?"

"What are you talking about?" said Xie Qingcheng. "Did you take the wrong fucking medicine today?"

He Yu only laughed, the sound so terrifying it could make one's blood run cold. When he finally stopped laughing, he reached out to Xie Qingcheng. "Come here."

For some reason, the moment he said those words, Xie Qingcheng—who had just imbibed a considerable amount of He Yu's blood—abruptly paled. His brow creased as if he was suddenly deeply uncomfortable, and his face took on a kind of sickly pallor.

But He Yu didn't notice. "Come here," he repeated. "I want you to listen to something—Xie Qingcheng, I'm telling you, there's nothing in this world that can stay hidden forever. Listen to this carefully, and you'll understand why I came to find you today."

Xie Qingcheng stood in place for a while, his face still pale, before finally, slowly, walking over to He Yu.

He Yu took out his cellphone and pulled up a recording. Before pressing play, however, he looked into Xie Qingcheng's pitch-black eyes. "Do you know who I ran into today?"

No reply.

"Would you like to take a guess?"

"...If there's something that you want to say, He Yu, then just say it."

He Yu smiled coldly. "Here's hoping you'll be able to maintain your composure once you finish listening. And here's hoping that when you hear this person's voice, you'll be able to remember the chance encounter you once shared." The corners of his mouth curved into a mocking smile, and he spoke his next words with deliberate emphasis: "Or rather, the farce you once enacted."

Click.

The recording began to play.

It was the entirety of the conversation between He Yu and the old woman at the café. The audio wasn't very long—in fact, the entire recording didn't last as long as Xie Qingcheng's silence after it finished playing.

For a long moment, neither of them spoke.

In the end, He Yu asked slowly, "What do you think? Did you like it?"

"...Where did you meet her?" Xie Qingcheng asked.

"In this very production." He Yu slowly set his phone down. "So you're not planning on denying it."

Xie Qingcheng said nothing.

"Why did you two act out a scene like that? Xie Qingcheng, what exactly were you trying to do? What are you hiding?"

Xie Qingcheng was silent for a moment longer. Then he closed his eyes. "It was a personal matter."

He Yu leaned his head back, wiping away the last of the blood staining the corners of his lips. Then his eyes landed back on Xie Qingcheng's figure. Provoked, he let out a cold, sneering laugh.

"Personal." He stared at him with his black eyes, no longer interested in wasting his breath on arguing about what constituted personal versus public. "Honestly, I'm well within my rights to ask you a few things about your personal matters." His eyes flickered slightly. "You already belong to me, so why shouldn't your business be mine?"

Being spoken to like this was the one thing Xie Qingcheng couldn't stand. He Yu was treating him like a woman. He opened his eyes and his expression swiftly darkened, becoming even more unsightly than it had been moments before. "I wish you had some sense of shame, He Yu."

"And I wish you'd tell the truth, Xie Qingcheng."

The words that left He Yu's bloodstained lips sounded vaguely like a command. For some reason, upon hearing those words, Xie Qingcheng's body swayed faintly, and his face abruptly blanched.

This time, very unfortunately...He Yu noticed.

He didn't pay it any mind at first, but a beat later, as though he'd suddenly realized something, he started in surprise. He narrowed his eyes, staring at Xie Qingcheng and his sudden onset of discomfort.

"... Xie Qingcheng," He Yu asked, "what's wrong?"

"I..." Xie Qingcheng's response was instantaneous, almost like he couldn't help but answer, but before he could finish speaking, he seemed to forcibly rein it in. His chest rose and fell as though he was trying to endure something, his expression clearly shifting as he gritted his teeth.

Then he abruptly turned his face away.

He Yu's expression turned even more unsightly as his voice hardened, determined to get to the bottom of this. "Speak. What's wrong?"

He didn't answer.

The sickly paleness of Xie Qingcheng's complexion became even more evident. Frozen in place, his back trembled slightly—it seemed like he did want to say something, but he was keeping himself firmly under control.

After a long stretch of silence, Xie Qingcheng suddenly erupted in a series of harsh coughs.

His coughing fit was so violent it made him list backward. Leaning against the icy ceramic tiles of the classroom wall, he looked up at He Yu through reddened eyes in what seemed to be genuine misery. At that moment, seeing his unusual reaction, He Yu's heart shuddered violently. Could it be...?

"Xie Qingcheng, you're..."

He didn't finish his sentence right away.

The way Xie Qingcheng looked right now suddenly called to mind something he'd experienced before, on a winter day several years ago...

Back when he had been studying overseas, he'd gone to a health facility and run into a mentally ill patient with severe symptoms. The doctors and nurses had tried to persuade him with words, but it was futile—they'd had no choice but to forcibly restrain and sedate him. But that foreign patient was very strong and struggled free in an instant, shouting and cursing in French at the top of his lungs as he swung at the staff.

"I'm going to kill you all—who told you to lock me up?! Who let you treat me like this?! Ha ha, ha ha ha ha!"

He Yu hadn't been feeling very well himself—that day, he'd sustained a minor injury that was still bleeding, so bloodthirsty violence was already on his mind. If he wanted to calm himself down as quickly as possible, watching a scene as hectic and intense as that obviously wouldn't do him any good.

He was too annoyed to keep quiet, so he said reproachfully in French, "Shut up."

Those words had been nothing more than a slip of the tongue as He Yu was passing by—but for some reason, this lunatic's face suddenly turned pale. He stared at He Yu as if he'd seen something terrifying.

The patient's suffering still seemed to be surging through his body, about to condense into a shriek and burst forth from his mouth. But as he stared attentively at He Yu, he actually managed to use all his strength to choke back the cries in his throat. In the wake of He Yu's "shut up," it was as though a massive, invisible hand had locked itself around his neck.

Back then, all the medical personnel present had been dumbfounded.

"D-do you know him?"

"...I do not," He Yu replied, just as taken aback.

For the doctors and nurses, the event passed just like that; later on, they assumed that it was likely just a coincidence. Only He Yu realized that it wasn't. He had looked carefully at the patient's deathly pale face, at the veins that bulged as he strained, and a tentative idea suddenly rose up in his heart, diffusing improbably through the air like early morning fog.

After the medical personnel left, he walked over to where the patient was still gasping for breath.

He Yu shot a sidelong look at the seated man. To confirm his suspicions, he issued him the cruelest possible order.

Testing the waters, he said softly, "Je veux que tu te suicides."

And then—like a horrifying truth breaking through the dense fog—suddenly, the patient's conscious mind began to resist, making his face turn bloodless with pain as his body swayed back and forth.

Like a pair of distant mirrors, He Yu's eyes reflected his struggle.

He stood very close to the patient, close enough that the man could smell the stench of blood on his body. After a few seconds, or perhaps a few dozen, the man lifted his hand as if finally overpowered by the nebulous force that was tearing him apart.

Eyes unfocused, he raised his hand—and ruthlessly seized his own neck.

He Yu was so astonished that it wasn't until the man had nearly choked himself to death that he snapped out of it. He immediately called out to him—

"Stop. Stop it!"

The man dropped his hand as if exhausted. His tall, sturdy physique looked as if it had come out of a red-hot forge, and he collapsed onto the ground like a heap of mud.

Afterward, He Yu found out that if he could make a mentally ill person smell his blood and then gave them a command, they would lose control of themself and carry out his orders. At Cheng Kang Psychiatric Hospital, he'd learned from Xie Qingcheng that this ability had a name: blood toxin.

In the present, He Yu's gaze was fixed unwaveringly on Xie Qingcheng's face.

This expression, the face of someone being compelled by the blood toxin but using all his strength to shake off those invisible chains... He knew it all too well.

There was no mistake.

Right now, Xie Qingcheng...was being affected by his blood toxin in the exact same way.

It was as if a sharp blade had cut through the fog and the darkness. A subtle flicker of light flashed through He Yu's eyes. Slowly rising from the floor, he murmured, "Xie Qingcheng, you..."

Xie Qingcheng had always been extremely calm. He Yu knew very well that it was easy for him to resolutely weather situations as absurd as the one that had just transpired, but at that moment, he didn't dare meet He Yu's eyes. Instead, he suddenly turned around and strode toward the door with an ashen expression on his face.

Xie Qingcheng's hand had already grabbed the doorknob and unlocked it with a *click*. He was about to pull the door open and leave.

But at that moment, He Yu caught up to him from behind and shut the classroom door again with a *bang*.

Pressing one hand against the door next to Xie Qingcheng's face and wordlessly grabbing the man's waist with his other, he forced him to turn around and face him.

He wasn't wrong...he wasn't wrong...

He Yu's pupils contracted—

There was no way he was wrong.

Xie Qingcheng was such a profoundly cold person—but at this moment, his body was shuddering violently in his grip, as if, despite losing control of himself in the face of He Yu's command, he refused to resign himself to his fate and was struggling with all his might like a butterfly caught in a spider's web. He was desperate to escape the compulsion of the blood toxin...

For a while, He Yu didn't know what to say.

Astonishment, fury, amazement, excitement, ecstasy, grief... In that moment, all of these emotions, as incompatible as fire and water, flooded into his heart.

"You... You're..." He Yu looked at the man trapped between his chest and the classroom door. This man who never had a hair out of place, who was always strong and severe...he simply didn't dare believe it. His voice came out mangled. "Are you the same as me?"

Xie Qingcheng said nothing.

"Xie Qingcheng, could it be you're the same as me?" Each syllable was more vicious, more sorrowful, more crazed, and more despairing than the last. "Are you?!"

His despair stemmed from his disbelief that Xie Qingcheng could also have psychological problems. In his eyes, Xie Qingcheng had always been an extremely strong person, someone who was endlessly capable of controlling his own emotions and state of mind.

Not to mention, he was a doctor. If even this kind of person could secretly buckle under the pressures of society and suffer from a mental illness, then how could He Yu believe that the human heart could prevail over such illnesses?

These demons could even defeat someone like Xie Qingcheng.

Panting, He Yu yanked on Xie Qingcheng's hair, forcing Xie Qingcheng to look at him. Almond eyes, filled with a trembling halo of light, met a pair of peach-blossom eyes that were as still as stagnant water. They were practically nose to nose.

Xie Qingcheng had inhaled more of the scent of He Yu's blood than anyone who had been affected by blood toxin before, so its effect on him was correspondingly much stronger.

He Yu's throat bobbed as he watched him, unable to stop himself from stroking Xie Qingcheng's hair over and over again in a deranged way. He strove for calm, lowering his volume, but still, his voice was shaking.

The emotions hidden within were even more terrifying than his voice itself.

His bloodstained lips hovered just above Xie Qingcheng's slightly panting mouth, with only a few centimeters between them. He mumbled, or said, or ordered...

"Tell me."

He Yu clutched at Xie Qingcheng so hard that, when the older man removed his police uniform later today, he'd doubtless find his waist covered in blue and purple bruises. He Yu gripped him firmly, like he had managed to grasp onto a vein of truth in the slipping, sliding quicksand. An intense light flashed through his eyes, but his voice grew softer and softer, like a shaman's murmured incantation.

"Tell me. Are you the same as me?"

Xie Qingcheng's brow creased in pain.

"Tell the truth, Xie Qingcheng." He Yu was desperate to uncover the secrets hidden within this man's body. His heart pounded, heating him up until his eyes burned scarlet.

"Are you mentally ill too?"

84

ARE YOU UNWILLING TO TELL THE TRUTH?

A SUDDEN HARSHNESS edged into He Yu's voice. "Say something!"

No response.

Under his repeated interrogation, Xie Qingcheng paled beneath him and slowly closed his eyes.

A man's man like Xie Qingcheng would otherwise never feel the slightest fear of He Yu, but the power of the blood toxin was brutal, overbearing, coursing through his body unrestrained.

This was different from the way it had been before. He'd never tasted all that much of it, but this time, he'd ingested so much of He Yu's blood. His mouth was still filled with the metallic taste He Yu had left behind from their passionate kiss. No matter how strong his willpower was, his body still felt an uncontrollable fear. In the face of this extremely invasive blood toxin, in spite of himself, he began to tremble.

"Xie Qingcheng..."

Xie Qingcheng's waist shivered in He Yu's grip. He even seemed somewhat pitiful, held like that. This was something He Yu had never felt before. He Yu looked down at the man's face, from his lowered lashes to his pale and slightly cool lips...but no matter how pitiful his body seemed, he still exuded an aura of strength.

Xie Qingcheng could actually still resist.

His forehead was quickly sheened with sweat. Against the navy blue of the formal police uniform he wore, his face seemed extraordinarily pale.

In the end, it seemed as if he had pushed through via sheer willpower; it looked like even blood toxin had its limitations. After the strongest surge of compulsion passed, its coercive power gradually faded.

Xie Qingcheng slowly stopped trembling. He was already soaked in sweat.

He lifted his quivering lashes and whispered, "He Yu." Though his voice was very weak and extremely hoarse, he still sounded lucid. "Didn't you know? Everyone living in modern society is mentally ill to some degree."

He Yu stared at him.

"The reason your blood toxin could affect me is because I didn't just smell your blood, I also drank it," he said very slowly, as if he lacked the strength to speak. "Even if I have only the mildest of mental issues, your ability still affects me if I swallow your blood. There's nothing strange about it."

At this point, he reached out and slowly tried to push He Yu away.

But He Yu didn't move. "You're still lying to me."

Xie Qingcheng said nothing.

"I bet half the things you've ever told me are lies. I know you're still lying this time—why do you have to be such a liar?! Xie Qingcheng? Everything you've told me—everything you've told *anyone*—is any of it true?!"

Xie Qingcheng didn't answer. Even though he'd escaped the overbearing power of the blood toxin, the residual terror of having his mind coerced and controlled remained within his blood. It made his head feel a little dizzy and his body a little weak. Leaning against the door, he took a moment to collect himself before straightening up and expressionlessly flinging He Yu's hand away without another word, determined to walk out.

But he'd accidentally poured oil on the flames raging in He Yu's already frustrated mind. He Yu grabbed Xie Qingcheng by the hips and yanked him back. With a *thud*, he pinned him hard against the wall.

"Don't even *think* about leaving this room without telling me the truth."

Xie Qingcheng's current state was like that of someone who had just gone through a life-or-death struggle. His eyes were somewhat blank, unable to focus as they gazed at He Yu vacantly, but his tone was still harsh: "Let go."

The response he received was He Yu clamping his wrists together and bringing them over his head where he pinned them against the door. He stared down at him.

And then, He Yu suddenly dipped his head to kiss him.

He kissed him very hard. Since Xie Qingcheng no longer had much strength to fight back, He Yu licked his way in quickly, twisting his tongue inside Xie Qingcheng's slick, soft mouth as he tried to force him to taste more of his blood. It was an utterly unbridled kiss, and because there was less resistance, he actually felt a sense of bone-deep intimacy.

By the time He Yu let up a little and pulled his mouth away from the lips that he'd kissed to the point of wetness, both their breaths had quickened slightly—but while this was urgency born of desire on He Yu's part, Xie Qingcheng's response was purely physiological due to a lack of oxygen.

"Listen up, Xie Qingcheng. If you don't tell me the truth, I'll use the blood toxin on you again." He Yu pressed his bloodstained lips softly to Xie Qingcheng's mouth, his lower jaw, then moved up once more, nudging against the high bridge of his nose. "I'll use it until you tell me."

"The answer will be the same no matter how many times you use it," Xie Qingcheng said. "If I can break free of it once, then I can do it again. Try it if you don't believe me."

He Yu stared at him with overwhelming hatred. He wanted to kill Xie Qingcheng and dig all his hidden secrets from his cold, frigid corpse. But he couldn't handle seeing Xie Qingcheng in this weakened state, a sight he saw so rarely.

Perhaps Xie Qingcheng possessed a toxin as well, some toxin related to desire. Why else would He Yu feel such a strong urge to hold him and kiss him when he saw him shivering and trembling with helpless vulnerability? When he didn't like men... He'd never liked men...

He Yu, who didn't like men, stared at Xie Qingcheng, who refused to obey. The young man's throat bobbed again as he took those lips, already rouged with his kisses, against his own once more.

"Either your body or your mouth is going to tell the truth—you can choose which one. The way I see it, seems like you prefer the first option."

Their lips intertwined wetly, and as He Yu kissed him, the taste changed to that of desire burning hotter and hotter. Xie Qingcheng didn't want to bite He Yu's tongue again, so He Yu took the opportunity to intensify the kiss and press in deeper. The kiss grew fiercely heated as their tongues entwined, and soft, wet noises permeated the room.

Xie Qingcheng was about to drive him insane.

The answers he wanted to hear.

The blood he wanted to drink.

The body he wanted to fuck.

They all belonged to one person—the person held beneath him, in his arms. But he was so stubborn and impenetrable that He Yu found himself driven close to madness with all kinds of complicated emotions, his mind and body manipulated by Xie Qingcheng's every move.

Just who was controlling who here?

Toward the end, the kiss transformed. The young man's desires were ready to burst out of him, and with Xie Qingcheng refusing to tell him the truth, He Yu was unwilling to let him go just like that. He had to gain something from Xie Qingcheng to stave off the emptiness in his heart. His ministrations intensified, one hand wandering freely while the other cradled the back of Xie Qingcheng's neck, angling his head as he kissed him again and again.

He was positive that Xie Qingcheng and Li Ruoqiu had never shared such a heated kiss before. It was obvious that Xie Qingcheng wasn't used to it. Xie Qingcheng clearly wasn't some-one who would take the initiative to kiss someone else, and it was unlikely that a woman like Li Ruoqiu would aggressively take the lead with a man like this. It was impossible that they had ever entangled this way.

He Yu went to strip Xie Qingcheng of his clothing as he kissed him—it'd been a long time since he'd slept with Xie Qingcheng.

Well, to him, it'd been a long time. With how provoked he felt by these secrets and emotions, He Yu's desire to touch Xie Qingcheng grew even stronger. He was panting slightly from how long they'd kissed, so he pulled back a little. Their lips were so wet that they made a soft smacking noise as they separated, a sound that made the rims of Xie Qingcheng's eyes redden. He Yu's eyes were even redder than Xie Qingcheng's, filled with desire, like an inescapable trawl that had yet to trap its prey, sweeping toward Xie Qingcheng to entangle him within its confines.

"If you refuse to be honest with me, then don't blame me for punishing you."

As He Yu spoke, he tightened his grip, his movements bordering on violent as he pressed his hand against the silver buckle of Xie Qingcheng's black leather uniform belt. The flames burning inside his chest were so hot that he was about to undo it immediately.

But how could Xie Qingcheng let him? He seized the belt tightly and refused to let He Yu move it, his knuckles turning white as he tussled soundlessly with He Yu. As the pair struggled in silence, Xie Qingcheng could feel the youth's scalding hardness pressing into him where it rubbed against his stomach through their clothes, making the veins at Xie Qingcheng's temples bulge and throb until they ached.

He resisted with all his might, as if being humiliated in a police uniform was something that he absolutely could not allow; He Yu wasn't quite able to gain the upper hand as they grappled with each other, simply because of the depth of Xie Qingcheng's fury. It was difficult to say whether the two of them were hooking up or fighting, as both ended up sustaining some considerable injuries.

At that very moment, He Yu's phone rang.

He Yu had no intention of answering. He continued to pull at Xie Qingcheng's uniform, turning his head to press kisses onto the man's pale neck. But the calls came in, one after another, unceasingly urgent, until finally He Yu began to feel somewhat vexed.

Furious, he took out his cellphone with the intention of turning it off.

When he looked down, however, he saw six missed calls from Executive Huang. The seventh was still ringing relentlessly.

He Yu had no choice. Shooting Xie Qingcheng a ferocious glare through eyes that had been seared red, he took a moment to catch his breath and then tapped his phone to accept the call. "Hello."

Lü Zhishu had arrived. Hoping to surprise her son, she hadn't given him a heads-up.

As Huang Zhilong told him this over the phone, He Yu stared at where he had Xie Qingcheng shoved against the door, at his rumpled uniform and the sweat beading on his forehead, and couldn't help but gnash his teeth.

Well, his mom had certainly given him a great fucking surprise.

"Hurry up and get over here. They mentioned that you're on set, so Executive Lü came over directly. She's waiting for you in the director's tent."

After he hung up, it took He Yu a long while to pull himself back together.

There were several beats of silence; in the end, He Yu lifted his eyes and said to Xie Qingcheng, "Officer Chen's leaving today, right?" His red lips were wet as he braced one hand against the door and lifted the other to pat Xie Qingcheng on the face. "Just wait. I'll come to your room tonight and finish what we started."

Lü Zhishu hadn't come alone.

He Li was on winter break and had returned home from school, as neither He Jiwei nor Lü Zhishu were spending the Spring Festival holiday in Yanzhou this year, instead choosing to remain in Huzhou.

He was different from He Yu in that over the course of his entire life, he had never once been treated with cold neglect. He'd cried and thrown a great tantrum over the phone, but in the end, unable to persuade his parents, he could only follow them down to Huzhou, sobbing and sniffling the whole while.

He Yu was still burning with rage over Xie Qingcheng's behavior, so when he suddenly came face-to-face with the little brother he hadn't seen in ages, his eyes couldn't help but abruptly cool by several degrees.

He Li was in middle school and far inferior to He Yu in terms of looks. However, his general facial features still carried a shadow of the He Family's genes, so he could still be considered fortunate on the whole.

"He Yu, you're here." Lü Zhishu and He Li were in the middle of watching something on the director's monitors. When she turned back and saw that He Yu had entered, Lü Zhishu hastily pasted on a freshly baked smile before pushing He Li forward. "Go say hi to your big brother."

He Li pouted. It made him look like a wretched tramp. "No way, I don't wanna..."

Luckily, He Yu had drunk some of Xie Qingcheng's blood and released some of his pent-up emotions, so he wasn't feeling particularly violent. Otherwise, given his condition that morning, there was truly no guarantee that he wouldn't have beaten his little brother to death in front of all these witnesses.

As it was, he could control himself now, so he smiled blandly, maintaining decorum. "Long time no see, He Li."

Just looking at him made He Li feel green with envy.

People always looked different in photos and videos than they did in the flesh. He Yu was even better-looking in person than he appeared on camera—he was stately and handsome with skin as white as snow, and for some reason his lips were more vividly red than normal, like plum blossoms in a snowy field. But he was tall in stature, and aside from his exquisitely refined face, his aura wasn't feminine in the least—in fact, he gave off an overwhelmingly domineering air.

Forget the fact that He Li couldn't beat him in any subject in school—even when it came to looks, he was inferior in multiple aspects.

How could He Li be at peace with this, when the two of them had been born to the same parents? If it wasn't for how much more his parents had doted on him all these years, he probably would have ended up even more unhinged than He Yu.

The only thing that pleased him was the knowledge that his brother was sick. He didn't know exactly what kind of illness it was, but he knew he was abnormal.

Sometimes, when he was in a dark mood, he would even think— if He Yu died from his illness, then there'd be no competition for his family's inheritance once he got older. Children who grew up in households like theirs would often end up no better than those from the most destitute of families; sons and daughters would cheat each other as a matter of course, and brothers would try to find ways to entrap and send one another to prison—none of that was out of the ordinary.

He Li had been deeply influenced by the pack of scoundrels he called friends in Yanzhou, so it was inevitable that he'd entertain such sinister ideas.

No wonder Wei Dongheng disliked He Yu so much. The older He Li became, the more clearly inferior he was to He Yu, and the more hostile he felt toward his elder brother. He grew to understand just how unpleasant it must have been for Young Master Wei to have spent his entire childhood being compared to He Yu by the people in their social circle.

He would have much rather had Wei Dongheng for a brother. Wei Dongheng was trash in every way, a perfect contrast to He Li's own excellence—that would be much more agreeable.

He Yu glanced down at the middle schooler from the corner of his eyes. He could tell what He Li was thinking with little to no effort, and he scoffed coldly and lifted a hand to pat He Li on the head—the gesture might have seemed affectionate, but the strength he used was considerable.

"You've gotten taller," he said.

"What are you doing?! Why did you hit me?!" He Li jumped, backing away abruptly and turning to his mom to tattle with a bashful expression. "Mom, he hit me—"

However, to He Li's shock, his mother refused to come to his aid. Instead, she just coughed quietly. "Your brother hasn't seen you for a long time, so he got too excited. What do you mean, he hit you? Why would he hit you? He's your brother. Come on."

Never mind how dumbstruck He Li was, even He Yu raised an eyebrow slightly, looking at Lü Zhishu with a complicated expression on his face.

Lü Zhishu walked over and gave He Yu a hug. "After I picked up He Li, I made a special trip here to see you. Tomorrow, I'll send someone to Huzhou to clean up the house."

To have his family constantly by his side had once been a dream that He Yu had yearned for day and night. But now that it was about to come true, he honestly didn't feel all that excited. He had probably waited so long he'd become numb to the idea. Too many things had happened since the days he'd held that dream, and people's hearts were prone to change.

"Let's have dinner together tonight," Lü Zhishu continued.

He Yu had finally managed to wait things out until Chen Man had left, but now his mother and brother had shown up—he truly couldn't muster any enthusiasm.

"All right," he said with an exceedingly indifferent expression, reluctant to even pretend to look happy. "Let's get dinner."

The meal passed by in a tedious fashion—it was almost embarrassing. The dishes didn't even taste as good as the wontons Xie Qingcheng had made him, and the occasion came to a boring end.

"Mom, I have work tomorrow, so I can't hang out with you guys. I'm going to go back to the hotel. I'm sorry." He Yu's words, at least, were polite.

Lü Zhishu accepted the excuse readily. The three of them being able to finish a meal together peacefully was an achievement in itself, so she didn't force it; she watched He Yu get into the van and leave without argument.

As soon as he left, He Li started sulking. "Mom, how come you're being so nice to him all of a sudden? I don't like it when you're nice to him."

"He's still your ge, and we didn't look after him enough before." Seeing He Li's expression, Lü Zhishu immediately added, "But you'll always be the one I love the most."

He Li was still grumbling under his breath—it was quite evident that his ambitions far exceeded He Yu's. He had been doted on all his life, after all. "The most" wasn't good enough for him. He wanted to be the only one.

He Yu, on the other hand, didn't attach any importance to such nonsense, because when it came to his family, his heart was dead to begin with. Even if you put a dead heart in a greenhouse, you couldn't warm it up.

For his part, He Yu went straight back to the hotel, where he used Executive Huang's privileges to obtain a key card to Xie Qingcheng's room.

Even though many unpleasant, unexpected things had taken place today, there was still one fact that made him very happy—Chen Man was gone.

Although the scent of alcohol lingered around him from dinner with his mother and his brother, he was completely sober. He checked the time on his phone when he stepped into the elevator—it was already past ten o'clock.

By now, Xie Qingcheng ought to have already washed up and should be getting ready for bed. As He Yu thought about this, for some reason that night in Hangshi floated up in his mind—he remembered the way Xie Qingcheng had looked in his bathrobe as He Yu pressed him beneath his body and kissed him by mistake.

The heart that Lü Zhishu hadn't managed to heat up suddenly stirred with warmth.

He Yu stood in the dark hallway before the door to Xie Qingcheng's room. When he shamelessly swiped the card, the door opened with a *click*. It was even darker inside than in the hallway, a night-light in the depths of the room the only source of illumination.

He Yu was a completely uninvited guest—but perhaps he didn't think of it that way. After all, the way he saw it, he'd fucked Xie Qingcheng before. Why shouldn't he enter his room?

However, as soon as he took a step inside, He Yu heard the faint sound of panting and soft, wet noises coming from the bed that lay within the room's murky darkness. He wasn't a virgin anymore; he knew perfectly well what those sounds signified. He immediately froze in shock.

85

WE CAME ACROSS ANOTHER HOMICIDE

BEFORE HE GOT AHOLD of himself, he nearly punched through the switch for the room's main light as rage surged through his head. As the room was flooded with brightness, He Yu rushed forward with bloodshot eyes and yanked aside the twisting blankets—

"Xie Qingcheng, you—"

"Mother*fucker*, the hell's wrong with you?!"

"Aaaaaah! Oh my god, what's going on?!"

The shrieks of a man and a woman rang out from the bed. In his rage-addled state, He Yu hadn't realized until that moment that the two lovers going at it on the bed weren't Xie Qingcheng and Chen Man at all, but rather two minor supporting cast members.

By this point, the actor and actress had also realized who he was, and their anger instantly turned into horrified shock.

He Yu stared at the couple, and the couple stared back. All three of them were speechless.

They were both playing minor roles, but this kind of major production would hardly recruit D-listers. The man and woman were both veteran actors with names He Yu recognized, and he knew that both of them were married to other people. The man's wife had even gotten pregnant recently; she'd trended on Weibo when she shared some sweet pregnancy photos.

But right now, they were both in bed with someone other than their spouse—these two laoshi were clearly having an affair out here.

"H-how did you get in here..."

He Yu stilled for a moment before saying indifferently, "I took the wrong room card. Isn't this 2209?"

"I-it's 2209," the actress said in a shaky voice. "I-I just switched rooms... The heat wasn't working in my room, so..."

"Wasn't there someone else staying in this room, though?" He Yu didn't care whether they were having an affair—he wasn't the least bit interested in such things, as extramarital affairs were completely unremarkable in the entertainment industry—so his face was completely devoid of surprise as he asked them directly, "Where is he?"

The actress cautiously drew the blanket securely over herself, then said in a trembling voice, "We don't know either—when I asked the front desk to change my room, the receptionist just gave me the card to this one... The...the previous guest must have checked out..."

Ashen-faced, He Yu turned around and left.

"Ah!" the actress cried out plaintively to his retreating back. "He-laoshi, *please* don't tell anyone about this—"

He Yu went to the front desk to ask which room the guest in 2209 had switched to.

Probably because his expression was very grave, the receptionist raised her head somewhat nervously after she looked it up.

"...He checked out."

"He checked..."

He Yu choked on his words.

Checked out?

He had looked at the remaining production schedule—barring unusual circumstances, Xie Qingcheng was supposed to continue supervising the production for quite a while. But if he'd checked out instead of just switching rooms, where was he staying?

Since he couldn't find him in person, He Yu gave Xie Qingcheng a call.

"Hello, Xie Qingcheng." He Yu had expected Xie Qingcheng to hang up on him and was surprised when he actually answered. He was so anxious, his whole body leaned forward slightly as he gripped his phone in his hand.

"Where are you?"

Xie Qingcheng was silent for a while before he said, "He Yu."

"Yes."

"Surely you're not so fucking narcissistic that you thought I'd really just stay in my room waiting for you to come back and fuck me."

The fucking actually wasn't all that important—he just wanted to speak to Xie Qingcheng alone.

"Did you get your head caught in a door or what?"

Once Xie Qingcheng was done cursing him out and letting off some steam, he hung up the phone, leaving He Yu rooted to the spot with an expression of displeasure on his face.

...You asked for it, He Yu thought.

He walked over to the resting area in the lobby, where he sat down and immediately opened the hacking software installed on his phone. Tracing the signal that had just been transmitted, He Yu took less than a minute to determine Xie Qingcheng's current location.

Xie Qingcheng was at a clay-pot congee restaurant on South Street.

He Yu didn't want anyone to follow him, so he didn't call the nanny van. Instead, he borrowed an ordinary car, a brand he didn't even recognize, from one of the production assistants, and drove it straight to the congee shop.

It was only once he arrived that he discovered Xie Qingcheng wasn't alone. He was accompanied by an assistant writer and a production manager. The three of them had just finished eating their late-night snack, and now they were standing outside the entrance waiting for a taxi. Xie Qingcheng must have walked away to take his call earlier—he definitely wouldn't have wanted anyone to overhear such a private conversation.

"Ah, Young Master He."

"He-laoban."

He Yu gave the two girls quite a shock when he rolled down his window. Even Xie Qingcheng was slightly surprised, but he quickly realized that He Yu must have used illicit methods to find him, and his expression turned grim.

"Did He-laoban come to have some congee?" the production manager asked.

He Yu paused, then smiled. "I was just passing by. It's so late— where are you guys headed?"

"We were just discussing tomorrow's shoot. It's that scene at the research institute tomorrow, but the director thinks there are still some issues with the props, so we were just about to take Professor Xie to the set to take a look."

"Well then, get in." He Yu unlocked the car doors with one hand, resting the other on the steering wheel as he stared unblinkingly at Xie Qingcheng. "I'm just out for a drive. I'll take you there."

Who wouldn't want to ride in a handsome guy's car? The two girls clambered happily into the back seat.

Naturally, they left the passenger seat open, as they couldn't allow a man as stoic as Xie Qingcheng to squeeze in with them in the back—not that they wouldn't have enjoyed it, but it would have been rather unbecoming.

Xie Qingcheng looked back at He Yu for several seconds as he stood there in the wind and snow, but in the end he had no choice but to grimly take a long-legged step into the car. He was so irritated that he forgot to put on his seatbelt after getting in, simply turning his head to look out the window with a dour expression.

It wasn't until He Yu's youthful scent pressed near that Xie Qingcheng suddenly snapped out of it. "What are you doing?" he said harshly.

He Yu leaned his entire body in until he was very close to him. The girls in the back couldn't see clearly from this angle as he lowered his lashes, indulged the desire in his eyes, and inhaled Xie Qingcheng's scent.

"I borrowed this car, so it'd be annoying if this got caught on camera and the owner's points were deducted. I hope you understand, Professor Xie." As he spoke, he reached over to pull down the seatbelt and fasten it with a *click*. "I'm buckling your seatbelt for you."

The writer and production manager thought nothing of it as they watched cheerfully from the back.

Xie Qingcheng didn't feel like wasting words with He Yu—even his anger was more than he wanted to offer. He only said coldly, "You have a mouth, and I have hands. Please remind me instead of doing it for me."

He Yu smiled. "Okay. Next time I definitely will."

The car whirred to life and sped off in the direction of the next day's set.

The studio where it was located wasn't all that far away, but it was surrounded by embankments. Aside from a handful of staff members, it was completely deserted.

He Yu's cousin was originally supposed to supervise this scene, but a position in a hospital's emergency department wasn't as predictable as one in a university's graduate school. When his cousin received a sudden summons to return to the hospital, the production had no choice but to let him go.

By the time they entered the studio, the workers had nearly finished assembling the next day's set according to the plans, but there were still a number of details that needed to be ironed out. Thus, the production manager and writer began making adjustments according to the discussion they'd had with Xie Qingcheng in the congee shop.

After explaining himself succinctly to the prop master, Xie Qingcheng watched calmly from the sidelines with He Yu.

The entire set had been designed to resemble a high-tech underground laboratory, with oxygen chambers, Petri dishes, operating tables, surgical lights... There were all kinds of highly realistic props. Some of it was even real equipment that the production had specially borrowed from collaborating hospitals.

Xie Qingcheng stood in their midst, looking at the massive specimen tanks looming in the corner. There were several of them crowded together, each two to three meters tall and containing a dummy made by the props department immersed in a chemical solution. The dummies were crafted to appear very lifelike, their hair floating like seaweed. It was one of these props that had been mistaken for an actual dead person in the glass cabinet back at the hotel. Now that they had been submerged in liquid, they seemed even creepier.

Xie Qingcheng's gaze wavered in uncertainty for an instant, but he quickly pulled his thoughts back under control.

"Where'd you move to?" He Yu asked softly as he stepped up beside him.

Xie Qingcheng knew that if he didn't tell He Yu, he would just find out on his own, so there was no point in hiding the truth from him. He told him the name of the hotel with an air of cool indifference.

"Why'd you move over there?"

"Because you don't have the privilege of obtaining the keycard to any room you want at other hotels."

...He'd hit the nail on the head.

"It must be expensive living somewhere else, and you're so stingy..." He Yu likewise poked at Xie Qingcheng's sore spot.

Xie Qingcheng lit a cigarette. "When I checked out, the production reimbursed me."

He had no reply to that.

This stupid production was really dumb as fuck—absolutely no foresight to speak of! Young Master He the capitalist wanted to fuck this man, yet they went ahead and reimbursed his room fees so he could live somewhere else!

"Cough cough cough cough!"

The hallway in this studio was so narrow that smoking indoors was bound to affect other people. Sure enough, the production manager couldn't handle it and started coughing. Xie Qingcheng immediately stubbed out his cigarette.

Seeing that his unfulfilled craving was bothering him, He Yu leaned back against the wall for a while, then said, "Let's take a walk outside." When he saw the look in Xie Qingcheng's eyes, he added, "Just out front by the door, where there are people. You don't need to be so afraid of me."

"When have I ever been afraid of you? You're giving yourself too much credit."

With that, Xie Qingcheng walked toward the exit.

He Yu chased after him. "If you're not afraid of me, then why did you switch hotels—?"

"You're a pain in the ass."

He had no response.

It was freezing outside, with snow drifting down through the crisp open air.

He Yu stood beside Xie Qingcheng the whole time he spent silently smoking a cigarette, leaning against the outside of the studio. There were so many things he wanted to ask Xie Qingcheng, but he knew he wouldn't receive a single answer.

There were also many things he wanted to do with Xie Qingcheng, but he didn't know why he had such desires.

The snow came down faster and faster as the night grew darker. The staff members left one after another as they completed their duties.

Xie Qingcheng hadn't smoked his fill yet and didn't feel like going back inside, so he took out his phone, intending to message the production manager to ask when they'd be finished, only to glance down and see—zero bars.

He asked a nearby staff member about it, one Xie Qingcheng hadn't seen before: a man in a raincoat who was loading some stuff into a car.

"It's always like that out here," the man said. He was packing a pile of props with no discernible purpose into the trunk. There was a large, heavy prop chest among them—even though he'd gotten a platform stepladder, he still seemed to be struggling somewhat, so Xie Qingcheng lent him a hand.

"Thank you," said the staff member.

"No problem," Xie Qingcheng replied.

"You're looking for cell service, right?" The man clapped the dust off his hands. "The coverage here is terrible, it comes and goes. You'll need to drive about half a kilometer out before the signal stabilizes. Are you leaving? Want me to give you guys a ride?"

"No need, thanks. We have a car."

The staff member stared at Xie Qingcheng some more, tugged down the hood of his raincoat, and smiled. Without saying anything more, he gathered his things and left.

This was the last large vehicle, which meant that there were very few people left inside the building now. Xie Qingcheng stood waiting outside for the writer and production manager to come out, but by the time he'd finished his third cigarette, the girls were still inside. He didn't know what sort of problem they could have run into that would require such a long discussion.

Xie Qingcheng originally wanted to go back inside, but when he saw that there was only one cigarette left in his pack, he couldn't help wanting to just polish it off.

Coughing slightly, he lit his Zippo and was just about to bring it to the cigarette when He Yu said, "Stop smoking. Let me have the last one."

He spoke conversationally, as though inviting discussion, but he really had no such intentions; he snatched the cigarette directly from between Xie Qingcheng's soft lips and took the lighter from his hand. Then he stepped further away, where the secondhand smoke couldn't reach Xie Qingcheng, and lit the cigarette.

That orange flame flickered between He Yu's fingers. Xie Qingcheng furrowed his pitch-black brows as he gazed at him.

He Yu's temperament was impossible to grasp. One moment he'd be smiling so gently as he spoke to you, the next he'd reveal a ferocious, predatory face. It wasn't necessarily a good thing when he smiled, nor was it necessarily hopeless when he lost his temper. In short, it was very difficult to get a glimpse into his heart.

Like right now. Xie Qingcheng had no idea what kind of madness had gotten into He Yu's head that would make him suddenly start smoking.

And it was his very last cigarette to boot.

He Yu tilted his head back to exhale a cloud of gray mist, gazing up at the boundless windblown snow. He looked very beautiful when he smoked, graceful and sensuous, without any of the greasy, unsavory vibes that men in the entertainment industry often gave off. But he wasn't like Xie Qingcheng either—when Xie Qingcheng smoked, he exuded an overwhelming aura of masculinity and looked incredibly handsome, like a rich liquor. He Yu was more like the mellow-hued silhouettes seen in Wong Kar-wai's films.

The last cigarette was finished.

He Yu walked back over the thin layer of snow on the ground. When he reached Xie Qingcheng, his eyelashes were dusted with frost. "They're still not done?"

"No."

"Let's go in and take a look."

There was practically no one left inside. Most of the lights in the studio had gone out, so it was very dark, with the only illumination coming from some weak continuous floodlights way up on the ceiling.

He Yu and Xie Qingcheng walked further into the building, gravel crunching beneath their feet.

Suddenly—

Thud.

Xie Qingcheng turned around at once. "Why did the main door close?"

"Maybe the wind is blowing too hard." He Yu looked back too, frowning slightly. He thought for a bit. "Let's find them and leave."

They followed the long walkway into the depths of the studio, where several rooms had been transformed into labs. The two girls had been talking to the set designer in the largest of these rooms, but when Xie Qingcheng and He Yu checked it, they discovered that no one was there.

The room was empty.

It was very quiet. He Yu called the girls' names, but there was no response. However, they could indistinctly hear a continuous susurration coming from one of the rooms in the distance.

"Did they leave just now?" asked Xie Qingcheng.

"Definitely not," said He Yu.

An ominous feeling flooded out from the bottoms of their hearts.

Xie Qingcheng took out his phone and looked at the screen. Seeing that his signal was still at zero bars, the ominous feeling intensified.

"Go check the other rooms," he told He Yu.

He Yu didn't move.

Xie Qingcheng turned around to see that he was staring fixedly at the giant specimen tanks in this "laboratory." In accordance with the script's specifications, each of them held a silicone rubber dummy immersed in liquid.

After a beat of silence, the muddy light at the top of the studio flickered. At nearly the exact same moment, Xie Qingcheng heard He Yu's quiet voice—

"Xie Qingcheng, look at the person in here." He Yu's voice had suddenly become very strained.

In the shadowy gloom, the light reflecting off of the solutions fluctuated unpredictably, and as it glanced over He Yu's face, it threw his pallid complexion into sharp relief.

"That looks like—"

86

AND WERE TRAPPED
TOGETHER

THE LIQUID INSIDE the tank was a murky reddish color, not fully transparent. But Xie Qingcheng could still tell at a glance that this wasn't a silicone dummy.

It was a man—or rather, a man's corpse.

This corpse was completely submerged inside the specimen tank, his hair drifting silently upward. It was obvious that he'd been dead for a while, as his skin was beginning to swell and his eyes were wide and vacant. But the Hello Kitty tattooed on his arm was still extremely vivid, gazing innocently yet sinisterly from the swollen skin.

It was Hu Yi.

It was fortunate that He Yu and Xie Qingcheng had been the ones to stumble across him. They both had far more experience with the macabre than the average person, so they reacted relatively calmly. If it had been another member of the film crew, they would have been scared out of their minds.

All the same, He Yu and Xie Qingcheng's faces turned exceedingly grim. They both stood frozen for a long while before Xie Qingcheng finally reacted, cursing under his breath as he began to look at the other specimen tanks. Examining them, he confirmed that the other glass containers were all filled with silicone dummies; there were no other corpses.

"...Let's hurry and check the other rooms for the writer and production manager," Xie Qingcheng said, his voice frigid.

Hu Yi's status was unique in that he was considered a big shot in entertainment circles. A descendant of senior party officials, both of his parents were prominent figures, and his skills were impressive in their own rights. If the murderer could make a move on someone like him, killing two little girls would be inconsequential.

The man in the container was long dead. No matter how unfortunate the circumstances, there was no use trying to save him now. They had to prioritize the people who might still be alive.

He Yu and Xie Qingcheng immediately went to the other rooms, calling out as they searched them one by one—but they found nothing, neither bodies nor living people. The two young women seemed to have disappeared into thin air.

"I can't find them."

"They're not in the rooms I checked, either."

When He Yu and Xie Qingcheng met up again, they turned together toward the last room—the one located in the furthest depths of the studio.

This room was very large and was separated into inner and outer chambers. It was often rented out for filming scenes set in cargo ships or treasure vaults, and it was built to the standards of a large, sealed-off storage space. The door was the electronic type and as thick as two adult fists.

On entering, the two of them realized that the rushing sound they'd heard from outside had gotten even louder—it seemed to be coming from within the inner room.

"What's that noise?" asked He Yu.

Xie Qingcheng shook his head. "I don't know. But searching for those two is more important—I'll look for them here, and you can check the inner room."

He Yu went to the inner room's door. The moment he entered, his expression immediately changed.

Water—that rushing noise was water!

The water main for the entire film studio had broken, and a steady stream of water was spurting out of the thick pipe.

He Yu watched all of this with a stiff expression—the inner room's structure was set low and the area was broad and deep, so for now, the water had yet to fill the room and overflow. But at its current rate, it probably would soon.

Xie Qingcheng joined him a short while later. "There's no one outside. What about in here? Did you..." He trailed off as he likewise caught sight of the wildly gushing water.

He Yu's voice was a bit cold. "...If they were in here, I'm afraid they've already drowned."

Xie Qingcheng beamed his phone's flashlight downward. The water was deep but clear, and it was obvious at a glance that the assistant writer and production manager weren't in this inner room.

The two young women had entered the film studio, but it was as if they'd evaporated into thin air. He Yu and Xie Qingcheng had searched the whole place and could be certain that the girls weren't here.

Snapping back to his senses, He Yu pulled Xie Qingcheng over. "Come on, let's get out of here first." It was clear to both men that the situation was grim, and they were about to turn back...when suddenly, they heard a low rumbling noise.

With a muffled sound, the room's electronic door descended—falling so quickly that it was already nearly closed before they could even move.

He Yu's expression changed abruptly. He immediately ran over to the electrical control panel, only to discover that the switch embedded inside the room had been cut off from the power source—the door had been closed using the main control panel outside.

"Xie Qingcheng, hurry! The door's about to close!"

But it was already too late... The automatic door crashed shut at an astonishing speed.

Boom—!

With the muffled thud of the door closing, the beam of light from outside was suddenly cut off. And just like that, he and Xie Qingcheng were trapped in the studio.

They both stood there in silence. Behind them came the gushing sound of an endless stream of water; it echoed like a requiem throughout the sealed chamber as though ushering them toward death.

The blood in their bodies seemed to freeze over at once. He Yu and Xie Qingcheng glanced at each other—neither had expected to encounter an incident like this at the studio tonight.

This was clearly no coincidence. This was a premeditated murder.

Water would be an excellent way to destroy evidence left behind at a crime scene, especially a large amount of water that could engulf the entire studio—if He Yu's guess was correct, after the murderer killed Hu Yi and submerged him in the film prop, he'd planned to destroy the water main and flood the site into a swamp, letting it soak in water for the entire night.

Both Xie Qingcheng and He Yu were very intelligent. As they stood in the dark, cramped space, the gears in their brains turned furiously. At nearly the exact same moment, they saw the answer in each other's eyes—

"It was that last staff member that came outside..."

"He was carrying a huge chest..."

He was probably the culprit!

The man whom Xie Qingcheng had asked about the terrible phone signal, the one who had looked unfamiliar because they'd never seen him among the crew before but could readily answer their question... If their guesses were correct, then that man was the one who had come to clean up the scene of Hu Yi's murder.

But after he'd set everything up so that a night of flooding would erase all the evidence and prepared to leave the studio, the murderer hadn't expected that a diligent writer and production manager would bring an advisor to the scene and request for some props to be rearranged...

Half an hour earlier...

"There's a problem with the setup of the sterile field on the operating table. Tomorrow, the actors are going to perform the scene where they collect and clean the kidney trays here. We asked the medical consultant... Yes, and right here, the recycling bin can't be placed like this. The scalpel needs to be swapped out for a real one during close-ups... Ah, that's right, where's Liu-laoshi? We can just tell him directly."

The production manager chattered at length, afraid that something might still go wrong the next day. After all, the man wearing the baseball cap and mask was entirely unfamiliar to her—she didn't know him, so in all likelihood, he was just some random part-timer under Mr. Liu, the person in charge of the set.

"Liu-laoshi was feeling unwell, so he went back to rest," said the man in the cap. "You can tell me, and I'll make a note of it."

"Unwell?" The production manager was unsatisfied with this response, but there was nothing she could do. She scratched her head. "My goodness..."

She could only continue talking to the man in the baseball cap.

Toward the end, when her spiel was almost over, she and the assistant writer prepared to leave. The man in the baseball cap walked them out, repeatedly promising that everything would be rearranged to their specifications before the next day's shoot began, otherwise he would shoulder the blame.

However, just as the two women were about to step out of the laboratory, the production manager suddenly stopped and slapped herself on the head. "Ah, I have such a bad memory."

She pulled the assistant writer back into the room, taking no notice of the malevolent gleam that flashed through the eyes of the man in the baseball cap as she passed him by.

"I almost forgot that these silicone dummies will have close-ups too, so I need to take pictures for the consultant so that he can make sure the pipes and things are in the right places... Hu-laoshi is very strict, so he'll be hopping mad if he finds any problems tomorrow."

As she spoke, she took out her phone and started snapping pictures of the dummies' faces in the specimen tanks.

Click, click...

She was so focused on zooming in, completely engrossed in taking pictures, that she didn't notice the horrifying, translucent image reflected on the glass: behind them, the man in the baseball cap was lifting a heavy club and raising it higher...

The production manager didn't notice a thing as she moved her cellphone to the next specimen tank. She focused, watching the details emerge as the picture appeared on her phone screen, framing the silicone dummy that she wanted to photograph, and then—

Clang!

When the production manager got a good look at the dummy's face, her blood ran cold for a few seconds, and she found herself completely unable to react. Her phone fell from her hands, smashing on the ground.

It felt as though her throat and lungs had been seized by a giant, invisible hand, brutally squeezing all the air from her lungs. She could neither inhale nor exhale, her mouth hanging silently open. Her soul seemed to be sucked right out of her, her entire body frozen and numb.

It was...

It was Hu Yi...?!

It was a real corpse!

Her wail had yet to burst out of her throat when she heard a muffled thump. She abruptly turned her head to see that her partner had already fallen to the ground, the back of her head covered in blood. As for the man in the baseball cap, he leered at her sinisterly as he raised the club once more...

"Namo ratna trayāya, namo āryĀvalokiteśvarāya..."

At that very moment, inside a disguised props transport vehicle with knockoff plates, the man in the baseball cap was driving expressionlessly with one hand on the steering wheel as the run-down radio played the Great Compassion Mantra. The man took off his hat, revealing a wanted criminal's face that had been obscured with makeup.

This was a homicidal maniac. The most frightening case that he'd perpetrated to date was a murder on a rainy night at a certain university in Huzhou. Back before criminal investigation technology had been thoroughly developed, this man had murdered a female student while wearing a raincoat. Then, under the cover of his raincoat, he carried her to the school's laboratory and dismembered her before casting her remains into the laboratory's drainage pipes.

Even all these years later, the police had yet to capture him and bring him to justice.

Meanwhile, his mental state had grown increasingly twisted. Whenever he killed and fled, he derived pleasure from provoking the authorities, and so he killed, again and again, making sure to wear a raincoat and rubber boots at the scene of each of his murders.

The first time he killed had just happened to be a rainy day, and he found that his waterproof attire made cleaning up after his crime much more convenient. Later, his mindset changed, and killing people in a raincoat simply became his signature.

Right now, inside the cargo bay behind him, lay the raincoat that he'd just removed. It had hidden the bloodstains covering his body, allowing him to successfully escape from right under Xie Qingcheng and He Yu's noses. Aside from the raincoat, there was also a massive props chest, which currently contained two unconscious young women: the missing writer and production manager.

"It's all been taken care of." The man in the baseball cap spoke into the phone in his other hand. "Though there were a few unexpected complications... Yeah, people from the production went in, mm-hm, looked like two staff members. I was originally planning on bringing them into the car and dealing with them, but they didn't wanna come—two tall guys, it wouldn't have been easy for me to take them by force either... It's fine, I ended up shutting them in the inner chamber and breaking the door. I set up a signal jammer over the whole area too, anyway, so they won't have any signal to call the police. There's no way they'll be able to get out. The only thing that anyone will see tomorrow will be their dead bodies."

The person on the phone gave him a few more instructions.

"Got it." The man in the baseball cap glanced subconsciously at the cargo bay through the rearview mirror, even though there was nothing to see.

"Oh yeah, I have two girls here, too. They also stumbled in by mistake. They're quite pretty, so I brought them both with me. Even though we only wanted to kill the big fish Hu Yi this time, there's nothing we can do about other little fishies taking the bait. I was planning on killing a little girl—I'd already arranged a pretty eye-catching murder display in the hotel hallway that day, but then the higher-ups said I couldn't just kill whoever I wanted, that I needed to make the kill count with a big one, and they gave me Hu Yi's name. Who would've thought that these little girls would come follow him into the grave? Do you think I should wait till he comes back to take care of them, or—"

When the man in the baseball cap finished listening to the instructions from the other end, he bared his yellowed teeth in a leer. "All right. I got it, I know what I need to do."

The truck sped along the road, blanketing the Buddhist chants in plumes of dust. It was ironic that these mantras about mercy could bring a trace of comfort even to fugitive criminals, making them feel like benevolent, enlightened people...

Inside the sealed chamber in the studio, the water had already flooded out of the inner room; it was spreading into a glimmering veneer at He Yu and Xie Qingcheng's feet in the outer room.

He Yu was trying to break through the signal jammer using his phone, but it was fruitless, as he didn't have a copy of the software that could counteract this type of hardware. No matter how skilled he was, he couldn't do anything without that essential component. He knew that this type of signal jammer was similar to the one he had used on Neverland, back when he wanted to confess to Xie Xue. Its coverage was so comprehensive that even calls to emergency numbers wouldn't go through—the police, fire, and first aid lines were all completely out of reach.

Turning to look at Xie Qingcheng, he put down his phone, leaned back against the ice-cold metal door, and silently shook his head.

His meaning was self-evident: they truly were trapped in this treacherous studio...with no way to escape.

87

YOU WERE ONCE ALL I COULD RELY ON

THE WATER LEVEL kept rising.

The room was very large, so there was still time left for them to escape. However, the lock on the door had been destroyed and their signal was being jammed. They had no way of opening the door or calling for help. He Yu and Xie Qingcheng tried everything they could, but it quickly became clear that they truly had no avenue of escape. The atmosphere in the studio grew extremely grave.

The water had already risen to their ankles. The winter was chilly, and the deathly cold was like a slippery snake flicking its tongue as it slithered up their legs, its icy bite stabbing into their bones.

He Yu suddenly picked up a spade from the corner and shoved it against the metal door.

"... Stop wasting your energy," said Xie Qingcheng. "It's impossible to get this kind of door open with brute force."

He Yu made no response. After scraping a few starkly visible lines on the door, he tossed the spade aside and took out his phone. He pulled up a stopwatch on the screen and started the timer.

The light of the phone's screen illuminated his face. He said softly, "I wasn't trying to open the door. I'm calculating how much longer our oxygen supply will last."

Xie Qingcheng hesitated.

"Two hours." With that, He Yu set down his stopwatch and turned back to look at Xie Qingcheng. "We still have two hours."

That was the answer to the math problem of their death. Unless something unexpected happened, the entire studio would be submerged in two hours.

Xie Qingcheng said nothing, subconsciously groping around in his pocket for a cigarette. But his pack was empty. He remembered— he'd let He Yu take his last cig when they were outside.

"... Fucking hell, why'd you have to smoke my cigarette?" Xie Qingcheng crushed the box in frustration and tossed it aside.

"We're about to drown here, and you're still talking about cigarettes?"

Xie Qingcheng looked up at He Yu, as irritated as ever. "Why the fuck are you always following me?"

He Yu didn't reply.

The more he talked, the more frustrated he got. "Seriously, He Yu. If you hadn't come, you wouldn't be stuck in a situation like this. You really brought this upon yourself."

"If I hadn't come," He Yu replied, "you'd probably be dead already."

"...At least that'd be neater." Xie Qingcheng spoke coldly and stiffly. "If that had happened, the only one who'd end up dead would be me."

He Yu's heart tensed inexplicably. "Xie Qingcheng, do you... think that it's a waste for me to die like this?"

Xie Qingcheng's expression was grim. "I think it'd be more clear-cut that way," he responded bluntly. "No one would owe anyone anything. And no one would've taken my last cigarette."

A brilliant series of emotions passed over He Yu's face as he walked toward him through the water. "Do you know what it means to die?"

"I'm a doctor. How could I *not* know what it means to die?"

"Really? But you seem like a madman to me."

The sound of water filling the studio continued uninterrupted.

Xie Qingcheng looked away from He Yu. Instead of continuing their argument, he took out his phone and swiped open the lock screen—but no miracle occurred. There were still no bars, and his emergency call couldn't break through the barrier.

However, as He Yu watched, he was surprised to see that, after Xie Qingcheng's call failed, he tapped open a jellyfish video from his camera roll and pressed play.

...For a moment, he wasn't sure whether he was more alarmed by Xie Qingcheng's excessively dark sense of humor, or by his terrifying composure. He stared at Xie Qingcheng's lowered lashes. "You're actually in the mood for that? If we can't get out in two hours, you won't need to look at jellyfish—the two of us will *become* jellyfish."

"What else can we do?" asked Xie Qingcheng.

He Yu choked.

Indeed, there was nothing they could do aside from waiting to be found.

He Yu leaned against the metal door next to Xie Qingcheng, standing shoulder-to-shoulder with him as he watched the floating jellyfish.

"Do you think this is the follow-up to what happened at the broadcasting tower?" he asked.

"Not necessarily. It probably isn't."

The jellyfish drifted gently. Accompanied by the ethereal music-box tinkling coming from the phone, it was really quite comforting.

"If this was their doing, there's no reason they'd wait this long," Xie Qingcheng added. "We would probably already be dead."

After the broadcasting tower incident, He Yu and Xie Qingcheng had been exposed before that mysterious organization, but their opponent hadn't moved against them since then. That meant the price of killing them was greater than the advantages gained—after all, the criminal organization wasn't a lone, deranged murderer. It usually acted with its own hidden motives, and its people didn't kill for fun, especially not highly visible public figures. The organization knew very well that if they did anything to people like that, they'd risk spraying themselves with blood at the slightest misstep. It wasn't worth the risk.

And He Yu and Xie Qingcheng had been trapped here entirely by coincidence too—Xie Qingcheng had wanted to come to the film studio on his own, and He Yu had randomly chosen to follow Xie Qingcheng. When they were outside earlier, they absolutely could have just left.

The murderer was probably trying to kill them simply because they had seen Hu-laoshi's murder scene. In that sense, they were just like the writer and production manager who were presently missing—collateral damage.

The first jellyfish video ended, and Xie Qingcheng opened another one.

He Yu suddenly spoke up. "Xie Qingcheng, the reason I follow you around all the time is actually because I still want to know the answer to those questions."

"The answers to which questions?"

"You know."

After a long moment of silence, Xie Qingcheng asked, "Can you give me a smoke?"

"...You know perfectly well that I don't—"

Xie Qingcheng's peach-blossom eyes were very calm. "And you know perfectly well that I won't."

With that, they stopped talking, and the studio sank back into silence.

In this silence, they didn't talk about Hu Yi, the assistant writer, or the production manager. He Yu and Xie Qingcheng were the same in this respect—it wasn't that they'd be motionless bystanders in the face of danger, but rather that they wouldn't waste time on fear or meaningless conjecture. Theorizing would only be meaningful if they made it out alive.

If they didn't...

Xie Qingcheng's choice was to watch jellyfish videos and wait things out calmly.

He Yu wondered—what would *he* do?

Even at that moment, He Yu still didn't feel like his life was about to end. The feeling of hopeless desperation was still very distant. But he couldn't help but think...

What if these really were his final two hours?

What did he want to do?

What was he going to do?

He Yu thought it over, but the fragmented scenes that flashed through his head seemed too absurd and somewhat pathetic. He tossed all those thoughts out of his head.

Time ticked away, second by second, and the water level rose to their chests.

The pressure made their chests feel tight, and the height of the water made it difficult to keep using their phones. All of the buoyant objects that were littered around the studio had floated to the surface. He Yu grabbed two plastic boxes and passed one to Xie Qingcheng, for him to put his phone inside.

"They're supposed to be waterproof, but it's best not to believe everything businessmen say."

Xie Qingcheng didn't waste his breath. In the glimmering water, his face was ashen. The color of his lips was far paler than usual. He couldn't tolerate the cold.

But it was more than just the cold. This enclosed space, along with the endlessly rising water level, was unsettling his mind.

He closed his eyes, pitch-black lashes lowering like curtains.

The water rose further. Now the water level had risen to over two meters, and He Yu and Xie Qingcheng had no choice but to float on the surface.

Xie Qingcheng shot a glance at the ceiling, which had drawn a bit closer. He still had some hope, because he thought that there might be some part of the ceiling through which they could break free.

The four walls of this place were completely smooth, with nowhere to gain any leverage, and so they could only wait until the water level rose high enough for them to float and take a better look at the ceiling's structure. The ceiling panels of a studio such as this often had a hollow space above that wasn't completely sealed off with bricks. If they could find that hollow space, they might be able to get out.

Xie Qingcheng didn't want to waste too much energy until that opportunity arose, much less lose his composure.

Time passed, little by little. The water level kept rising, higher and higher, lifting them closer and closer to the ceiling...

He Yu was floating on his back. It had to be said, he was the best possible companion for this kind of situation; anyone else would have cried themselves to death if they weren't terrified out of their wits. But He Yu was different. He viewed death like an unstoppable car passing by on the street. He would do his best to avoid a head-on collision, but he didn't fear the car itself.

"Xie Qingcheng, I know what you're thinking. You think we can escape through the ceiling."

Xie Qingcheng was silent.

So much water had collected that the broken pipe was now submerged, water pouring directly into the pool. The sound of rushing water was no longer as loud. The room seemed even quieter, like they were in an entirely different world in the depths of the sea.

"But what if we can't find that hollow board...? What if this last chance is just another dead end?"

He didn't reply.

He Yu picked up his phone from the plastic box floating beside him, displaying the countdown timer he had set.

"In that case, we have less than an hour left. And then we'll die. Did you ever imagine that we'd die so unexpectedly—and together like this? In a place like this? I know you're not afraid, but don't you have any regrets?"

Xie Qingcheng closed his eyes and said quietly, "Stop blathering."

"If I die, I won't be able to speak anymore."

"...Don't overthink this."

He Yu suddenly asked, "Xie Qingcheng, aren't you freezing?"

Xie Qingcheng didn't reply.

"I can hear your voice shaking. Actually, I'm pretty cold too. I'm glad it's only two hours. If it were four, in these temperatures, we wouldn't have to wait to drown—we'd freeze to death first. We'd die of hypothermia."

In the end, young men and fully grown men weren't the same. Faced with the threat of death, young men would always have more to say.

He Yu was too young, Xie Qingcheng thought. It was already quite impressive that he could maintain this amount of composure despite glimpsing the robes of the reaper drawing near. But his next thought was that He Yu was truly unlucky, insisting on trailing him to this cursed place, seeking his own demise.

In the end, not one, but two of them had been caught in this single trap.

"We can get out," Xie Qingcheng said. "There's an open pipe near the edge. I can already see the gap in the ceiling; it's very thin. There's no need to be so nervous."

He Yu laughed. "I'm not nervous."

Xie Qingcheng's only response was skeptical silence.

"I just think I'd have a lot of regrets. Xie Qingcheng, there's just so much to regret. There are so many things I want to tell people, and so many things I want to know. If we really can't get out—"

"We'll definitely get out."

"... How can you be sure?"

"Because it's not the time to give up yet. If we're not planning to give up, then doubt is pointless."

He Yu went quiet for a moment, then sighed softly. "Don't you understand? I'm not doubting, I just want to plan for the worst—if I'm really going to drown here, then I want to at least live with a little bit more clarity before I die. What about you? Will you still refuse to tell me just a little bit of the truth, even if you're going to die?"

"What will the truth matter when our bodies have already gone cold?"

He Yu looked quietly up at the ceiling, at the light reflecting off the rippling water. It was such a perilous scene, yet those patterns of light were very beautiful. "Someone once said that the truth is never meaningless. The truth can determine whether what's laid to rest is regret or closure."

Xie Qingcheng said nothing.

"If you don't want to talk, then I have quite a lot to say."

"You sure have a lot of energy," said Xie Qingcheng.

He Yu chuckled. "Ah, you'd know firsthand just how much energy I have."

Xie Qingcheng really had to hand it to him—to be able to crack off-color jokes even at a time like this...

He Yu laughed for a while, floating on his back on the crystal-clear surface of the water. With a misty look in his eyes, he said, "Xie Qingcheng, all this time, I've never been able to have a proper chat with you. Do you know why I dislike you so much? I've never disliked anyone this much before."

"I know. It's because you think I lied to you."

"That's not it."

Their surroundings were very quiet and cold, and their breaths fogged in the air as they spoke.

"That's not it," He Yu murmured. "...It's because I've never trusted anyone as much as I used to trust you."

He'd never spoken so frankly before.

"You have no idea how much of my courage to live came from the fundamental principles you once taught me... But then you tore that courage right out of me."

Xie Qingcheng was silent.

"I'm so cold, Xie Qingcheng... I don't understand why you had to lie to me like that, how you managed to pretend so convincingly."

The water was so cold, so bone-chillingly cold.

He Yu was still for a long moment, then said, "Actually, that day at the Skynight Club, I poured that first cup of wine by accident. At first, I hadn't planned on doing that to you. But—" With a splash, he flipped from floating on his back to treading water, with only his head above the surface.

Xie Qingcheng was still lying on his back. He Yu swam forward slightly, until his chest touched the top of Xie Qingcheng's head.

He Yu looked down, water dripping from his face, the translucent droplets trickling along his cheeks and falling onto Xie Qingcheng's forehead. Just like that, he gazed down at Xie Qingcheng, whose eyes were still closed. He felt so resentful—even now, Xie Qingcheng could still be so cold, unwilling to even open his eyes and look at him.

The impulse to tease him rose in He Yu's heart, so he abruptly dipped his head to kiss Xie Qingcheng on his ice-cold lips.

One of them lay on the surface, while the other floated upright in the water. The moment he lowered his head and kissed him, Xie Qingcheng's eyes flew open.

"You—"

"I don't regret anything that I did. I don't like men, I've never liked men, but I felt very content with you." He Yu looked at him, his warm breath brushing over Xie Qingcheng's ice-cold skin. "Even though I don't know why I feel this way."

Xie Qingcheng glared up at him.

"If we do manage to get out of here, I'm going to book a room and spend an entire day in bed with you. I've given up on prying any honest words out of your mouth, but I'm sure I'll be able to tease out some other sounds I like hearing. I'm going to fuck you all day and night—once the New Year's holiday rolls around and we go back to Huzhou, I'm going to come over to your house every single day, and we're gonna spend the entire break having sex. Every single day. Unless you leave your phone at home when you go out—otherwise I'll always have a way to track you down."

Xie Qingcheng didn't expect him to be so unreasonable. He straightened up in the water with a *splash*, changing his position from lying flat to treading water face-to-face with He Yu.

"Is there something wrong with you?" he demanded.

"Probably. A new disease, I don't know what it is either." He Yu drifted closer in the water, the dim light spilling over his eyelashes. The light rippling off the water gathered and dissipated around them. "When we get out of here, help cure me. Lie underneath me and treat me..."

Xie Qingcheng didn't want to hear any more—he simply shoved He Yu's head underwater instead. "Why don't you just die here?"

After being pushed down for a bit, He Yu floated back up, sending beads of water flying when he surfaced—Xie Qingcheng had only wanted to scold him, so he had some semblance of self-control and hadn't used too much strength.

As He Yu surfaced, he was like a mermaid coming out of the water. Covered in glimmering droplets, he took Xie Qingcheng into his arms and pressed his damp mouth to his again, angling his head to take those chilly, shivering lips between his own. This kiss seemed different from their previous ones—passionate and lingering, suppressed within it was some sort of emotion that neither of them quite understood, as if they were trying to stave off the bone-chilling surroundings and seize onto hope.

"Ge..."

In the midst of this uncertainty, not knowing whether the god of death was about to descend upon them, He Yu softly uttered a few words to Xie Qingcheng. There was resentment, dissatisfaction, disappointment, and bewilderment in his words. But among them, the most prevalent emotion was one that had not appeared in a very long time, one that sounded a lot like hurt.

"Did you know? To you, those words were just a handful of trivial lies. But for the last ten years, they were all I could rely on."

88

MY HEART WILL GO ON

XIE QINGCHENG FROZE for a moment, unsure of exactly what he was feeling.

He watched He Yu. All along, it had always been He Yu who didn't dare look him in the eyes; Xie Qingcheng's pupils were too cold and too sharp, capable of dissecting hearts like a surgical scalpel. But in this moment, the chaotic, intense emotions in He Yu's eyes were too strong, like lava.

No matter how sharp the blade, it was still common steel—it couldn't withstand the heat of molten rock. This time, it was Xie Qingcheng who looked away first.

He felt intensely conflicted. He wouldn't have had such a drastic reaction if He Yu had said this to him under normal circumstances, but now, he knew that it meant something different.

This was the one thing that He Yu wanted to tell him the most.

If they couldn't make it out, if they died in an hour, these would be the words that He Yu most wanted to say to him at the very end—they would represent his farewell to the world of the living.

The weight of those words struck him right in the heart.

Xie Qingcheng didn't curse him out, nor did he mock him—this was the first time Xie Qingcheng had faced He Yu's candid words with this kind of attitude since that night at the club.

But he didn't know how to respond to him, either.

After all the misplaced love and entanglement that had taken place between them, Xie Qingcheng didn't know how to face He Yu's borderline pathological reliance on him.

In the end, he simply turned away. He swam to a place closer to the wall, then looked up fixedly at the studio ceiling as it loomed closer and closer.

Some scattered light glanced over his handsome, yet ashen, face. He was bloodless from the cold, like a drifting floe of ice—even his lips seemed nearly translucent.

A dozen centimeters... Another dozen centimeters... Closer and closer.

Xie Qingcheng could already make out the pipes and metal panels, the joints and nails of the ceiling.

Struck by a sudden idea, he looked down through the clear water—and found what he was looking for.

"Give me a moment."

Xie Qingcheng passed the plastic box with his phone inside to He Yu, in order to keep it from falling into the water and being rendered completely useless. Then he plunged into the water, his slender body raising a series of ripples as he dove straight down. After a while, he rose back to the surface, flinging wet droplets from his hair with a toss of his head, a discarded length of metal tube in his hand.

The tube was over a meter long. At the current water level, it could easily touch the ceiling when he held it up in his hand.

With bated breath, Xie Qingcheng began to tentatively strike at the ceiling with the metal pipe.

Hollow ceiling boards could be identified by ear—they were louder and crisper than solid panels when they were struck, emitting a resonant, cavernous noise.

Xie Qingcheng very stoically began his inspection.

He Yu also stopped talking, watching as he used the pipe to slowly test each panel, starting from the side closest to the door.

Centimeter by centimeter, second by second.

Solid.

Solid.

Yet another solid panel...

...Fifteen minutes later, Xie Qingcheng laid down the metal pipe he was using to reach the boards. He didn't need it anymore, as he could already touch the ceiling with his bare hands.

But he didn't move, his face hidden amongst the rippling waves.

He Yu saw that his face was paler than before.

There was no hollow space.

The roof of this building had been sealed with poured concrete...

Anyone, no matter how fearless, would feel shaken when truly facing death's knell. The ceiling was sealed shut, which meant that their final glimmer of hope had been extinguished.

As he watched Xie Qingcheng's face, even He Yu's own breathing seemed to catch for a moment. After swimming closer and gazing up at the ceiling, he could now see everything clearly. Even though the damaged covering over the pipes that had previously given them hope was indeed made of hollow wooden boards, there was still a layer of cement plastered on top of it. With only the strength of ordinary men, there was no way they'd make it out in a hundred years, let alone in under an hour...

It seemed as if they really were going to die, just like this.

"Xie Qingcheng." He Yu looked at him, his throat tightening up slightly. At that moment, he wanted to say many things, but what ended up leaving his mouth was: "The headlines for tomorrow's paper...what do you think they'll say?"

Xie Qingcheng looked up, gazing once more at the ceiling as it drew ever closer. The glimmering ripples cast light over his jawline. His hair had become slightly mussed by the water—although his features were as immaculate as ever, dark locks of soaking wet hair fell into his eyes.

He didn't respond to He Yu's nonsensical question. But after a while, He Yu heard him speak softly. "...He Yu, a lot of things have happened between us. We've both hurt each other and we owe each other debts. It's not a simple matter of keeping score, but looking back now, there is at least one thing for which I must apologize to you."

Suddenly hearing him talk like this, He Yu actually found himself momentarily dumbfounded. "...I was the one who followed you. This isn't the same as what happened at the broadcasting tower, so you don't need to blame yourself."

"I'm talking about what happened before. What happened five years ago."

He Yu fell silent for a short while, feeling like something was churning in his heart. "...If you say it like that, then haven't I done a ton of unforgivable, beastly things to you? And anyway, apologizing to each other in the face of death seems a little too scrupulous— living so methodically and rationally for an entire lifetime, with everything laid out so clearly? You must be exhausted."

As he spoke, He Yu finally allowed his mind—which had been tense for over an hour—to relax.

He'd accepted his fate.

A death like this came as a surprise to He Yu, but he'd always been able to accept dying. He wouldn't lose his composure in the face of death or succumb pathetically to panic, for in his short nineteen years of life, he'd already faced pain and loneliness far more terrifying than death.

His whole life, he'd been anticipating death. Since birth, death had always been an old friend waiting for him, one he'd inevitably have to reunite with one day. And compared to going mad and losing control in an insane asylum before a miserable end, absent of dignity like all the cases before him, a death like this was honestly not hard to accept.

It couldn't scare someone who had spent most of his young life going insane in desolate solitude.

He Yu decided to assume a more comfortable backstroke position and lie back on the surface of the water once more. Picking up his phone, he suddenly thought of something—

"Hey Xie Qingcheng, what if we trust in those businessmen for once?"

This time, it was Xie Qingcheng's turn to be dumbfounded. "What?"

"Waterproofing." He Yu waved his phone. "After this water submerges us entirely, our phones will get soaked as well. But in case it turns out that the manufacturers weren't too unscrupulous and they actually are waterproof, why don't we leave behind some last words or something... We still have plenty of time. Our fates aren't that bad."

As he spoke, he opened the notes app on his phone. Then he tapped on a music app.

Unlike Xie Qingcheng, He Yu was a romantic aesthete. If he was really going to be buried right there in the water and leave his mortal body behind, upon accepting his fate, he'd want to properly welcome his death with calm elegance.

"Did you know? Right before prisoners on death row are subjected to lethal injection, the prison wardens let them listen to music. Apparently, the song that gets chosen the most is 'Don't Look Down on Me Just Because I'm a Goat.'"[9]

Xie Qingcheng floated calmly for a while. He hadn't expected He Yu to face death this way.

When people were born, they were still innocent, and they couldn't control when they laughed or cried. With just a slap from the nurse, they came into the world with a wail. But when people died, they were filled with all their love and hatred, their learning and knowledge, their past experiences... People had to say goodbye to these intangible friends that had accompanied them to the end. Perhaps He Yu thought that he ought to part ways with those old friends with a smile.

"Don't you think it's very strange that criminals on death row like 'Don't Look Down on Me Just Because I'm a Goat' so much?"

He Yu swiped at his phone screen and looked at the songs he had saved, speaking in an increasingly calm voice.

"But actually, it's because they know they're about to die and they don't really want to go through the effort of making a decision, so they just choose the first song that comes up. Alphabetically, 'Don't Look Down on Me Just Because I'm a Goat' is the first song on the list. In my opinion, those people were still defeated by death—caring so little you don't even bother to make a choice even as you're about to die is tasteless and cowardly... Here, I think this song is quite nice. Do you like it?"

He tapped the speaker button on the screen, and a sweeping melody drifted out of the phone, sentimental and timeless—it was "My Heart Will Go On."

---

9   The theme song to Pleasant Goat and Big Big Wolf, a popular children's cartoon that first aired in 2005.

Xie Qingcheng was speechless.

"You jump, I jump." He Yu started reciting the movie lines he could remember at random in a slightly nasal voice. "You're going to get out of here. You're going to go on... Not here. Not this night. Not like this."

The water surrounding them was very cold, thanks to the freezing Jiangnan winter outside.

He Yu laughed. "How fitting for the occasion... Did you know I loved Rose when I was little? I wondered—how could she brave all those people's condescending stares and overlook all those mundane barriers to be with that penniless bastard? If there was a girl who treated me like that, when the Titanic sank, I'd put her on a floating plank and stay in the water by myself too. I wouldn't want to watch her die.

"You know Rose got married later and lived a very happy life—the time she spent with Jack on the Titanic was like a single dream over the course of her long lifetime. And then, when she woke up, beside her bed there was a photo of her wearing pants and riding a horse exactly the way Jack described to her in that dream. How wonderful it must be to have a dream like that..." He Yu sighed. "I don't even have any dreams."

The soaring music lingered distantly, like the sonorous whistle sending off the great liner on her maiden voyage a century ago, floating across space and time to echo within this sealed, flooded film studio.

As he listened to the song, He Yu opened the notes app on his phone and pondered what he should write.

But in the end, he realized that his farewell message would be completely meaningless. There wasn't anyone in the world he especially cared about—or there was, but that person was already by his side. And even with death imminent, he still didn't know what his feelings and desires toward Xie Qingcheng ultimately meant.

He also still didn't know what Xie Qingcheng had kept hidden from him for all those years.

In the end, these would all be regrets that he would bring to Meng-po[10] to be forgotten.

He Yu put his phone back in the plastic box. Closing his eyes, he hummed the melody softly, seemingly relaxed as he waited for the moment to arrive.

The ceiling loomed closer...

It was just then that he heard a distinct splash of water.

He opened his eyes—Xie Qingcheng had swum over and flipped onto his back, stretching out beside him.

Xie Qingcheng had put his phone down too.

He Yu was a bit surprised. "You're not writing anything...? For Xie Xue."

"She'll only be sadder if she sees it," he said calmly. "I don't want her to live the rest of her life haunted by my last words. Sometimes, the words of the deceased aren't a kindness. My last conversation with her was very unremarkable—it's a good way to end things. If it's up to me, I don't want to use a message written before I died to hurt her one last time."

In a sense, they were one another's most suitable companion on this road to the Yellow Springs.[11] They were both capable of quietly and serenely facing their own deaths, which was beyond the abilities of most people in the world.

Xie Qingcheng checked the time on his phone. He and He Yu were just like jellyfish floating silently—moon jellies, peach blossom jellies, flame jellies... The ripples of light seemed to transform into

---

10 *The goddess of forgetfulness, who serves soup to the dead that removes all memories of past lives so that their souls can be reincarnated with a blank slate.*

11 *The underworld in Chinese mythology.*

the jellyfish in those videos, peaceful creatures that tenderly healed the hearts of those that watched them.

"Every night in my dreams,
I see you,
I feel you,
That is how I know you go on..."

As He Yu listened to the song on repeat, he suddenly recalled the door that kept appearing in his dreams.

From ages seven to fourteen, he'd opened that door countless times—just as from ages fourteen to nineteen, he'd dreamed of that door countless times.

Back when Xie Qingcheng had been by his side, he could open the door and see the man standing by the window, tall and handsome, looking back at him quietly. And later, when the room beyond that door became completely empty, as he stood inside with his eyes closed, he almost felt like he could still detect a faint trace of the doctor's presence...

Doctor Xie had said to him, "Sooner or later, you'll have to depend on yourself to walk out of the shadows in your heart."

At the desk next to the window, Xie Qingcheng had inscribed stroke after beautiful stroke of profound words with his fountain pen.

He had written, "To He Yu, From Xie Qingcheng."

Then, Xie Qingcheng had left.

And after he left, for many nights, and in many dreams, He Yu had dreamed of him.

He Yu's expression slowly relaxed. He was lying in the cold water, but he knew that right now, he wasn't alone. Xie Qingcheng was right by his side. He only had to reach out a hand, and he would feel a hint of another person's warmth. It was a warmth that wouldn't leave...a warmth that could only be taken away by death.

"Once more, you open the door,
And you're here in my heart..."

As that voice sang on, the door engraved with countless summer hydrangeas seemed to open again, revealing the rays of summer, the snow of winter, and a beautiful silhouette that remained unchanged through spring and autumn. It was as if he'd never left the room in his heart.

He Yu didn't recognize the emotion that surged up within him, but it felt at once bitter and complicated. He felt an unexpected urge to cry, but he knew that it wasn't because he was afraid of dying.

He suddenly wanted to talk. He suddenly wanted to reach his hand out to Xie Qingcheng. He suddenly wanted to say to him, "Doctor Xie, Xie Qingcheng, I'm sorry."

He'd just been the one who criticized Xie Qingcheng for apologizing before death, though; he'd described it as worthless and clichéd. So the words remained stuck in his throat, going neither up nor down.

But his hand had already reached over, drawing ripples through the water much like the waves stirring through his heart. And then—

He grabbed hold of Xie Qingcheng's fingertips.

Xie Qingcheng's hand twitched slightly. But he didn't shake him off.

"...Xie Qingcheng, don't be afraid. Death isn't scary. I've had several near-death experiences, you know? It's just like falling asleep, faster and simpler than falling asleep..."

He'd opened his mouth, but the words were different from what he intended. They were more like what a stoic, masculine man ought to say.

He gripped Xie Qingcheng's hand tightly, feeling a slight tremor in the clasp of their hands—but he didn't know if it was him or Xie Qingcheng.

"I'll stay with you. It'll be fine...I'll stay with you..."

Xie Qingcheng remained silent. He Yu didn't look at him, instead staring at the ceiling as it drew closer and closer, whispering those words. But Xie Qingcheng turned his head to look at He Yu.

Of course he knew that He Yu wasn't afraid of death, that there were times when the younger man even longed for it. But right now, He Yu seemed a little upset: relaxed, but unable to shake his distress.

Why?

Xie Qingcheng looked at him for a long while, just like that. In the end, perhaps he knew the reason...

As the romantic melody from Titanic played across a span of ninety years of history, in the face of imminent death, his indestructible, unconquerable heart finally softened—

"He Yu," Xie Qingcheng suddenly said. There was a faint serenity to his voice, a serenity that only came with a certain degree of resolution.

"Hm?"

"Five years ago, when I left Huzhou First Hospital. When I left you..." Xie Qingcheng paused, then softly continued. "There was indeed a secret reason." He paused again. "If this truth is the last thing that I can restore to you, if this truth can give you some final relief..."

Their surroundings were so cold. Even the dim light shining from above was a lonely, faint blue color; it cast a layer of frost over Xie Qingcheng's features that, despite it all, only served to highlight the fact that his eyes were less frigid than usual.

Despite it all, he was still very calm.

As their imminent death grew nearer, he finally opened his mouth. He tilted his face to the side, his eyelashes trembling faintly as he turned to speak to the boy who was gazing back at him.

"I'll tell you."

Meatbun's Mini Theatre

Magical Pet Shop

ONCE UPON A TIME, there was a pet store full of pretty little creatures waiting to catch a buyer's eye.

The puppydragon was the strangest-looking one of all, because he was both puppy and dragon. He had a dragon's tail and sharp little fangs, but a puppy's almond eyes. The puppydragon thought he was very cute, but as the customers came and went, as the days passed on and on, there was no one who wanted him.

The puppies and kitties around him had all been taken home by their new owners, and he was the only one left behind to sit in the store and stare into space.

Why doesn't anyone want me? he wondered.

Time passed, and the pet store was going to move elsewhere. There weren't any new little animals coming into the store, and the puppydragon was the only older animal left behind.

The puppydragon finally began to feel hurt. Could he actually be a very unlikable little creature? He wanted to bring an end to this anchorless waiting; he wanted to sell himself to someone. And so he asked the shopkeeper for a wooden board and a crayon.

Using the crayon, the puppydragon clumsily wrote, "Puppydragon for sale, super cheap." And then he trotted out of the store with the wooden board in his arms to go sit by the doorway, staring wide-eyed at the people passing by.

Gradually, the sky grew dark, but still, there was no one willing to take the puppydragon home. They probably thought that he was diseased—how else could such a strange creature exist? In the glow of the setting sun, the puppydragon's head began to droop.

But just as the shop was about to close up for the night, he suddenly heard the sound of footsteps approaching and then stopping in front of him. He looked up immediately, clutching the wooden board in hopeful anticipation as he stared at the newcomer.

Wah...it was a very tall, handsome man who looked like a doctor. He was carefully assessing him with a lowered head.

The puppydragon's ears pricked up and he wagged his tail, hastily lifting the board to show him the sign. The doctor calmly read over the text on the board. Even though he didn't want to buy him, he still asked, "...Are you really very cheap?"

"Mm-hm!"

"How much?"

The puppydragon wagged his tail and piped up in a childish voice, "1.68 million!"

"...I'm broke."

The puppydragon grew anxious, his tail wagging more furiously as he jumped up and clung to his waist. "Free of charge! Free of charge!"

The doctor didn't want to keep a little pet at all. He was too busy and didn't have much free time, but the puppydragon had buried his head in his stomach, and those little claws clutched him like he'd never let go.

The doctor looked up at the pet store's sign and realized that the store was about to relocate to somewhere very, very far away.

"Are you afraid of car rides?"

"Mm-hm!"

"Do you get carsick?"

"Mm-hm!"

"...I guess I don't have a choice." The doctor sighed, fumbling his wallet out of his pocket. Even though the puppydragon did say he was free, there was no way he could leave without paying a single cent.

He put the puppydragon down. After taking a few steps forward, he beckoned for the puppydragon, whose tail had immediately drooped the moment he thought he was being abandoned.

"Walk by yourself, and come with me to the cashier. By the way, what's your name?"

The puppydragon stood dazedly in the golden-red sunset for a very long time. Then his ears perked up all at once, eyes shining with light as he showed off his sharp little canines and ran toward him in delight, throwing himself once more at the doctor's waist. "Hi! My name is He Yu!"

The doctor's body smelled faintly of disinfectant, but the scent didn't seem harsh at all.

"...Hello, little devil," the doctor said. "My name is Xie Qingcheng."

THE STORY CONTINUES IN

CASE FILE COMPENDIUM
VOLUME 4

THE STORY CONTINUES IN

GREEN LANTERN OMNIBUS
VOLUME

CHARACTERS, NAMES, AND LOCATIONS

CHARACTERS

MAIN CHARACTERS

HE YU: 贺予: A nineteen-year-old university student with a rare mental illness.

XIE QINGCHENG 谢清呈: He Yu's former doctor, who currently works as a medical school professor.

SUPPORTING CHARACTERS

XIE XUE 谢雪: Xie Qingcheng's younger sister, and a lecturer at He Yu's university.

JIANG LIPING 蒋丽: The morality advisor in charge of He Yu's screenwriting/directing class.

WEI DONGHENG 卫冬恒: A senior drama student at Huzhou University.

CHEN YAN 陈衍: A police officer and family friend of Xie Qingcheng. Nicknamed "Chen Man."

QIN CIYAN 秦慈岩: Xie Qingcheng's former colleague, who was killed by the angry son of a patient.

LI RUOQIU 李若秋: Xie Qingcheng's ex-wife.

LÜ ZHISHU 吕芝书: He Yu's mother, a wealthy businesswoman.

HE JIWEI 贺继威: He Yu's father, a wealthy businessman who is often away from home.

HU YI 胡毅: A screenwriter and producer of *The Trial*.

HUANG ZHILONG 黄志龙: A powerful entertainment executive.

ZHENG JINGFENG 郑敬风: A veteran criminal investigator and former colleague of Xie Qingcheng's parents.

DUAN-LAOBAN 段老板: A mysterious figure working in the shadows.

NAME GUIDE

Diminutives, Nicknames, and Name Tags

DA-: A prefix meaning "big" or "elder," which can be added before titles for elders, like "dage" or "dajie," or before a name.

DI/DIDI: A word meaning "younger brother." It can also be used to address an unrelated (usually younger) male peer, and optionally used as a suffix.

GE/GEGE: A word meaning "older brother." It can also be used to address an unrelated male peer, and optionally used as a suffix.

JIE/JIEJIE: A word meaning "elder sister." It can also be used to address an unrelated female peer, and optionally used as a suffix.

LAO-: A prefix meaning "old." Usually added to a surname and used in informal contexts.

LAOSHI: A word meaning "teacher" that can be used to refer to any educator, often in deference. Can also be attached to someone's name as a suffix.

LAOBAN: A word meaning "boss" that can be used to refer to one's superior or the proprietor of a business. Can also be attached to someone's name as a suffix.

SAOZI/-SAO: A word meaning "elder brother's wife." It can be used to address the wife (or informally, girlfriend) of an unrelated male peer.

XIAO-: A prefix meaning "little" or "younger." Often used in an affectionate and familiar context.

XUEZHANG: Older male classmate.

XUEDI: Younger male classmate.

XUEJIE: Older female classmate.

XUEMEI: Younger female classmate.

APPENDIX

GLOSSARY

GLOSSARY

EYES: Descriptions like "almond eyes" or "peach-blossom eyes" refer to eye shape. Almond eyes have a balanced shape, like that of an almond, whereas peach-blossom eyes have a rounded upper lid and are often considered particularly alluring.

FACE: *Mianzi* (面子), generally translated as "face," is an important concept in Chinese society. It is a metaphor for a person's reputation and can be extended to further descriptive metaphors. For example, "having face" refers to having a good reputation, and "losing face" refers to having one's reputation hurt. Meanwhile, "giving face" means deferring to someone else to help improve their reputation, while "not wanting face" implies that a person is acting so poorly or shamelessly that they clearly don't care about their reputation at all. "Thin face" refers to someone easily embarrassed or prone to offense at perceived slights. Conversely, "thick face" refers to someone not easily embarrassed and immune to insults.

JADE: Jade is a semi-precious mineral with a long history of ornamental and functional usage in China. The word "jade" can refer to two distinct minerals, nephrite and jadeite, which both range in color from white to gray to a wide spectrum of greens.

UNIVERSITIES AND CLASS STRUCTURE: In Chinese universities, students are assigned to a class of students in their major. Each class takes their major courses together for the duration of their university career.

WECHAT: A Chinese instant messaging, social media, and mobile payment app ubiquitous in modern Chinese society. People use its text, call, and voice message functions for both personal and business communications. Many vendors in China prefer its mobile payment capabilities to cash.

WEIBO: A popular Chinese microblogging social media platform similar to Twitter.

XUEBA: 学霸, literally "academic tyrant," is a slang term for high-achieving students. Usually complimentary.